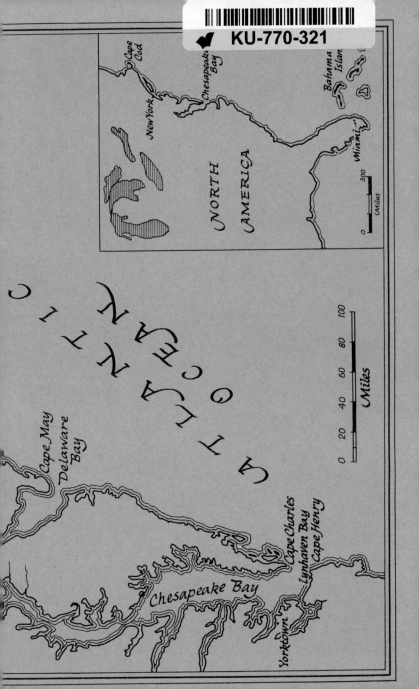

SLOOP OF WAR

For the young Richard Bolitho, the spring of 1778 marked a complete transformation for himself and his future. It was the year in which the American War of Independence changed to an all-out struggle for freedom from British rule—and the year when Bolitho took command of the *Sparrow*, a small, fast and well-armed sloop of war. Inevitably, as the pace of war increased, the *Sparrow* was called from one crisis to another—and when the great fleets of Britain and France converged on the Chesapeake, Bolitho had to throw aside the early dreams of his first command to find maturity in a sea battle that might well decide the fate of a whole continent.

SLOOP OF WAR

*

ALEXANDER KENT

THE
COMPANION BOOK CLUB
LONDON

This edition, published in 1973 by
The Hamlyn Publishing Group Ltd,
is issued by arrangement with
Hutchinson & Co. (Publishers) Ltd.

THE COMPANION BOOK CLUB

*Made and printed in Great Britain
for the Companion Book Club
by Odhams (Watford) Ltd.*
600871649
7·73/264

For Walter J. Minton,
with thanks for firing the starting gun
on this series

The author wishes to thank: the U.S. Navy for their help and co-operation during his visit to the Chesapeake in 1970; Captain A. G. Ellis, Director of the U.S. Naval Academy Museum, Annapolis; the Hall of Records, Annapolis; the Mariners Museum, Newport News, Va.; and the Mugar Memorial Library, Boston University.

A.K.

'It seems to be a law inflexible and inexorable that he who will not risk cannot win.'

JOHN PAUL JONES

PART ONE: 1778

1. The Most Coveted Gift

IT WAS A LITTLE MORE than a hundred yards' walk from
the busy foreshore to the elegant white building at the top
of the coast road, but within a minute of leaving the launch
Richard Bolitho was damp with sweat. In the broad expanse
of English Harbour there had been an illusion of a breeze,
but here, as the noon sun stood high above Monk's Hill and
bathed the island of Antigua in a shimmering haze, there was
no such comfort.

Nevertheless, Bolitho quickened his pace, conscious of his
rising excitement and a sense of unreality which had been with
him since his arrival just a week earlier. Events had moved
so fast that he felt unable to keep a grip on them, as if he was
a spectator watching somebody else, a being quite alien to his
own resources.

Through wide gates, the sand and dust covering his new
shoes with a pale layer, and across some well-tended gardens
towards the building itself. But for the flag which hung
limply from its staff it could have been the residence of some
rich merchant or shipowner. From the number of Negro
servants who were working amidst the flowers and shrubs he
guessed that the previous occupant had probably been a dealer
in African slaves.

Within the deep porch it felt almost cold after the sun's
fierce glare, and he found himself confronted by a red-faced
sergeant of marines who, after a cursory glance which covered
Bolitho from top to toe, said, 'If you will step into this room,
sir.'

His tone, if not offhand, was that of a man so used to
dealing with the comings and goings of sea-officers that he
could no longer be excited by anything or anyone.

Bolitho entered the small room and heard the door slam
behind him. For the first time since he could recall he was

7

quite alone. Alone, and poised on what might be the most important step in his life.

He made himself walk very slowly to the window and stood looking down at the harbour spread below him like some great painting. English Harbour. The headquarters and linchpin of England's sea power in the Indies and Caribbean. Every type of ship seemed to be here. Stately two-deckers in the deep anchorage, their awnings spread and every gun port open to catch the merest breath of air. Lithe frigates and supply vessels, and a whole collection of smaller craft from brigs to schooners, between which countless oared boats plied back and forth like water-beetles.

Somewhere in the building a man shouted loudly and feet clattered in a passageway. Bolitho tore his eyes from the anchored ships and crossed to a wall mirror, his mind suddenly very aware of what the next minutes might bring or take away.

He still could not get used to his change of appearance. He had never imagined that a uniform would alter a man's outward image so much yet leave him inwardly the same. Just weeks ago he had been second lieutenant in the *Trojan*, an eighty-gun ship-of-the-line. For three years he had lived, worked and nearly died within her crowded hull, rising from his original position of fourth lieutenant by way of one man's death and the promotion of another. He had become used to the *Trojan*, even though he had had to fight off the yearning to free himself from her ponderous authority to find more individual scope for his ideas.

Like everyone aboard he had been kept busy enough. With the rebellion in America every ship-of-war was needed as never before. As the rebellion grew and spread and some real hint of its purpose filtered through to the fleet the *Trojan* was called from one crisis to another.

It seemed incredible that disorganized bands of men could be welded into armies. Armies strong and agile enough to out-manœuvre some of the best troops from England. But like most of his companions Bolitho had firmly believed that some sort of compromise would still present itself. That was until six months ago in October 1777, when the news of Burgoyne's surrender had burst upon them. Overnight, or so it seemed, the rebellion

8

had developed into a new and bitter conflict. On the one hand the British with their overstretched resources, and on the other the armies of the American Revolution backed as they were by a whole fleet of privateers from France and Spain. No supply ship could sail alone without the real risk of being taken by such privateers. Even troop convoys were not immune from attack.

It was in the middle of this new hit-and-run war that Bolitho's own life had changed. *Trojan* had run down and boarded a prize, a handsome brig, off the coast of Puerto Rico, her holds jammed with contraband goods and powder for the Americans. Caught between two sets of shoals, and confronted by the *Trojan's* impressive artillery, her master decided to surrender without fuss.

Trojan's first lieutenant was badly needed in his own ship as most of the officers were newly appointed and without much experience. To Bolitho fell the lot of prize-master, with orders to take her to Antigua and await further instructions. It was like the beginning to some impossible dream. Freedom, excitement, the room to move and act without his captain's eye upon him, the little brig seemed to offer unlimited possibilities, even though he knew it would not last.

But fate had other ideas. Within a few days they had sighted another, larger brig, well handled, and displaying a heavier armament than was usual for such a craft. There had been no doubt that she was a privateer, and, further, it had seemed likely she was approaching to rendezvous with the prize.

There was little time to think, let alone plan. The other ship would outsail and outshoot anything Bolitho's small prize-crew could offer. To fight and die to no purpose was unthinkable, and to surrender without doing so was equally so.

It had turned out to be so simple that looking back it too seemed like part of the dream. Closing the unsuspecting privateer, apparently to pass despatches, they had run alongside and grappled her, both vessels being buried under a mass of fallen spars and canvas in the collision. A volley of musket fire, a wildly yelling rush of boarders, and the other ship was taken, even though her company outnumbered Bolitho's party by four to one. *Trojan's* seamen were well used to this sort of game. The privateer's crew were not. In fact, it was her captain's first voyage in that capacity.

So instead of one prize Bolitho entered harbour with a pair. With the war going badly on land, and affairs at sea so confused as to be equally disheartening, his arrival under the guns of the harbour's battery was like a tonic. Handshakes from a rear-admiral, smiling greetings from senior captains, Bolitho had been staggered by the welcome.

With the prizes handed over to the dockyard he had been found accommodation in an old hulk called *Octavia*. Originally a two-decker, she had been all but sunk in a hurricane the previous year and now served as accommodation ship. Junior officers whiled away the time gambling, sleeping, or drinking to excess as they awaited their next appointments. Promotion and transfers, courts martial or passage home as a crippled victim of some encounter with the enemy, the old *Octavia* had seen them all.

As the days passed, Bolitho began to imagine he had been forgotten. Soon the *Trojan* would arrive and he would find himself back again in her tight community. Living from day to day. Hoping, yet not daring to hope for too much.

The orders, when they were delivered by an immaculate flag lieutenant, were as brief as they were astounding. By consent of the Commander-in-Chief, Richard Bolitho would take upon himself the appointment of commander with the rank and benefits attached. The appointment would take effect forthwith. He would furnish himself with all necessary vestments and report to the newly acquired headquarters building in two days' time.

He stared at himself in the glass. *Today.*

It seemed that in Antigua you could obtain everything even at such short notice, for a price. And now, instead of his faded lieutenant's uniform, he was looking at the broad blue lapels of commander, the single gold stripe on each sleeve which showed him to be what was to all intent a junior captain. Behind him on the chair a gold-laced cocked hat shone in the filtered sunlight, and like everything else about him, his white waistcoat and breeches, a tight neckcloth and his dusty shoes, even the handsome basket-hilted sword which he had chosen with such care, were so new that they felt like borrowed finery. He had not dared to contemplate the cost, the bribes required to obtain everything within the allotted time. An advance on his well-earned prize money had sufficed for the present.

He touched the lock of black hair which hung rebelliously above his right eye. Beneath it the deep, savage scar which ran to his hairline felt hot, as if it had been a matter of weeks rather than years when he had been struck down by a cutlass.

In spite of his inner tension he grinned at himself. Junior or not, he had taken the first real step. One which would bring him either fame or disgrace, but which like all his family before him he had awaited with both anxiety and eagerness.

More footsteps sounded in the passageway and he adjusted his neckcloth and settled the new sword more comfortably on his hip. Once again his image in the mirror was like a stranger's. The uniform, the tense way he was holding his slim figure as if on parade, displayed more apprehension than he had believed he harboured.

The footsteps halted outside the door, and in one movement Bolitho swept up the cocked hat and jammed it beneath one arm, trying to ignore his heart pounding against his ribs like a hammer. His mouth was bone dry, yet he could feel the sweat running between his shoulder-blades like warm rain.

Richard Bolitho was twenty-two years old and had been in the King's Navy since the age of twelve. But as he stared fixedly at the gilt door-handle he felt more like a frightened midshipman than the man who was about to receive the most coveted gift to be bestowed on any living creature. A command of his own.

The marine sergeant stared at him woodenly. 'When you're ready, sir. Cap'n Colquhoun will see you now.'

'I'm ready, thank you.'

The marine eyed him with the merest hint of a smile. 'He'll be glad to know that, I'm sure, sir.'

Bolitho did not hear a word. Following the sergeant he strode out into the passageway, and another world.

Captain Vere Colquhoun rose briefly from behind a large desk, made as if to offer his hand, and then sank back into his chair.

'Pray be seated, Bolitho.'

He had his back to a window and it was impossible to see his expression. But as Bolitho arranged himself into a narrow, high-backed chair he was well aware of the other man's scrutiny.

Colquhoun said, 'You have a good report.' He opened a canvas folder and ran his eye across the attached papers. 'I see that you were commissioned lieutenant in 'seventy-four.' He glanced up sharply. 'Well?'

Bolitho replied, 'Yes, sir. The *Destiny*, frigate.'

He had been long enough in the Navy to realize that interviews with superior officers took time. Each had his own way, but all seemed to result in being kept hanging on a thread of uneasy expectation. He tried to ignore Colquhoun's bowed head and made himself look instead at the room. White walls and a colourful tiled floor. Some pieces of dark, heavy furniture and one table which was almost covered with handsome decanters. Colquhoun, it appeared, enjoyed life. He shifted his gaze to his new superior. At a guess he was about thirty, and from what he could see from the sunlit window he had finely cut features with a small, aggressive chin. He had fair hair, pulled back to the nape of his neck like his own, in the current fashion, and Bolitho noticed that in spite of his service on the station his skin was remarkably pale.

Colquhoun said, 'Your captain speaks well of you.' He rustled his papers. 'Quite well.'

Bolitho tried not to swallow and display the dryness in his throat. Captain Pears of the *Trojan* had sent a report with him aboard the prize. Had he been aware of Bolitho's later luck with the privateer his report might have been even better. It was strange, he thought. In his three years aboard Pears's ship he had never really understood the man. Sometimes he had imagined his captain disliked him, and at best only tolerated his efforts. Yet now, on this desk, under the eyes of a new superior, Pears's words were showing him in a different light.

'Thank you, sir.'

'Hmph.' Colquhoun stood up and walked towards the table and then changed his mind. Instead he moved to the window and stared absently at the anchorage. 'I am commanded to give you your new appointment. It will be up to you to prove your worth, an ability to carry out orders rather than to make play with them for your own advantage.'

Bolitho waited. It was impossible to follow this man.

Colquhoun added, 'Since the military disaster at Saratoga last year we have seen all the signs of the French increasing their aid to the Americans. Originally they sent supplies and military advisers. Then privateers and soldiers-of-fortune, mercenaries.' He spat out the words. 'Now they are more open in their efforts to use the Americans to further their own ends and regain territory lost to us in the Seven Years War.'

Bolitho gripped the hilt of his new sword and tried to remain outwardly calm. Somewhere outside this room was a ship awaiting her new captain. Old or new, large or insignificant as a fighting unit, she was to be all his own. And he had to remain quite still, listening to Captain Colquhoun's observations on the war. Bolitho had been involved in the war since its beginning, and he had already learned from a fellow officer in the *Octavia* that Colquhoun had arrived from England just six months ago.

Colquhoun was saying in the same dry tone, 'But while we command the sea-lanes and supply routes neither the French nor the damned Pope can stop us regaining overall control of the mainland.' He turned slightly, the sun glinting across the gold lace of his coat. 'Don't you agree?'

Bolitho shifted in his chair.

'Up to a point, sir. But . . .'

Colquhoun snapped, '*But* is not a word which appeals to me. Either you agree or you disagree.'

'I think more should be done to seek out the privateers and destroy them in their bases, sir.' He paused, anticipating some caustic remark. Then he continued, 'We have too few ships to spare for convoy work. Any attack on merchantmen, pressed home by two or more vessels at once, can play the devil with a solitary escort.'

'Really. You surprise me.'

Bolitho bit his lip. He had allowed himself to be drawn. Perhaps Colquhoun had been hoping that one of his friends or protégés would be given the new appointment, and saw

13

Bolitho as an intruder. Whatever it was, there seemed to be no doubting his hostility.

'I have, of course, heard of your family, Bolitho. Seafaring stock. None of 'em ever afraid to risk his neck. And out here at this moment we need the best fighting officers we can get.'

He turned abruptly to the window. 'Come over here.'

Bolitho crossed to his side and followed his glance towards the ships at anchor.

'Look impressive, don't they?' Colquhoun gave what might have been a sigh. 'But once at sea, scattered to the winds, they are just a handful. With the Frogs at our backs and threatening England once more we are stretched beyond any safety limit.' He gestured across the harbour. A frigate was being careened, heeled right over on her beam, her bilges covered with busy figures, their naked backs shining in the glare like polished mahogany. Colquhoun said, quietly, '*Bacchante*, thirty-six.' He tightened his jaw. '*My* ship. First time I've been able to get her underwater repairs done since I assumed command.'

Bolitho darted a quick glance at him. He had always dreamed of commanding a frigate since his first and only experience in the little twenty-eight-gun *Destiny*. Freedom to move and hit hard at anything but a ship-of-the-line, with all the dash and agility that any young captain could ask for. But Colquhoun did not seem to fit the role. Slightly built, with the pale, petulant good looks of a true aristocrat. His clothes were beautifully made, and the sword at his hip must be worth two hundred guineas.

Colquhoun raised his arm. 'Look yonder. Beyond my ship you will see the rest of our flotilla. With these and nothing more I am expected to patrol and seek out the enemy, run errands for the fleet, dab away the tears of rich merchantmen whenever they sight an unfamiliar sail. It would need a force five times as large, and even then I would hope for more.'

He turned to watch Bolitho's expression as he stared across the shimmering water.

Bolitho said slowly, 'Three sloops-of-war.' He saw a tiny armed schooner anchored beyond the others. Was she to be his? He swallowed hard. 'And a schooner.'

'Correct.' Colquhoun moved to his table and picked up a

heavy decanter. As he held it against the sunlight he said, 'You are being given the *Sparrow*, Bolitho. Eighteen guns and only two years old.' He eyed him flatly. 'Next to my frigate, she is the best under my command.'

Bolitho could only stare at him.

'I do not know what to say, sir.'

The other man grimaced. 'Then say nought.' He poured two glasses of brandy.

'I have no doubt of your ability as a sea-officer, Bolitho. Your past record is proof of that. To obey and carry out orders without question is one thing, however. To lead others, to hold their skills and lives in your hands without ever losing grip, is something else entirely.' He offered him a glass. 'To your first command, Bolitho. I wish you more of the luck which has guided your feet to this year of 'seventy-eight, for I *promise* you will need it!'

The brandy was like fire, but Bolitho's head was still reeling and he hardly noticed it. A new sloop. The best under Colquhoun's command. In a moment he would awake aboard *Octavia* to find today just beginning.

Colquhoun said calmly, 'Your predecessor in *Sparrow* died recently.'

'I am sorry to hear it, sir.'

'Hmm.' Colquhoun studied him thoughtfully. 'Fever. His first lieutenant is too junior even for temporary command.' He shrugged. 'Your timely arrival, the blessing of our devoted admiral, and, of course, Bolitho, your obvious qualities for the appointment, made you an immediate choice, eh?' He was not smiling.

Bolitho looked away. It would be safer to assume from the beginning that Colquhoun had no sense of humour.

He said, 'I will do my best, sir.'

'Be sure of that.' Colquhoun took out his watch and flicked it open. '*Sparrow* is at full complement. For seamen, that is. I will have to send your prize-crew to other vessels in greater need. Unless you have any particular fellow you wish to keep?'

'Yes, sir. Just one. I appreciate that.'

Colquhoun sighed. 'You are a curious mixture. A Cornishman, I believe?'

'Aye, sir.'

'Ah well . . .' He did not continue. Instead he said, 'I have made arrangements for a boat to collect you in a half-hour. Your documents will be ready by then.'

Bolitho waited, half expecting some fresh advice.

Colquhoun seemed to read his thoughts and said quietly, 'From time to time you will receive written instructions. But you will only be told *what* to do. How you achieve success and carry them out will be your burden alone.' He turned back to the window, his eyes on the careened frigate. 'I have held four different commands. The first was, of course, the most exciting. But also, as I recall, the loneliest. No more could I ask for help from my companions in the wardroom. Nor could I seek freedom outside my hours of duty. In earlier days I always imagined a captain to be a kind of god, put on earth to command and to leave all worry of execution to mere subordinates. Now, I know different, as you will.'

Bolitho picked up his hat. 'I shall try and remember that, sir.'

Colquhoun did not face him. 'You will not. You will think you know better than everyone else, which is as it should be. But somewhere along the way, in the teeth of a gale, or facing an enemy broadside, or becalmed perhaps with the ship's people near mad with thirst, you will know the true meaning of command. When you need help and advice most, and there is none. When all others are looking aft at you, and you have the power of life and death in your fingers. *Then* you will know, believe me.'

He added shortly, 'You may wait in the room by the entrance.'

The interview was ended.

Bolitho crossed to the door, his eyes on the silhouette against the bright window. It was such an important moment that he wanted to hold on to every part of it. Even the furniture and the well-stocked decanters.

Then he closed the door behind him and returned to the waiting room. When he looked at his watch he saw he had been just twenty minutes in the building.

At the window he stood staring at the small ships on the

far side of the anchorage, trying to distinguish one from the other, wondering what she would be like. What his company would think of him.

Eventually the door opened and an elderly lieutenant peered into the room.

'*Sparrow*, sir?'

Bolitho saw the sealed envelope in the man's hands and took a deep breath.

He nodded. 'Yes.'

The lieutenant bobbed his head and smiled. 'Your orders, sir. The boat has been sighted approaching the jetty. I will arrange for your gear to be collected from *Trojan* when she reaches here.' He shrugged. 'I am not so sure it will ever catch up with you, however.'

Bolitho grinned, unable to maintain his outward calm.

'Have it sold for me, eh? Put it towards helping some of those wounded seamen awaiting passage to England.'

As he strode towards the sunlight the lieutenant took out a pair of steel-rimmed glasses and peered after him. Then he shook his head very slowly. A remarkable young man, he thought. It was to be hoped he would remain so.

After the shadowy cool of the building Bolitho found the sun's glare harsher than before. As he strode down the coast road, his mind half dwelling on the interview with Colquhoun, he was already wondering what his new command would offer. With, but not *of* the fleet, there should at least be room to move, freedom from the daily flow of signals and requirements which had been his lot in the powerful *Trojan*.

He paused at a curve in the road and shaded his eyes to watch the boat which was already drawing near to the jetty. He shivered in spite of the heat and started to walk more quickly towards the sea. To anybody else it was just one more boat going about its ship's affairs, but to him it represented far more. A first contact. Some of his men. *His* men.

He saw the familiar shape of Stockdale standing beside some of his newly bought belongings and felt a sudden touch of warmth. Even if Colquhoun had said that not one single man of Bolitho's prize-crew could be spared for his first

17

command he felt sure Stockdale would have arrived aboard in his own way. Thickset and muscular, in his broad white trousers and blue jacket, he reminded him of some indestructible oak. He, too, was watching the approaching boat, his eyes slitted against the light with critical interest.

Bolitho had been junior lieutenant in the frigate *Destiny* when their paths had first crossed. Sent ashore on the thankless task of drumming up recruits for the ship, and with little hope of much success, he had arrived at a small inn with his party of seamen to set up headquarters, and, more to the point, to find some peace and a moment to refresh himself for the next attempt to obtain volunteers. Tramping from village to village, inn to inn, the system rarely changed. It usually resulted in a collection of those who were either too young for the harsh demands of a frigate or old sailors who had failed to find fortune or success ashore and merely wanted to return and end their days in surroundings they had originally sworn to forsake forever.

Stockdale had been none of these. He had been a prize-fighter, and stripped to the waist had been standing like a patient ox outside the inn while his sharp-faced barker had called upon all and sundry to risk a battering and win a guinea.

Tired and thirsty, Bolitho had entered the inn, momentarily leaving his small party to their own devices. Exactly what had happened next was not quite clear, but on hearing a string of curses, mingled with the loud laughter of the sailors, he had hurried outside to find one of his men pocketing the guinea and the enraged barker beating Stockdale round the head and shoulders with a length of chain. Whether the victorious seaman, a powerful gunner's mate well used to enforcing authority with brute force, had tripped Stockdale or gained a lucky blow was never discovered. Certainly, Bolitho had never seen Stockdale beaten in any fight, fair or otherwise, since that day. As he had shouted at his men to fall in line again he had realized that Stockdale had been standing as before, taking the unjust punishment, when with one stroke he could have killed the barker who was tormenting him.

Sickened by the spectacle, and angry with himself at the

same time, he had asked Stockdale to volunteer for the King's service. The man's dumb gratitude had been almost as embarrassing as the grins on the sailors' faces, but he had found some comfort in the barker's stunned disbelief as without a word Stockdale had picked up his shirt and followed the party away from the inn.

If he had imagined that was the end of the matter he was soon to discover otherwise. Stockdale took to a life at sea in a manner born. As strong as two men, he was gentle and patient, and whenever Bolitho was in danger he always seemed to be there. When a cutlass had hacked Bolitho to the ground and his boat's crew had retreated in panic, it had been Stockdale who had rallied them, had fought off the attackers and carried his unconscious lieutenant to safety. When Bolitho had left the frigate for the *Trojan* Stockdale had somehow contrived to transfer also. Never far away, he had been his servant as well as a gun captain, and when aboard the prize ship he had merely to glare at the captured crew to obtain instant respect. He spoke very little, and then only with a husky whisper. His vocal cords had been maimed over the years of fighting for others in booths and fair grounds up and down the country.

But when Bolitho's promotion had been delivered he had said simply, 'You'll be needing a good cox'n, sir.' He had given his lazy, lopsided grin. 'Whatever sort of a ship they gives you.'

And so it was settled. Not that there would have been any doubt in Bolitho's mind either.

He turned as Bolitho strode down the jetty and touched his hat.

'All ready.' He ran his eyes over Bolitho's new uniform and nodded with obvious approval. 'No more'n you deserve, sir.'

Bolitho smiled. 'We shall have to see about that.'

With oars tossed, and a seaman already scrambling ashore with a line, the cutter eased gently against the piles.

Stockdale stooped and steadied the gunwale with his fist, his eyes on the motionless oarsmen as he said hoarsely, 'A fine day for it, sir.'

A slim midshipman leapt from the boat and removed his hat with a flourish. About eighteen, he was a pleasant looking youth, and as tanned as a native.

'I'm Heyward, sir.' He shifted under Bolitho's impassive gaze. 'I—I've been sent to collect you, sir.'

Bolitho nodded. 'Thank you, Mr Heyward. You can tell me about the ship as we go.'

He waited for the midshipman and Stockdale to follow his sea-chest and bags into the boat and then stepped after them.

'Shove off forrard! Out oars!' Heyward seemed very conscious of Bolitho's nearness. 'Give way all!'

Like pale bones the oars rose and fell in regular precision. Bolitho glanced swiftly at the two lines of oarsmen. Neatly dressed in check shirts and white trousers, they looked fit and healthy enough. A ship could always be judged by her boats, some people contended. Bolitho knew otherwise. Some captains kept their boats as outward showpieces, while within their own ships the people lived little better than animals. Their expressions gave nothing away. The usual, homely faces of British sailors, set in careful masks to avoid his scrutiny. Each man was probably wondering about the new captain. To any seaman his captain was not much junior to God. He could lead, and use his skills on their behalf in battle. He might just as easily turn their lives into a daily hell with no one to whom they could protest or plead their cause.

The midshipman said haltingly, 'We have been at anchor for three days, sir.'

'Before that?'

'Patrol duty off Guadeloupe. We did sight a French brig but lost her, sir.'

'How long, have you been in *Sparrow*?'

'Two years, sir. Since she commissioned on the Thames at Greenwich.'

Stockdale craned round. 'There she is, sir. Fine on the larboard bow.'

Bolitho sat upright in the sternsheets, knowing that as soon as his eyes left the boat every man would be staring at him. He could barely contain his excitement as he peered towards the anchored sloop which was now fully in view beyond a heavy transport. She was riding almost motionless above the twin of her own reflection, her ensign making a scarlet patch of colour against the haze-shrouded hills beyond.

Bolitho had seen sloops in plenty during his service. Like frigates, they were everywhere and always in demand. Maids of all work, the eyes of the fleet, they were familiar in most naval harbours. But right at this moment in time he also knew that the *Sparrow* was going to be different from all those others. From her gently spiralling mastheads to the single line of open gun ports she was a thing of beauty. A thoroughbred, a miniature frigate, a vessel which seemed eager to be free of the land. She was all and none of these things.

He heard himself say, 'Steer round her bows.'

As the tiller went over he was conscious of the silence, broken only by the sluice of water around the cutter's stern and the rhythmic creak of oars. As if he was sharing this moment with nobody. Like a raked black finger the sloop's long jib-boom swept out and over his head, and for a few more moments he stared up at the figurehead below the bowsprit.

A man-sized sparrow, beak wide in fury and with wings spread as if to fight, its curved claws firmly gripping a gilded cluster of oak leaves and acorns. Bolitho watched until the boat had moved around and under the starboard cathead. He had never thought a mere sparrow could be depicted as being so warlike.

He started with surprise as his eyes fell on a gun muzzle in the first port.

Heyward said respectfully, 'We have a thirty-two-pounder on either bow, sir. The rest of the gun deck is made up of sixteen twelve-pounders.' He flinched as Bolitho turned to look at him. 'I beg your pardon, sir, I did not mean to intrude.'

Bolitho smiled and touched his arm. 'I was merely surprised. She seems to have very heavy artillery for such a small ship.' He shook his head. 'Those two bow-chasers must have brought many an enemy aback with shock. Nine-pounders are more common in sloops, I believe.'

The midshipman nodded, but his eyes were on the ship's side, his lips in an anxious line as he gauged the moment.

'Put her about!'

The cutter swung in a tight arc and headed for the main chains. There were many heads lining the gangway, and

Bolitho saw the blue and white of an officer's uniform by the entry port, a press of more figures by the mainmast.

'Toss your oars!'

The boat idled towards the chains where the bowman brought down his boathook with a well-timed slash.

Bolitho stood up in the sternsheets, conscious of all the eyes above and around him. Of Stockdale's hand, half-raised, ready to steady him if he lost his balance. Of the new sword at his hip and not wanting to look down to make sure it would not tangle with his legs as he climbed up the sleek tumblehome.

With a quick breath he reached out and hauled himself from the boat. He had been prepared for almost everything but was still taken totally off guard by the piercing shrill of pipes as his head and shoulders rose through the port. Perhaps, more than anything else, the time-honoured salute from a ship to her captain made him realize just how great was the step from lieutenant's berth to command.

It was all too much to take in and comprehend in this small cameo. The drawn swords, the boatswain's mates with their silver calls to their lips, the bare-backed seamen on the gangways and high in the shrouds. Below his feet he felt the deck lift easily, and once more was aware of the change this ship had brought him. After the *Trojan*'s fat bulk, her massive weight of guns and spars, this sloop even *felt* alive.

One officer stepped forward as Bolitho removed his hat to the quarterdeck and said, 'Welcome aboard, sir. I am Graves, second lieutenant.'

Bolitho regarded him searchingly. The lieutenant was young and alert, but had the controlled caution on his dark features of a man much older.

He half turned and added, 'The others are awaiting your pleasure, sir.'

Bolitho asked, 'And the first lieutenant?'

Graves looked away. 'In the flagship, sir. He had an appointment.' He faced him quickly. 'He meant no disrespect, sir, I am quite sure of that.'

Bolitho nodded. Graves's explanation was too swift, too glib. Or that of a man who wished to draw attention to the absent officer's behaviour by excusing it.

Graves hurried on, 'This is Mr Buckle, the sailing master, sir. Mr Dalkeith, surgeon.' His voice followed Bolitho down the small line of senior warrant officers.

Bolitho marked each face but checked himself from further contact. That would come soon enough, but now his own impression on them was far more vital.

He stood by the quarterdeck rail and stared down at the gun deck. The *Sparrow* was one hundred and ten feet long on that deck, but had a broad beam of thirty feet, almost that of a frigate. No wonder she could contain such powerful armament for her size.

He said, 'Have the hands lay aft, Mr Graves.'

As the order was passed and the men came pressing down on those already assembled, he drew his commission from his pocket and spread it on the rail. How hot the wood felt beneath his hands.

Again he darted a glance at the faces beneath him. In so small a ship how did they all manage to exist? There were one hundred and fifteen souls crammed aboard *Sparrow*, and as they jostled together below the quarterdeck there appeared to be twice that number.

Graves touched his hat. 'All present, sir.'

Bolitho replied with equal formality, 'Thank you.' Then in a steady voice he began to read himself in.

He had heard other captains do it often enough, but as he read the beautifully penned words he felt once more like a spectator.

It was addressed to Richard Bolitho, Esquire, and required him forthwith to go on board and take upon him the charge and command of captain in His Britannic Majesty's Sloop-of-War *Sparrow*.

Once or twice as his voice carried along the deck he heard a man cough or move his feet, and aboard another sloop close by he saw an officer watching the proceedings through a telescope.

He put the commission in his coat and said, 'I will go to my quarters, Mr Graves.'

He replaced his hat and walked slowly towards a covered hatch just forward of the mizzen mast. He noticed that the ship's wheel was completely unsheltered. A bad place in a storm, he thought, or when the balls begin to fly.

At his back he heard the rising murmur of voices as the men were dismissed, and noticed, too, the heavy smell of cooking in the listless air. He was glad he had restrained himself from making a speech. It would have been vanity, and he knew it. All the same, it was so precious a day that he wanted to share it with all of them in some way.

In his excitement he had forgotten about the time. Now as he made his way down a ladder to the gun deck and aft behind Graves's crouched figure he was more than glad he had restricted himself to the formal reading of his appointment. Men kept standing in the sun to hear a pompous speech were one thing. Men kept also from their well-earned meal were something else entirely.

He gasped as his head crashed against a deck beam.

Graves spun round. 'I beg your pardon, sir!' He seemed terrified Bolitho should blame him for the lack of headroom.

'I will remember next time.'

He reached the stern cabin and stepped inside. For an instant he stood motionless, taking in the graceful sloping stern windows which spread from quarter to quarter, displaying the anchorage and the headland like some glistening panorama. The cabin was beautifully painted in pale green, the panels picked out with gold leaf. The deck was concealed with a black and white checked canvas covering, and arranged on either side was a selection of well-made furniture. Gingerly he raised his head and found he could just stand upright between the beams above.

Graves was watching him worriedly. 'I am afraid that after a ship-of-the-line, sir, you'll find this somewhat cramped.'

Bolitho smiled. 'Have the ship's books brought to me after you have dined, Mr Graves. I will also want to meet the other officers informally sometime today.' He paused, seeing again the caution in his eyes. '*Including* the first lieutenant.'

Graves bowed himself out and Bolitho turned his back to the closed door.

Cramped, after a ship-of-the-line, Graves had said. He hurled his hat across the cabin on to the bench seat below the windows. His sword he unbuckled and dropped in a green velvet chair. He was laughing aloud, and the effort to restrain it was almost painful.

Cramped. He walked, ducking between the beams. It was a *palace* after the *Trojan*'s wardroom.

He sat down beside his hat and stared around the neat, cheerful-looking cabin.

And it was his own.

2. Freedom

IT WAS LATE AFTERNOON when Bolitho finally decided he had read all that there was available about the ship around him. Muster and punishment books, watch-bills and ledgers of stores and victualling returns, the list seemed endless. But at no time was he bored. With his new coat hanging on a chair-back, his neckcloth loosened and shirt unbuttoned, he found each item fascinating.

His predecessor, Captain Ransome, had kept a smart and well-run ship on the face of things. The punishment book had all the usual culprits and awards for minor misdemeanours. A few for drunkenness, even less for insolence and insubordination, and the worst recorded crime was that of a seaman who had struck a petty officer during gun drill.

Ransome had been extremely lucky in one thing. With the ship being commissioned on the Thames he had been able to secure the cream of the press. Men off incoming merchant ships, transfers from vessels laid up in ordinary, he had been in a position to complete his company with far less difficulty than most captains.

Against the apparent taut atmosphere in the ship was a rather negative list of reports in the log books. Only once had *Sparrow* been called to action in the two years since leaving England, and then as secondary reinforcement to a frigate attacking a blockade runner. It was little wonder that Midshipman Heyward had showed some concern at his remarks about the big bow-chasers. He had probably imagined his words to be some sort of criticism at their lack of use.

There were the usual lists of men transferred to other ships because of promotion and the like. Their places had been filled by what Ransome had termed 'local colonist volunteers' in his personal log. Bolitho had lingered a good deal on the previous captain's daily records. His comments were extremely brief and it was impossible to get even a feel of the man. As he paused to glance around the cabin from time to time Bolitho found himself wondering about Ransome. An experienced and competent officer, obviously a man of good breeding and therefore influence, the cabin seemed at odds with his mental portrait. Extremely attractive, comfortable, yet just that too much removed from what you might expect in a ship-of-war.

He sighed and leaned back in the chair as his cabin servant, Fitch, padded into the shafted sunlight to remove the remains of his meal.

Fitch was tiny. A miserable scrap of a man, who had already confessed to having been a petty thief in his unfortunate past. Saved from transportation or worse by the timely arrival of a King's ship as he awaited sentence at the Assizes, he had accepted life at sea more as an extension to his punishment than any love of service. But he seemed a capable servant, and was probably well pleased with his work. It kept him from the heavier tasks on deck, and provided his current master was a humane man he had little to fear.

Bolitho watched him as he collected the crockery on to a tray. It had been an excellent meal. Cold tongue and fresh vegetables from ashore, and the claret which Fitch had mournfully observed was 'the last of Cap'n Ransome's stock' had been a touch of perfection.

'Your late captain.' Bolitho saw the small man stiffen. 'Did he leave any instruction as to his property aboard?'

Fitch dropped his eyes.

'Mr Tyrrell 'as attended to it, sir. It's been sent to a transport for passage 'ome.'

'He must have been an officer of some consequence.'

Bolitho hated this form of questioning, but he felt he needed some link, no matter how small, with the man who had controlled this ship from the day she had slid into the water.

Fitch bit his lip. ''E were a strict cap'n, sir. 'E saw that the 'ands took fairly to their work. If they obeyed, 'e was 'appy. If not . . .' he shrugged his frail shoulders, 'then 'e tended to swear a piece.'

Bolitho nodded. 'You may leave.'

It was useless to proceed with Fitch. His life concerned only the comings and goings. Food and drink, a warm cot, or a swift curse if things were not to his master's liking.

Feet padded overhead and he had to restrain himself from running to the stern windows or standing on a chair to peer through the skylight above the table. He thought of his old companions in the *Trojan*'s wardroom and wondered if they were missing him. Probably not. His promotion would mean a gap, and therefore a step up the ladder for another. He smiled to himself. It would take time to fit himself into this new role. Time and vigilance.

There was a tap at the door and Mathias Buckle, the sailing master, stepped inside.

'Do you have a moment, sir?'

Bolitho gestured to a chair. Again this was so unlike a bigger ship-of-war. There were no marines in the company, and visitors to the captain's quarters seemed free to come and go almost as they pleased. Perhaps Ransome had encouraged such informality.

He watched Buckle fitting himself into the chair. He was a short, square-built man, with steady eyes and hair almost as dark as his own. Aged forty, he was the oldest man in the ship.

Buckle said, 'I'd not trouble you, sir, but as the first lieutenant's away, I thought . . .' He shifted in the chair. 'I thought I should settle the matter of promotion for one of the hands.'

Bolitho listened in silence as Buckle ran through the points which concerned a man named Raven. It was an internal matter, but he was conscious of the importance it represented. The very first time as captain he was being confronted with the affairs of one of his own company.

Buckle was saying, 'I thought, begging your pardon, sir, that we might advance him to master's mate for a trial period.'

Bolitho asked, 'How long have you been master?'

'Just in this ship, sir.' Buckle's clear eyes were distant. 'Before that I was master's mate in the old *Warrior*, seventy-four.'

'You've done well, Mr Buckle.' He was trying to place the dialect. London, or further east. Kent.

'How does she handle?'

Buckle seemed to consider it. 'She's heavy for her size, sir. All of four hundred and thirty tons. But the better the wind, the livelier she goes. You can even get the stunsails and royals on her in anything but a true blow.' He frowned. 'In a calm she can be the devil's daughter.' He gestured vaguely. 'You've probably seen the little port alongside each gun port, sir?'

Bolitho had not. He said slowly, 'I am not too sure.'

Buckle smiled for the first time. 'If you gets becalmed you may run a sweep through each o' those ports, sir. Clear lower deck and get every man-jack on the sweeps and you can still get a knot or two out of her.'

Bolitho looked away. Reading the ship's books and correspondence had not even told him the half of it. He felt vaguely angry that his first lieutenant was still not present. Normally the departing captain would have been aboard to tell him the ship's behaviour and failings, or at least the senior lieutenant.

Buckle said, 'You'll soon get the feel of her, sir. She's the best yet.'

Bolitho eyed him thoughtfully. The master was nobody's fool, and yet, like Graves, he seemed to be holding back. Maybe waiting for him to display his strength or weakness to them.

He made himself reply coldly, 'We shall see about that, Mr Buckle.'

When he glanced up he saw the man watching him with sudden anxiety. He added, 'Any other matter?'

Buckle rose to his feet. 'No, sir.'

'Good. I anticipate that sailing orders will be arriving shortly. I will expect the ship to be ready.'

Buckle nodded. 'Aye, sir. Have no fear.'

Bolitho relented slightly. It was just possible his own uncertainty was making him unnecessarily harsh towards his sailing master. And it was equally likely he would need Buckle's guiding hand very much until he got the feel of his new command.

He said, 'I have no doubt that I will be as satisfied with your appointment as Captain Ransome was.'

Buckle swallowed hard. 'Yes, sir.' He stared round the low cabin. 'Thank you, sir.'

The door closed behind him and Bolitho ran his fingers through his hair. Just a few hours since he had climbed aboard to the squeal of pipes and already he was beginning to *feel* different.

It was all so alien to his past life when you could argue and compete with your companions, curse your captain behind his back or reveal his weakness which only you really understood. As from today a mere word could bring a shutter across a man's eyes or make him fear for his own safety. Buckle was eighteen years his senior, yet at the first hint of Bolitho's displeasure had almost cringed.

He closed his eyes and tried to fathom out how he should proceed. To try to be too popular was to be a fool. To hold unswervingly to matters of discipline and order was to be a tyrant. He recalled Colquhoun's words and grinned ruefully. Until you reached Colquhoun's lofty post-rank you could never be certain of anything.

Somewhere beyond the bulkhead he heard a challenge and a shouted reply from a boat. Then the squeak of a hull along-side, the patter of feet on a gangway. It seemed unreal and incredible that the ship, his ship, was running her affairs while he just sat here at the table. He sighed again and stared at the pile of papers and books. It would take longer than he had imagined to adjust.

There was another rap at the door and Graves ducked inside, removing his hat and jamming it under his arm as he announced, 'The guardboat has just been alongside, sir.' He held out a heavily sealed canvas envelope. 'From the flag, sir.'

Bolitho took it and laid it carelessly on the table. His sailing orders without doubt, and he had to restrain himself from acting as he truly felt. He wanted to rip them open, to know and understand what was required of him.

He saw Graves looking round the cabin, his eyes passing swiftly over the discarded dress coat, the hat lying on the bench seat, and finally on Bolitho's unbuttoned shirt.

Graves said quickly, 'Will you wish me to stay, sir?'

'No. I will inform you of their content when I have had time to study them.'

Graves nodded. 'I am waiting for the last water-lighter to

come out to us, sir. I have sent the cooper ashore to speed them up, but . . .'

Bolitho smiled. 'Then attend to it, if you please.'

Bolitho watched him leave and then slit open the envelope. He was still reading the neatly worded orders when he heard voices in the passageway beyond the door. Graves first, curt and resentful, then another, calm to begin with and then loud with anger. The latter finished with, 'Well, how in God's name was I to know? You could have made a signal, you bloody fool!'

There was a sudden silence and then a further tap on the door.

The lieutenant who stepped into the cabin was not at all what Bolitho had been expecting. Too junior for temporary command, Colquhoun had said, and yet this man was probably two years older than himself. He was tall, broad-shouldered, and deeply tanned. His thick auburn hair brushed the deckhead between the beams so that he seemed to fill the cabin.

Bolitho glanced up at him calmly. 'Mr Tyrrell?'

The lieutenant nodded briefly. 'Sir.' He took a quick breath. 'I must apologize for my late arrival aboard. I have been in th' flagship.'

Bolitho looked down at the table. Tyrrell had an easy drawl, the mark of a man born and bred in the American colony. He was like a half-tamed animal, and the quickness of his breathing betrayed the anger which he still harboured.

Bolitho added, 'Our sailing orders have just arrived.'

Tyrrell did not seem to hear. 'It was personal business, sir, I hadn't th' time to arrange otherwise.'

'I see.'

He waited, watching the man as he stared restlessly towards the stern windows. He had a strange way of standing, with one arm hanging down his side, the other inclined towards his sword. Relaxed, but wary. Like someone expecting an attack.

He continued, 'I would have preferred to meet my first lieutenant on board when I arrived.'

'I have sent Cap'n Ransome's remains ashore to be conveyed home with his possessions, sir. As you were not yet in command I felt personally free to act as I thought fit.' He looked at Bolitho evenly. 'I was aboard th' flagship to ask, plead if required, for a transfer to another ship. It was refused.'

'You felt that by being passed over for command that your talents would be better suited elsewhere, is that it?'

Tyrrell gave a slow smile. It changed him instantly from an angry man to one of obvious charm, with the inbuilt recklessness of a fighter.

'I really am sorry, sir. But no, it was not that. As you no doubt know, I am what th' late Cap'n Ransome would term a *"local colonist".*' He added bitterly, 'Although when I came aboard a year back it appeared we were all on th' same side against th' rebels.'

Bolitho stiffened. It was strange he had never considered the feelings of those like Tyrrell before. Good American families, loyal to the Crown, the first to stand together against the sudden revolution in their midst. But as the war had spread, and Britain had fought to retain a grip, then a foothold in the colony, the loyal ones like Tyrrell had all at once become the outsiders.

He asked quietly, 'Where is your home?'

'Virginia. Gloucester County. My father came out from England to found a coastal shipping trade. I was master of one of his schooners when th' war began. I have been in th' King's service since that time.

'And your family?'

Tyrrell looked away. 'God knows. I have heard nothing of them.'

'And you wished to transfer to a ship nearer home? To take yourself back to what you now consider your own people?' Bolitho did not conceal the bite in his tone.

'No, sir. That ain't it.' He raised one arm and dropped it again, his voice angry. 'I am a King's officer, no matter what Ransome chose to believe, damn his eyes!'

Bolitho stood up. 'I will not have talk of your late captain!'

Tyrrell replied stubbornly, 'Cap'n Ransome is safe now in his cask of spirits in th' hold of a transport. His widow at his great London residence will weep for him, his service which

32

cost him his life.' He laughed shortly. '*Fever*, they said.' He looked round the cabin. 'See all this, sir? A woman's hand. We barely logged a mile in *Sparrow* without him having some damned doxy aboard for company!' He seemed unable to stop himself. 'That's th' sort of *fever* which killed him in th' end, and damned good riddance, if you ask me.'

Bolitho sat down. Once again the ground had been cut from under him. Women, here in this cabin. He had heard of such things in grander ships, but only occasionally. But in *Sparrow*, where there could be little safety if called to do battle, it was unthinkable.

Tyrrell was studying him grimly. 'I had to tell you, sir. It's my way. But I'll say this one thing more. If disease hadn't taken him, I'd have killed him myself.'

Bolitho looked up sharply. 'Then you're a fool! If you have no more strength than in your bare hands then *I* will ask for your transfer, and make no mistake about it!'

Tyrrell stared at a point beyond Bolitho's shoulder.

'Would you behave so calmly, sir, if one of th' women had been *your* sister?'

The door opened a bare inch and Stockdale's battered face peered in at them. In his hand was balanced a small silver tray, two glasses and a decanter.

He wheezed, 'Thought you might want a bit o' refreshment, sir.' He watched the two men and added, 'Sort o' celebration like.'

Bolitho gestured to the table and waited until Stockdale had left. Still without speaking he filled the glasses, conscious of Tyrrell's eyes following every movement. A bad start. For both of them. If there was still time to make amends it was now. This minute. If Tyrrell took advantage of his surrender, there was no saying where it would lead.

He handed him a glass and said gravely, 'I have two sisters, Mr Tyrrell. In answer to your question, I daresay that I would not.' He smiled, seeing the sudden surprise in the lieutenant's eyes. 'I suggest you propose a toast for the pair of us, eh?'

Tyrrell reached out and held his glass against Bolitho's.

'Then let's drink to a new beginning, sir.'

Bolitho held his glass steady. 'No transfer?'

33

He shook his head. 'None.'

Bolitho raised the glass. 'Then, to a new beginning.' He took a sip and added quietly, 'Which is well for you, Mr Tyrrell. We are sailing tomorrow to join the inshore squadron.' He paused, seeing the sudden desperation on the other man's features. 'Not so very far from the coast of Maryland.'

Tyrrell said, 'Thank God. I know I'm being stupid, but just being off that shoreline again will make th' world of difference.'

Bolitho put down his glass. 'Then I will meet our officers informally at the close of the first dog watch.' He was careful to make his tone formal again. Each of them had shown enough of his inner reserves for the present. 'In the meantime you can take me on an inspection around the ship. And I will want to see everything, good and bad.'

Tyrrell nodded. 'So you shall, sir.' A slow grin spread across his face. 'I have a shrewd feeling that *Sparrow* is going to fly like she's never done before.' He stood aside as Bolitho threw on his coat and buttoned his shirt. 'Now if you will follow me, sir.'

Bolitho looked at Tyrrell's broad shoulders as they walked towards the sunlight on the gun deck and held down a sigh. If each day was going to present a battle of wills, it would make the privilege of command a testing experience.

He said, 'We will begin with the starboard battery, Mr Tyrrell.'

The first lieutenant paused below the break in the quarter-deck. 'As you said, sir. Everything.' He grinned again. 'Good and bad.'

Stockdale picked up Bolitho's shaving bowl and peered at the untouched breakfast on the cabin table. Overhead and throughout the ship the air was alive with noise and bustle. To a landsman the activity of preparing to get under way would appear haphazard and disorganized, but to the practised eye each man had his place, and his reason for being there. The miles of cordage and rigging, each scrap of sail had a vital part to play if a ship was to move and act to perfection.

Bolitho crossed to the stern windows and stared at the nearest strip of land. It was a bright morning, with the sky above the hills very pale, washed-out and clean. He could just see the staff above the headland battery, its flag no longer list-less but lifting and curling to a fair north-easterly. It was almost physical pain to stay sealed in the cabin, waiting and fretting for the exact moment to show himself.

Voices pealed along the upper deck and shadows flitted busily across the skylight. Occasionally he could hear the plaintive squeak of a fiddle, the distorted rumble of a shanty as the men tramped around the capstan.

In the past hours and for most of the night he had tossed and turned in his cot, listening to the sea noises, the creak of timbers and rigging, his mind exploring every contingency, his brain bursting to the mental picture of his chart. Every unemployed eye would be watching him this morning. From the flagship's quarterdeck to some unknown lieutenant who probably hated Bolitho for getting the golden chance which he considered should have been his.

'The coffee, sir.' Stockdale hovered by the table. 'While it's still 'ot.'

Bolitho swung round to curse him for breaking his racing thoughts, but the sight of his anxious face was too much for him. As was so often the case.

He sat down at the table and tried to relax. Stockdale was right. If he had forgotten anything it was already too late. You could cram your head just so much. After that the mind became awash and confused beyond reason.

He sipped his coffee and stared at the cold meat. He could not touch that. His stomach was already twisting with appre-hension, the lean slices of pork would be just enough to tip the balance.

Stockdale peered through the windows. 'It will be a good passage, sir. Long enough to get the measure of these fellows.'

Bolitho glanced up at him. He must be a mind-reader. In company with another sloop they were to escort two fat transports with supplies for the troops at Philadelphia once a rendezvous with the inshore squadron had been made. Two thousand miles, mostly in open waters, would certainly allow him time to test himself and his company. He had met his officers in the small wardroom the previous evening. With the exception of Tyrrell, all had been aboard since commissioning at Greenwich. He felt vaguely jealous of their obvious familiarity with the *Sparrow*. The two midshipmen, each eighteen years old, had joined as untrained novices. They had grown up in the *Sparrow*, and were now hopefully awaiting promotion. It was a pity they were only midshipmen, he thought. They might vie too much for their captain's approval, where in a larger ship and with more competition amongst the 'young gentlemen' it would be less direct.

Buckle had said little during their informal meeting. Reserved, and no doubt waiting to see how his captain would behave under sail, he had restricted himself to matters of navigation.

Robert Dalkeith, the surgeon, was an odd one. Young, but already too plump for his own good, he was also completely bald, and wore a bright red wig. But he appeared more skilled in his trade than was usual in a King's ship, as well as cultivated, and Bolitho imagined there was more to him than he showed at face value.

Lock, the purser, a bobbing, genial stick of a man, completed the gathering.

Graves had joined them later, making a good deal of noise about his trouble with the water-lighters, the difficulties in obtaining help ashore for loading boats, in fact the list had been formidable.

Tyrrell had interrupted cheerfully, 'It ain't fair, Hector. You being singled out to be a bloody martyr like this!'

Graves had frowned and then forced a smile when the others had joined Tyrrell in the laughter.

Bolitho leaned back and stared at the skylight. He was not sure of Graves either. A hard worker. Ransome's toady? It was hard to see where the latent bad feeling had started between him and Tyrrell. But it *was* there right enough.

'Captain, sir?'

Bolitho started and looked at the door. Midshipman Bethune was standing with his hat under his arm, his free hand grasping the hilt of his dirk. He was a round-faced, sturdy youth, and his face was a mass of dark freckles.

'Well?'

Bethune swallowed. 'Mr Tyrrell's respects, sir, and the transports have weighed. *Fawn* has her preparative hoisted, sir.' He glanced curiously round the cabin.

Bolitho nodded gravely. 'I will be up directly.'

With elaborate care he forced himself to take another sip of coffee. It almost choked him. *Fawn* was the other sloop for the escort and would be carrying Colquhoun, in addition to her commander, as senior officer.

The midshipman was still inside the cabin. He added awkwardly, 'I am from Cornwall, too, sir.'

Bolitho smiled in spite of his tension. The competition had begun already.

He replied, 'I will try not to hold it against you, Mr Bethune.' He dropped his eyes as the boy fled from the cabin.

He stood up and took his hat from Stockdale. Then with a brief nod he strode out towards the waiting sunlight.

The gangways and decks seemed more crowded than ever as seamen ran this way and that, pursued by the hoarse shouts of their petty officers. As he reached the quarterdeck he saw two heavy transports idling towards the headland, their tan sails flapping and billowing in the breeze.

Tyrrell touched his hat.

'Anchor's hove short, sir.'

'Thank you.'

Bolitho strode to the larboard side and stared towards the anchored *Fawn*. He could see the muddle of men at her capstan, the scurrying preparations as the cable became bar-taut beneath her bulkhead.

He crossed to the opposite side, trying to ignore the seamen who were poised at their stations on every hand. Beyond the nearest headland towards the hard blue horizon he saw a lively pattern of small white horses. Once outside this sheltered anchorage it would be good sailing weather. He glanced at the sluggish swirl of currents around a nearby storeship and bit his lip. He had to get free of all the shipping first.

'*Fawn*'s signal is close up, sir!' Bethune was clinging to the shrouds with his telescope, although Colquhoun's signal was clear enough to be seen without any glass.

'Stand by on the capstan!'

Tyrrell ran to the rail and cupped his big hands. 'Loose th' heads'ls!'

Beside the wheel Buckle stood near the two helmsmen, his eyes watching Bolitho.

'Breeze is freshening a mite, sir.'

'Yes.'

Bolitho walked to the rail and stared along his command. He saw Graves watching over the anchor party, Midshipman Heyward at the foot of the mainmast with his division of seamen.

'Signal, sir! *Up anchor!*'

'Hands aloft and loose tops'ls!'

He stood back to watch the seamen surging up the shrouds and out along the swaying yards, their bodies black against the sky. Tyrrell said very little, and Bolitho observed that the topmen were well able to manage without added inducement from the deck. As canvas thundered loosely from the yards and the ship gave a long-drawn shudder, he saw the *Fawn*'s masts already swinging across the stern, her foretopsail filling to the wind as she heeled over.

Bethune called, 'Signal! *Make haste*, sir!' He lowered his glass, trying to avoid Bolitho's eye.'

'Man the braces!'

He tried to shut out Colquhoun's last signal. Maybe he was endeavouring to goad him into doing something foolish. Perhaps he was always the same. But nothing must or would spoil this moment.

From forward came the cry, 'Anchor's aweigh, sir!'

Free of the land the *Sparrow* tilted steeply to the wind, the headland sliding across her jib-boom as with more and more canvas thundering and hardening from her yards she paid off into the wind.

Blocks clattered and whined, and high above the decks the seamen sprang about like monkeys.

Bolitho looked at Buckle. 'Lay her on the larboard tack. Then set a course to weather the headland.' He held the master's gaze and added, 'We will get the courses on her directly and see if we can take the edge off *Fawn*'s lead.'

Moments later, with her courses and topsails filling to the

morning breeze, the *Sparrow* glided swiftly past an anchored two-decker which wore a vice-admiral's flag at the fore.

Bolitho glanced at Tyrrell and saw him give a quick grimace. He might have cause to regret his application for transfer, Bolitho thought. And so, if his trust in Tyrrell proved false, would he.

Between two anchored Indiamen and on down the fairway towards that beckoning headland. Small craft bobbed astern in the frothing wake, and when Bolitho moved from studying the compass he saw they had already cut *Fawn*'s lead by half a cable.

Buckle glanced at the surgeon who was clinging to the mizzen shrouds with one hand and holding on to his outrageous wig with the other.

He winked. 'We have a rare one here, Mr Dalkeith.'

Dalkeith kept his face immobile as Bolitho glanced aft towards him before replying, 'Poor Captain Ransome would never have left port with such dash, eh?' He gave a sly grin. 'But then, at this time o' morning he would have been somewhat *tired*!'

They both laughed.

Bolitho's voice brought them up with a jerk.

'There is a yawl on the larboard bow, *Mr* Buckle. Laugh later with my blessing, but run her down within sight of the flagship and you will laugh to another tune!'

He turned back to the rail as Buckle hurled himself towards his helmsman.

The tip of the headland was already dropping abeam, and he felt the *Sparrow*'s stem bite into the first gentle roller, her deck tilting still further under her press of canvas.

Tyrrell shouted, 'Anchor's secured, sir!' Spray had soaked his face and shirt but he was grinning broadly.

Bolitho nodded. 'Good. Now get the forecourse trimmed. It looks like a piece of untidy linen.' But he could not hold his severity. 'By God, she *flies*, does she not?'

He looked aloft at the squared sails and braced yards, the masthead pendant which flicked out like a coachman's whip. He had seen it all before so many times, but now it felt as if it was unique.

Bethune called, 'From *Fawn*, sir. *Take station to wind'rd!*'

Bolitho smiled at him. 'Acknowledge.'

To the quarterdeck at large he added, 'A *fine* morning.'

By the hatchway Stockdale watched Bolitho's pleasure and felt inwardly happy. He ran his eye over the hurrying seamen as they slithered down once more to the deck. Tanned and healthy, what did they know about anything? He picked his uneven teeth with an ivory pin. The captain had seen more action in the past years than they knew about. He watched Bolitho's squared shoulders as he paced restlessly on the weather side. Given time, they'd come to find out, he decided.

3. The Privateer

BOLITHO opened his eyes and stared for several seconds at the unlit lantern spiralling above his cot. Despite the weariness in his limbs and the fact he had been on deck repeatedly during the night he found it hard to sleep. Beyond the screen which partitioned his sleeping quarters from the cabin he could see the pale light of dawn, and knew from the lantern's sluggish movement and the uneasy creak of timbers that the wind was little more than a breeze. He tried to relax, wondering how long it would take to break the habit of awakening with each dawn, to enjoy his new-found privacy.

Feet thudded on the quarterdeck above, and he guessed that soon now the seamen would be turning to for another day It had been two weeks since the little convoy had sailed from Antigua, and in that time they had covered only half their set distance. One thousand miles in open waters, and each mile marked by perverse winds and no winds at all. Barely an hour passed without the need to call the hands to make or shorten sail, to trim yards in the hope of catching a dying breeze, or to reef against one violent and taunting squall.

Buckle's gloomy prediction about *Sparrow*'s sailing qualities in a poor wind had proved only too true. Time and time again she had paid off, her canvas flapping in confusion as yet one more wind had died and left them almost becalmed. Hard work and angry words had eventually brought her back on station again, only to have the whole thing repeated before the end of a watch.

Patrol and scouting duty had been the lot of *Sparrow*'s company for most of their commission and they had yet to learn the true misery of convoy over long passages. The two transports had not helped. They appeared totally unwilling to realize the importance of staying in close company, so that if they became scattered by a swift squall it took many hours to

41

urge, threaten and finally drive them back into formation. Colquhoun's curt signals had only succeeded in antagonizing the master of one of them, a big transport named *Golden Fleece*. On more than one occasion he had ignored the signals altogether or had caused the *Fawn* to withdraw from her proper station at the head of the convoy in order to commence a verbal exchange which could be heard by everyone else nearby.

Bolitho climbed from the cot and walked slowly into the cabin, feeling the deck lifting gently beneath his bare feet before slipping away in a trough, the motion bringing the usual clatter of blocks, the drawn-out groan of the rudder as the helmsman brought the sloop back under command.

He leaned his hands on the sill of the stern windows and stared out at the empty sea. The two transports, if they were still together, would be somewhere on *Sparrow*'s starboard bow. Bolitho's orders were to stay to windward of the well-laden ships so as to be ready to run down on any suspicious vessel and hold the maximum advantage until she was proved friend or foe.

In fact they had sighted an unknown sail on three separate occasions. Far astern, it had been impossible to know if it was the same on each sighting or three individual vessels. Either way, Colquhoun had refused to be drawn to investigate. Bolitho could sympathize with his unwillingness to leave the valuable transports, especially as the wind might choose the very moment when his sparse forces were scattered to play a new trick or bring some real enemy amongst them. On the other hand, he was very conscious of a sense of uneasiness after each call from the masthead. The strange sail was like a will-o'-the-wisp, and if it was hostile could be methodically following the little convoy, awaiting exactly the right moment to attack.

The door opened and Fitch padded into the cabin carrying two jugs. One was coffee, and the other contained water from the galley for Bolitho's shave. In the pale light from the windows he looked smaller and scrawnier than ever, and as usual kept his eyes averted while he prepared the necessary cup for Bolitho's first coffee of the day.

'How is it on deck?'

Fitch raised his eyes only slightly. 'Mr Tilby reckons it'll be another roastin' day, sir.'

Tilby was the boatswain, a great untidy hulk of a man who was given to some of the most profane language Bolitho had heard in ten years at sea. But his knowledge of weather, his forecast of what each dawn might bring, had been only too accurate.

And under a blazing sun, with little space to find shade or comfort, the *Sparrow*'s seamen had more torment to face before night found them again. It was amazing how they all managed to survive in such a small hull. What with extra stores and spare spars, powder and shot, and countless other requirements for keeping a ship at sea, some of the men were hard put to find space for a hammock. In addition the *Sparrow* had all the great lengths of anchor cable to be neatly stowed when she was under way. Several hundred fathoms of thirteen-inch hemp for the main anchors and another hundred of eight inch for the kedge took up more space than fifty human beings required for even the most basic needs.

But if this or any other ship was to survive and live from her own resources then such discomforts had to be endured.

He sipped the coffee. If only the wind would freshen and stay with them. It would help drive away the weariness and drudgery of work aloft, and also give him time to drill the guns' crews to better advantage. They had had few such drills during the first days out of harbour, and once more he had been made aware of the strange attitude of acceptance he had originally noticed. Perhaps they had been so long without actually being called to do battle they had taken the drills as merely something to be tolerated, even expected from a new captain. Their timing had been good enough, if somewhat rigid, they had gone through all the motions of running out, traversing and pointing, but again and again he had felt something was badly lacking. As the crews had faced outboard through their open ports he had sensed their indifference There was nothing to fight, so what was the point of it all, their relaxed bodies seemed to indicate.

He had tackled Tyrrell about it but the first lieutenant had said cheerfully, 'Hell, sir, it don't signify they won't be able to fight if th' time calls for it.'

Bolitho's sharp reply brought a new barrier between them, and for the moment he was prepared to let it remain.

Captain Ransome must have used the sloop like a personal possession, a yacht, he thought. Sometimes during the night when Bolitho had come down to the cabin after a frustrating hour on deck watching the hands shortening sail yet again he had pictured Ransome with some woman or other. Or Tyrrell pacing the quarterdeck, tearing himself apart as he imagined his sister just a few feet below him. He had not mentioned the matter to Tyrrell since his first outburst, but had found himself wondering about the real story, and what had happened to the girl after Ransome's sudden death.

Stockdale came into the cabin with the shaving bowl. He glared at Fitch and wheezed, 'Get the cap'n's breakfast!'

To Bolitho he added, ' 'Nother clear morning', sir.' He waited until Bolitho was in his chair and then held the razor against the window. He seemed content with its edge. 'Wot we need is a real good blow.' He showed his uneven teeth. 'Make some o' these young puppies jump about!'

Bolitho relaxed as the razor moved precisely over his chin. Stockdale said very little but he always seemed to hit the exact point.

In between strokes he replied, 'In another month we'll be in the hurricane season again, Stockdale. I hope *that* will satisfy you.'

The big coxswain grunted. 'Seen 'em afore. Us'll see 'em again an' live to tell of it.'

Bolitho gave up. Nothing, it seemed, could break the man's supreme confidence in his ability to produce a miracle, even in the face of a hurricane.

Voices rang out overhead, and then he heard feet dashing down the companion ladder from the quarterdeck.

It was Midshipman Heyward, impeccable as ever in spite of being on his feet for much of the night.

'Captain, sir.' He watched Stockdale's razor poised in mid-air. 'Mr Graves's respects and *Fawn* has just signalled. Sail to the nor'-east.'

44

Bolitho snatched the towel. 'Very well. I will come up.'

Stockdale laid down the bowl. 'That same one, sir?'

Bolitho shook his head. 'Unlikely. She'd never overreach us in one night, even if she was after our blood.' He rubbed his face vigorously. 'But in this empty sea a sight of anything is welcome.'

When he reached the quarterdeck he found Tyrrell and most of the others already there. Below the mainmast the hands had just been mustered in readiness for the morning assault on the decks with holystones and swabs, while others were waiting by the pumps or just staring up at the barely filled sails.

Graves touched his hat.

'Masthead lookout has not yet sighted anything, sir.'

Bolitho nodded and strode to the compass. North-west by north. It seemed as if it had been riveted in that direction since time began. It was hardly surprising *Fawn* had sighted the newcomer first. In her position ahead and slightly to starboard of the transports she was better placed. All the same, he would have wished otherwise. *Fawn*'s signals and execution of Colquhoun's orders always seemed to be that much quicker than his.

Through the criss-cross of rigging and shrouds and slightly to starboard of the rearmost transport he saw the other sloop tacking awkwardly in the gentle westerly breeze. With every stitch of canvas on her braced yards she was barely making headway.

From aloft came the sudden cry, 'Deck there! Sail on the starboard beam!'

Tyrrell crossed to Bolitho's side.

'What d'you think? One of our own?'

Graves said swiftly, 'Or a damned Yankee, eh?'

Bolitho saw the exchange of glances, the sudden hostility between them like something physical.

He said calmly, 'We will know directly, *gentlemen*.'

Midshipman Bethune called, 'From *Fawn*, sir. *Remain on station.*'

Graves said complacently, 'There goes *Fawn*. She's going about to take a soldier's wind under her tail.'

Bolitho said, 'Get aloft, Mr Graves. I want to know everything you can discover about that sail.'

Graves stared at him. 'I've a good hand aloft, sir.'

Bolitho met his resentment gravely. 'And now I require a good officer there, too, Mr Graves. An experienced eye and not just a clear one.'

Graves moved stiffly to the weather shrouds and after the merest hesitation began to climb.

Tyrrell said quietly, 'Do him good, that one!'

Bolitho glanced around the crowded quarterdeck.

'Maybe, Mr Tyrrell. But if you imagine I am using my authority to foster some petty spite between you then I must assure you otherwise.' He lowered his voice. 'It is an enemy we are fighting, not each other!'

Then he took a telescope from the rack and walked to the foot of the mizzen mast. Steadying his legs against the uncomfortable motion he trained the glass on the *Fawn* and then very slowly beyond her. Minutes passed, and then as the distant ship lifted on some large roller he saw her topgallant sails shining in the first sunlight like matched pink shells. She was clawing her way close-hauled on a converging course, her yards braced so tightly they were almost fore-and-aft.

Graves yelled down, 'Frigate, sir!' A pause as every man looked up at his tiny silhouette against the sky. 'English built!'

Bolitho stayed silent. English built perhaps. But who now stood behind her guns? He watched *Fawn* edging round, her masthead pendant lifting and curling listlessly. More flags shot up her yards and Bethune yelled, 'From *Fawn*, sir. Recognition signal.' A further pause as he groped through his grubby book. 'She's the *Miranda*, thirty-two, Captain Selby, sir.'

Buckle said to the deck at large, 'From England most likely.'

The light was already stronger, and as he stared across the brightening water Bolitho could feel the first warm rays against his face. From England. Every man aboard was probably thinking of those words. Except for Tyrrell and the colonists in the company. But all the rest would be picturing his own past way of life. Village or farm, some ale house outside a harbour or fishing port. A woman's face, a child's last grip before the harder hands of the press-gang.

46

He found himself thinking of his own home in Falmouth. The great stone house below Pendennis Castle where his father would be waiting and wondering about him and his brother Hugh, while he remained in Cornwall. Like all the Bolitho ancestors, his father had been a sea-officer, but having lost an arm and his health was now confined to a landbound existence, always within sight of the ships and the sea which had forsaken him.

'From *Fawn*, sir. *General. Heave to.*'

Colquhoun, it seemed, was quite satisfied with the other ship's identity. For once the two transports needed no extra goading to obey the signal. Perhaps like the rest they, too, were eager for news from that other world.

Bolitho closed the glass and handed it to a boatswain's mate.

'Shorten sail, Mr Tyrrell, and heave to as ordered.' He waited until the lieutenant had shouted for the topmen to get aloft and then added, 'That frigate has been hard worked so her mission must be important.'

He had watched the newcomer while she had forged towards the uneven cluster of ships, had seen the great scars on her hull where the sea had pared away the paintwork like a giant knife. Her sails, too, looked much repaired, evidence of a rapid voyage.

Bethune shouted, '*Miranda*'s hoisted another signal, sir!' He swayed in the shrouds as he tried to level his big telescope. 'To *Fawn. Captain repair on board.*'

Once again *Fawn*'s response was swift, her big gig being swayed out within minutes of the signal. Bolitho could imagine Colquhoun hurrying to the other ship and the *Miranda*'s consternation when they discovered that he was senior to their own captain.

Whatever it entailed, the matter was obviously urgent, and not merely an exchange of gossip at this chance encounter in open waters.

Bolitho rubbed his chin and said, 'I'm going below. Call me if anything happens.'

In the cabin he found Stockdale waiting with his coat and sword, his lopsided grin very broad as he muttered, 'Thought you'd be wantin' these sir.'

Fitch was gripping the table, his legs spread apart as the sloop rolled and staggered in the uncomfortable troughs, the power gone from her sails. He was staring at the breakfast he had just brought, his narrow features resigned.

Bolitho smiled.

'Never fear, I'll find time to eat it later.'

It was strange that the mere sight of another ship, the obscure hint of excitement, had given him an appetite at last. He gulped down some coffee as Stockdale adjusted his sword-belt before handing him the coat.

Perhaps *Miranda* had discovered an enemy and needed help to attack them. Maybe the war was over, or another had broken out elsewhere. The possibilities seemed endless.

He looked up and saw Tyrrell peering through the open skylight.

'Cap'n, sir! The *Fawn*'s gig is shoving off from th' frigate.'

Bolitho replied, 'Thank you.' He forcibly disguised his disappointment. 'That was quick.'

Tyrrell vanished and he added quietly, 'There'll be time for breakfast after all.'

He was mistaken. Even as he began to unfasten his sword-belt Tyrrell's face reappeared at the skylight, his words filling the cabin as he shouted, 'From *Fawn*, sir. *Repair on board forthwith.*'

Stockdale bounded from the cabin, his hoarse voice bellowing for the gig's crew which the boatswain had already thought prudent to muster.

With frantic haste the boat was swung outboard and dropped alongside, where with little thought for dignity or safety, Bolitho hurled himself into the sternsheets, his sword clattering against the gunwale and almost tripping him on top of the oarsmen.

Stockdale bawled, 'Give way all!' In a lower but no less menacing tone he added, 'An' remember, my beauties, if one o' you misses a stroke you'll 'ave me to answer!'

The gig seemed to fly across the water, and when at last Bolitho regained his composure and looked astern he saw the *Sparrow* was already a cable clear. She was pitching steeply in the swell, her sails rippling and flashing in disorder while

48

she lay hove to in the pale sunlight. In spite of his own busy thoughts and anxiety he could still find time to admire her. In the past he had often watched the stern cabin of a passing man-of-war and pondered about her captain, what sort of person, his qualities or lack of them. It was very hard to accept that the *Sparrow*'s cabin was his own and that others might be wondering about him.

He turned and saw *Fawn*'s outline overlapping that of the idling frigate, figures moving round her entry port to receive him with all formality. He smiled to himself. In the face of hell it seemed likely that no captain, no matter how junior, was expected to go without his proper acknowledgement.

Bolitho was met at the entry port by Maulby, *Fawn*'s commander. He was very thin, and but for a pronounced stoop would have stood well over six feet. Life between a sloop's decks must be uncomfortable for such a man, Bolitho thought.

He appeared a few years older than himself and had a drawling, bored manner of speaking. But he seemed pleasant enough and made him welcome.

As they ducked beneath the quarterdeck Maulby said, 'The little admiral is excited, it would seem.'

Bolitho paused and stared at him.

'Who?'

Maulby shrugged loosely. 'In the flotilla we *always* refer to Colquhoun as our little admiral. He has a way of inserting himself in the role without actually holding the necessary rank!' He laughed, his bent shoulders touching a deckhead beam so that he appeared to be supporting it with his own frame. 'You look shocked, my friend?'

Bolitho grinned. Maulby, he decided, was a man you could like and trust on sight. But he had never before heard such comments made about a superior by two subordinates meeting for the first time. In some ships it would be inviting disaster and oblivion.

He replied, 'No, but I am refreshed!'

The stern cabin was much the same size as his own. There was no other similarity. Plain, even spartan, he was reminded of Tyrrell's anger, his bitter attack on the *woman's touch*. He

49

saw Colquhoun sitting at a table, his chin in his hands as he stared at some newly opened despatches.

Without pausing he said, 'Sit down, both of you. I must give this matter my attention.'

Maulby looked gravely at Bolitho and dropped one eyelid in a quick wink.

Bolitho glanced away, Maulby's easy acceptance of their superior was daunting. *The little admiral.* It suited Colquhoun very well.

Maulby seemed well able to remain relaxed, yet he was nobody's fool. Bolitho had noted the smart way his men had moved about the gun deck, the crisp passing and execution of orders. Bolitho had not met the other captains of Colquhoun's flotilla. If they were all such odd birds as Maulby it was hardly surprising that Colquhoun was showing signs of strain. Or maybe in such small ships individual characters were more noticeable. He thought of Pears in the old *Trojan*, his rugged features which had never seemed to alter under any circumstances. In a gale, close to a lee shore, or under enemy fire, witnessing a flogging, or commending some sailor on promotion, he had always seemed remote and beyond personal contact. It was hard to imagine Maulby, he paused, or himself either, with such aloof and godlike powers.

Colquhoun's voice broke across his thoughts, sharp and incisive. '*Miranda*'s captain has brought serious news.' He still did not lift his head. 'France has signed an alliance with the Americans. It means that General Washington will have the full support of French regular troops *and* a powerful fleet.'

Bolitho shifted in his chair, his mind grappling with Colquhoun's announcement. The French had already done much to help their new ally, but this would mean that the war was now firmly in the open. It also implied that the French were showing fresh confidence in the Americans' chance of victory.

Colquhoun stood up quickly and stared through the stern windows. 'The *Miranda* is carrying despatches and intelligence for the Commander-in-Chief at New York. When he left Plymouth he had a brig in company with duplicate information for Antigua. The ships were caught in a storm shortly after clearing the Channel and the brig was not seen again.'

Maulby asked quietly, 'Taken by the French, sir?'

Colquhoun swung on him with unexpected anger. 'What the hell does it matter? Taken or wrecked, dismasted or bloody well eaten by worms, it makes no difference to us, does it!'

Suddenly Bolitho realized the cause of his attack. Had Colquhoun remained at Antigua until his own ship had refitted, Maulby would have been in charge of the convoy's escort. *Miranda*'s captain, desperate to carry his news to New York, and senior to Maulby, would have ordered him to make arrangements for the information to be taken without delay to Antigua. Nobody could rely on the brig's survival as an excuse for doing nothing. By a mere twist of fate, or Colquhoun's determination to keep control of his ships at sea, *Miranda*'s captain had been able to pass on the decision to him.

In a calmer tone Colquhoun continued, 'It has been reported that the French have been preparing ships for months. From Toulon a whole squadron set sail weeks ago and slipped through the Gibraltar patrols without so much as a squeak of news getting out.' He looked at each of them in turn. 'They could be on their way here, to the American coast, anywhere, for all we know, damn their eyes!'

The *Fawn* had swung slightly in the slow procession of troughs, and through the swaying windows Bolitho could see the two transports, huge and ungainly, their yards askew as they awaited the next signal. Each transport was filled to the deck seams with much needed supplies for the army in Philadelphia. In the wrong hands they would represent a tremendous prize, and the realization must be foremost in Colquhoun's mind.

Colquhoun said, '*Miranda* has agreed to stand by the convoy until we contact the inshore squadron. But in this damned weather it might take weeks.'

Bolitho imagined Colquhoun was picturing the distance like a mental chart. All those miles, with the knowledge that he must eventually make the long passage back to Antigua to resume control of his small force.

Maulby drawled, 'May I suggest that I continue with the transports, sir? With *Miranda* in company we will be safe enough.' He glanced at Bolitho. 'You could then return in

Sparrow to English Harbour, pass the news to the admiral and prepare our own ships for further work.'

Colquhoun stared at him, his eyes unseeing.

'God damn the complacency of our precious Government! For years this has been brewing, and while the French have been building new ships, ours have been allowed to go rotten for want of money. If the Channel Fleet were to be ordered to sea tomorrow I doubt that more than twenty sail of the line would be capable!' He saw their surprise and nodded vehemently. 'Oh yes, gentlemen, while you have been out here imagining that all would be ready if once the call came, I have been made to stay silent and watch it happening.' He struck the table with his fist. 'Some flag officers are too concerned with political power and gracious living to care for the wants of the fleet!'

He sat down heavily. 'I must decide . . .'

The door opened slightly and a frightened-looking midshipman said, 'From *Miranda*, sir. She requests instructions . . .' He got no further.

'Tell him to mind his manners!' Colquhoun glared at him hotly. 'It is *my* decision!'

Bolitho glanced at Maulby. For the first time in his life he was beginning to realize the meaning of command. Whatever Colquhoun decided could be equally right or wrong. Bolitho had learned one thing well. If you made a right decision, others often received the credit. But make a wrong one and you were in no doubt where the blame would lie.

Colquhoun said suddenly, 'Send for your clerk, Maulby. I will dictate new orders for . . .' he looked at Bolitho, 'for *Sparrow*.'

He seemed to be speaking his thoughts aloud. 'I do not doubt your ability, Bolitho, but you lack experience. I will need Maulby's *Fawn* with me until I know what is to happen next.' He gestured to the table as the ship's clerk entered the cabin. 'You must remain with the transports. *Miranda's* captain will give you guidance, and you will obey him to the best of your skill. Your orders will allow you to return to the flotilla when the transports have been delivered.' He paused and added softly, 'Delivered.'

Bolitho rose to his feet. 'Aye, sir.'

'Now get out and leave me to draft these orders.'

Maulby took Bolitho's elbow and guided him towards the gun deck.

'I think the little admiral is worried, my friend.' He sighed. 'I was hoping to rid my ship of his presence and pass him on to you.' He turned and gave a quick grin. 'There is no justice in this world!'

Bolitho saw his gig falling and rising in the swell, Stockdale shading his eyes as he watched the sloop for a recall.

He said, 'The news is bad, but not unexpected. At least the pretence is done with.'

Maulby nodded gravely. 'No comfort, I fear, to the lamb about to be devoured.'

Bolitho stared at him. 'Not that serious surely?'

'I am not certain. What the Frogs do today the damned Spaniards will copy tomorrow. Soon we will have the whole world at our throats.' He frowned. 'The little admiral is right on one score. It seems that our Government is run by demons, most of whom appear determined to drive the rest of us to madness.'

The first lieutenant hurried into view and proffered a freshly sealed envelope.

Maulby clapped Bolitho on the shoulder and said cheerfully, 'Think of us sometimes. While you enjoy your leisurely voyage, I will be forced to share my table with *him*.' He rubbed his hands. 'But with any luck he may get promotion and vanish forever.'

The lieutenant said urgently, 'Captain Colquhoun's compliments, and will you join him immediately?'

Maulby nodded and held out his hand.

'Until we meet again, Bolitho.' He seemed unwilling to let him leave. Then he said awkwardly, 'Be warned, my friend. You have a fine command, but you also have a large number of colonists in your company.' He tried to smile. 'If the war goes badly, there are some who might be tempted to change allegiance. In their shoes I could perhaps feel the same.'

Bolitho met his gaze and nodded. 'Thank you. I will remember it.'

Maulby did not hide his relief. 'There, I knew you were a good fellow! Not one to treat my clumsy advice as patronage.'

Bolitho grinned. 'You took a risk. I might have gone to Colquhoun and told him of your name for him.'

'I would have denied it!'

'Naturally!'

They both laughed.

Then as the gig hooked on to the chains they became formal again. Even before Bolitho had reached the boat, flags were soaring up the *Fawn*'s yards, and an acknowledgement appeared above the frigate with equal speed.

Bolitho settled himself in the sternsheets and stared towards his ship. Colquhoun had taken the responsibility and made a decision. His own responsibility was just beginning.

Lieutenant Tyrrell turned as Bolitho's head and shoulders rose through the quarterdeck hatch and waited until he had made his usual inspection of the sails and compass before remarking, 'She's running well, sir.'

Bolitho walked across the tilting deck and rested his hands on the rail, feeling the hull quivering beneath him like a living creature. The noon sun stood high over the ship, but he was able to ignore it, conscious only of the well-filled sails, the leap of spray up and over the bowsprit. It had been five days since *Fawn* had turned back for Antigua, and it seemed as if Colquhoun's disappearance from their midst had brought a change of luck and weather. Perverse as ever, but for once on their side, the wind had backed suddenly to south-south-west and had freshened into a lively blow which had hardly dropped during the whole time. Under bulging canvas the ships had driven on towards the American coast, which according to the most recent calculations now lay some two hundred and fifty miles away. The heavy merchantmen had maintained a good five knots, satisfied perhaps that *Miranda*'s captain was content to leave them to their own devices. The frigate's signals had been confined for the most part to *Sparrow*. For within twenty-four hours of leaving *Fawn* the masthead lookout had sighted a solitary sail once again, far astern of the convoy, a tiny white flaw on the horizon.

Bolitho had sent Graves aloft with a telescope, but even he had been unable to identify the mysterious follower. Next he signalled to the frigate, requesting permission to investigate. He had been refused. *Miranda*'s captain was probably regretting his meeting with the convoy. But for their dragging weight he would have reached his objective by now and would have borne no blame for failing to pass his news to Antigua. But once in contact with the slower vessels he had no choice but to act as he had. Also, he would be fully aware that once beyond his control *Sparrow* might become too involved with a separate situation to return, and thus leave him with total responsibility for the transports.

The unknown sail had not been sighted again, and Bolitho had accepted that *Miranda*'s captain had been right, if over cautious, to restrain his efforts.

He looked at Tyrrell's bronzed features and nodded. 'I am well satisfied.'

He watched some foretopmen sliding down the backstays, racing each other to the deck after their work aloft. Buckle was right. She moved like a bird with any sort of wind. He watched the *Bear*, the transport closest to his own ship, and wished they were free of the convoy. Then he could really put *Sparrow* to the test. Royals, even studding sails could be rigged, if only to find out what she could accomplish under every stitch of canvas.

Most of the unemployed officers were on deck enjoying their usual gossip before the midday meal, careful to stay on the lee side and as much out of his way as possible.

He saw Dalkeith, the surgeon, laughing with Buckle, his head very white in its baldness under the harsh light. The red wig was being vigorously shaken by the wardroom servant, and Bolitho guessed it had been given some sort of a wash. Lock, the purser, was in a more serious conversation with young Heyward, opening and ruffling a big ledger in the wind as he explained some point of victualling which might place the midshipman's knowledge above that of his friend Bethune. The latter, being on watch, stood untidily by the quarterdeck rail, his shirt open to his waist and massaging his stomach with one hand.

Bolitho smiled. The boy was no doubt hungry. Midshipmen like Bethune usually were.

Down on the gun deck many of the seamen were lounging beneath the sails' great shadows or passing the time like their officers. The boatswain was with his own friend Yule, the gunner, and together they would have made a frightening pair of highwaymen, Bolitho thought. Whereas Tilby was vast and ungainly, his heavy features seamed with too much drink, Yule was swarthy and lithe, like a stoat, with darting, flinty eyes which were forever on the move.

As he glanced from group to group he was again reminded of his new-found isolation. Privacy which could lead to loneliness. Privilege which might become a burden.

He thrust his hands behind him and began to pace slowly along the weather side, letting the warm wind ruffle his hair and play with his open shirt. Somewhere out there beyond the hammock nettings was the coast of America. It would be strange to drop anchor only to find the war had finished, that blood had proved too strong in the face of France's new challenge. If England were to admit to America's independence then perhaps both nations would unite against France and settle her ambitions once and for all. He glanced at Tyrrell's profile and wondered if he was thinking the same.

He shut Tyrrell's personal problems from his mind and tried to concentrate on the string of affairs which daily needed his attention. The water supply should be replenished as soon as possible. The casks were poor, and water soon became rancid in this climate. And he would purchase fresh fruit whenever they contacted the land or some supply vessel. It was amazing that the ship's company had stayed so healthy when Ransome had failed to take such simple precautions. Aboard the old *Trojan* he had not seen one case of scurvy in the three years he had been in her, evidence of Captain Pears's concern for his men and a valuable lesson to all his subordinates. He had already spoken about it to Lock, and after some hesitation the purser had muttered, 'A *costly* affair, sir.'

'Costlier if our people go down with disease, Mr Lock. I have known a whole squadron rendered useless because of such skinflint methods.'

Then there was the matter of a flogging, his first as captain. He had always disliked unnecessary use of punishment even though he knew it to be necessary on occasions. In the Navy discipline was harsh and instant, and when a ship was miles from home and other authority, it was a captain's deterrent to insubordination and final confusion. Some captains used it without thought. Brutal and inhuman floggings were commonplace in many ships, and as a young midshipman Bolitho had nearly fainted after one such spectacle. Other captains, weak and inefficient, left authority to subordinates and shut their ears to its misuse.

But for the most part the English seaman knew the measure of his service, and if he took chances was prepared to accept the consequences. And if one man thieved or cheated another of his messmates he had no mercy at all. The justice of the lower deck was equally feared to that of a captain.

But this case was different, or could be from what he knew of it. A seaman had defied Lieutenant Graves during a night watch when the hands had been called to reef topsails in an unexpected squall. He had shouted at the officer and called him a 'heartless bugger' within earshot of some twenty other people.

In confidence Tyrrell had asked Bolitho to accept the seaman's explanation. He was a good hand, and Graves had provoked him in a fit of anger when he had failed to reach his station on the mainyard with his companions.

A dirty Yankee bastard. They were the words Graves had used. Too lazy to do his proper duty, and no doubt too gutless to fight when the time came.

All this and Tyrrell's heated attack on Graves's handling of the matter were fresh proof of the latent tension amongst the company under his command.

Graves had been adamant. The man had insulted him in front of his watch and must be punished.

He was right in one respect. His authority had to be upheld or he would never be able to retain control again.

Bolitho blamed himself. If he had had more time to consider this unusual situation, or had taken less comfort from his own new position, he could have prevented it. By example or by forcing his will on his officers he might have made them realize

57

that such behaviour would not be tolerated. But that was all too late now. It had happened.

He had compromised by standing the man over, knowing then as at this moment that he was merely postponing the inevitable.

He glanced up towards the mainyard, braced hard round as the ship heeled close-hauled on a larboard tack. He could see the man now, naked but for a scrap of canvas, working with some others on the endless business of re-splicing and repairs high above the deck. Did Tyrrell really think the man was provoked? he wondered. Or was he standing up for him because he imagined Graves was getting at him by punishing another colonist?

'Deck there!' The masthead lookout's cry was muffled by the wind and the lively crack of sails. '*Miranda*'s signallin'!'

Bolitho swung round. 'Jump to it, Mr Bethune! You are half asleep today!'

Tyrrell stood aside as the midshipman ran to the lee shrouds with his telescope.

'Thinking of his next meal!' He was smiling at the boy's confusion.

'It seems that the masthead lookout was the only one in *this* watch thinking of his duty, Mr Tyrrell!'

The edge of his voice brought a flush to the lieutenant's face and he turned away without answering.

Bethune called, 'From *Miranda*, sir! *Sail to the nor'-west!*'

'Acknowledge.'

Bolitho was angry with Tyrrell's careless attitude, angrier still more with his own unfair outburst.

Some two miles ahead of the *Golden Fleece*, her patched sails hard-bellied and drawing well, the *Miranda* was already setting her topgallants in readiness to investigate. The unknown ship, whatever she was, lay somewhere across the larboard bow, and as she had not been seen before it seemed likely she was on a converging course.

'Deck there! Sail in sight! Fine on th' weather bow!'

Bolitho looked round at the intent faces. For an instant he toyed with the idea of making his way to the dizzy mainmast crosstrees himself, in spite of his fear of heights which he had never been able to overcome. The long climb up those shivering, vibrating shrouds might drive his anger away and leave his mind clear once again.

He saw Raven, the newly appointed master's mate, and said, 'Go aloft. Take a glass and tell me what you see.'

Buckle had told him that the man was an experienced sailor, one who had already served in several King's ships and would not be easily fooled by first appearances.

Before Raven had even reached the mainyard the lookout called again, 'Two ships! Close in company!'

Every eye was on Raven's body as he swarmed out and around the futtock shrouds and up towards the topmast head.

Bethune, still smarting over his failure to see *Miranda*'s signal, suddenly stiffened and called, 'Gunfire, sir!' He had his hands cupped round his ears, giving his round face the appearance of a freckled goblin.

Bolitho looked down at him. Then as his hearing adjusted itself beyond the crack of sails and the plunging sweep of spray around the hull, he, too, heard the deeper, discordant thud of cannon fire. He was almost beside himself with impatience, but he knew if he hurried Raven he might become too confused to make a proper assessment.

'Deck there!' It was Raven at last. 'First ship's a merchantman! She's under attack from a brig!'

Buckle exclaimed thickly, 'Privateer, by God!'

Bolitho snatched a telescope and trained it through the dark mass of rigging and beyond some men who were grouped on the forecastle. A trick of the light. He blinked and tried again. No, there it was, a tiny white speck which seemed to mingle with the unending pattern of crisp wavecrests. The lonely merchantman had been unlucky, but now with any sort of good fortune they might turn the tables on her attacker.

The *Miranda* was already tacking violently, her sails in confusion as she headed away from her original station. Even as her sails refilled and hardened on the new tack Bolitho saw her signal flags breaking to the wind.

Bethune said quickly, 'General signal, sir. *Remain on station.*'

Buckle swore. 'After the bloody prize money himself, the greedy bugger!'

The gunfire was clearer now, and as he raised the glass again Bolitho saw smoke drifting down-wind from the two ships, the lithe shape of the attacking brig as she endeavoured to close the range still further.

He shut the glass with a snap, aware of the muttering behind him, disappointment which matched his own. *Miranda*'s captain was probably making the attack more to break the frustration of a slow passage than to humiliate the *Sparrow*.

He looked at Tyrrell's broad shoulders and said, 'Signal the *Bear* to make more sail. She's dropping astern badly.'

Then he turned back to watch the frigate. She was moving fast in spite of the wind being almost abeam of her sails, and he could see her port lids opening, the single line of muzzles catching the sunlight as they were run out in readiness to fight.

The brig's captain must have realized what was happening. Even so, he was probably unwilling to lose his prize with victory almost in his grasp.

On the gangways and gun deck his own seamen were chattering and waving their arms about, and he guessed they were discussing how they would have acted had they been given the chance to go for the privateer.

Bolitho recalled Raven to the deck and said, 'You did well.'

The man grinned uncomfortably. 'Thank you, sir. The brig's a Yankee right enough. Seen many like her in me time. T'other one's an Indiaman by her looks, 'though her gunnery ain't so good as some on 'em. There's never a mark on the Yankee's canvas.'

Tyrrell shouted, 'Th' brig's broken off the action! He's going to make a run for it!'

Bolitho sighed. The merchantman was already turning steadily towards the little convoy while the *Miranda* under full sail charged towards her attacker. The brig, if well handled, stood a fair chance against a frigate in matters of speed and manœuvrability. But this one had waited just that much too long.

Converging like prongs of a trap the three vessels would pass beam to beam, the frigate shielding the merchantman and well able to rake the brig from stem to stern as they passed.

Provided the brig was not too badly damaged she might be

useful to the fleet. Either way, *Miranda*'s captain would gain a nice purse of prize money.

He tore his eyes away as sounds of angry voices came up the quarterdeck ladder at his side.

It was Tilby, flushed from some secret hoard of rum, his face heavy with rage as he said, 'Beg pardon, sir, but this 'ere man says 'e wants to speak to 'ee.' He glared severely at the seaman in question. 'I told 'im that no man under punishment can speak to an officer without permission.'

Bolitho saw that the seaman behind Tilby was the one waiting to be flogged. He was a young, well-made man and was dragging at the boatswain's arm with frantic determination.

'What is it, Yelverton?' Bolitho nodded to Tilby. 'Is it *so* important?'

The seaman reached the quarterdeck, and swallowed hard. 'That ship, sir! She ain't no Indiaman! She's a damned Frenchie! I seen her in Boston some years back!'

Bolitho swung round. 'God in heaven!'

It was at that moment the oncoming merchantman fired a full broadside into the *Miranda*'s unmanned side as she passed, the sound going on and on until it reached the heart of every man in the convoy.

4. A Total Responsibility

EVEN AT TWO MILES' RANGE Bolitho saw the *Miranda* give
a violent shiver as the broadside swept across her. It must have
been aimed high, for as the smoke fanned away he saw the
havoc left by the sudden onslaught, maintopmast gone, and
most of her sails ripped and punctured like rags in a gale.

He thrust himself from the nettings and noticed that the
men near him were still standing like groups of statues, or
people so stricken they were unable to think or respond.

He shouted, 'Mr Tyrrell! Beat to quarters and clear for
action!' He gripped Bethune's arm, seeing his dazed expression
as he added, 'Run up the colours!'

A ship's boy seized his drum and began to beat out the
staccato tattoo. The men on deck, and poised in the bows
where they had waited to watch *Miranda*'s swift victory, came
alive and began to run to their stations. But gone was the
automatic movement of men at drill, or the grim silence of old
hands facing one more battle. They hurried like those already
too confused to act for a set purpose. Some cannoned into one
another, others stood momentarily at the wrong gun, or
groping with unfamiliar equipment until a petty officer kicked
them away.

Bolitho looked at Buckle, trying to keep his tone level
amidst the din around him. 'Get the courses off her and set
the t'gallants. There'll be enough risk of fire without having
the canvas burn around our ears.'

Below the quarterdeck he heard the thud and bang of screens
being torn down, a patter of feet as the boys dashed from the
magazine with powder for each waiting gun.

He made himself face the approaching ships, knowing it
was taking far too long to prepare for action. How near they
looked. There was more gunfire, the smoke writhing between
the vessels making it impossible to see what was happening.

He held his breath as he saw the *Miranda*'s yards swinging above the smoke, and knew her captain was trying to go about and run parallel with his attacker. Guns roared through the drifting fog, their long orange tongues flashing above the churned water, some of the balls whipping away over open sea, leaving vicious spurts of spray to mark their progress.

Miranda was still edging round, her pockmarked sails flapping weakly as she began to swing past the wind's eye. Her captain was either going to fight the bigger ship gun to gun, or intended to slip past her stern and rake her with a broadside as he did so.

Bolitho heard someone groan as the enemy fired into the smoke. Gun by gun down her hidden side, the balls could almost be felt across the tumbling white-horses.

It was superbly timed, catching the frigate even as she was beginning to pass across the wind. The enemy was using langridge or chain-shot, for as the slow broadside smashed home Bolitho saw the *Miranda*'s fore and mainmasts stagger and then begin to topple sideways into the smoke, the sails jerking to the bombardment. From a lithe and beautiful ship to a crippled wreck, the *Miranda* was still trying to turn, her bow-chaser firing blindly, the ensign showing scarlet from her mizzen.

Tyrrell shouted wildly, 'Cleared for action!'

Bolitho looked at him. 'Load and run out, if you please.'

The lieutenant stayed facing him, his eyes very bright in the sunlight.

'You ain't going to fight *both* of 'em, surely?'

'If necessary.'

Bolitho turned as more shots echoed and murmured across the shortening distance. He saw the brig clawing away from the two larger ships, her maintopgallant leaning at a dangerous angle where *Miranda*'s first balls had found their mark.

The planks vibrated under his shoes, and as the port lids opened the *Sparrow*'s eighteen guns squeaked and rumbled towards the sunlight, the bare-backed seamen slipping on sanded decks as they tried to keep in time to the shouted commands from their captains.

Bolitho stared along the length of his ship with something

like despair. In moments now, all would be finished. His ship, his precious *Sparrow*, would be sharing the frigate's fate.

And it had all been so easy. It had happened so often in the past that the sight of a helpless merchantman being harried by a well-armed privateer had not even aroused the faintest suspicion. No wonder the privateer's sails had been unmarked in their carefully staged battle. How the two American captains must have laughed when *Miranda* had swept in to defend her own murderer.

He felt Stockdale breathing noisily beside him, the sudden grip of the swordbelt around his waist.

He said huskily, 'By God, sir, them's bad odds!'

'Deck there!' The masthead lookout had been forgotten in the sight of disaster. '*Miranda*'s goin' to grapple!' The unseen lookout gave a cracked cheer. 'She's goin' to close with the bugger!'

Bolitho ran to the rail. The frigate was almost hidden by the heavier shape of the enemy ship, but he could tell from the set of her mizzen that she was indeed lurching towards her attacker. Another crash of gunfire made the smoke spout upwards between them, and the frigate's remaining mast vanished in a welter of rigging and ripped canvas. But Bolitho could see the sudden activity on the enemy's gangways, the surge of figures by her foremast, and pictured the battered frigate heading her bows straight for the forecastle. Muskets cracked feebly across the water, and he saw the telltale flash of steel as the two vessels ground momentarily together and the fight became hand to hand.

He grasped Tyrrell's arm and shouted, '*Miranda*'s given us time!' He saw no understanding in his eyes, only disbelief. 'If she can hold on, we will close with the brig!'

He shaded his face against the glare and watched the brig as she swept down towards the two transports.

'She'll cross *Golden Fleece*'s bows, and rake her as she passes.' He was shouting his thoughts aloud. 'We will wear ship directly, pass between the transports, and return the compliment!'

Tyrrell bit his lip. 'But we might collide with th' privateer, sir!'

Bolitho swung him round, pointing him at the embattled ships. 'Do you want those lads to die for nothing, man?' He pushed him to the rail. 'Now get ready to wear when I give the order!'

The brig was already dead ahead of *Sparrow's* raked jib-boom, no more than a mile away. Aboard the leading transport Bolitho could see smoke from a solitary gun, although he saw no sign of a ball.

'Signal the transports to keep station, Mr Bethune!' He repeated the order to break the midshipman from his unmoving stance. '*Lively!*' If either of the transports' captains lost his head now all would fail. The enemy would destroy or capture at leisure. Even now there was little room for hope of any kind. And all of it, from the first hint of surprise to this moment, had been merely minutes.

He made himself walk aft towards the taffrail, his eyes passing over the crouching swivel gunners, the two helmsmen at their unprotected wheel, Buckle grim-faced and staring at the sails above. All of them.

He saw Raven, the new master's mate, watching him wretchedly, and paused to say, 'You weren't to know. She *was* an Indiaman after all, but not, I fear, as she was intended.'

Raven shook his head, so concerned with his failure to recognize the enemy that he seemed oblivious to the sporadic crash of cannon fire.

'I should've *seen* 'er, sir. But I saw what I *expected* to see, an' I'm powerful sorry on it after you givin' me a chance to better meself.'

Bolitho smiled, feeling his lips cracking with the effort.

'And I will expect you to do even better this day, Mr Raven!' He strode aft, hands behind his back, the new sword flapping against his thigh.

Buckle pursed his lips in a silent whistle. 'He's a calm one. Death coming up the hawse an' he just walks about like he was enjoying himself.'

Behind the fixed smile Bolitho continued to pace the deck, his ears pitched above the gunfire to catch the news that the brig had reached the first transport. If her captain saw through his frail plan it would be pointless to continue with it. He would either have to run away from the fight and carry *Miranda*'s important news to the admiral, or stay and await the final meeting with the converted Indiaman. A few of the *Miranda*'s guns were still firing here and there, their muzzles almost overlapping those of the other ship. Between decks it must be a slaughterhouse, he thought despairingly.

Tyrrell shouted, 'Brig's crossing her bows!'

Sharper explosions echoed over the water, and Bolitho knew the brig was firing her starboard battery as she ran easily across the transport's bowsprit. Before she had vanished beyond *Golden Fleece*'s great bulk he saw the American flag whipping jauntily from her gaff, the sudden stab of musket fire from her low deck as sharpshooters practised their aim.

'*Now!*' Bolitho sliced the air. 'Wear ship!'

As the helm went over and along the *Sparrow*'s crowded decks the men threw themselves on the braces, the hull seemed to stagger violently under the shock. Blocks screamed, and above the decks the great yards creaked round with such speed that Bolitho could feel the whole fabric shaking in protest. But nothing carried away, and as she heeled steeply to take the wind under her stern the sails lifted then filled to its thrust.

Bolitho cupped his hands. 'Mr Graves! Engage with the larboard guns first! You will point the thirty-two-pounder yourself!' He saw Graves nod before vanishing beneath the forecastle in the direction of the bow-chaser.

How fast she was moving, despite both her courses being brailed up to the yards for fear of fire when the guns started to engage. The maintopgallant seemed to bend forward, the masthead pendant flicking straight out towards the bows as if to point the way.

Already the jib-boom must be crossing the leading transport's quarter, and to starboard Bolitho saw the second one, *Bear*, altering course slightly as if fearful of a collision with the sloop which was dashing across her path. More shots came from beyond the first transport, and he saw smoke funnelling down her hull to mark the brig's progress.

From forward came the cry, 'Thar she be! On th' larboard bow!'

The *Sparrow*'s unexpected appearance between the two

transports seemed to have caught the brig's captain totally by surprise. The privateer was passing down the transport's side, about a cable clear, her yards braced round to hold her on a starboard tack.

Bolitho yelled, 'We'll cross the enemy's hawse and rake him as we go!' He saw some of his men staring at him from their guns, faces strained and confused. He drew his sword and held it over his head. 'As you bear, lads! Make each ball strike home!'

The brig was barely half a cable away, her bowsprit pointing at right angles towards *Sparrow*'s figurehead. The distance seemed to be falling away at a tremendous speed, and Bolitho knew that if he had misjudged it, or if the wind chose this instant to drop, the enemy would drive into the sloop's side like a battering ram and split her seams wide open.

The big thirty-two-pounder in the bows broke the spell, the crash of the explosion transmitting itself through the deck until it reached Bolitho's feet. He saw the brig's shrouds slashed open, the whirl of bright wood splinters as the ball ploughed into her tiered boats. Then gun by gun down *Sparrow*'s side the broadside continued, with Graves bursting into the smoky sunlight, waving his sword and yelling orders to each crew.

Frantically the enemy captain tried to wear ship and follow *Sparrow*'s onrushing charge. Unable to get her own guns to bear, and with most of the forward shrouds and rigging hanging like black weed above her deck, the brig was staggering drunkenly under the well-aimed barrage.

Then with the helm over and some wind still alive in the torn sails the brig finally came under command. Here and there a gun banged out, but in their haste the privateers were firing haphazardly into the whirling smoke.

'Load and run out!' Tyrrell was yelling above the din. 'Roundly!'

Bolitho shouted, 'Don't wait for a broadside! Let each captain fire whenever he has loaded!' It was useless to expect these men to keep on firing as a team once they, too, were under the enemy's metal.

Graves rasped, 'Sponge out, you stupid bugger!' He had to drag a dazed man to the rear of his gun. 'Are you mad?' He pushed the luckless seaman towards the gun captain. 'I'll put you in irons if I see you . . .'

Bolitho did not hear the rest of it. The brig was slowly edging round until she was lying almost diagonally across the larboard quarter. Smoke fanned down around him and he felt musket balls thudding into the deck planks, the maniac whine as one ricocheted from a swivel gun just feet away.

Stockdale said desperately, 'Keep on the move, sir! Them buggers'll mark you down else!'

Bolitho stared at him, knowing his own face was set in a wild grin. It never failed to amaze him that it was so easy to lose control and reason once a battle had begun. Later perhaps . . . He shook himself. There would be no later when they closed with the bigger ship.

He yelled, 'They are shooting blind, Stockdale!' He waved his sword around the quarterdeck. None of the officers had found time to get their uniform coats or hats and like himself were dressed only in shirts and breeches, and those were already grimy with drifting powder-smoke. 'See? They can take their pick of us today!'

A seaman at the mizzen braces gave a terrible scream and was hurled on to his side by the force of a musket ball. Blood spurted from his chest, and as he rolled about in agony Bolitho called, 'See to that man, Mr Bethune!' When the midshipman hesitated, his face like chalk under the freckles, he added harshly, 'Your mother is at home, boy, so you can weep alone *after* you have done your duty!'

Bethune dropped to his knees, his breeches spattered with the blood, but his face suddenly determined as the dying sailor groped for his hand.

Buckle yelled, 'The Yankee will try to work across our stern, sir!'

Bolitho nodded. There was nothing else the enemy could do. With most of his sails damaged by cannon fire, and already overreached by *Sparrow*'s maddened attack through the transports, the brig's captain must either try to cross astern or tack and risk his own poop coming under fire.

He snapped, 'We will wear ship, Mr Buckle. Lay her to the larboard tack and follow the brig round, nose to tail!'

He was still grinning, but could feel his mouth raw with tension as once again the men hurled themselves on the braces, their smoke-grimed bodies glistening in the glare as they angled back above the deck, their eyes on the yards above them.

'Helm a'lee!' Buckle was adding his own weight to the wheel.

Bolitho watched the bowsprit swinging, heard the immediate crash of guns as Graves directed his newly loaded battery towards the other ship.

Through the dense gunsmoke Bolitho saw the murky shape of the leading transport, now some two cables away.

'Steady as you go, Mr Buckle!' A ball whimpered overhead, and when he glanced up he saw a neat hole in the centre of the big spanker. 'Keep station on *Golden Fleece*, she is better than any compass today!'

He winced as the hull jumped once, twice and yet again, as some enemy shots smashed into it. But the brig was in a bad way, and she was drifting stern-first, her complete foremast dragging over the side like a fallen tree. Men were working in the wreckage, axes flashing, while others continued to fire and reload the guns as before.

'Steady, sir! Nor'-west by north!'

Bolitho raised his sword, his eyes narrowed against the reflected sunlight as he watched the brig swinging drunkenly on the tow of fallen spars.

'Easy!' The sword held the sunlight. '*Easy*, lads!' Not a gun fired, and along the deck only at the weapons not yet reloaded was there any sort of movement.

Another ball slammed into the lower hull, and somewhere a man screamed in torment as he was clawed down by flying splinters.

The sun was shining into his eyes now, and through the drifting smoke he saw the outline of the brig's tattered main-topsail, the glint of gla-- as she helplessly presented her stern.

'Fire as you bear!'

Driven by the wind, the smoke came funnelling inboard through port after port as Graves ran along the gun deck, his voice cracking from the strain of shouting directions.

A shadow passed briefly above the smoke, and through the

din Bolitho heard the splintering crash of a complete mast falling, and guessed it had been sheared off between decks by the *Sparrow*'s merciless bombardment.

Then as the *Sparrow* forged ahead once more he heard cheering and knew it was from the *Golden Fleece*. As wind drove the smoke apart he saw the brig very clearly and someone on her splintered deck waving the flag in surrender. Mastless, and with her stern gouged open by the slow broadside, she was little better than a hulk. Within her small hull her company must have been savagely mauled.

Tyrrell was staring at it, his eyes bright with concentration, and by his side Heyward was almost jumping up and down, his voice half choked by smoke.

Then, almost before the *Sparrow*'s dazed company could feel the taste of their conquest, the air was blasted apart with one deafening explosion. Spars, complete sections of timber and deck planking, all whirled above an angry scarlet core, and across the water a shock wave rolled towards the sloop like a miniature typhoon. When the smoke and flying fragments subsided there was nothing to show of the privateer but for a few pieces of charred flotsam and an upended jolly boat which was miraculously undamaged. A sudden spark, an upended lantern, or someone so crazed in the horror between the shattered decks that he had ignited a fuse, the brig's end was terrible in its completeness.

Bolitho said, 'Get the maincourse on her, Mr Tyrrell! We must make haste to assist *Miranda*.' He waited until Tyrrell had brought the stunned seamen to their senses, his voice hoarse through his speaking trumpet, and then added, 'They will know that we can still sell our lives dearly.'

It took little time to overhaul the *Golden Fleece* and to see the two embattled ships about a mile distant. They had drifted in the fury of combat, their hulls masked in smoke, through which the flash of musket fire, the occasional glare of a swivel, were clear to see.

The frigate was listing against her heavier adversary, like a hulk already dead, and without using a glass Bolitho could see that the fighting had spread down across the fore deck as more boarders hacked their way between the grappled ships.

'We will go about, Mr Tyrrell. Lay her on the starboard tack once we have gained some room and prepare to engage with the other battery.'

He bit his lip to steady his racing thoughts. A quick glance aloft told him that the masthead pendant was lifting as firmly as ever. The wind was steady from south-south-west.

'Pass the word for Mr Graves to lay aft.'

When the lieutenant arrived, his face gaunt with fatigue, Bolitho said, 'I want the starboard bow-chaser to keep firing at the enemy. As soon as we have gone about I'll expect it to concentrate on that ship, no matter what.'

Buckle called, 'Ready on th' quarterdeck, sir.'

Bolitho nodded. 'Put the helm down, if you please.'

'Helm a'lee, sir!'

Tyrrell was already bellowing through his trumpet, and forward the seamen were leaping like demons at the headsail sheets, and with canvas flapping the *Sparrow* started to swing into the wind.

'Man the braces!' Bolitho gripped the rail, his eyes smarting as the sun lanced between the shrouds.

'Heave there! With all your weight!'

Across the wind and still further round, the yards groaning in unison. Then as the sails refilled and laid the deck over in the opposite angle he watched the distant ships edging very slowly between the foremast shrouds as if caught in a giant web. 'Steady, Mr Buckle! Hold her!'

He paced a few steps this way and that, aware that Tyrrell was urging the men at the braces to trim the yards still further, that the dead seaman had gone from the quarterdeck, and that Ben Garby, the carpenter, with his mates, was slithering through the after hatch to inspect the damage there. Aware of all this and more, yet not a part of it as he had once been.

'Steady, sir! Full an' bye!'

He nodded, his mind busy with the two ships. Close-hauled it would take thirty minutes to reach them, maybe more. *Miranda* was almost overrun by enemy boarders. Outnumbered from the start, she would have lost many good men in that first savage broadside.

'*Fire!*'

71

As the muffled cry came from forward he saw the puff of smoke beneath the starboard cathead, felt the sharp convulsion as the thirty-two-pounder crashed inboard on its tackles. He snatched up a glass and saw the ball plunge close to the enemy's hull, throwing up a tall waterspout.

Heyward muttered hoarsely, 'Near!'

Bolitho looked away. The big ex-Indiaman mounted anything up to forty guns, at a guess. She could finish *Sparrow*, if ever she could bring her artillery to bear, with even a badly aimed broadside. Less.

Bang. Another ball crashed away from the bow-chaser, and he watched the feathers of spray lifting from wave to wave until it plunged hard alongside the other ship.

They should hear us and see we are coming. He tried to clear his brain. What should he do? Signal the transports to run? No. They were helplessly overladen and slow. It would merely prolong their agony.

Overhead, the spanker cracked noisily, and Buckle cursed it before allowing the helm to be eased still further.

Bolitho knew without looking that sailing so close to the wind was cutting away his chances of reaching the ships in time to help.

Someone walked past him. It was Bethune, his arms hanging at his sides, his breeches covered with dark blood blotches and a smear where the seaman's fingers had made their last agonized grip on this earth. Bolitho stared at him.

'Mr Bethune!' He saw the youth jump. 'Come here!'

He walked to the rail and back again. It was worth an attempt. Anything was, now. If they arrived alongside after *Miranda* had struck to the enemy, *Sparrow*'s decks would be as red as the flag above his head.

The midshipman waited. 'Sir?'

'Make this signal at once.' He rested his hand on Bethune's plump shoulder. He could feel the skin through his shirt. Like ice, in spite of the sun.

'*Signal*, sir?' He stared up at him as if he had misheard. Or his captain had gone mad.

'Yes. To *Miranda*. Sail in sight to the nor'-east!' He tightened his grip. 'Then *move* yourself!'

Bethune fled, calling shrilly for his assistants, and within a minute the bright signal flags broke to the wind, while Tyrrell stared from them to Bolitho, first with incredulity and then with slow understanding.

Buckle said, 'There's few poor devils'll see that aboard *Miranda*.'

Tyrrell was studying Bolitho. 'No. But th' privateer will. He might just think that a patrol from th' squadron has come to join th' fight!'

Bolitho waited until Graves's bow-chaser had fired yet again and said, 'It is all we can do at present.'

Minutes dragged by like hours, and then as a freak down-draught of wind swept across the two snared ships Bolitho caught his breath. A thin shaft of light where there had been none. Then a glint of water. Wider still, as the ships drifted apart and the big privateer set her foresail and jib to work clear. Then *Miranda* was quite separate, the water between her and the other ship dotted with wreckage and torn canvas, where here and there a man thrashed to stay afloat amidst a litter of bobbing corpses.

A ragged cheer came up from *Sparrow*'s gun deck, and several ran to the gangways to watch while the enemy spread more canvas and lengthened her outline against the wind.

Tyrrell's grin froze as Bolitho snapped, 'Keep those men *silent*!' He realized he was still holding his sword, that his hand was aching with the force of his grip. 'Look yonder, Mr Tyrrell. There's no call for cheers this day.'

Tyrrell turned to stare at the *Miranda*'s dark shape. The rising clouds of smoke as her remaining hands quenched fires and groped amidst the wreckage of their ship. As *Sparrow* drew closer they could all see the thin tendrils of scarlet which ran from her scuppers, the great pitted holes along every part of her hull.

'Pass the word for Mr Tilby to prepare boats for lowering. Call the surgeon and send him with them.' Bolitho hardly recognized his own voice. Clipped, dull, inhuman. 'Then shorten sail and get the t'gallants off her. We will stand under *Miranda*'s lee for the present.'

He ignored the rush of feet as Tilby's men dashed to the

boat shackles. He saw Graves walking aft towards the quarterdeck, wiping his face and chest with a wet rag. Above the
activity the sails were still drawing well, but there were plenty
of holes which would need attention before nightfall. A few
stays and halyards were broken, and he knew the hull had been
hit several times on or near the waterline. But the pumps
sounded normal enough. She was taking it like a veteran.

Dalkeith came hurrying up the ladder, his heavy bag gripped
against his chest, face streaming with exertion.

'How many, Mr Dalkeith?' Again he heard his own voice
as a stranger's.

The plump surgeon was staring at the frigate, his eyes dull.
'Two killed, sir. Five wounded by splinters.'

Bolitho tried to recall the man who was killed by his side.
Manners. That was his name.

He said, 'Manners. Who was the other?'

'Yelverton, sir. He was killed by a ball at the foremast.'
He looked down. 'Took his head off.'

Graves was halfway up the ladder but recoiled as Bolitho
said, 'Yelverton. Did you hear that, Mr Graves? The one
man who kept his senses when all others were too blind to see
the truth. The one you wanted to flog?' He turned away.
'Well, he'll not trouble you further, Mr Graves. Nor we him.'

Blindly he saw Stockdale watching from the foot of the
mizzen mast. 'Call away the gig. I will visit Captain Selby and
see what must be done.'

'Aye, sir.'

Stockdale glanced back at him as he hurried to the boat tier.
He had never seen Bolitho so stricken or so moved before.
And for once he did not know what to do to help.

Bolitho entered his cabin and unbuckled his sword before
throwing it on to the bench seat below the windows. Fitch
and a young seaman were busy replacing the furniture, and
another was mopping away smoke stains from the low deckhead. For in action even the captain's quarters were not spared.
With the hasty removal of screens the cabin became an extension of the gun deck: on either side of it a squat twelve-
pounder, now once again hidden by discreet chintz covers.

He stared at the nearest gun, his eyes blurred with strain. *A woman's touch.* Then he turned abruptly to face Tyrrell and Graves who had followed him into the cabin upon his return from the crippled *Miranda*.

His mind was so filled with questions and suppositions, his brain so racked by the sights and sounds aboard the frigate, that for a moment he was unable to speak at all.

Beyond the bulkhead he could hear the steady thud of hammers, the rasp of saws as the ship's company continued work on repairs. After a full hour aboard the *Miranda* he had returned to find his own command settling down to the task of making good the damage from their encounter with the privateer with such orderly dedication that he had been unable to compare the scene with what he had just left. The sailmaker and his mates had already replaced the punctured canvas, and with their needles and palms flashing in the sunlight covered every foot of deck space as they patched the others sent down from the yards.

Garby, the carpenter, had greeted him at the entry port and had told him that the brig's gunnery had not been too damaging. Two shot holes below the waterline which his men were already plugging, and several others which he would repair before sunset. Garby had spoken quickly, professionally, as if like the rest he was unwilling to think about the *Miranda* and the fate which could have been theirs.

Graves was the first to break the silence.

'All guns secured, sir. No damage to tackles or ports.' He dropped his eyes under Bolitho's unmoving stare. 'Better'n we could have hoped.'

Tyrrell asked quietly, 'How was it, sir?'

Bolitho let himself drop into a chair and thrust out his legs in front of him. The breeches were black with powder stains and his climb up the frigate's side. *How was it?* Once again he saw the pictures of death and horror, the few uninjured men who were trying even now to put the frigate to rights. Smoke stains and great patches of drying blood, gaping corpses littered amongst the fallen spars and broken planking. It was a miracle that *Miranda* was still able to keep afloat.

He said, 'They hope to get a jury rig hoisted by sometime

tomorrow. Provided the wind doesn't get up, or the pumps foul, they will obtain steerage way.' He rubbed his eyes with his knuckles, feeling the weariness enclosing him like a vice. 'Some of the wounded will be transferred to the transports directly. There they will have more room to recover.'

He tried again to shut the agony from his mind. Men so badly mutilated by splinters that they should be dead already. Midshipmen and even seamen in charge of repairs because of the carnage on the quarterdeck. He had found the frigate's first lieutenant supervising the recovery of the mizzen topmast when he had climbed aboard. The man had had one arm in a sling and his forehead had looked as if it had been laid open by a hot iron.

Graves breathed out very slowly. 'They did well against such odds.'

'Yes.' Bolitho wanted to get them out of the cabin. Seal the door and shut them a·vay from his uncertainty.

Tyrrell said, 'I've passed th' word around th' ship, sir. I think our people know how satisfied you . . .'

Bolitho's tone made him fall back. '*Satisfied?*' He lurched to his feet. 'If you feel cause for complacency, Mr Tyrrell, then please contain it!' He moved to the windows and back again. 'I have seen it for myself. Our people are not moved by a sense of victory. They are *relieved*, and nothing deeper than that! Thankful to be spared a similar mauling, and all too eager to overlook their own shortcomings!'

Tyrrell said quickly, 'But that's a mite unfair, surely.'

'You think so?' He sank down at the table, his anger spent. 'Raven had the measure of it. He saw what he expected to see, as did Captain Selby in *Miranda*. And like you, Mr Tyrrell, our people thought that fighting an enemy was just an extension of drill, a few cuts and a few curses, and all would be well. Perhaps we have been too victorious in the past and have been overreached by this newer kind of warfare.'

There was another silence, so that the hammering deep in the hull became insistent, and to Bolitho suddenly urgent.

Graves asked, 'What will we do now, sir?' He sounded wary.

Bolitho faced them gravely. 'Captain Selby is dead. Killed in the first broadside.'

He walked to the quarter windows and stared towards the drifting frigate. Without effort he could picture the wounded first lieutenant, the man who had somehow fought his ship alongside the enemy. Knowing it was all he could do despite the crippling losses and damage already suffered. Now, without a single lieutenant, aided by a mere handful of junior warrant officers, he was doing his utmost to repair the ship. To get her to safety before the sea or an enemy found him again.

In the shattered chaos of Selby's cabin he had unlocked the safe and handed Bolitho the despatches without hesitation. Even now that he was back in his own cabin he found it hard to believe. Junior command, and then, almost in the twinkling of an eye, he was to shoulder the total responsibility for them all. Colquhoun and Maulby were beyond reach. And Selby was dead. He had seen his corpse on the splintered quarterdeck, pinned beneath an upended nine-pounder, one hand still clutching his sword like a useless talisman.

Tyrrell's voice made him turn towards them again.

'Then *you* are in command, sir?'

The lieutenants were watching him intently, their faces showing both doubt and apprehension.

Bolitho nodded slowly. 'We will continue with the transports before dusk. After we have ferried the *Miranda*'s wounded across to them and done what we can for their own ship.' He tried not to think of the endless problems which lay ahead. 'When we have made contact with the squadron as ordered we will proceed with the despatches to the Commander-in-Chief.' He let his eyes stray around the cabin. All at once it was smaller, the sloop more vulnerable.

'And *Miranda*, sir?' Tyrrell's tone was hushed.

Bolitho kept his voice level and without emotion, knowing that if he showed them even for an instant, his true feelings, they would lose what small faith they still retained.

'Her people will do what they must. We cannot stay with her, nor would they wish it.'

Spray pattered against the thick windows. The wind was already freshening slightly. Tyrrell licked his lips, his eyes distant as he stared towards the dismasted frigate.

Bolitho added, 'That will be all. Keep the hands working until the last minute.' The two lieutenants, in their filthy shirts and breeches, turned and left the cabin without another word. Bolitho looked at Fitch and said, 'You may go, too. I wish to think.'

When Fitch and his helpers had gone he rested his head in his hands and allowed his body to sway with the ship's uncomfortable motion.

Tyrrell probably thought him heartless for leaving the other ship without company or aid. Graves, too, would no doubt be finding plenty of fuel for his own personal fires.

He stood up, fighting back the tiredness and strain, knowing he must not heed nor care about their considerations. They were in a war which for too long they had only skirted like spectators. If learn they must, it were better to be done at once.

Then he recalled the *Miranda*'s lieutenant, the bitterness in his voice as he had described the action. He was able to add little to what Bolitho already knew and guessed. But for **one** thing, the name of the big privateer. *Bonaventure*. It was a name he would not forget.

There was a tap at the door. It was Lock, his face dark with gloom as he began to recount a list of stores damaged in the brief fight with the brig.

Bolitho faced him and said quietly, 'Now let me have a full list, Mr Lock, and I will give you my opinion.'

It was useless to think of what had passed. He was alone now, and only the future, like the next horizon, had any true meaning for him.

5. All The Luck . . .

Bolitho nodded. 'Very well.'

He had already seen it, but was concentrating instead on the overlapping lines of anchored ships, the nearest of which, a two-decker, wore a rear-admiral's flag at her mizzen.

Then he took a quick glance along the busy gun deck, the preparations to drop anchor for the first time since leaving Antigua. It was ten days since they had watched the *Miranda*'s battered outline fall further and further astern until they had lost it altogether. Days of fretting impatience as they repeatedly shortened sail to keep station on the two transports. And when at last they had found a frigate of the inshore squadron they had received not freedom but yet another unexplained leg to the journey. *Sparrow* would not hand over her charge of the transports, nor would she close with the shore to supervise their unloading. Instead she was to proceed with all despatch to New York. The frigate's captain had been impatient to be away and had merely sent a midshipman across to *Sparrow* with his orders. From what little he had discovered, Bolitho gathered the frigate had been waiting and patrolling for three weeks in order that his message could be passed on to the convoy, and had no wish to be involved further.

He shifted his gaze to the guardboat, rocking gently in the offshore swell, a large blue flag lifting and curling from her bows to mark where the sloop should anchor.

The wheel creaked as Buckle passed his directions to the helmsmen, and forward on the beakhead, framed against the glittering water, he saw Graves waiting for the command to anchor. He heard someone laugh and saw the two transports idling awkwardly towards another anchorage, their yards alive with men as they shortened sail.

Dalkeith saw him turn and remarked, 'Glad to see the back

of 'em, eh, sir?' He mopped his face with a handkerchief. 'They've been with us so long I felt we were towing the beasts.'

The gunner climbed halfway up the ladder and called, 'Permission to begin the salute, sir?'

Bolitho nodded. 'If you please, Mr Yule.' He turned away, knowing that but for the gunner's request he would have forgotten about it in his concern for what would happen next.

While the *Sparrow* continued easily towards the guardboat, her canvas clewed up but for topsails and jib, the air shook to the regular bang of cannon fire as she paid her respects to the rear-admiral's flag.

Bolitho wanted to take Bethune's big telescope and study the other ships, but guessed too many glasses would now be on him. His natural curiosity might be seen as uncertainty, or the apprehension of a young commander approaching an unfamiliar anchorage. Instead he made himself walk a few paces along the weather side, noting with satisfaction that the nettings were neatly filled with hammocks and every unused line and halliard was either belayed or flaked down on the decks. Of their clash with the brig there was little or no visible sign. The ten days had been well used to replace woodwork and apply fresh paint.

Tyrrell was standing at the rail, a speaking trumpet under one arm. In his blue coat and cocked hat he seemed unfamiliar again, a stranger, like the day he had come into the cabin after his visit to the flagship.

The last wisp of gunsmoke drifted forward above the anchor party, and he concentrated his attention on the last half cable of distance. The other ships were spread out on either bow and looked impressive, indestructible.

He raised one hand slowly. 'Lee braces, Mr Tyrrell. Hands wear ship!'

Why then was he so apprehensive? Perhaps the frigate's curt orders had hidden something deeper? He tried to disregard it. After all, he had been sick to death of the slow passage with the transports, so how much worse it must have been for the solitary frigate.

Tyrrell's voice brought a screaming chorus from the circling gulls which had been with them for several days.

'Tops'l sheets!' He was squinting into the sunlight, watching the darting figures high above the deck. 'Tops'l clew lines! Roundly does it, lads!'

Bethune's voice cut across the shouted orders and the flapping crack of canvas.

'From *Flag* to *Sparrow*, sir. *Repair on board.*'

Bolitho nodded. 'Acknowledge.' The admiral did not believe in wasting time.

'Helm a'lee!'

Gently, easily, the *Sparrow* turned her jib-boom into the wind, her sails vanishing as the topmen vied with each other to fist the unruly canvas under control.

'Let go!'

From forward came a brief splash as the anchor plunged to the bottom, and before Graves had turned to signal the quarterdeck, Tilby, the boatswain, was already urging the boat-lowerers to sway out the gig.

Tyrrell came aft and touched his hat. 'I hope you get good news, sir.'

'Thank you.'

Bolitho wondered what it must be like for Tyrrell. He was back off his own coastline. Sandy Hook. He must have sailed this way many times in his father's schooner. But there was nothing on his features to betray whatever he was thinking. The usual controlled respect which he had shown since the battle.

Tyrrell had not spared himself in his efforts to get the damage repaired. He had a manner which at first glance seemed easy going, even casual, but there was no doubting his ability, or the edge of his tongue if someone was foolish enough to mistake his attitude for weakness.

'I doubt that I will be long in the flagship.' Bolitho watched the gig's crew tumbling down the side.

'Th' admiral may ask you to take lunch, sir.' Tyrrell's eyes crinkled in a rare smile. 'I gather th' old *Parthian* is known for a good table.'

Stockdale called, 'Gig's ready, sir.'

Bolitho looked at Tyrrell. 'Make arrangements for taking in fresh water and casks. I have told Mr Lock to see what he can do about fruit.'

Tyrrell followed him to the entry port where the side party were assembled. He hesitated and then asked quietly, 'If you could find out anything about . . .' He shrugged. 'But then I guess you'll be too busy, sir.'

Bolitho ran his eye over the nearby seamen. Had he learned anything about them since he had taken command? Did he even know what they thought of him?

He replied, 'I will do what I can. Perhaps your father has sent some message for you.'

Tyrrell was still staring after him as he clambered into the boat, his ears ringing to the squeal of pipes.

When Bolitho climbed up through the *Parthian*'s gilded entry port and doffed his hat to the quarterdeck he was immediately reminded of the *Trojan*, the life he had so recently left behind. All the old smells and sights came crowding back, and he marvelled that he had forgotten so much in so brief a time. A lieutenant guided him to the flag captain's cabin and relieved him of the despatches and a bag of letters which *Miranda* had brought from England.

He said, 'The admiral will read these first, sir.' His eyes moved swiftly over Bolitho's new uniform coat. Searching perhaps for the same old answer. *Why him and not me?*

The admiral did not send for him for a full hour, although it felt twice as long. To avoid repeatedly examining his watch he made himself listen to the sounds around and above him. The old, familiar noises of a teeming community encased in one great hull. It took little imagination to hear Captain Pears's harsh voice complaining, 'Mr Bolitho! Are you aware that the weather forebrace is as slack as a sow's tail? 'Pon my soul, sir, you'll have to do better if you wish to make something of yourself!'

He was smiling ruefully when the lieutenant returned and without further ceremony led him aft to the great cabin.

Sir Evelyn Christie, Rear-Admiral of the Red, and commanding the Inshore Squadron, was fanning his face with a napkin, and after a searching examination of Bolitho's general appearance said, 'A glass of claret, Commander.' He did not wait for an answer but gestured to his servant, a splendid-looking man in scarlet jacket and brilliant yellow breeches.

'I was somewhat surprised to see *your* name affixed to the report.' The admiral's eyes were fastened on the claret, as if daring the servant to spill even a drip. 'You say in it that Ransome died of fever.' He took a glass and examined it critically. 'Damn good job, if you ask me. Young popinjay. Too much money and no damn integrity.' Ransome disposed of he continued calmly, 'I expect you're concerned about the change of plans, eh?'

Bolitho felt a chair nudg thee back of his legs and realized the silent servant had somehow managed to arrange a glass of claret on a small table, fetch a chair, and all without apparently moving or uttering a sound.

The admiral scowled. 'Take no notice. The man's a fool.' He added sharply, '*Well?*'

Bolitho replied, 'I was expecting to . . .'

Rear-Admiral Christie interrupted, 'Yes, I imagine you were.' He paused, his head on one side like an irritable bird. 'The claret. Well?'

'Very good, Sir Evelyn.'

'Hmm.' The admiral seated himself carefully on a gilt chair. 'Took it off a blockade runner last month. Palatable.'

Something metallic crashed across a deck beyond the bulkhead and he snapped savagely, 'Go and tell the officer of the watch, with my *compliments*, that if I hear one more unseemly sound during this interview I will personally take him to task!'

The servant fled from the cabin and the admiral gave a slow smile. 'Keep them jumping. That's the answer. Don't give 'em too much time to think.'

In the very next breath he changed the tack yet again.

'Fact is, Bolitho, things are not going too well. Thank God you at least are a man who knows how to abide by the letter of his orders. In your place I might have said to hell with waiting around for some damn patrol to find out what was happening. I might even have gone so far as to take those transports direct to the army.'

Bolitho stiffened. It sounded genuine enough, but perhaps the admiral was merely hinting at a criticism. Maybe he thought he should have made straight for the exact rendezvous, used his initiative instead of acting as he had.

The admiral's next words changed that.

'You were not to know, of course, but the army is in the process of evacuating Philadelphia. Falling back.' He looked down at the empty glass. 'Sounds better than a retreat, but it amounts to the same.'

Bolitho was stunned. Reverses he could accept. This war was so extended, the areas so vast and little known, that no plan of battle of the old style could be expected. But to quit Philadelphia, the vital command garrison of the Delaware, was unthinkable. In spite of his caution he said, 'Surely that was unnecessary, sir? I thought we had destroyed all the American forts and outposts on the Delaware last year.'

The admiral eyed him shrewdly. 'That was *last* year, before Burgoyne surrendered at Saratoga. The whole of this area is overrun with bands of raiders and enemy informers.' He threw open the chart. 'With my squadron I must patrol and keep watch over the whole three hundred miles of coastline, from New York down to Cape Henry on Chesapeake Bay. It is a labyrinth. Inlets and rivers, coves and hiding places where you could fail to sight a three-decker at a mile's range. And every day the sea teems with shipping. From the north, and as far south as the Spanish Main and Caribbean. Dutch, Portuguese, Spanish, and most of 'em intent on slipping past my patrols with stores and guns for the enemy.'

He poured two more glasses of claret.

'However, now that you have brought these despatches we are aware of the extent of our dangers. The French are out in the open at last. I have already sent word to the Commander-in-Chief and all senior officers here.'

He smiled. 'You did well, Bolitho. No one could have expected so newly appointed a commander to act as you did.'

'Thank you, sir.'

Bolitho thrust away the opposite side of the picture. If he had sailed with the rich transports into an enemy trap, the admiral would have spoken very differently.

'Pity about *Miranda*. We are cruelly short of frigates.'

'About the *Bonaventure*, sir, I was wondering . . .'

'You are a man who does a lot of wondering.' The admiral continued to smile. 'Not too bad a fault in some. I knew your father. I hope he is well?' He did not wait for or expect an answer. He hurried on, 'I am drafting fresh orders for you. The military, in their haste, unfortunately allowed an headquarters company to become lost.' He added dryly, 'Between ourselves, I, too, have done a certain amount of *wondering*. About some of our military colleagues ashore. Some, or so it would appear, did not obtain the necessary brains to match their appointments.'

He gave an elaborate sigh. 'But then, who am I to judge? We are fortunate. We carry our homes, our manner of existence, around with us like sea-turtles. It is hard to compare that with some wretched infantryman, loaded down with pack and musket, footsore and half starved. He has to contend with living off the land, fighting shadows, being shot at by American woodsmen as well as coming to grips with well-trained troops.'

Bolitho watched him curiously. On the face of it the admiral was nothing out of the ordinary, no more than you would expect of one backed up by his power and authority. But his features certainly hid a razor-sharp mind, the way he could throw it around from one aspect to the next without losing sight of anything.

'What about the *Bonaventure*, by the way?'

'She's big and fast, sir.' Bolitho readjusted his mind again. 'At least forty guns and well handled. I am sure she was the one which followed us, yet was well able to outsail us when the time came.' He waited, but the admiral's face was a mask. 'A match for any frigate.'

'Point taken. I will make inquiries about her pedigree.' He opened his watch. 'I want you to sail today and find that missing company of foot-soldiers before they are captured.'

Bolitho stared at him. 'But, sir, I have my orders.'

'Ah, yes.' He bobbed his head. 'Now you have *mine*, eh?'

Bolitho sank back in the chair, 'Yes, sir.'

'I neglected to mention that the soldiers are transporting gold bullion. God knows the exact amount, I find it difficult on occasions to crack the military mind into precise details. But it is a great deal. Fortunes of war, army pay, booty, whatever it is, you may be sure it is valuable.' He smiled. 'It has a complete general with it!'

85

Bolitho swallowed the claret in one gulp. 'A general, sir?'

'No less. Take care, he is well connected, and not given to much tolerance.' He continued evenly, 'Your arrival is a godsend. I have only one small brig available, and I was loath to send her.'

Bolitho stayed silent. *Lose* her, was probably what he really meant.

'Arrangements have been made for some army scouts to accompany you, and a small detachment is already trying to make contact with the missing company.' He paused before saying quietly, 'You will be under the instruction of one Colonel Foley. He knows the area well, so you must abide by his experience.'

'I understand, sir.'

'Good. I will have your written orders sent to you without delay.' Another glance at the watch. 'I will expect you to be ready to weigh before dusk.'

'May I ask where I am to go, sir.'

'You may not. It will be clear in your orders. I do not want the whole of New York to learn of it yet. General Washington has many friends here, just as we have many who are waiting to change sides if things go badly for us.'

He held out his hand. It was over.

'Take care, Bolitho, England will need all her sons if she is to survive, let alone win this damn war. But if you succeed in this venture you will be more than able to face whatever lies ahead. You can rejoin your own squadron with much more than seniority to your credit.'

In something like a daze Bolitho found his way to the entry port, his mind grappling with the admiral's words.

This time he was greeted by the flag captain in person who asked quickly, 'Has he told you what he wants of you?'

'Yes.'

The captain studied Bolitho thoughtfully. 'The general's brother is a member of the Government. I thought I should tell you.'

Bolitho tugged his hat down on his forehead. 'Thank you, sir. I will try to remember.'

The captain grinned at his grave expression. 'You youngsters have all the luck!' His laughter was drowned by the trilling pipes as Bolitho climbed once more into his gig.

It was towards the end of the last dogwatch when Bolitho's passenger, Colonel Hector Foley, climbed aboard from the guardboat. In his early thirties, he had the dark, even swarthy good looks of a Spaniard, set off with a hooked nose and deep-set brown eyes. The appearance seemed totally at odds with the impeccable scarlet coat and close-fitting white breeches of an infantry officer. He glanced around the stern cabin, and accepted Bolitho's offer of the sleeping compartment and cot with little more than a nod, before seating himself in one of the chairs. He was tall and straight-backed, and like Bolitho had to be careful when moving between the deckhead beams.

He took out his watch and said calmly, 'I suggest you read your orders, Captain. Given luck, your part of the game should be no more than transport.'

He did not smile or show any emotion which Bolitho could recognize. His contained, aloof manner was vaguely disturbing. Irritating. It made Bolitho feel cut off from the more vital aspects of his strange mission.

The orders took little time to read. He was to proceed with as much despatch as possible, some one hundred and fifty miles southward along the coastline of New Jersey. Under cover of darkness, if considered possible and prudent, he would then enter Delaware Bay to such distance and position as would be directed by Colonel Foley. He re-read the orders more slowly, conscious the whole time of Foley's polished boots tapping gently on the deck beside the table.

If considered possible and prudent. That passage seemed to stand out more than all the rest, and he was again reminded of Colquhoun's prophecy. It meant simply that it was his responsibility. Foley could suggest what he liked, pick any landing place or rendezvous with equal indifference to the problems of sailing the ship close inshore through badly charted channels where in places the sea-bed was visible even to a man nearly blind. He looked up. 'Can you tell me nothing more, sir?'

Foley shrugged. 'I have twenty scouts aboard. They will have to make the first contact.'

The scouts had arrived some time before the colonel. They were Canadians, and in their buckskin clothing and fur caps, their outward appearance of slovenly ease, gave little hint of being soldiers. Bolitho had seen them sprawled around the gun deck, cleaning their assortment of weapons or idly watching the busy seamen with amused contempt.

Foley seemed to read his mind. 'They are good soldiers, Captain. Well used to this sort of warfare.'

'I should have thought you could have obtained similar assistance locally, sir?'

Foley regarded him coldly. 'An American is an American. I do not choose to trust any of them if I can obtain an alternative.'

'Then there seems little point in continuing the war, sir.'

For the first time Foley smiled. 'I need to have perfect trust in my men. Idealists I do *not* need at present.'

Stockdale opened the door and asked huskily, 'Are you ready for the officers, sir?' He glanced at Foley. 'Eight bells 'ave just struck.'

'Yes.'

Bolitho pulled at his neckcloth, angry that he could rise so easily to Foley's arrogance.

Fitch hurried into the cabin and lit two lanterns, for although it was early evening the sky was unusually overcast and the wind veered to the west with a hint of rain in it. It was also hot and stuffy, and when the other officers had somehow crammed themselves into the cabin it was almost unbearable.

He waited, watching Foley's gently tapping boots as there were more delays while chairs were brought from the wardroom and in awkward, shuffling silence they got themselves sorted out. Then he said, 'We will weigh as soon as this meeting is over. Is everything prepared, Mr Tyrrell?'

Tyrrell had his eyes fixed on the colonel. 'Aye, sir.'

'Mr Buckle?'

'Ready, sir.'

Bolitho looked at the carefully worded orders, recalling Tyrrell's astonishment when he had returned from the flagship. He had blurted out, 'But we ain't had time to take on water, sir.'

The admiral had kept to his word on the matter of secrecy. He was not even going to allow the *Sparrow*'s boats in contact with the shore, no matter for what purpose.

What he would have said if he had learned that Lock had begged a trip ashore in a passing lighter, Bolitho could not imagine. Lock had returned just as secretly with several large casks of lemons, and a more mournful face than usual as he had told of their cost.

He said, 'We will proceed to the south'rd and enter Delaware Bay. There we will act in co-operation with the army and take aboard . . .'

Foley interrupted calmly, 'I think that will suffice for the present, Captain.' Without looking at Bolitho he added, 'So, gentlemen, your duty is to ensure that this vessel is in the right place at the right time, and ready to fight if necessary to complete the mission.'

The others shifted in their seats, and Bolitho saw the two midshipmen staring at him with surprise. To them, Foley's obvious control must seem strange.

Buckle muttered, 'Bad bit o' coast down there, sir. Shoals and sandbars a'plenty.' He sucked his teeth noisily. 'Bad.'

Foley glanced at Bolitho, his deepset eyes showing annoyance. 'We are not here to discuss the competence or otherwise of your officers, surely?'

Bolitho met his gaze steadily, suddenly very calm. 'Indeed not, sir. I will vouch for my people.' He paused. 'Just as I am sure you will vouch for yours when the time comes.'

In the stiff silence Bolitho heard Tilby's booming voice along the upper deck, driving some unfortunate man about his work. Again, he had made a bad start, but he was unrepentant.

Foley nodded slowly. 'We shall see.'

Graves asked, 'May I speak, sir?'

Bolitho nodded.

'Why cannot one of the inshore squadron do this mission, sir?'

Foley stood up, his head lowered between the beams. 'Because your vessel is the more suitable, Lieutenant. Not, I assure you, because you are at all outstanding in such work.'

Bolitho looked at their faces. Resentment, surprise, even hurt. It was all there. He said slowly, 'Carry on, gentlemen. Call all hands in ten minutes.'

When they had filed out he said, 'You have said that my duty is to act as your transport. How I do it is my responsibility, and I am not required to remain quiet while you insult my officers.' When the soldier stayed silent he continued, 'These same men helped to save two transports which are needed so badly for the military. They fought and sank a privateer and helped to drive away another, more powerful ship.'

'For which you will receive the credit, no doubt?'

Bolitho faced him quickly, his voice low with anger. 'Thank you, Colonel. I had no doubt you expected me to say that in front of the others, just so you could make such a suggestion.' He picked up his hat. 'Had I known that the army was already quitting Philadelphia, I might have spent more time in harrying that privateer than dragging my heels with your transports!'

Foley smiled. 'Well said, Captain. I like a man who can still show some feeling.'

Bolitho slammed out of the cabin and strode unseeingly to the companion ladder. He could tell from the way some seamen avoided his eye, the alert manner with which young Bethune was studying the flagship, that they could all recognize his fury.

Had he changed so much? Before he would have laughed or cursed at Foley's rudeness once his back was turned. Now, at the mention of some criticism, the merest hint of an attack on his subordinates, and therefore his ship, was enough to drive away control and reason.

Tyrrell came aft and said quietly, 'I know those waters well enough, sir. Mr Buckle is a mite bothered, but I can stand by him.'

'I know. Thank you.'

He had seen Tyrrell's expression when Buckle had voiced his concern at the meeting. He had been about to make the same suggestion. Perhaps that was why he had rushed in to defend the master against Foley's sarcasm. Foley had already made it clear what he thought of Americans. Rebels, colonists, or those unwillingly caught between the cross-fire of different factions and divided families, any of them.

Tyrrell turned to watch the gig being swayed up and over the starboard gangway. 'Bit of a bastard, that one, sir.' He shrugged. 'I've met 'em before.'

Bolitho bit back the reproof he should have given. But what was the use? Even Bethune must have seen the antagonism between himself and Foley. 'Let us hope he knows what he is doing, Mr Tyrrell. For all our sakes.'

The boatswain's mates charged along the gun deck and hovered over hatchways as they bawled, 'All hands! All hands! Clear lower deck!'

Bolitho said, 'I did not get time to discover any news of your family.'

'Ah well.' Tyrrell tilted his hat to shade his eyes in a shaft of dying sunlight. 'Maybe later.'

The hatch casing slid open and Foley appeared at the top of the companion.

Bolitho said evenly, 'I must ask you to leave the quarterdeck, sir.' He saw him start angrily and added, 'Or cover your red coat. It will not help if we are seen to be carrying even one soldier with us.'

Foley withdrew and Tyrrell said happily, 'One to you, sir!'

'It was unintended.' Bolitho took a telescope and trained it beyond the anchored shipping. 'Our sailing must be seen as normal. Spies will have reported our arrival and no doubt will think only of our despatches. I don't intend to have the news abroad that we are going on some special mission. The world may soon know of it, but the later the better.'

He walked to the quarterdeck rail, watching the seamen being mustered at their stations by the petty officers, but wondering at the truth of his words. Could a man like Foley really make him so quick to hit back as Tyrrell believed?

'Man the capstan!' Tilby was clinging to the foremast shrouds, his mottled face shining with sweat as he yelled at the scurrying seamen. 'Jump to it, you idle buggers, or I'll be amongst you with my starter!' Caught off guard by the unexpected sailing orders, he was showing signs of a recent drinking bout.

Bolitho looked at Buckle. 'Once we have worked clear of the land we will get the t'gallants on her. The wind seems steady enough, but we'll have rain before nightfall, I'm thinking.'

Buckle tugged his hat. 'Aye, sir.' He hesitated. 'I'm sorry I spoke out as I did. I should have known different.'

Bolitho smiled. 'Better to speak your doubts before you meet trouble. It is too late when you are hard aground, eh?' He touched his arm lightly. 'But before we draw that close to land we will see what *Sparrow* can do under full canvas.'

He walked away, hoping Buckle felt less worried. It could not be easy for him either. His first ship as master, and about to plunge into dangerous waters he had never seen before.

'Anchor's hove short, sir!' Graves's voice was loud on the blustery wind.

Bolitho looked at Tyrrell. 'Get the ship under way, if you please.'

He swung round as a chorus of derisive laughter burst from the deck below. A seaman had caught his foot on one of the army scout's muskets and gone sprawling into the scuppers. It seemed to amuse the soldiers greatly.

Bolitho added coldly, 'With this fresh wind you'll need plenty of weight on the capstan bars.' He let his eyes rest on the Canadians.

Tyrrell grinned. 'Right away, sir!' He cupped his hands. 'Bosun! Put those men on th' capstan!' He silenced the immediate protests by adding, 'Don't hesitate to start 'em if you find 'em slacking!'

Bolitho thrust his hands beneath his coat tails and walked away from the rail so that he could watch the topmen more easily. He had taken enough insults from Foley. There was no good reason for his own seamen to suffer also.

'Anchor's aweigh, sir!'

He stared up at the thundering pattern of canvas as the ship heeled over, free to the wind.

Once clear of the land's sheltering arm the motion became more violent, the waves shorter and the colour of straw in the dull light. Spray lifted and dashed over the busy seamen and pattered across the quarterdeck like heavy rain. Bolitho felt it on his lips and wet against his shirt, sensing the released power as the courses and then the topgallant sails filled and bellied to the wind.

He watched the jib-boom rise towards the scudding clouds, stagger and then plunge forward and down over the next line of crests, the stays and shrouds gleaming like wet ebony. He pictured the angry sparrow beneath the beakhead clutching its oak leaves and acorns, and wondered if the *Bonaventure*'s captain had seen it when he had broken off the action, and would remember it.

Tyrrell lurched aft, his body angled steeply to the deck. He yelled to the mizzen topmen before pausing to check those working at the weather braces. Fitch scurried past carrying a bucket and Tyrrell called after him.

Bolitho shouted above the thunder of canvas, 'What is it?'

Tyrrell laughed. 'Th' colonel's being sick, sir! A shame, ain't it?'

'Terrible.' Bolitho turned away to hide a grin. 'Especially as it seems to be blowing harder now!'

Buckle clung to the binnacle and yelled, 'Steady she goes, sir! Sou'-east by south!'

'Hold her so!' Bolitho removed his hat and let the wind press the hair against his forehead. 'We will wear ship soon.' He walked up the deck and rapped the half-hour glass beside the compass. 'I am going below to inform the colonel.'

As he swung down the ladder he heard Tyrrell laughing and Buckle's equally cheerful chuckle. It was a small thing. But it was a beginning.

93

6. Scarlet and Gold

BOLITHO entered his cabin and was surprised to see Foley seated at the table studying a chart. He was fully dressed, and his features had regained most of their colour. After leaving Sandy Hook he had spent most of the passage sprawled on the bench seat, unable or unwilling to climb into the cot, eyes half closed and his face like a wax mask.

He glanced up and grimaced. 'The motion feels easier.'

Bolitho nodded. 'We are standing into the bay. Cape May lies about five miles off the starboard beam.'

'I see.' Foley peered at the chart for several seconds, his fingers drumming a little tattoo across Bolitho's calculations and bearings. 'What is your opinion, Captain?'

Bolitho looked at his lowered head. It was the first time he had asked him for his views on anything. Under full canvas the *Sparrow* had lived up to her name, so that on the passage southward Bolitho had been able to put aside his apprehensions, if not forget them, while he had enjoyed the sloop's vitality and freedom of movement. Then as they had closed the land to fix their position a great squall had risen, bleating and moaning with such violence that it had taken all hands to reef down and gain more sea room. After the untroubled sailing with even the royals set to catch the wind it was a severe disappointment. They had arrived off Cape May at the entrance to Delaware Bay precisely as Bolitho had planned, one full day after weighing anchor. Yet even as Buckle had been taking his bearings the squall had swept offshore, flattening the wave-crests and cloaking the distant land more effectively than night itself. It had taken another day, beating and clawing round in a great circle, the land hidden to all but the masthead lookout by rainsqualls and low cloud.

He heard himself answer, 'The wind has backed again, sir. To the sou'-west, and it is dropping.'

94

He listened to the groan of yoke lines as the rudder went over beneath the transom, and thought of Tyrrell and Buckle beside the wheel. He could also imagine the chart, the great bay opening up on either beam as the *Sparrow*, under close-reefed topsails, headed further and further away from the sea. Tyrrell was a tower of strength, and seemed to remember these waters as if every sandbar and current was imprinted on his brain.

Foley looked up, his face grim. 'It has already taken too long. I must know if you think we can proceed.' He laid one finger on the chart. 'Here, directly north of where you say we are now. I estimate it to be about six leagues. There is a cove.' He was speaking quickly and Bolitho could feel his agitation.

Bolitho leaned over the table. 'To the west of Maurice River?' He paused, visualizing the set of the yards, the weakening wind across the quarter. 'It will take at least four hours. More if the wind goes.'

He stood back and tugged his neckcloth. With the shutters tightly closed to mask the chance of showing even a glimmer of light, the cabin was like a small oven. On deck, as he had been for much of the passage, he had not felt either fatigue or strain. Now, he was not so sure, and could even pity Foley's misery during the journey. Outside the hull it was pitch-black, and once the ship had slipped past the protective headland he had felt the same sensation as a man striding blindly into an unlit cave.

He asked, 'How long will your scouts need?'

'Six hours maybe.'

Foley stretched his arms and yawned. He was giving little away.

Bolitho made up his mind. 'In that case we will have to anchor and wait for tomorrow night before we can leave the bay. There may be enemy ships nearby, and I can't risk a conflict in these confined waters. Especially if your scouts fail to find our missing soldiers and need one more day.'

'Handling the ship is *your* concern.' Foley regarded him evenly. 'Well?'

'The tide is right and if we wait further we might lose the wind altogether.' He nodded. 'I am ready.'

Foley stood up and massaged his stomach. 'Good. By God, I think I have recovered my appetite.'

'I am sorry, sir.' Bolitho smiled. 'For the galley fire has been doused.' He added, 'Unless you would care for some salt beef from the cask?'

Foley eyed him ruefully. 'You have a cruel streak. One sight of that muck would render me as weak as a rat.'

Bolitho made for the door. 'In a King's ship the rats are rarely that!'

On deck he had to wait several seconds before he could see further than the rail. Below on the gun deck he could just make out the waiting seamen, their bodies etched against the darker shapes of the nearest guns.

He walked aft and held his hand above the shaded compass light.

Buckle said, 'Due north, sir. Full an' bye.'

'Good.' He beckoned to Tyrrell. 'I want our two best leadsmen in the chains.'

'Already done, sir.' Tyrrell shrugged. 'Seemed th' thing to do.'

'When we draw closer to the northern shore we will slip the gig.' Bolitho sought out Stockdale's thick outline by the hammock nettings. 'You will take the gig and a boat's lead and line. The waters hereabouts are so shallow and treacherous that you must keep ahead of the ship, sounding all the while. Understood?'

Stockdale said stubbornly, 'I should be 'ere, sir. Just in case.'

'Your place is where I *say*, Stockdale.' He relented immediately. 'Do as I ask, and keep a shaded lantern with you. You may need to signal us.' He glanced towards Tyrrell. 'If that happens we will drop the kedge anchor and pray.'

The sails flapped loosely above the deck, and Bolitho knew the wind was still dropping, its touch clammy across his face. He pushed the nightmare of *Sparrow* grinding aground from his mind. He was committed. No, he had committed all of them.

'When we reach our destination, Mr Tyrrell, you may have the starboard cutter lowered. Mr Heyward will convey our passengers ashore and return when all is well.'

Tyrrell said, 'They'll have to wade th' last few yards, I'm thinking. It's shallow up there.'

'You've guessed the place then?'

He grinned, his teeth white in the gloom. 'There ain't no other suitable for this sort of game, sir.'

From forward, hollow-toned like a lost spirit's, came the leadsman's cry. 'By th' mark five!'

Tyrrell muttered, 'Bring her up a point, Mr Buckle.' His palm rasped over his chin. 'We must have drifted a piece.'

Bolitho remained silent. They were doing all they could. Thank God *Sparrow* had such shallow draught. Otherwise . . .

'Deep six!'

Tyrrell grunted. 'Fair enough. In bad times I've seen a tide race turn a schooner round like a bit o' flotsam.'

'Thank you.' Bolitho watched the faint splash beyond the bows as another lead went down. 'That is a comfort.'

'By th' mark five.'

'Trust a soldier to choose such a place.' Tyrrell leaned over the compass. 'To th' west still further and in th' main Delaware channel there's depth to spare for us, even if th' tide's wrong.'

'A quarter less five!'

Buckle whispered, 'Hell's teeth!'

Boots scraped on the planking and Foley asked crisply, 'How are we getting along, Captain?'

'By th' mark three!'

'Is it necessary for that man to make so much noise?' Foley stared round at the figures grouped by the wheel.

Tyrrell drawled calmly, 'It's either that, Colonel, or we rip our keel out.'

Bolitho said, 'A man as tall as yourself, sir, could just about walk twixt the keel and the ground below if he had a mind to.'

Foley did not speak for a full minute. Then he said, 'I'm sorry. It was a foolish thing to say.'

'Deep four!'

Buckle breathed out slowly. 'Better.'

Bolitho felt Tyrrell's fingers on his arm as he said, 'If we can keep her steady we should rest easy, with some room to swing at anchor. The bottom's safe and we might touch without too much danger.'

'Captain!' Foley's tone was as before. Sharp and impatient. He waited by the nettings and then said, 'Tyrrell. Is he an American?'

'A colonist, sir. Like a good many of the hands.'

'God damn!'

Bolitho added, 'He is also a King's officer, sir. I hope you will remember that.'

Foley's white breeches vanished into the hatchway, and Tyrrell said bitterly, 'Thinks I'm running th' ship aground just to spite him, I suppose.'

'That will be enough.' Bolitho stared past him at the dancing phosphorescence below the closed gun ports. Like magic weed, changing shape and vanishing only to reappear elsewhere along the slow-moving hull. 'I do not envy him his work.' Surprisingly, he found that he meant it.

Somewhere out there in the darkness was the great mass of land. Hills and rivers, forest and scrub which could tear out a man's eye if he was careless. There had been many stories of attacks and ambushes in this area, and even allowing for their being magnified in the telling, they were enough to chill even a seasoned fighter. Indians who were used to scout for Washington's army, who moved as silently as foxes and struck with the savagery of tigers. A world of shadows and strange noises, cries which would bring a drowsy sentry wide awake in a cold sweat, if he was lucky. If not, he would be found dead, his weapons gone.

'Deep eight!'

Tyrrell moved restlessly.

'We can leave th' channel now. I suggest we steer nor'-east.'

'Very well. Man the braces and bring her round.'

And so it went on, hour by hour, with the leads going and the reefed topsails being trimmed and re-trimmed to hold the fading wind like something precious. Occasionally Tyrrell would hurry forward to feel the tallow in one of the leads, rubbing particles from it between his fingers or sniffing it like a hunting-dog.

Without his uncanny knowledge of the sea bottom, his complete confidence despite the shallow water beneath the keel,

Bolitho knew he would have anchored long ago and waited for the dawn.

Foley came and went several times but said nothing more about Tyrrell. He mustered the Canadian scouts and spoke for several minutes with their sergeant. Later he remarked, 'Good men. If I had a regiment of them I could retake half of America.'

Bolitho let him talk without interruption. It broke the tension of waiting. It also helped to discover the man behind the disciplined arrogance which Foley wore like a shield.

'I have fought the Americans in many places, Captain. They learn quickly and know how to use their knowledge.' He added with sudden bitterness, 'So they should, they have a hard core of English deserters and soldiers-of-fortune. Whereas I have had to manage with dregs. In one battle most of my men spoke only a few words of English. Imagine it, Captain, in the King's uniform, yet their tongues were more used to German dialect than ours!'

'I did not know there were so many English deserters, sir?'

'Some were stationed here before the rebellion. Their families are with them. They have found roots in this country. Others pin their hopes on rich pickings later, land, maybe, or some abandoned farmstead.' Again the harsh bitterness. 'But they will fight dearly, no matter what their conviction. For if they are taken and are found to be deserters, they will leave this world on a noose and with Jack Ketch to speed their passing!'

Tyrrell loomed out of the darkness, his voice hushed. 'Ready to slip th' gig, sir. Th' cove will be fine on th' larboard bow, by my reckoning.'

The tension was momentarily removed as with whispered commands and groping fingers the waiting seamen hoisted the gig over the gangway to tow jerkily alongside.

Midshipman Heyward was standing nearby as the gig idled clear, and Bolitho said quietly, 'Take good care when you land with the cutter. Keep your wits about you, and no heroics.' He gripped his arm, feeling the tension like the spring of a cocked pistol. 'I want to see you leave *Sparrow* as a lieutenant and in one piece.'

Heyward nodded. 'Thank you, sir.'

99

Graves climbed lightly up the ladder. 'Cutter's hoisted out and ready.' He glanced at the midshipman. 'Send me, sir. He's no match for this sort of thing.'

Bolitho tried to see Graves's expression but it was impossible. Maybe he really cared about the midshipman. Or perhaps he saw the prospect of action as his first chance of quick promotion. Bolitho could sympathize with him on either count.

But he replied, 'When I was his age I was already commissioned lieutenant. It was not easy then, and it will not be so for him until he has learned to accept all that goes with his authority.'

Bethune said quickly, 'Signal from gig, sir! Three flashes!'

Tyrrell snapped, 'Th' bottom has changed, most likely.' He became calm again. 'I suggest you anchor, sir.'

'Very well.' Bolitho saw the black outline of the gig bobbing slowly off the larboard bow. 'Back the mizzen tops'l. Prepare to go about. We will let go the anchor and then take the kedge away in the other cutter. Lively there, or we'll be joining Stockdale in the gig!'

Feet thudded on the gangways, and somewhere above the deck a man yelped with pain as he almost fell headlong. The mizzen topsail was flapping and cracking in spite of the wind's weak pressure, and the noise seemed loud enough to wake the dead.

On darkened decks the men ran to braces and halliards, each so familiar that there was hardly any more delay than if they had been in bright sunlight.

Unsteadily, drunkenly, the sloop rode into her cable, the water beneath the stem alive with swirling phosphorescence. Both cutters were already swaying up and over the gangways, their crews tumbling into them, groping for oars and each other in the rush to get clear.

Then, and it all seemed to happen in a matter of minutes, everything was quiet again. Sails furled, and the hull rocking gently to a pair of anchors, while close by the boats moved warily, like predators around a tethered whale.

Foley stood beside the nettings and said, 'Send my scouts ashore, Captain. You have done your part.'

Then he strode to the larboard gangway to watch Heyward's

cutter hooking on to the chains where the army scouts were already clinging like so many untidy bundles.

Bolitho asked softly, 'What is this cove like, Mr Tyrrell? Describe it.'

The lieutenant ran his fingers through his thick hair. 'It's well sheltered, 'less some other vessel comes close by. Inland it's heavily wooded, and as I recall, there's two rivers running down towards us.' He peered over the side. 'Th' cutter's nearly there. If we hear shooting we'll know we're in for a spell of bother.' He forced a grin. 'One thing. We don't need no wind to work clear. We can run out th' sweeps and *pull* her to safety.'

Bolitho nodded. In almost any other vessel this mission would have been madness. Close inshore and with little chance of beating clear into the centre of the bay, they would have been as good as wrecked.

He said, 'Get Tilby to grease the sweeps while we are waiting. If go we must, then I think we had best do it silently.'

Tyrrell strode away, his head jutting forward to seek out the boatswain.

Foley reappeared and remarked, 'I think I will get some sleep. There is nothing more we can do but wait.'

Bolitho watched him go. You will not sleep, Colonel. For now it is your turn to bear the load.

Bethune said excitedly, 'Cutter's returning, sir. All's well.'

Bolitho smiled. 'Pass the word that our people will remain at quarters during the night, but may sleep watch by watch. Then find the cook and see what he can produce without relighting his fires.'

The midshipman hurried away and Graves said sourly, 'He'd eat anything. Even if he cannot see the damn maggots in the dark.'

Bolitho sat down on the hatch casing and loosened his shirt. As his head lolled in a doze he heard a heavy body lower itself to the deck nearby. Stockdale had returned. Waiting. *Just in case*, as he always put it.

The very next instant Bolitho fell into a dreamless sleep.

*　　　*　　　*

'Where th' *hell* are they?' Tyrrell trained a glass over the nettings and moved it slowly from side to side.

It was approaching noon, and lying at two anchors the *Sparrow* held the heat like a kiln. The cloud, like the wind, had gone overnight, and beneath an empty sky and dazzling sunlight it was impossible to move without sweating badly.

Bolitho plucked his shirt away from his waist. He had been on deck since awakening at dawn, and like Tyrrell was uneasy about the lack of results. How different it was in daylight. At the first glimmer of sunrise he had watched the nearby land growing from the shadows, the rounded hills and thick green trees beyond. Pleasant crescents of beach, shaded by thick foliage which ran almost to the water's edge. It had all seemed quiet and harmless. Perhaps too quiet.

He made himself walk to the opposite side of the quarter-deck, wincing as the sun burned his shoulders like fire. The bay looked vast. The water was unbroken by crests, and but for a swirling uneasiness of currents it could have been one large lake. It measured about twenty miles across and as much from the headland to the north, where the great Delaware River gave it its substance. Beyond the jutting point which made the cove and protected *Sparrow* from any passing vessel, the river curved and twisted in an ever-changing concourse, with a full seventy miles before you could sight the outskirts of Philadelphia.

He looked along the gun deck, seeing the men on watch, some protruding legs to mark where others lay resting beneath the gangways to escape the merciless glare. He let his gaze move upwards, where the yards were now festooned with branches and leaves brought aboard soon after first light. They might help disguise her outline and deceive all but the professional observer.

Between the ship and the nearest beach a cutter pulled slowly and painfully back and forth, Midshipman Bethune squatting in the sternsheets watching the shore. Foolishly he had stripped to the waist, and despite his tan would suffer for it later.

Tyrrell followed him as he returned to the shelter of the hammock nettings.

'I'd like to go ashore, sir.' He waited until Bolitho faced him. 'I could take a small party of men. Try and find out what's happening.' He opened the front of his soiled shirt and sucked in a lungful of air. 'Better'n waiting like bloody cattle for slaughter.'

'I'm not sure.' Bolitho shaded his eyes as a movement made the trees shimmer by the beach. But it was only a large bird.

Tyrrell persisted, 'Look, sir, I guess th' orders are supposed to be secret, but th' whole ship knows why we're here. Them scouts spoke freely enough with a tot of rum under their belts.'

Bolitho smiled wryly. 'I thought as much.'

'Yes. An' it seems we're expected to rescue a whole crowd of soldiers who've got lost coming overland.' He grimaced. 'I can well believe it, too. It ain't no barrack square.'

Bolitho studied his strong profile and pondered over the suggestion. He had not mentioned the gold bullion, so that was obviously a secret which Foley had not even shared with his own men. And it was just as well. Some might be tempted to try for it rather than any kind of rescue.

'Very well. Pick your men quietly and take the gig. You will need arms and provisions, too, otherwise . . .'

Tyrrell smiled. 'Otherwise it might be too bad for us if *Sparrow* sails without waiting, eh?'

'It is a risk. Do you want to reconsider?'

He shook his head.

'I'll start now.'

Bolitho said, 'I'll make a report of this in the log.'

'No need, sir. If I come to grief it'd be best left unwritten.' He smiled sadly. 'I'd not want for you to face a court martial on my account.'

'I will make it, none the less.' Bolitho forced a grin. 'So be off with you.'

The gig had covered less than a cable from the side when Foley burst on deck, his face screwed up in the glare.

'Where is he going?' He clung to the nettings, staring after the small boat which was almost shapeless in a drifting haze. 'Did you give him permission?'

'I did.'

'Then you are a bigger fool than I imagined!' Foley's

103

anxiety was pushing aside his self-control. 'How dare you take it on yourself?'

'Colonel Foley, I have no doubt you are an excellent field officer. Experienced enough to realize that if your scouts have failed to make contact with those landed here earlier they must either be dead or taken.' He kept his voice level. 'You will also appreciate that I am not going to risk my ship and company to comply with a plan already misfired.'

Foley opened his mouth and then shut it again. He said flatly, 'I have my orders. The general must be rescued.'

'And the gold.' Bolitho could not hide the bitterness. 'That too, surely?'

Foley rubbed his eyes, his face suddenly showing the strain. 'You'd need a regiment to search this area. Even then . . .' His voice trailed away.

Bolitho took a glass and swung it over the rail. There was no sign of the gig now.

He said, 'Mr Tyrrell has my confidence. At least *he* might discover something.'

Foley glanced around the sunlit deck. 'I hope so, Captain. Otherwise you will lose this ship, and that will be the very least of your worries.'

Graves appeared on the ladder, saw them together and walked away.

Bolitho frowned. So he had been the one to inform Foley of Tyrrell's expedition.

He asked, 'This general. Who is he, sir?'

Foley dragged himself from his brooding thoughts. 'Sir James Blundell. He came out here on a tour of inspection!' He laughed shortly. 'By the time he reached New York there was less to inspect than he had anticipated. He owned a great deal of property in Pennsylvania, enough to buy a thousand ships like this one.'

Bolitho turned away. He had never heard of the man, but this was more than he wanted to know. Foley would never speak his mind more clearly than he had already done. But it was enough. Blundell had obviously been caught in the middle of retrieving some of his personal wealth by the sudden military evacuation. Worse, he had been using his role of an inspector-general for his own ends and had involved a company of desperately needed soldiers.

Foley looked at him for several seconds. 'The men with him are mine. All that are left from the whole battalion. So you see why I must do this thing.'

Bolitho replied quietly, 'Had you told me that from the beginning, Colonel, it might have been better for both of us.'

Foley did not seem to hear. 'They were the best men I have commanded here and we've seen a dozen skirmishes together. By God, when it comes to the line of battle there is nothing to beat the English foot soldier. Even a small square of them will withstand the cream of French cavalry.' He spread his hands. 'But out here, they are like lost children. They cannot compete with men who have lived all their lives in the woods and plains, who have known times when one musket ball was the margin between survival and starvation!'

Bolitho did not know how to phrase the next question. He said slowly, 'But you were not with your men when it all happened?'

'No.' Foley stared at two gulls diving and screaming around the topgallant yards. 'I had been sent to New York with a convoy. Mostly it consisted of unwanted supplies and the soldiers' women.' He looked hard at him. 'And the general's niece, I should not forget to mention *her*.' He was speaking quickly. 'Even on a safe trail we were dogged by enemy skirmishers, and there was never a day without some poor devil being brought down by one of their long muskets. By God, I think some of them can knock the eye out of a fly at fifty paces!'

The deck moved very slightly, and when he looked aloft Bolitho saw the masthead pendant flicking out feebly before falling lifeless once more. But it was the first hint of a breeze so far.

He said, 'I suggest you get some rest while you can, Colonel. I will inform you when I hear anything.'

Foley said heavily, '*If* your Mr Tyrrell returns.' In the same breath he added, 'That was unfair. I have been so unbalanced by all this I am not myself.'

Bolitho watched him walk to the hatchway and then seated himself on a bollard. If nothing happened soon Foley would have to make a fresh decision. With Tyrrell out of the ship and the mission a failure, there would be little hope for his own future once they returned to Sandy Hook.

All afternoon and into the evening the *Sparrow* lay pinned down by the unwavering glare. Deck seams were so sticky that they gripped a man's foot, and the gun barrels were as hot as if they had been in action for many hours. The watches changed and sentries came and went, hearing and seeing nothing.

The first rosy glow of sunset had settled over the cove, and the hillside beyond was deep in purple when Foley came on deck again.

He said, 'There is nothing more we can do.'

Bolitho bit his lip. Tyrrell had not returned. Perhaps he was already on his way south overland. Or even now guiding American scouts towards the cove. He shook himself like a dog. His tiredness and disappointment were tearing down his reserves. His trust.

Midshipman Heyward was standing by the starboard gangway, his body limp against the rail like a man half asleep. Suddenly he jerked upright, his voice hoarse as he called, 'Gig, sir! Coming from the point!'

Bolitho ran to his side, caring nothing for what Tyrrell may or may not have discovered. He had come back. That was more than enough.

When the gig ground alongside he saw the oarsmen lolling on the thwarts like puppets, faces and arms raw from the harsh sunlight of the day.

Tyrrell climbed to the quarterdeck, his legs and feet filthy, his clothing torn.

He said thickly, 'Your scouts couldn't find th' ones sent on ahead, Colonel. But we did.' He took a mug of water and gulped it down gratefully. 'They're all dead. Up river in a burned-out fort.'

Foley stared at the dark trees beyond the cove. 'So my men are still out searching.'

Tyrrell ignored him. 'We pulled th' gig into th' inlet and tumbled on this old fort by accident.' He looked away. 'An' that ain't all, by a potful.'

106

Bolitho waited, seeing the tension, the pain of what he had found.

Tyrrell said slowly, 'Just up th' channel, sitting as bold as you please, is a bloody frigate!'

Foley swung round. 'American?'

'No, Colonel, not American.' He looked at Bolitho gravely. 'A Frenchie by th' cut of her. No colours, so I guess she's a privateer.'

Bolitho steadied his racing thoughts. But for their stealthy entry into the bay under Tyrrell's guidance, they would have run under the frigate's guns, or at best been attacked when they had anchored.

Tyrrell was saying, 'So it looks as if your general has been took, Colonel. Not much use in us staying here to follow his example, eh?'

'Did you see what they were doing?' Bolitho tried to picture the great river sweeping around the point. The frigate anchored in the safe knowledge she could fight off an attacker from either direction.

Tyrrell shrugged. 'There were marks on th' beach. I guess they'd had boats ashore getting fresh water. But no sign of prisoners.'

'Then it would appear that the missing soldiers are *still* missing.' Bolitho glanced at the colonel. 'If the wind gets up it is my guess that the frigate will weigh. She'd not risk a night passage, so we're safe here 'til dawn at least. After that . . .' He did not have to explain further.

Heyward called, 'Cutter's signalling, sir!'

They all turned and stared at the darkening beach as the oars came to life and the cutter started towards the shore. A solitary figure was just visible waving his musket back and forth towards Bethune. It was one of Foley's scouts.

Foley snapped, 'I must go ashore at once.' He ran towards the entry port. 'They have found the general!'

Bolitho hurried after him, and with Stockdale on his heels plunged into the waiting gig.

When the boat had grounded in the shallows Bolitho leapt over the gunwale and waded the last yards through clear water, vaguely aware that it was the first time he had been on land,

107

apart from a few occasions in Antigua, for months. He stood beneath a tree as Foley questioned the scout, knowing the man would probably become flustered with both of them present.

Foley walked towards him, his boots squeaking in the sand. 'They found them.' He gestured to the wall of trees. 'The first party will arrive in about an hour.'

'First party?' Bolitho saw the despair in Foley's eyes.

'The general is coming with my scouts and all the fit men.' He took a deep breath. 'But there are some sixty sick and wounded following behind at a slower pace. They've been on the move for days. They ran into an ambush in a gully the night before last but fought their attackers off. The general says they were French.'

'Off that frigate most likely.' Bolitho tried to imagine what it must be like for the sick and injured soldiers. Not knowing where they were. How they would survive.

He said, 'The cat is out of the bag now. That ship will be expecting some rescue attempt. *I* would be in their shoes.'

Foley sighed. 'I agree. What will you do?'

Bolitho did not reply directly. He beckoned to Bethune who was giving the weary scout some water from his flask.

'Return to the ship at once. My compliments to Mr Tyrrell. Tell him to stand by to receive the first party in an hour. I want one watch of the hands ashore and all the boats. It must be well handled and these men fitted into the ship if we have to jettison the stores to do it.'

He watched the youth running to the cutter, his shoulder glowing like a ripe fruit.

Foley said quietly, 'It'll be a miracle if we can get them off in time.'

Bolitho smiled. 'Miracles do happen, Colonel. Just occasionally.'

He walked towards the gig, his tiredness forgotten. Then he realized that Foley had not followed but was standing with his scout.

The colonel called after him, 'I'm going inland.' He looked away. 'To meet my men. Or what is left of them.'

His scarlet coat faded between the trees and he was gone.

*　　*　　*

General Sir James Blundell lay back in one of Bolitho's chairs and thrust a leg towards his orderly.

'For God's sake get these damn boots off!' He stared up at a deckhead lantern and added, 'I could relish a glass of something. I am as dry as dust!' He cursed the orderly and pushed him in the shoulder with his boot. '*Easy*, you damn fool!'

Foley turned and looked at Bolitho by the door, his eyes showing anger and embarrassment.

'Could you arrange something for the general?'

Bolitho nodded, and saw Fitch scurrying away for some wine. It was all like a part of a dream. A nightmare.

As the last of the daylight had begun to fade, the soldiers who had accompanied the general had appeared along the beach. Even *Sparrow*'s seamen, who moments before had been skylarking and chattering while they enjoyed their unusual freedom of dry land, had fallen still and silent.

Torn and bedraggled, red coats filthy from forced marches and sleeping when they could in the undergrowth, they had shuffled into lines like obedient animals. Others had followed with pack mules, so loaded that it was a wonder they had survived.

Bolitho had been on the beach with Dalkeith, explaining the needs and preparations for this mass of passengers, and had watched in silence as Foley had stood with his face like stone while a solitary lieutenant had lurched towards him, the regimental colours across one shoulder, his sword dangling from his wrist on a lanyard. Foley had been unable to speak. He had merely touched the lieutenant's shoulder and nodded towards the dull-eyed soldiers along the edge of the trees before saying to Bolitho, 'For God's sake, do what you can for these fellows.'

As the seamen had hurried forward to help the soldiers into the waiting boats the last reserve had cracked. Along the swaying lines of red coats men had dropped like corpses, while others had merely stared speechlessly at the bronzed sailors, their filthy faces running with tears, hands outstretched like men seeing messengers of salvation itself.

It had been pitiful and moving just to watch while they had lurched into the shallows and the boats. The lieutenant carry-

ing his regiment's colours, as he must have done all the way
south from Philadelphia, trying to show some last control but
his face reversing the lie, the despair and the disbelief.

Now, as he stood watching the general it was hard to connect the two scenes together. Blundell was a rotund but power-
fully built man, and apart from dirt on his boots, his uniform
looked as if it had been only recently pressed. His iron-grey
hair was neat, and his heavy, florid features must have been
shaved within the day.

So far, he had given Bolitho little more than a cursory glance,
and was content to make his needs known through Foley.

He touched the glass of wine with his tongue and grimaced.
'I suppose one cannot hope for too much in a craft of this
size, what?'

Foley looked again at Bolitho, his expression one of physical
pain.

Overhead and deep in the hull the timbers were alive with
thudding boots, the occasional bellow of orders and the squeak
of tackles above the boats.

The general said, 'You should have put those men to work,
Foley. No sense in letting 'em lie about like squires of the
manor.'

Bolitho said, 'My people can manage the loading, sir.'

'Hmm.' The general seemed to consider him for the first
time. 'Well, make sure that every mule is properly checked.
Some careless or greedy fool might be thinking of stealing
their loads. There's a king's ransom in those packs. So think
on these things when you report you're ready for sea.'

Graves appeared in the door.

'All the soldiers are on board, sir. Some of them are in a
poor way.'

Bolitho tore his eyes from the general, the droplets of wine
on his lips.

'Have the cook light the galley fire, Mr Graves. That French
frigate will not attempt to weigh in the dark, even if the wind
gets up. I want those men to get something hot to eat. Rum,
too, while they are waiting. Tell Mr Lock to arrange it.'

He thought of the staggering men, the fallen redcoats by
the trees. And this was the party of *fit* men.

Foley asked quietly, 'When will you be raising anchor, Captain?'

Bolitho saw the anguish in his eyes, the way he lingered on his question.

'An hour after dawn the tide will be right, as will the current hereabouts, according to my information.'

The general's glass hovered in mid-air, so that his orderly allowed the wine to pour from the decanter and across the deck.

'What the hell are you talking about?' He struggled up in the chair. 'You can sail *now*. I heard your men saying the time was as good as any for it.'

Bolitho faced him coldly. 'That is true only up to a point, sir. But if I am to wait for the sick and wounded to reach the cove, I must prepare for the next tide.' He hardened his tone. 'I have sent my first lieutenant and forty seamen to aid their passage here. I pray to God we can save them from more suffering.'

The general lurched to his feet, his eyes flashing angrily. 'Tell this young upstart, Foley! There is an enemy ship up-channel and no time to be wasted. I have gone through enough in the last few days, and I command you to . . .'

Bolitho said, 'My orders say that I am in command of *transportation* for this mission, sir. They make no distinction between gold bullion or men.' He paused, the anger churning his stomach like brandy. 'Even those too weak and sick to fend for themselves. Is that not so, Colonel?'

Foley was staring at him, his eyes in dark shadow. When he spoke his voice was different, husky. 'It is true, Captain. You are in command.' He swung round and faced his astonished superior. '*We*, Sir James, are just so much cargo.'

Bolitho turned and walked from the cabin. On deck the air seemed cleaner, and he made himself stand quite still by the rail above the nearest twelve-pounders for several minutes.

Below he could see figures moving in all directions, and from the galley funnel he caught the aroma of meat stew. Even Lock must have been too overcome by the tattered, starving soldiers to restrain the cook.

He heard Foley's boots beside him but did not turn.

'Thank you, Captain. From me and my men. And those who will owe their lives to your humanity. And courage.' He held up his hand as Bolitho turned to reply. 'You could risk your very future because of this action, as well you know.'

Bolitho shrugged. 'Rather that than live with a foul memory.'

Someone called in the darkness and a nearby cutter began to pull inshore.

'I'd not leave those men behind.' He walked towards the gangway. 'If needs be, I'll drop the gold overboard first!'

'Yes. I believe you would, Captain.'

But Foley was speaking to the darkness. And when he reached the side he saw the gig already on its way to the beach, Bolitho sitting beside Stockdale at the tiller. He peered down at the gun deck. Where would Bolitho put all these men? He heard the creak of oars as the first boat thrust off from the beach. One thing was certain. He would find the space somehow, if it cost him his commission.

7. To Dare or to Die

BOLITHO opened his eyes and stared at the mug of steaming coffee which Stockdale was holding above the side of the cot. He struggled upright, his mind and vision readjusting to the unfamiliar surroundings, the awareness that it must already be dawn. He was in Tyrrell's small screened cabin adjoining the wardroom, and as he held the mug to his lips he realized he could not remember how he came to be there.

Stockdale wheezed, 'You've 'ad a good hour's sleep, sir. I was fair loath to wake you.' He shrugged heavily. 'But your last orders was to rouse all 'ands afore dawn.'

Bolitho's aching mind suddenly cleared. He could feel the uneven motion around him, the creak of stays and shrouds.

'The wind? How is it?' He threw his legs over the side of the cot, feeling crumpled and unclean.

'Risin', sir.' Stockdale sounded unhappy. 'From the west'rd.'

Bolitho looked at him. '*Damn!*'

With the mug still in his hand he hurried from the cabin and almost fell across a line of sleeping soldiers. Despite the need to know what was happening he stood motionless looking at them. Remembering the long night, the stream of sick and wounded men he had watched brought aboard by his sailors. Some would not see another day pass, others were like skeletons, racked with fever or the agony of wounds gone rotten. He still felt that same cold anger and shame which he had endured then. The realization that most of the men could have been carried on the mules instead of being left to stagger further and still further in the rear of their comrades. And the general.

He stepped over the inert shapes and continued to the quarterdeck.

Tyrrell saw him and said, 'You know about th' wind?'

Bolitho nodded and walked to the nettings, seeing the bay opening up in the pale early light like ruffled steel, the dancing cat's-paws against the hull, pushing it gently but insistently on the taut anchor cables.

Buckle came to his side, his face grey with fatigue.

'We can't set even a scrap o' canvas, sir. We're on a lee shore an' no mistake.'

Bolitho was staring along the larboard gangway and away towards the dark slab of land emerging from the shadows. The point, around which lay the river and the deep channel.

Graves said, 'We will have to stay where we are and hope that Frog has a mind to do likewise.'

He sounded doubtful.

Bolitho shook his head, thinking aloud. 'No. The Frenchman will have guessed we are about, even if he does not realize our exact strength. Either way he will up anchor soon and make for open water. If he sees us in passing he will have little difficulty in aiming his broadsides.'

He peered up at the yards where some topmen were casting away the last of their leafy camouflage. Above their heads the masthead pendant was whipping towards the cove, and he saw the beach regaining shape in the light, the marks of many feet, the small humps to show where some of the soldiers had been buried within sight of rescue. *Rescue*. He rubbed his chin and tried to think more logically.

Once out in the bay they could make sail and tack towards the entrance and open sea. The Frenchman, on the other hand, already had the advantage of the wind. Could even anchor if desired and pound *Sparrow* to fragments while she lay helpless in the cove. She would sink with her masts above water. It was a cruel picture.

He said, 'Break out the kedge anchor, Mr Tyrrell, and then hoist all boats.' He looked at the long racks of sweeps. 'We will have to see what those will achieve this morning.'

Once free of the kedge the hull swung sternwards towards the beach, the current swirling around her stern as if she was already under way.

The gun deck and gangways were crowded with men, and he knew that below every space was filled with exhausted soldiers. He watched the gig rising above the gangway before dropping neatly on its chocks between the cutters, the seamen working in unusual silence, glancing occasionally towards him by the rail as if to see his intentions.

He was able to pick out individual faces in the strengthening light, and realized he now knew most of them by name. The reliable and the lazy, the malcontents and those who were able to accept their calling, enforced or otherwise, with varying degrees of trust. He remembered that first day, the sea of unknown men, with Graves excusing Tyrrell's absence. It seemed so long ago.

Tyrrell reported, 'Boats secured, sir!'

Bolitho walked to the rail and leaned on it. The wood was moist and clammy, but within a few hours would be like a furnace bar. If it was still above water.

He said, 'You all know of that frigate, lads. She's up there now, taking her time, as Frogs do in such matters.' He paused, seeing some of the older men nudging each other and grinning at his feeble wit. 'You can also see that we are unable to loose tops'ls without driving ashore. But if soldiers can march all the way across country to us, I reckon we should be able to get 'em home again, what d'you say?'

For a long moment nobody moved or spoke, and he felt despair rising as if to mock him. Why should they care? After his displeasure following the fight with the privateers they might simply see it as a just rebuff.

Surprisingly, it was the boatswain who was the first to break the silence.

Bursting from the larboard gangway with his face glowing like a grotesque heated shot, he bellowed, 'What are we waiting for, my lovelies? A huzza for the cap'n! An' another for *Sparrow*!'

The cheering spread along the decks and up to the topmen on the yards. To the dazed soldiers below and in the cramped holds, and wherever a foot or so had been found for them.

Tilby yelled, 'An' to 'ell with them bloody Frogs!' He was already cutting the lashings on the nearest sweeps, pushing men towards them while others scampered to open the small ports on either beam.

Bolitho turned away, seeing Tyrrell's great grin and Buckle nodding his head and beaming as if they were already at sea and away under full sail. Even Graves was smiling, his tired face both dazed and pleased by the din.

He said, 'Man the capstan.' He wished they would stop cheering. That Tyrrell would obey and leave him to his thoughts. 'Run out the sweeps, if you please.'

Tyrrell shouted the order, and as the helmsmen stood to the wheel and the capstan took the first slow strain, he turned and said, 'They'll not let you down. Not after what you've done for those poor redcoats. Not now. Not ever, Cap'n.'

Bolitho could not face him. Instead he stared along the larboard side at the wavering line of sweeps poised above the swirling water like the oars of some ancient galley. It would take a great deal of effort to move her into the bay. With the wind against her and the dead weight of all her guns and extra passengers it might prove impossible.

'Stand by!'

The sweeps swung gingerly forward, the seamen clinging to the long looms and gripping the deck with their bare toes.

'Anchor's aweigh!' Graves came running aft above the seamen and yelled, 'She's paying off, sir!'

'Give way all!' Tilby threw his own weight on the aftermost sweep, his bulging muscles showing evidence of the strain. "*Eave!* Come on, boyos, 'eave! Agin now!'

Rising and falling, the lines of sweeps thrust and slashed at the water to hold the *Sparrow*'s drift towards the beach, and then very slowly, painfully brought her under command and towards the bay.

Bolitho called, 'Mr Buckle, take the wheel!' To Tyrrell he added, 'Every officer and man on the sweeps! *Everyone!*'

As the anchor was catted home and Graves led his own party to the sweeps others slithered down backstays or ran from their stations elsewhere to give weight to the stroke.

Bolitho tried not to watch the point, green and brown now in the light. It was stationary and the sloop was hardly making headway. Yet already the men were gasping for breath, and only Buckle and himself were not helping. The wind was too strong, the current too insistent.

Tyrrell's voice carried like a trumpet. 'Heave! Heave! An' one more lads!' But it was no use.

116

Buckle called softly, 'We'll have to anchor again, sir! They'll be beat in a moment!'

Several seamen missed their grip and almost fell as a voice shouted above the plunge and creak of sweeps.

'Quickly there! Spread yourselves out with the seamen!'

Bolitho stared with disbelief as Foley emerged below the quarterdeck, and following him, two by two, some limping, others blinded by bandages, came the remnants of his company.

Foley looked up. 'The 51st have never been known to fail in showing up the Navy, Captain!' He steadied one of his men who was groping past him before adding, 'You spoke earlier of miracles. But sometimes they, too, need a little help.' He turned away and put himself beside a master's mate on the end of a sweep.

Bolitho gripped the rail, wanting to hide his face from them, but unable to tear his eyes from their combined efforts.

Buckle called huskily, 'I've got steerage way, sir. She's answering now!'

Bolitho said softly, 'The colonel told me he could take half the continent with the right men. With men such as these he could conquer the world.'

When he looked again he saw that the point was slipping across the starboard quarter as with great care Buckle eased the helm over and watched the jib-boom pointing towards deeper water.

Here and there a man fell exhausted from a sweep, but the stroke barely faltered.

When the full rim of sunlight eventually broke above the distant hills, *Sparrow* was well out into the bay.

Bolitho shouted, 'Topmen aloft! Stand by to make sail!'

The jib cracked and flapped angrily, then hardened into a firm crescent, and as the long sweeps were withdrawn from their ports the deck tilted to a small but satisfying angle.

'Lay her on the starboard tack, Mr Buckle. As close to the wind as you can. We will need all the room possible to weather Cape May.'

Tyrrell came aft and stood beside the compass, his eyes fixed on the hazy shoreline. He looked strangely contented. Reassured.

He saw Bolitho watching him and remarked, 'It was a good feeling to get ashore again. But then I guess you feel th' same about England.'

Bolitho nodded gravely. Maybe Tyrrell had been tempted after all. But he had come back, and that was what counted.

He said, 'You did well, Mr Tyrrell. You all did.'

Tyrrell gave his lazy grin. 'If you'll pardon th' liberty, sir, you ain't no hoof-dragger yourself.'

'Deck there! Sail on th' starboard quarter!'

Bolitho looked at Buckle. 'The Frenchman is after us sooner than I thought. Get the t'gallants on her, if you please.' He walked up the slanting deck and shaded his eyes. 'We'll give him a run for his money.'

Tyrrell was still grinning. 'For th' *general's* money, you mean!'

Bolitho glanced down at his stained breeches. 'I'm going to shave.' But the mood persisted for him also. 'In case we have visitors this morning, eh?'

Buckle watched him go and then said, 'Nothing ever seems to worry that one.'

Tyrrell was peering up at the topmen, his eyes critical. He recalled Bolitho's face when the wounded soldiers had staggered on deck to help man the sweeps. For just those few moments he had seen beyond the brittle composure, the mantle of command, to the real man beneath.

Half to himself he murmured, 'Don't be too sure of that, Mr Buckle. He *feels* it right enough. Just like th' rest of us.'

Bolitho closed the telescope with a snap and steadied himself against a belaying-pin rack.

'Alter course two points, Mr Buckle. Steer due east.'

It had taken another two hours from sighting the French frigate to tacking dangerously close around Cape May. With the nearest spur of that untidy headland barely two cables under the lee side they had surged towards the open sea, close enough to see smoke from some inland fire and the morning sunlight flashing on a hidden window or an unseen watcher's telescope.

It had been harder than he could have imagined to remain in a wardroom chair while Stockdale shaved him and laid out a clean shirt. Now, as he watched the men running to the braces, the lifting, dipping bowsprit beyond the taut rigging, he wondered why he had made himself waste time below. Pride or conceit, the need to relax even for minutes, or a greater need that his seamen should think him so calm he could concentrate on his own comfort?

As the sloop plunged round still further until she had the wind directly astern, he could feel every spar and timber quaking to the motion. Above the quarterdeck rail he saw the mainyard bending like one huge bow, the splayed legs of the topmen denoting the savage vibration aloft, the need for care when one false step could mean instant death. Or the longer agony of watching the ship ploughing away to leave the fallen man to drown alone.

'Steady she be, sir! Due east!'

He walked to the compass and then took a careful glance at the set of the sails. Every inch of canvas was fully drawn, the bellies so rounded and hard they looked about to burst.

He gestured with the telescope. 'Another pull on the larboard forebrace, Mr Tyrrell, and then belay.'

As the men ran to obey he took one more glance astern. The enemy had gained on them during the dash from the bay, had cut away their early advantage while *Sparrow* had lost valuable time clawing around the last headland. Now, as he steadied the glass across the taffrail he could see their pursuer rising and driving over the lively white-horses, her hull bathed in spray, the gun ports awash as she surged on a starboard tack, showing her sleek hull and full pyramids of canvas. She had set her royals once away from the headland and was heading into deeper water before continuing the chase.

Tyrrell came aft, wiping droplets of salt from his arms and face.

'We're standing well afore th' wind, sir. There's naught else we can do at present.'

Bolitho did not reply. At the quarterdeck rail he leaned over and saw the uneven lines of wounded soldiers, and others less handicapped, helping with food and bandages. Two of Dalkeith's assistants came on deck and hurled a bundle over the gangway and vanished down a hatchway with hardly a glance. Bolitho watched the bundle bobbing away on *Sparrow*'s creamy wake and felt his stomach contract violently. Some bloodied bandages, but most likely the amputated limb of one more luckless soldier. Dalkeith was in his makeshift sickbay, as he had been since the sloop had weighed anchor, working in almost total darkness with saw and swabs while the ship yawed and staggered around him.

Graves called above the boom of canvas, 'The Frenchman's wore, sir!'

The frigate was now about eight cables off the starboard quarter. Certainly no more, and steering a parallel course, her royals fully squared and straining at their bolts like pale breastplates.

Bolitho said, 'She's pulling up, Mr Tyrrell. Not a great deal, but enough to worry about.'

Tyrrell rested at the rail and kept his eyes forward, away from the enemy frigate.

'Will I clear for action?'

He shook his head. 'We cannot. Every bit of space is packed with soldiers. There is barely room on the gun deck for a twelve-pounder to recoil.'

He thought of the big thirty-two-pounders pointing from either bow. With the enemy astern they were impotent. Just so much extra weight. Had the enemy been in their line of fire they might have been able to cripple her, if only temporarily, or until some ship of the inshore squadron could give them support.

Tyrrell looked at him worriedly. 'You have a choice, sir. You close th' shore now and risk losing th' wind altogether. Or you alter course to seaward within th' hour.' He angled his thigh against the rail as *Sparrow* plunged heavily, the spray dashing aft over the decks, rattling against the courses like lead pellets. 'There's a long ridge of sandbars running north to south. You take one side or t'other. But in an hour you'll have to decide which.'

Bolitho nodded. Even with the barest information he had discovered on his charts he knew Tyrrell's estimate was only too true. The sandbars, like uneven humps, ran for over twenty miles across their line of advance. To wear ship north or south to avoid them would mean loss of time, and with the enemy so near, it could represent the measure of disaster.

Tyrrell said, 'We could wait and see what th' Frenchie intends.' He rubbed his chin. 'But it would be too late for us by then.' He shrugged helplessly. 'I'm sorry, sir. I ain't much help.'

Bolitho stared past him towards the land. As the coast turned north-east it was falling away. Ten, fifteen miles, it was hard to gauge in the bright sunlight and low sea haze.

'You have been helpful.'

He walked aft to the compass and saw Buckle watching him grimly. The earlier laughter, the sudden relaxation of clearing the land, had all gone now. From a rumour to the sight of a sail. From a distant ship to real, deadly menace in the frigate's line of gun ports. It had all changed against them so quickly.

'Deck there! Sail fine on th' starboard bow!'

Graves said excitedly, 'The squadron! By God, that's better!'

Moments later, 'Deck! She's a lugger, sir! Headin' away!'

Bolitho clasped his hands behind his back. Some frightened trader, no doubt. If still within sight she might witness a swift one-sided fight within the hour.

'The Frenchman's altered course apiece!' Buckle was peering astern through a telescope. 'His yards are coming back!'

Bolitho waited, counting seconds. The frigate had swung off her original course, her speed and drive taking her away slightly further off *Sparrow*'s quarter. He tensed, seeing the telltale puff of brown smoke, driven away instantly by the following wind.

The heavy ball plunged short by a cable, the waterspout rising violently as if to mark a spouting whale.

Bolitho shut the seamen's jeers from his thoughts. No matter what they believed, it was a fair shot. She had fired nearly two miles with what must be a powerful bow-chaser like his own.

Foley appeared at his side. 'I heard the cannon.' He shaded his eyes to peer over the nettings. 'He means to unnerve you.'

Bolitho smiled gravely. 'He intends much more than that, Colonel.'

He heard more footfalls on the quarterdeck and saw Dalkeith blinking in the sunlight, wiping his face on his big handkerchief. He had removed his heavy apron, but there were dark stains on his legs and shoes, not yet dry.

He saw Bolitho and reported, 'That is all for now, sir. Ten have died. More will follow, I fear.'

Foley said admiringly, 'Thank you, Mr Dalkeith. It is better than I dared hope.'

They all looked round as another dull bang echoed across the cruising white-caps. It was nearer, and level with the starboard quarter.

Dalkeith shrugged. 'On dry land I might have saved more, Colonel.' He walked away towards the taffrail, his brilliant wig askew, his shoulders sagging as if from a great weight.

Bolitho said, 'A good surgeon. Usually the calling attracts the failure or the drunkard. He is neither.'

Foley was studying the frigate with a telescope. 'A woman drove him to sea maybe.' He ducked involuntarily as the other ship fired and the ball whimpered high overhead before throwing up a shark's fin of spray on the opposite side.

Bolitho said, 'Hoist the colours, Mr Tyrrell. He has the feel of us now.' He watched the scarlet flag break from the gaff. 'Mr Dalkeith! Have your helpers move those wounded men to the larboard side.' He silenced his unspoken protest with, 'Better now than when we are in real trouble.'

Graves came running aft along a gangway. 'Run out, sir?'

'No.' He looked up as another ball fanned above the deck. 'Load the starboard battery. Double-shotted and with grape for good measure.' He ignored Graves's puzzled expression and added to Foley, 'If we must fire it will have to be the one broadside. You have been below yourself. You know we cannot indulge in close action with the hull filled to its brim with sick men.'

Foley looked away. 'I am sorry, Captain.'

Bolitho studied him gravely. 'Do not be. My orders said little of fighting. Transportation was the ideal arrangement.' He forced a smile. 'Unfortunately, the Frenchman has not read them also!'

He turned to watch the wounded being carried to the

opposite side, while Graves and Yule, the gunner, supervised the slow loading of every starboard gun which was not impeded by either passengers or cargo.

Graves came to the ladder eventually and called, 'All but four guns loaded and ready, sir.' He broke off with a gasp as the air overhead came alive with a long-drawn-out shriek, as if a thousand devils had been freed from the sea itself.

Rigging and shrouds jerked savagely, and men ducked holding their hands above them as torn cordage and several severed blocks hurtled amongst them.

Bolitho gripped his hands together behind him still tighter until the pain helped to steady him. Langridge shot, as used by the big *Bonaventure*. It was vicious and very dangerous. Consisting of fragments of iron bound together, it could cut away rigging and tear down spars with ease. But unlike chain-shot, which was more generally used, it could also do terrible damage to men otherwise hidden by gangway or bulwark. The Frenchman obviously wanted to dismast *Sparrow* and take her and cargo intact. The gold would pay for many requirements in the future, and *Sparrow* would make a valuable addition to the enemy's fleet. It had happened before. Within the hour he might see it happen again. To him.

The bow-chaser threw out a spurt of smoke and the *Sparrow*'s main course burst open with a searing explosion, the great sail ripping itself to a hundred fragments in the wind even before the enemy's iron had finished falling alongside.

Bolitho could feel the difference instantly, the heavier motion between each lift and plunge, the increase of turns on the wheel as Buckle's helmsmen fought to hold her on course.

Yet again that demoniac scream of whirling fragments, the thud and clatter of falling rope and halliards. Men were working feverishly far above the decks to make good the severed rigging, but the frigate was much nearer, and as Bolitho swung round he saw three of her foremost guns belching fire and smoke, proof that she was overhauling rapidly to bring more of her armament to bear.

Balls shrieked and whimpered overhead and one ripped through the mizzen topsail with the slap of a whip against wood. Men yelled and cursed to control it as once again the wind explored the damage, tearing the shot-hole in an uneven gash from head to foot.

Bolitho gripped the rail hard. If only there was sight of a friendly sail, anything which might make the frigate lose heart or change tack even for a few moments.

He saw a ball skipping across the wave-crests, its progress clearly marked by the leaping feathers of spray; winced as the deck jumped beneath him as the shot slammed into the lower hull.

From below the gun deck he heard muffled cries, and pictured the sick and wounded, some with limbs only just cut away by Dalkeith, enduring the menacing roar of gunfire, the increasing accuracy of each successive shot.

Bethune came running from the ladder. 'Captain, sir! The general wishes to be kept informed . . .' He ducked as a ball burst through the taffrail and hurled two seamen in a tangle of writhing limbs and horrifying spurts of blood.

Bolitho turned from the sight. He had been speaking to one of them just several minutes ago. Now he was less than a man. Nothing.

'Tell the general to stay below and . . .'

He broke off as with a splintering crash the maintopgallant canted over, the sail whipping madly in a web of parted rigging, while the yard itself snapped into equal halves before pitching towards the deck. Men ran in confusion until the avalanche of wood and cordage had draped itself over the larboard gangway to trail alongside in a maelstrom of spray. A man, it must have been the lookout, was hurled bodily to the topsail yard, and even above the din Bolitho heard his shrill scream, saw him roll over and fall the rest of the way to the gun deck.

Another rugged burst of cannon fire, and Tilby dashed amongst the struggling seamen, his arms flailing as he pushed and drove them with their axes to free the ship from its torn rigging.

Tyrrell shouted, 'We will have to alter course, sir!' He was yelling to make himself heard as men rushed past him, faces screwed into tight masks, their eyes blind even to the butchered corpses beside the nettings.

Bolitho stared at him. 'How much water is there over those bars?'

Tyrrell seemed to think he had misheard. 'At *this* time? Next to nothing!' He peered wildly at the sails as more jagged iron screamed amongst them.

A topman had slipped and was being suspended by his hands by two of his companions while his legs kicked helplessly in the air. Sweat, fear or a flying splinter cut the contact, and with a brief cry the man fell head over heels, seemingly very slowly, until he hit the sea by the hull. Bolitho saw him passing below the quarterdeck, arms outspread, his eyes very white as the water closed over them.

'I must risk it!' He was shouting aloud without realizing it was more than a murmur. 'Tack either way and that frigate will rake us!'

Tyrrell nodded jerkily. 'As you say! I'll get a leadsman in th' chains and . . .'

Bolitho seized his arm. '*No!* Do that, or shorten sail, and that bastard will know what we're about!' He shook him violently. 'If I fall, you must try to take her through.'

A ball crashed into the nettings and sliced behind him. Splinters and fragments filled the air, and he saw Foley throw one hand to his shoulder where the epaulette had been torn cleanly away.

He faced Bolitho and said, 'Warm work, Captain.'

Bolitho stared at him, feeling that same fixed grin on his mouth and jaw like a cruel vice. Like him, the ship was acting like something beyond control, the remaining sails driving her onwards towards the hidden menace of those hard sandbars. He was banking everything on Tyrrell's knowledge, and the hope that the Frenchman was ignorant of his danger, or so blinded by all else but *Sparrow*'s closeness to defeat that he was totally absorbed.

Yet in spite of the intermittent gunfire, the responding crashes and thuds of balls striking home, he was able to see small but important details on every side.

A badly wounded seaman, his shoulder mashed to bloody pulp, was being held in the arms of a wounded soldier. The latter was blinded from some previous fight and his face

125

covered by bandages. But his hands seemed to stand out even in all the confusion around him. Moving and calming, shielding the sailor and groping for a flask of water to ease his suffering. And Dalkeith, his wig screwed into one pocket while he knelt beside another injured man, his fingers like scarlet claws as he felt the extent of the wound, while his eyes rested on the next victim, and the one after that.

And through it all Graves walking behind the loaded guns, chin on chest, pausing only to check a particular crew or to step astride a corpse or fallen rigging.

From forward came the frightened cry, 'I kin see th' bottom!'

Bolitho ran to the nettings and pulled himself above the tightly stowed hammocks. In the bright sunlight he saw the spray bursting from the rounded bilge, trailing ropes and a complete section of a broken cutter dragging alongside. Then he saw the darting, shadowy shapes gliding deeper still, weed and rock clusters, some of which seemed to be rising towards the keel like disturbed monsters.

If she struck now the masts would be ripped out of her, and she would plough forward, grinding and breaking open to the waiting sea.

He turned to seek out the enemy. How near she looked. Less than three cables off the quarter, her complete battery run out in readiness to finish the contest.

Buckle muttered hoarsely, 'By the living God, the Frenchie's in a safe channel!' There was a break in his voice. 'The bastards have done for us!'

Bolitho looked at Tyrrell. 'Get the t'gallants off her.' He could not hide the despair this time.

As the men swarmed aloft to shorten sail, Tyrrell shouted, 'There was nothing else you could do . . .'

He broke off as Buckle and Midshipman Heyward yelled together, '*She's struck!*'

Bolitho pushed between them and stared with sick disbelief at the other ship. She had been changing tack, either because her captain had at last seen his danger or was about to rake the sloop with his first full broadside, and had struck one of the bars at full speed. Across the strip of water they could hear the jarring crashes, the awful rumble of her hull pounding aground. And as she began to slew round, her foremast, followed and entangled with her main and mizzen topmasts, came down in one mighty curtain of leaping spray.

Bolitho had to yell several times to stop his men from shouting and cheering, to make them understand that their own danger was just as real.

'Alter course five points to starboard!' He dashed the sweat from his eyes to peer at the compass, his mind dulled by the crash of spars and groaning timbers. 'Steer sou' sou'-east!'

With only her torn course and topsails set, the *Sparrow* came round sluggishly, as if she, too, was beyond reason.

Gear flapped and banged, and men clambered over the scattered debris like dazed animals in their efforts to obey the shouts from aft.

Bolitho cupped his hands and yelled, 'Mr Graves! Run out!'

The ports squeaked open, and on their trucks the guns which could be manned trundled into the sunlight. With the sloop leaning over on her new tack each cannon moved quickly down the deck until with a shout of, 'All run out!' Graves stared once again towards Bolitho.

Bolitho watched narrowly, his hand lifting while he forced himself to see the other ship as a target and not a once living creature writhing in agony.

'As you bear, Mr Graves! Full elevation!'

He saw the listing, dismasted frigate falling past *Sparrow*'s starboard bow, the churned sand around her beakhead to mark the extent of her charge on to the bar.

His hand came down. '*Fire!*'

The hull jerked and bucked as gun by gun the double-shotted charges ripped over the wave crests to smash into the helpless enemy. A few shots from swivel guns answered the first onslaught, but as the heavy balls, coupled with a full load of grape, swept into her side and decks, those, too, fell silent.

Bolitho held up his hand. 'Cease firing! Secure guns!' To Buckle he added, 'We will wear ship directly. Nor'-east by north.' He glanced astern at the smoking wreck. 'She will rest there until someone comes, friend or foe, it makes little difference for her.'

Tyrrell watched him gravely. 'Aye, aye, sir.'

He appeared to be waiting for something more.

Bolitho walked to the rail and studied the men below him. Restoring lashings on the guns, working to repair damage and sort out the tangle of rigging, everywhere something was happening to prepare *Sparrow* for her next challenge. There was no cheering, in fact little sound of voices at all. Just a few grins as seamen discovered good friends still alive. A nod here, a casual thump of the shoulder there. Together they told him more than words.

'They've learned well, Mr Tyrrell.' He saw Dalkeith coming aft again and steeled himself for the list of dead and dying. 'After this they will be ready for anything.'

He handed his sword to Stockdale, who had been near him the whole time although he could not recall seeing him.

'As *I* will.'

8. A Captain's Decision

THE *Sparrow*'s stay at New York proved to be the most frustrating and testing time Bolitho could remember. Instead of weeks, as he had hoped, to carry out his repairs and replace stores, he was forced to wait and watch with mounting impatience while every other ship, or so it appeared, took precedence.

As the time dragged into one and then a second month, he found himself ready to plead rather than demand, beg instead of awaiting his rightful aid from the shore authorities, and from what he could gather elsewhere, it seemed that most other junior vessels were in the same situation.

Work aboard continued without pause, and already *Sparrow* had taken on the appearance of a tried veteran. Sails were carefully patched rather than being replaced without thought of cost. Nobody seemed to know when more replenishments were arriving from England, and those already in New York were jealously guarded or, he suspected, hoarded for some suitable bribe. The maintopgallant yard had been fished, and from the deck appeared as good as new. How it would withstand a real storm, or a chase after some blockade runner, was often in Bolitho's mind, along with the endless stream of reports to be made, requisition and victualling lists to be checked and argued over with the supply yard, until he began to think neither he nor his ship would ever move again.

Most of the pride and excitement at running the French frigate aground, of seeing the rescued soldiers safely landed, had given way to resigned gloom. Day after day, the ship's company endured the heat and the work, knowing there was no chance of setting foot on land unless under close supervision and then only on matters of duty. Bolitho knew the reasons for this rule were sound up to a point. Every vessel which came and went from Sandy Hook was shorthanded, and unscrupulous captains had been known to steal seamen from other ships if offered half a chance.

Since assuming command he, too, was short of fifteen men, those killed or so badly injured as to be unfit for further service.

And the news was not encouraging. Everywhere on the mainland the British forces were in trouble. In June a complete army was forced to retreat from General Washington's attacks at the battle of Monmouth, and the reports which filtered to the anchored ships showed little hope of improvement.

To add to the fleet's troubles had come the first hurricane of the season. Sweeping up from the Caribbean like a scythe through corn it had destroyed several ships in its path, and so damaged others they were out of commission when most needed. Bolitho was able to appreciate the admiral's concern for his patrols and prowling frigates, for the whole management of strategy along the American coast depended on their vigilance, their ability to act like his eyes and an extension to his brain.

He was thankful for one thing only. That his ship had not been so seriously damaged below the waterline as he had first feared. As Garby, the carpenter, had said, 'She's like a little fortress, sir.'

On his regular inspections below decks to watch the work's progress Bolitho had understood the carpenter's pride. For *Sparrow* had been built as a sloop of war, quite unlike most of her contemporaries which had been purchased for the Navy from the less demanding tasks of merchant service. Even her stout frames had been grown to the right proportions and not cut with a saw, so that the hull had all the added security of natural strength. The fact that but for a few ragged shot-holes below the quarter which needed the aid and tools of the New York shipwrights his ship could sail and fight as before, made the delay all the more unbearable.

He had been to see Rear-Admiral Christie aboard his flagship, but had gained little idea of when he could complete repairs. The admiral had said wryly, 'If you had been less, er, difficult with General Blundell, things might be different.'

When Bolitho had tried to draw him further he had snapped, 'I know the general was wrong to act as he did. The whole of

New York knows it by now. He may even be censured when he returns to England, although knowing his influence in certain regions, I doubt that.' He had shrugged wearily. '*You*, Bolitho, had to be the one to humble him. You did right, and I have already written a report to show my confidence in you. However, the *right* way is not always the most popular.'

One item of news hung over Bolitho like a cloud and seemed to torment him as day by day he tried to prepare his ship for sea. An incoming brig had brought news of the privateer *Bonaventure*. She had fought several actions against supply vessels and ships-of-war alike. She had seized two prizes and destroyed an escorting sloop. Just as he had predicted, as he had feared. But to him the worst part was that the privateer had returned to the same area where they had exchanged shots, and had found the crippled frigate *Miranda*.

A handful of survivors had been discovered drifting in a small boat, some wounded or half-mad with thirst, the rest stunned by the suddenness of their ship's end, when they had done so much to repair and save her.

Over and over again Bolitho searched his mind to examine his actions, to discover what else he might or should have done. By carrying out his orders, by putting duty before the true desire to help the damaged frigate, he had left her like a helpless animal before the tiger.

In his heart he believed he could have made no other decision. But if he had realized that the two transports were no longer so desperately needed, he also knew he would have acted differently. When he had admitted as much to the brig's captain he had replied, 'Then your *Sparrow*, too, would be at the bottom, for *Bonaventure* is more than a match for anything but a ship of the line!'

Apart from matters of duty, errands to use his presence or his purse on shipyard clerks, Bolitho refrained from going ashore. Partly because he thought it unfair when his men were penned in their ship, the size of which seemed to shrink with each passing day, and partly because of what he saw there. The military preparations were usual enough. Artillery wheeling and exercising, the horse-drawn limbers charging at full tilt, to the delight of idlers and yelling children. Foot soldiers drilling and sweating in the grinding heat, he had even seen cavalry on several occasions.

No, it went far deeper. The worsening news from inland seemed to reach just so far and then stop. In the great houses, rarely a night passed without some fine ball or reception being held. Staff officers and rich traders, ladies in full gowns and glittering jewels, it was hard to realize they were so close to a full-scale war. Equally, he knew his disgust came from his own inability to mix in such circles. In his home town of Falmouth his family had always been respected, but more as seafarers than local residents. He had gone to sea at the age of twelve, and his education had been more concerned with navigation and learning the mysteries of every eye and cleat, each foot of cordage required to sail a ship under all conditions, than the art of making small-talk and mingling with some of the bewigged jackadandies he had seen in New York. The women, too, seemed different. Beyond reach. Unlike the outspoken countrywomen in Cornwall or the wives and daughters of fellow sea-officers, they appeared to give off a power all of their own. A boldness, a certain amused contempt which both irritated and confused him whenever he came in contact with their perfumed, privileged world.

He had allowed Tyrrell to go ashore whenever possible, and had been surprised to see the change in him. Instead of showing excitement or relief at being amongst men like himself, places he had often visited in his father's schooner, he withdrew still further, until eventually he avoided leaving the ship unless on some particular duty. Bolitho knew he had been making inquiries about his family's whereabouts, anything which might give him some hint of their safety or otherwise. Also, he believed that Tyrrell would tell him in his own good time, if that was what he wished.

And then, three months almost to the exact day after watching the French frigate pounding herself to fragments on the hidden bar, *Sparrow* was once more ready for sea. When the last shipwright had been escorted ashore, each watched to make certain he took no more than he had brought with him, and the water-lighters and yard hoys had pulled clear of the side, Bolitho wrote his report for the admiral. Another special mission, to carry despatches, or merely to return to Captain Colquhoun's command, he now cared very little which it was to be. Just to be under sail again, free of urbane flag officers and inscrutable clerks, it was all he wanted.

When Tyrrell came aft to report the ship cleared of shore workers Bolitho asked, 'Will you dine with me this evening? We may be too occupied in the near future.'

Tyrrell looked at him dully. 'My pleasure, sir.' He sounded worn out. Spent.

Bolitho stared through the open stern windows towards the anchored ships and the pale houses beyond.

'You may share your worries with me, Mr Tyrrell, if you wish.' He had not meant to say what he did. But the look of despair on the lieutenant's face had pushed all caution aside.

Tyrrell watched him by the windows, his eyes in shadow. 'I did get news. My father lost his schooners, but that was expected. They went to one side or t'other. Makes no difference. My father also owned a small farmstead. Always said it was like th' one he had once in England.'

Bolitho turned slowly. 'Is that gone, too?'

Tyrrell shrugged. 'Th' war reached th' territory some months back.' His voice became distant, toneless. 'We had a neighbour called Luke Mason. He an' I grew up together. Like brothers. When th' rebellion began Luke was up north selling cattle an' I was at sea. Luke was always a bit wild, an' I guess he got carried along by all the excitement. Anyway, he joined up to fight th' English. But things got bad for his company, they were almost wiped out in some battle or t'other. Luke decided to go home. He had had enough of war, I guess.'

Bolitho bit his lip. 'He went to your father?'

'Aye. Trouble was, my father was apparently helping th' English soldiers with fodder an' remounts. But he was fond of Luke. He was like family.' He gave a long sigh. 'Th' local colonel heard about it from some goddamn informer. He had my father hanged on a tree and burned th' house down for good measure.'

Bolitho exclaimed, 'My God, I'm sorry!'

Tyrrell did not seem to hear. 'Then th' Americans attacked an' th' redcoats retreated.' He looked up at the deckhead and

133

added fiercely, 'But Luke was safe. He got out of th' house before it burned around him. An' you know what? Th' American colonel hanged Luke as a deserter!'

He dropped on a chair and fell against the table. 'In th' name of hell, where's th' goddamn sense in it all?'

'And your mother?' He watched Tyrrell's lowered head. His anguish was breaking him apart.

'She died two years back, so she was spared all this. There's just me now, an' my sister Jane.' He looked up, his eyes reflecting the sunlight like fires. 'After Cap'n Ransome had done with her, she disappeared. Christ alone knows where she is!'

In the sudden silence Bolitho tried to discover how he would feel if, like Tyrrell, he was faced with such an appalling discovery. Ever since he could remember he had been taught to accept the possibility of death and not shirk from it. Most of his ancestors had died at sea in one manner or another. It was an easy thing to do. Quite apart from a brutal end under cannon fire or the plunge of an enemy's sword, there were countless traps for the unwary. A fall from aloft, drowning, fever, men died as much from these as anything fired from a gun. His brother Hugh had been a lieutenant in the Channel Fleet when he had last seen him. He could be commanding a ship against the French, or at this very moment lying many fathoms down with his men. But the roots would still be there. The house in Falmouth, his father and married sisters. What would he be suffering if, like Tyrrell, he knew all that was broken and trodden down in a country where brother fought brother and men cursed each other in the same language as they struggled and died?

Now Tyrrell, and many more besides, had nothing left. Not even a country.

There was a rap on the door and Graves stepped into the cabin. 'This was delivered by the guardboat, sir.' He held out a canvas envelope.

Bolitho walked to the windows again and slit it open with a knife. He hoped Graves would not notice Tyrrell's misery, that the time taken to read the message would give him a moment to recover.

It was very brief.

He said quietly, 'We are ordered to weigh at first light tomorrow. We will be carrying important despatches to the admiral in Antigua.'

He had a mental picture of the endless sea miles, the long passage back to English Harbour and Colquhoun. It was a pity they had ever left in the first place.

Graves said, 'I'm not sorry. We'll have something to boast about this time.'

Bolitho studied him gravely. What an unimaginative man he is.

'My compliments to the master. Tell him to make preparations at once.'

When Graves had gone Bolitho added, 'Maybe you'll wish to postpone dining with me?'

Tyrrell stood up, his fingers touching the table as if to test his own balance.

'No, sir. I'd like to come.' He looked round the cabin. 'This was th' last place I saw Jane. It helps a bit now.'

Bolitho watched him leave and heard the slam of a cabin door. Then with a sigh he sat down at the table and began to write in his log.

For seven untroubled days the *Sparrow* pushed her bowsprit southwards, taking full advantage of a fresh wind which hardly varied in bearing or substance throughout that time. The regrets and brooding despondency which most of the company had felt at New York seemed to have blown away on the wind, and their new freedom shone in the straining canvas which gleamed beneath a cloudless sky. Even the memory of the last fight, the faces of those killed or left behind crippled to await passage home had become part of the past, like old scars which took just so much time to heal.

As Bolitho studied his chart and checked the daily sunsights he felt cause for satisfaction in *Sparrow*'s performance. She had already logged over a thousand miles, and like himself seemed eager to leave the land as far away as possible. They had not sighted even a solitary sail, and the last hopeful gulls had left them two days earlier.

The routine aboard such a small ship-of-war was regular and carefully planned, so that the overcrowded conditions could be made as comfortable as possible. When not working aloft on sails and rigging the hands spent their time at gun drill or in harmless contests of wrestling and fighting with staves under Stockdale's professional eye.

On the quarterdeck, too, there was usually some diversion to break the monotony of empty horizons, and Bolitho came to know even more about his officers. Midshipman Heyward had proved himself to be an excellent and skilful swordsman, and spent several of the dog watches instructing Bethune and the master's mates in the art of fencing. The biggest surprise was Robert Dalkeith. The plump surgeon had come on deck with the finest pair of pistols Bolitho had ever seen. Perfectly matched and made by Dodson of London, they must have cost a small fortune. While one of the ship's boys had thrown pieces of wood chippings from a gangway, Dalkeith had waited by the nettings and when they had bobbed past on the wash had despatched them without seeming to take aim. Such marksmanship was rare for any ship's surgeon, and added to the price of the pistols made Bolitho think more deeply about Dalkeith's past.

Towards the end of the seventh day Bolitho received his first warning that the weather was changing. The sky, clear and pale blue for so long, became smeared by long tongues of cloud, and the ship reeled more heavily in a deep swell. The glass was unsteady, but it was more the feel of things which told him they were in for a real blow. The wind had backed to the north-west and showed every sign of strengthening, and as he faced it across the taffrail he could sense the mounting power, its clamminess on his skin.

Buckle observed, 'Another hurricane, I wonder?'

'Maybe.' Bolitho walked to the compass. 'Let her fall off a point.' He left Buckle to his helmsmen and joined Tyrrell by the quarterdeck rail. 'The fringe of a storm perhaps. Either way we will have to reef down before dark, maybe sooner.'

Tyrrell nodded, his eyes on the bulging canvas. 'Th' main-to'gan'sl seems to be drawing well. They did good work aloft while we were in port.' He watched the masthead pendant as it twisted and then flapped out more firmly towards the larboard bow. 'Goddamn th' wind. It backs still further by th' looks of it.'

Buckle smiled glumly. 'Course sou' sou'-east, sir.' He cursed as the deck tilted steeply and a tall spectre of spray burst above the nettings.

Bolitho considered the matter. They had made a good passage so far. There was no point in tearing the sails off her just to spite the wind. He sighed. Perhaps it would ease again soon. 'Get the t'gallants off her, Mr Tyrrell. It's coming down on us now.'

He stood aside as Tyrrell ran for his trumpet. Out from the swaying hull he saw the telltale haze of rain advancing across the uneven swell and blotting out the horizon like a fence of chain-mail.

Within an hour the wind had backed even further and had risen to gale force, with the sea and sky joined together in a torment of bursting wave-crests and torrential rain. It was useless to fight it, and as the clouds gathered and entwined above the swooping mastheads *Sparrow* turned and ran before it, her topmen fighting and fisting the sodden canvas as yet another reef was made fast. Half-blinded by rain and spray, their feet groping for toeholds, while with curses and yells they used brute strength to bring the sails under control.

Night came prematurely, and under close-reefed topsails they drove on into the darkness, their world surrounded by huge wave-crests, their lives menaced at every step by the sea as it surged over the gangways and boiled along the decks like a river in flood. Even when the hands were dismissed in watches to find a moment of rest and shelter below there was little to sustain them. Everything was dripping or damp, and the cook had long since given up any idea of producing a hot meal.

Bolitho remained on the quarterdeck, his tarpaulin coat plastered to his body like a shroud while the wind howled and screamed around him. Shrouds and rigging whined like the strings of some mad orchestra, and above the deck, hidden in darkness, the crack and boom of canvas told its own story. In brief lulls the wind seemed to drop, holding its breath as if to consider its efforts against the embattled sloop. In those small moments Bolitho could feel the salt warming on his face, raw to the touch. He could hear the clank of pumps, the muffled shouts from below and on the hidden forecastle as unseen men fought to make fast lashings, seek out severed cordage, or merely to reassure each other they were alive.

All night the wind battered against them, driving them further and still further to the south-east. Hour by hour, as Bolitho peered at the compass or reeled below to examine his chart, there was neither rest nor relief from its pounding. Bolitho felt bruised and sick, as if he had been fighting a physical battle, or dragged half-drowned from the sea itself. Despite his reeling mind he thanked God he had not tried to lie to and ride out the storm under a solitary reefed topsail. With this strength of wind and sea *Sparrow* would never have recovered, could have been all aback and dismasted before anyone had realized what they were truly against.

He could even find a moment to marvel at *Sparrow*'s behaviour. Uncomfortable she was to every man aboard. Fighting the jerking canvas or working on the pumps with sea and bilge water swirling amongst them like rats in a sewer, their lives were made worse by the motion. Up, higher still, and then down with the sound of thunder across a great crest, every spar and timber shaking as if to rip free of the hull. Food, a few precious possessions, clothing, all surged about the decks in wild abandon, but not a gun tore away from its lashings, not a bolt snapped, nor was any hatch stove in by the attacking sea. *Sparrow* took it all, rode each assault with the unsteady belligerence of a drunken marine.

By the time they sighted a first hint of grey in the sky the sea had begun to ease, and when the sun peeped languidly above the horizon it was hard to believe they were in the same ocean.

The wind had veered again to the north-west and as they stared with salt-caked eyes at the patches of blue between the clouds they knew they were being left in comparative peace.

Bolitho realized that if he allowed the hands to rest now they would not be able to move again for hours. He looked down at the gun deck and gangways, seeing their tired faces and torn clothing, the way the topmen's tarred hands were held like claws after their repeated journeys to those treacherous yards to battle with the sails.

He said, 'Pass the word for the galley fire to be lit. We must get some hot food into them directly.' He looked up as a shaft of sunlight touched the upper yards so that they shone above the retreating darkness like a triple crucifix. 'It will be warm enough soon, Mr Tyrrell. Rig wind-sails above each hatch and open the weather gun ports.' He let his salt-stiffened lips crack into a smile. 'I suggest you forget your usual concern for the ship's looks and have the hands run their spare clothing aloft to dry out.'

Graves came aft and touched his hat. 'Able Seaman Marsh is missing.' He swayed and added wearily, 'Foretopman, sir.'

Bolitho let his eyes stray over the starboard quarter. The seaman must have been hurled overboard during the night, and they had not even heard a cry. Which was just as well. They could have done nothing to save him.

'Thank you, Mr Graves. Note it in the log, if you please.'

He was still watching the sea, the way the night appeared to withdraw itself before the first gold rays, like some retreating assassin. The seaman was out there somewhere, dead and remembered by just a few. His shipmates, and those at home he had left so long ago.

He shook himself and turned to the master. 'Mr Buckle, I hope we can fix our position today. Somewhere to the sou'-west of the Bermudas, I have no doubt.' He smiled gently at Buckle's gloomy expression. 'But fifty miles or five hundred, I am not sure.'

Bolitho waited another hour until the ship had been laid on a new tack, her jib-boom prodding towards the southern horizon, her decks and upperworks steaming in the early sunlight as if she was smouldering.

Then he nodded to Tyrrell. 'I will take some breakfast.' He sniffed the greasy aroma from the galley funnel. 'Even that smell has given me an appetite.'

With the cabin door firmly closed and Stockdale padding around the table with fresh coffee and a pewter plate of fried pork, Bolitho was able to relax, to weigh the value and cost of the night's work. He had faced his first storm in command. A man had died, but many others had stayed alive. And the *Sparrow* was once again dipping and creaking around him as if nothing out of the ordinary had happened at all.

Stockdale put a plate with half a loaf of stale bread on it beside a crock of yellow butter. The bread was the last of that brought aboard at New York, the butter probably rancid from the cask. But as Bolitho leaned back in his chair he felt like a king, and the meagre breakfast seemed a banquet.

He stared idly around the cabin. He had survived much in so short a time. It was luck, more than he deserved.

He asked, 'Where is Fitch?'

Stockdale showed his teeth. 'Dryin' your sleepin' gear, sir.' He rarely spoke when Bolitho was eating and thinking. He had learned all about Bolitho's odd habits long back. He added, 'Woman's work.'

Bolitho laughed, the sound carrying up through the open skylight where Tyrrell had the watch and Buckle was scribbling on his slate beside the binnacle.

Buckle shook his head. 'What did I tell you? No worries, that one!'

'Deck there!' Tyrrell stared up at the masthead as the cry came. 'Sail! Fine on th' starboard quarter!'

Feet clattered on the ladder and Bolitho appeared beside him, his jaw still working on some buttered bread.

He said, 'I have a feeling about this morning.' He saw a master's mate by the mainmast trunk and called, 'Mr Raven! Aloft with you!' He held up his hand, halting the man as he ran to the shrouds. 'Remember your lesson, as I will.'

Graves had also come on deck, partly shaved and naked to the waist. Bolitho looked around the waiting men, studying each in turn if only to contain his impatience while Raven clawed his way to the masthead. Changed. They were all different in some way. Toughened, more confident perhaps. Like bronzed pirates, held together by their trade—he hesitated—their loyalty.

'Deck there!' Another maddening wait and then Raven yelled down, 'It's her right enough! The *Bonaventure*!'

Something like a growl came from the watching seamen.

One man shouted, 'The bloody *Bonaventure*, is it? Us'll give that bugger a quiltin' today an' that's for sure!'

Several others cheered, and even Bethune called excitedly, 'Huzza, lads!'

Bolitho turned to look at them again, his heart suddenly heavy, the promise of the morning sour and spoiled.

'Get the t'gallants on her, Mr Tyrrell. The royals, too, if the wind stays friendly.'

He saw Tyrrell's eyes, worried, even sad, and snapped, 'We have orders. To carry despatches to our admiral.' He gestured angrily towards the taffrail. 'Do you want to match guns with her?' He turned away, adding vehemently, 'By God, I'd like nothing better than to see her strike!'

Tyrrell took his trumpet and shouted, 'Call th' hands! All hands make sail!'

He glanced quickly at Bolitho who was staring astern. The privateer was not visible from anywhere but the masthead. Nor would she be now. But Bolitho was staring fixedly, as if he could see every gun, each gaping muzzle, like the day she had swept *Miranda*'s defences aside like so much rubbish.

Graves moved to his side, his eyes on the seamen as they hurried to their various stations, some still puzzled by their orders.

Tyrrell said quietly, 'It ain't easy to run before an enemy.'

Graves shrugged. 'How about you? I'd have thought you should be somewhat comforted by the fact.' He fell back before Tyrrell's cold stare but added smoothly, 'It would have been less easy for you to fight a Yankee, eh?' Then he hurried down the ladder towards his men at the foremast.

Tyrrell followed him with his eyes. 'Bastard.' He spoke only to himself and was surprised to find he was so calm. '*Bastard*.'

When he turned his head he saw that Bolitho had left the deck.

Buckle dipped his thumb to the skylight. 'He's not laughing now, Mr Tyrrell.' He sounded grim. 'I'd not have his rank for all the whores in Plymouth!'

Tyrrell tapped the half-hour glass and said nothing.

How different from Captain Ransome, he thought. He would have shared neither hopes nor fears with any of them.

And these same seamen who were already swarming up the ratlines on either beam would have shown no surprise if he made a similar decision as Bolitho. It was because they seemed to think Bolitho could lead them anywhere, and with all odds against them, that they were puzzled by his action. The sudden realization troubled him. Partly because Bolitho did not understand, but mainly because he should have been the one to make Bolitho realise how they all felt for him.

Ransome had always used and never led them. Instead of example he had laid down rules. Whereas he . . . Tyrrell glanced at the cabin skylight now shut, and imagined he could hear a girl's voice again.

Graves strode aft and touched his hat, his tone formal in front of the watching eyes.

'Permission to dismiss the watch below, sir?'

'Aye. Carry on, Mr Graves.' They held each other's gaze then Tyrrell turned his back.

He walked to the rail and stared up at the freshly trimmed sails, the seamen on the upper yards, their skins brown in the sunlight.

The privateer would never catch them now, even if she so intended. It would be another ship, a fat merchantman, or some unsuspecting trader from the Bahamas.

He saw the captain's coxswain beside the nettings and asked, 'How is he, Stockdale?'

Stockdale regarded him warily, like a watchdog examining a possible intruder.

Then he relaxed slightly, his big hands loose at his sides. ''E's in irons at th' moment, sir.' He stared angrily at the blue water. 'But we've come through worse afore. A lot worse.'

Tyrrell nodded, seeing the certainty in Stockdale's eyes like something written.

'He has a good friend in you, Stockdale.'

The coxswain turned his broken face away. 'Aye. I could tell you things I seen 'im do that'd make some of these Jacks run to their mothers and pray.'

Tyrrell kept quiet and very still, watching the man's profile as he relived some memory, an incident so vivid it was like yesterday.

Stockdale said in his wheezing voice, 'I've carried' im like a child, seen 'im so beside hisself with anger there's not a man-jack'd draw near. Other times I've seen 'im 'old a man in 'is arms until 'e died, even though there was nought anyone cou'd do for th' poor bugger.' He swung round, his eyes fierce. 'I ain't got the words for it, else I'd make 'em all listen.'

Tyrrell reached out and touched his massive arm.

'You're wrong. You've got th' words right enough. And thanks for telling *me*.'

Stockdale grunted and walked heavily towards the hatch. He had never spoken like that before, but somehow he trusted Tyrrell. Like Bolitho, he was a man, not just an officer, and for him that was more than enough.

All that day the *Sparrow* ran freely towards an empty horizon. The watches changed, drills were carried out, and one man was flogged for drawing his knife against a messmate after an argument. But there were no contests on deck, and when Heyward appeared with his swords to begin another period of instruction he found no takers, nor did Dalkeith leave his sickbay for a pistol shoot.

In his cabin Bolitho remained with his thoughts, wondering why a simple action was so hard to bear, merely because he had been the one to dictate it. Command, leadership, authority, they were mere words. At no time could they explain his true feelings, or wipe away inner misgivings.

As Rear-Admiral Christie had said, the right way was not always the most popular, or the easiest to accept.

When the bell chimed out for the first dogwatch he heard another cry from the masthead.

'Deck there! Sail on the lee bow!'

He made himself remain seated at the table until Midshipman Bethune came down to report that the sail was barely moving and was perhaps hove-to.

Even then he delayed before going on deck. Another disappointment, a fresh need to take avoiding action from one more enemy, only time and distance would tell him.

Graves, who had the watch, said, 'If it's one of our frigates we could turn and close with the *Bonaventure*, sir.'

Heyward added, 'Maybe we could take her as a prize.'

Bolitho faced them coldly. 'And if she's a *French* frigate, what then?' He saw them stiffen under his stare. 'I suggest you hold your suppositions until later.'

But it was neither privateer nor patrolling ship-of-war. As *Sparrow* sped down towards her Bolitho watched the stranger through his glass, seeing the gap in her outline where her main topmast had been torn away like a branch from a tree, and the huge scars along her tumblehome to show the battering she had received from sea and wind.

Buckle said quietly, 'By God, she must have taken the storm full on herself. She's in a poor way, I'm thinking.'

Tyrrell, who had climbed to the main topmast yard, shinned down a backstay and reported, 'I know her, sir. She's th' *Royal Anne*, West Indiaman.'

Buckle agreed. 'Aye, that's so. She set sail from Sandy Hook three days afore us. Bound for Bristol, I heard.'

'Run up the colours.'

Bolitho shifted the glass carefully, watching the tiny figures swarming along the other ship's decks, the broken gangway where a great sea had thundered inboard like a falling cliff. She made a pitiful sight. Spars missing, sails in ribbons. She must have ridden out the same storm which they had skirted just a night ago.

Bethune exclaimed, 'I have her here in my book, sir. She is under warrant to the Commander-in-Chief.'

But Bolitho barely heard him. He saw the figures along the vessel's upper deck pausing to stare at the approaching sloop, while here and there a man was waving, perhaps cheering to see a friendly flag.

He stiffened and then said, 'There are women aboard that ship.' He lowered the glass and looked at Tyrrell questioningly. 'Under warrant, is she?'

Tyrrell nodded slowly. 'Indiamen do take a government charter when it suits, sir.' He glanced away. 'Th' *Royal Anne*'ll be carrying folk from New York to England. And away from th' war, no doubt.'

Bolitho raised the glass again, his mind working on Tyrrell's words.

He said, 'We will close her now, Mr Tyrrell, and keep her under our lee. Have the starboard cutter cleared for lowering. The surgeon will accompany me on board.' He glanced at Bethune. 'Signal her to that effect. If she fails to understand, then hail her when we draw nearer.'

He walked away from the rail as the flags soared aloft on their halliards.

Tyrrell followed him and said gravely, 'She'll not be able to outsail th' *Bonaventure*, sir. Even if she was without damage.'

Bolitho faced him. 'I know.'

He tried to sound composed even though his mind was screaming. Turn after all and face the big privateer. The facts had not altered. *Sparrow* would still be outgunned and sunk without too much difficulty. The *Royal Anne* was so badly damaged that a respite brought about by sacrificing this ship and all her company would make no difference. But to run once more. Leave her helpless and allow the enemy to take her at leisure was too cruel even to contemplate.

He *must* contemplate it. It was his decision. *His.*

Buckle called, 'She's standing by, sir! We'd best take the way off us.'

'Very well.' Bolitho walked slowly along the side. 'Get the royals and t'gallants off her, Mr Tyrrell. We will heave-to directly.'

He saw Stockdale hurrying towards him with his coat and sword. It would be dark in five hours. If they were to do anything, they would need haste and luck. Especially the latter.

He slipped into his coat and said, 'Mr Tyrrell, you will come with me.'

Then as the boat was hoisted over the gangway and lowered alongside he looked astern, almost expecting to see a sliver of sail, or hear the masthead's call.

'Cutter alongside, sir!'

He nodded and strode towards the gangway.

'Let us be about it then.'

And without a glance at the others he followed Tyrrell down into the boat.

9. 'Boarders Away!'

AS HE PULLED HIMSELF up a dangling rope ladder to the *Royal Anne*'s thick bulwark Bolitho was conscious of the tension which awaited him. There were many people on the upper and poop decks, passengers and sailors, singly and in large groups, but all joined together in some way as they stared at him, then at the seamen who followed him up from the cutter.

Bolitho paused to collect his thoughts, and while he adjusted the sword on his hip and Tyrrell mustered the boarding party into line, he took a slow appraisal of the ship around him. Fallen rigging and broken spars, whole strips of torn canvas and cordage littered the decks in profusion, and he could tell by the heavy motion that she had taken a good deal of water in the bilges.

A tall, gangling man in a blue coat stepped forward and touched his forehead.

'I'm Jennis, sir.' He swallowed hard. 'Mate and senior officer.'

'Where is the Master?'

Jennis gestured wearily towards the rail. 'He went overboard in the storm. Him and twenty more besides.'

Boots thudded on a companion ladder and Bolitho stiffened as a familiar figure thrust the others aside and strode towards him.

It was General Blundell, impeccable as ever, but with two pistols at his belt.

Bolitho touched his hat. 'I am surprised to see you, Sir James.' He tried to mask his dislike. 'You appear to be in some trouble.'

The general glared around him then across at the *Sparrow* as she swayed easily in the swell, her sails flapping loosely as if resting.

He barked, 'And about time, too! This damn ship should

never have been allowed out of harbour!' He pointed at the mate. 'That fool cannot even keep order!'

Bolitho looked at Tyrrell. 'Take your men and examine the hull and other damage. Quick as you can.' He glanced narrowly at a group of sailors lolling by the forward hatch, noticing how they swayed out of time with the deck, their eyes devoid of interest in his arrival or the disorder which lay on every hand.

The mate explained hurriedly, 'We've had to use pistols, sir. Some men ran wild when the storm broke. We've a full cargo of rum and other spirits, as well as molasses and coffee. While the rest of us were working the ship they and a few passengers broached holds and began drinking.' He shuddered 'What with women crying an' screaming, the ship falling about us, an' Cap'n Harper lost overboard, I was hard put to watch everything at once.'

Blundell snapped, 'You're bloody useless! I'd have you shot for your incompetence!'

As the first of *Sparrow*'s seamen approached the fore hatch the drunken figures seemed to come to life. With jeers and taunts they blocked the way across the deck, and from right forward an unseen hand hurled a bottle which shattered against a ring bolt, bringing bright droplets of blood down a sailor's chest.

Bolitho said sharply, 'Carry on, Mr. Tyrrell!'

The lieutenant nodded. 'Party! Draw cutlasses!' He took his pistol and pointed it at the line of swaying figures. 'Kill anyone who interferes! Bosun's mate, take 'em below and put 'em on the pumps!'

One made as if to run amongst the small party, but fell senseless as the boatswain's mate brought the flat of his blade hard down on the side of his head.

Bolitho said, 'There is much to do. Mr Jennis, turn the hands to and replace your fores'l. Have all this clutter cut adrift so that the injured may be laid on deck where my surgeon can attend them.' He waited until the mate had shouted his instructions before adding, 'How are you armed?'

Jennis waved vaguely around him. 'Not much, sir. Twenty six-pounders and some swivels. We aim to steer clear of trouble. These guns are all we need for fighting off the *boucanier* or would-be pirate.' He looked up, startled. 'Why do you ask?'

General Blundell interrupted, 'Hell's teeth, must I stand here while you people discuss the fittings of this wretched ship? I have had all I can tolerate and . . .'

Bolitho said abruptly, 'Sir James, there is an enemy privateer to the north. She is probably still following us. The *fittings*, as you call them, will be very useful if that enemy comes our way.'

He turned, cocking his head, as the clank of pumps told him Tyrrell had the mutinous seamen in hand.

To Stockdale he said, 'Go aft, see what you can discover.' Blundell sounded less confident.

'Privateer? Attack us?'

Bolitho replied, 'The *Sparrow* is very small, sir. The enemy more than twice our strength.'

The general grunted. 'Well, better than nothing. If fight you must, it will be for the finest reasons.'

Bolitho ignored him as Tyrrell came on deck again.

'I have sounded th' well. Th' hull is taking water steadily, but th' pumps seem to be containing it. It's all hell below. Cabins broken open, drunks, and two dead from knife wounds.' He frowned towards the mate who was urging his men to clear away fallen spars. 'He must have been mad with worry.' He saw Bolitho's expression. 'What'll we do?'

Blundell said, 'Your captain will do his duty. If we are attacked he will defend this ship and passengers. Do you need telling, man?'

Tyrrell eyed him coolly. 'Not by *you*, General.'

Bolitho snapped, 'How many women are there?' He was watching Stockdale ushering them from the poop, his voice barely audible as he tried to placate them.

There were children, too. More than he had realized.

'For God's sake, how much longer are you going to stand like this?' The general was shouting, his face almost as red as his tunic. 'What does it matter how many this or that we have on board, or what colour their eyes are?' He got no further.

148

Tyrrell stepped between them, his head lowered so that their faces were nearly touching.

'Look here, General, what th' cap'n says is right. Th' enemy can outshoot anything we have to offer, an' this Indiaman is a damn sight worse off.'

'Not my concern, and I'll tell you once more to mind your manners!'

'Warn me, General?' Tyrrell laughed silently. 'But for you meddling with us at Sandy Hook th' *Sparrow* would have completed repairs an' been away at sea a month back. So but for that you would be alone out here, sitting like a fat duck waiting to be shot for th' pot.' His tone hardened. 'So mind *your* damn manners, *sir*!'

Bolitho was standing apart from them, only half listening to their hushed anger. Once again Blundell's interference was to put him and the ship in real jeopardy. But the facts were unchanged. He turned to conceal his despair. All he had was the hope that *Bonaventure* would not find them. That he could set sail on the battered Indiaman and leave the area with all possible haste.

The mate, Jennis, came aft again. 'I've got the hands bending on a new fores'l, sir. Apart from that we've little spare canvas aboard, not made up that is. This is a Company ship, and we were expecting to have a complete overhaul once we reached Bristol. That's why we sailed short-handed and one officer under strength.' He wiped his hand across his lined face. 'If you hadn't found us I think more of the men might have gone mad and mutinied. We've a fair sprinkling of rogues amongst the passengers as well as honest ones.'

Bolitho looked up as a block swayed and clattered against the mizzen topmast. He saw the torn sails stirring like ragged banners, the sudden movement in the bright Company flag. He frowned. The wind was freshening. Very slightly, but it made things harder if he was to face the decision which had to be made.

And yet, there was still a chance he might be wrong. If so, all this would do nothing but harm and cause more suffering to the passengers.

He pulled out his watch and flipped open the cover.

Less than four hours of visibility left.

'Mr Tyrrell, have the *Royal Anne*'s boats lowered at once. Send a message to Graves and tell him I want our boats and fifty seamen here without delay. We must work like the devil if we are to get this ship fit to make sail again.' He waited until Tyrrell and the Indiaman's mate had hurried away before saying, 'Well, Sir James, I must see what needs to be done.'

The general called after him, 'And if as you fear the enemy appears, do you intend to steal away and leave us?' He sounded hoarse with suppressed anger. 'Will written orders save your disgrace after taking such a course?'

Bolitho stopped and faced him again. 'No, Sir James, to both questions. If we are allowed time I will transfer all *Royal Anne*'s passengers and additional hands to my own ship.'

The general's eyes were bulging. '*What?* Leave the cargo and sail away without it?' He seemed stunned in disbelief.

Bolitho shifted his gaze outboard, watching the boats alongside, the slow return of order as his own men took control.

Of course, he should have realized. The general's booty was on board, too. Surprisingly, the thought helped to steady him. He could even smile as he said, 'You can appreciate the need for haste, sir. For both our reasons!'

Tyrrell fell in step beside him. 'That took th' wind from his sails!'

Bolitho said, 'It is no joke. If we can get under way in company at dawn we will have a fair chance. It may be that the *Bonaventure* changed tack altogether when we lost her. She could be many leagues away by now.'

Tyrrell glanced at him. 'But you don't think so?'

'No.' He stepped aside as broken rigging was dragged like black snakes from an upended boat. 'It is the *when* rather than the *if* which troubles me.'

Tyrrell pointed across the bulwark. 'Graves is sending th' first of th' men over.' He grimaced. 'It'll leave him short-handed in *Sparrow*. Barely enough to work ship.'

Bolitho shrugged. 'If the company was halved by fever the rest would *have* to manage.'

He added, 'Now let us meet the ladies. They will be more worried than the general, I should imagine.'

There were about fifty of them. Crowded together below the high poop, but separated by their rank and station in that other world outside the ship. Old and young, plain and beautiful, they watched Bolitho in silence, as if he had risen from the sea like a messenger from Neptune.

'Ladies.' He licked his lips as a strikingly beautiful girl in a gown of yellow silk smiled at him. He tried again. 'I must regret the inconvenience, but there is much to do before we can see you safely on your voyage.' She was still smiling. Direct. Amused. Just the way which always reduced him to confusion. 'If anyone is injured my surgeon will do his best for her. A meal is being prepared, and my own men will stand guard over your quarters.'

The girl asked, 'Do you think the enemy will come, Captain?' She had a cool, confident voice which spoke of education and breeding.

He hesitated. 'It is always possible.'

She showed her even teeth. 'There now. What profound words from so young a King's officer!' Several of the others smiled. Some even laughed aloud.

Bolitho said stiffly, 'If you will excuse me, ladies.' He shot the girl a fierce stare. 'I have work to do.'

Tyrrell hid a smile as he strode past him, recalling Stockdale's words. *So angry that not a man-jack would draw near.* He was angry now. Blazing. It was good, Tyrrell concluded. It might take his mind off the real danger.

A servant girl touched his arm. 'Beggin' yer pardon, sir, but there's a lady below in a poor way. Very feverish.'

Bolitho stopped and looked at them. 'Fetch the surgeon.'

He tensed as the other girl came towards him, her face suddenly grave.

'I am sorry I made you angry, Captain. It was unforgivable.'

'Angry?' Bolitho plucked at his swordbelt. 'I do not recollect . . .'

She touched his hand. 'Now that is beneath you, Captain. Unsure maybe, but never pompous. I see you quite differently.'

'When you have *quite* finished . . .'

Again she stopped him without even raising her voice. 'The other women were close on hysteria, Captain. One minute the storm was throwing us about like rag dolls, the very next instant there is the cry of mutiny and riot. Men fighting each other, for the drink and for what they might take from us when they were too crazed to know otherwise.' She dropped her eyes. 'It was horrible. Terrifying.' The eyes came up again and levelled on his face. They were the colour of violets. 'Then all at once there was a shout. Someone called, "A ship! A King's ship!" and we ran on deck despite the dangers.'

She turned to look across the bulwark. 'And there you were. Little *Sparrow*. It was almost too much for most of us. Had I not made that jest at your expense, I think some might have broken down.'

Bolitho's defences wavered. 'Er, yes. Quite so.' He toyed with his sword-hilt, seeing Dalkeith hurry past and giving him a curious glance as he went. 'You thought quickly, ma'am.'

'I know about some things, Captain. I saw your eyes when you spoke to your lieutenant and Sir James. There is worse to come, is there not?'

Bolitho shrugged. 'In truth I do not know.'

He heard the general shouting angrily at a seaman and said, 'That man is bad enough for me!'

She gave a mock curtsy, smiling again. 'Sir James? He can be difficult, I agree.'

'You know him?'

She moved back towards the other women. 'My uncle, Captain.' She laughed. 'Really you must try to hide your emotions better! Or else you will never be an admiral!'

Tyrrell came on deck and said, 'That woman in th' cabin is ill. But Dalkeith is managing well enough.' He frowned. 'Are you all right, sir?'

Bolitho rasped, 'In God's name stop asking me stupid questions!'

'Aye, sir.' He grinned, seeing the girl by the rail and far more beside. 'I understand, sir.'

There was a dull bang, and as they all turned Bolitho saw a puff of smoke drifting from one of *Sparrow*'s larboard batteries.

The general came panting up a ladder and shouted, 'What was that?'

Bolitho replied quietly, 'The signal, sir. My lookout has sighted the enemy.'

He ignored the general and those near him as his mind accepted the one important fact. In a way it was almost a relief to meet it. Recognize what must be done.

'Mr. Tyrrell, *Bonaventure* will take several hours to show her intentions. By then it will be too dark for her captain to attack. Why should he? He merely has to await the dawn and then pounce.'

Tyrrell watched him, fascinated by his even tone.

Bolitho continued, 'If the wind does not act against us, we will be able to transfer the passengers to *Sparrow*. I want every boat working, and all who are neither sick nor injured to take fairly to their tasks.'

'I understand.' Tyrrell studied him impassively. 'There's nothing else you could do. Many would leave 'em to their own devices.'

Bolitho shook his head. 'You have *not* understood. I am not going to abandon the *Royal Anne* or scuttle her to avoid capture as a prize.' He saw Tyrrell's jaw tighten, the quick anxiety in his eyes. 'I intend to stay in her with sixty volunteers. What happens later will depend very much on *Bonaventure*'s captain.'

He had not noticed that the others had crowded round him, but turned as the general exclaimed, 'You cannot! You dare not risk this ship and cargo! I'll see you damned first!'

Silk rustled against Bolitho's arm and he heard the girl say calmly, 'Be still, Uncle. The captain intends to do more than dare.' She did not turn her face. 'He intends to *die* for us. Is that not enough, even for you?'

Bolitho nodded curtly and strode aft, hearing Stockdale's voice as he hurried to cover his retreat. He had to think. Plan every last moment until the actual second of death. He paused and leaned against the ornate taffrail. Death. Was it so soon upon him?

He turned angrily and said, 'Pass the word for those boats to begin loading immediately! Women and children, then the injured.' He glanced past the ship's mate and saw the girl staring after him. 'And no arguments from anyone!'

He walked to the opposite side and looked at his own command. How beautiful she was as she edged carefully across the Indiaman's quarter. Soon now he would be able to see the enemy's sails on the horizon. Closing, like the hunter, for his kill. There was so much to do. Orders for *Sparrow* to carry to Antigua. Perhaps even a quick letter to his father. But not just yet. He must stand quite still a little longer to watch his ship. Hold her in his memory before she was taken from him.

Bolitho was still staring across the water when Tyrrell came aft to report that all available boats were working, carrying the passengers and Indiaman's company over to the waiting sloop.

He added, 'She'll be a mite more crowded than when we rescued th' redcoats.' He hesitated and then said, 'I'd like to stay with you, sir.'

Bolitho did not look at him. 'You realize what you are saying? There is more at stake than your life.'

Tyrrell tried to grin. 'Hector Graves will make a better commander, sir.'

Bolitho faced him. 'You will be called on to fight some of your own people.'

Tyrrell smiled. 'I knew that was what you were thinking.' He gestured towards some of *Sparrow*'s seamen as they carried an elderly woman towards the boat tackles. 'These are my people. Then can I stay?'

Bolitho nodded. 'Gladly.' He removed his hat and ran his fingers through his hair. 'Now I'll go and write Graves's orders.'

'Deck there! Sail on th' larboard quarter!'

They looked at each other and then Bolitho said quietly, 'Hurry our people along. I do not want the enemy to see what we are about.'

As he strode away Tyrrell stared after him and then murmured, 'So be it, Cap'n.'

He heard a sudden cry and saw the girl who had made Bolitho angry struggling to push her way through a cordon of seamen.

154

A boatswain's mate bellowed, 'She don't want to go, sir!'

The girl punched the sailor's arm but he did not seem to feel it.

Then she shouted at Tyrrell, 'Let me stay! I want to be here!'

He grinned down at her and then pointed at the boat alongside. Kicking and protesting she was picked up bodily and carried to the rail, where with little ceremony she was passed down the side like a bright silk parcel.

The sky was much darker when Bolitho came on deck with a sealed envelope for the boat still hooked on to the chains. All other boats were hoisted, and the ship around him seemed very quiet and empty.

He raised a telescope and trained it over the quarter. The *Bonaventure* was visible now, some six miles distant. But she had already shortened sail, waiting, as he had expected, for the new day.

Tyrrell touched his hat. 'Our men are aboard, sir.' He gestured to the main deck where Midshipman Heyward was speaking to a petty officer. 'I picked 'em myself, but you could have had volunteers a'plenty.'

Bolitho handed the envelope to a seaman. 'Pass this to the boat.' To Tyrrell he added slowly, 'Go and take some rest. I shall think awhile.'

Later as Tyrrell lay in an abandoned cabin, the deck of which was littered with open chests and discarded clothing, he heard Bolitho's shoes on the planking overhead. Back and forth, up and down. Thinking. Eventually the sound of his pacing made his eyelids droop, and he fell into a dreamless sleep.

Bolitho stood straddle-legged on the *Royal Anne*'s poop, seeing his own shadow for the first time across the taffrail. How long the night had been, but at the hint of dawn everything seemed to begin at once, like the start of some ill-rehearsed drama. Away on the larboard quarter he saw the hardening pyramid of sails where the big privateer moved purposefully before the wind. Strangely, her hull was still lost in shadow, with only a bone of white around her stem to reveal her growing speed. About three miles distant. He turned his glass to the opposite quarter, to the little sloop. *Sparrow* was much closer, yet in spite of this seemed even smaller.

Tyrrell joined him and said, 'Th' wind seems steady enough, sir. Nor'-west by north, by my reckoning.' He was speaking in a hushed voice, as if afraid to disturb the ships and their deliberate preparations to fight.

Bolitho nodded. 'We will steer sou'-east. It is what the enemy will expect.'

He tore his eyes from the privateer and turned to look along the Indiaman's deck. The new foresail was drawing well, as were spanker and jib. The rest were little better than shreds, and to try to tack more than a point or so would be a waste of time.

Tyrrell sighed. 'I've checked th' guns myself. Loaded as ordered.' He scratched his stomach. 'Some of 'em look so old they'd split if we double-shotted 'em.'

Bolitho faced aft again to watch the other ships. Raising his glass he moved it slowly over *Sparrow*'s deck, seeing the figures on the gangways, a solitary seaman at her mainmast cross-trees. Then aft, as a freak gust lifted the foot of the main-course like a miller's apron, he saw Graves. He was standing beside the wheel, arms folded, looking every inch a captain. Bolitho breathed out very slowly. So much depended on Graves. If he lost his head, or misinterpreted his carefully worded instructions, the enemy would still catch two for the price of one. But Graves had got the first part right. He was wearing Bolitho's new uniform, the gold lace showing clearly in spite of the feeble light. The enemy captain would be wary, watchful. Nothing must go wrong at the beginning. Heaven alone knew how all the extra passengers had been crammed below and out of sight. It would be like a sealed tomb, a nightmare for the women and children once the gunfire began.

Midshipman Heyward came to the poop and said, 'All our boarding party are ready, sir.' Like Bolitho and Tyrrell he had discarded his uniform and looked even younger in his open shirt and breeches.

'Thank you.' Bolitho noticed that instead of a midshipman's dirk Heyward had thought fit to wear one of his precious swords.

There was a bang, and he saw a ball ricocheting across the lively wave crests before throwing up a quill of spray between him and the *Sparrow*'s bows. A sighting shot, a declaration of intent, probably both, he thought grimly.

Over the water, and audible above the rustle of torn canvas, he heard the staccato beat of drums, and pictured the scene aboard *Sparrow* as her men ran to quarters. Phase two. He saw the patch of scarlet as the ensign broke jauntily from her gaff, felt a catch in his throat as the ports opened to reveal her line of guns. With less than half a company available, Graves must have pressed some of the Indiaman's crew into service to get the guns out so smartly. But it had to look exactly right. As if the sloop was preparing to show defiance and trying to defend her heavy consort.

Another bang, and the ball ploughed into the sea about a cable clear of *Sparrow*'s stem.

Bolitho clenched his jaw. Graves was cutting it fine. If the wind chose this moment to veer he would be unable to go about, would be in irons if he tried to fall back and try again.

Tyrrell said hoarsely, 'There she goes!'

The sloop's yards were swinging and as her lee gangway dipped heavily into the swell she began to tack close-hauled to larboard, crossing *Royal Anne*'s stern like a small protective terrier. Flags broke from her yards, and Bolitho imagined Bethune yelling at his party to make haste and hoist the meaningless signal. The enemy would think *Sparrow* was preparing to fight to the death and was ordering the Indiaman to make a run for it.

Cannon fire ripped along the *Bonaventure*'s foremost battery and more splashes leapt closer to the heeling sloop. Graves was shortening sail, clearing away the hampering canvas from his guns, even though it was unlikely he had more than a quarter of them manned.

Tyrrell spoke between his teeth.

'That's close enough, Hector! For God's sake don't make a meal of it!'

One heavy bang rolled across the shark-blue water, and even though the flash was hidden by *Sparrow*'s hull, Bolitho knew it was one of her bow-chasers. He saw the ball slap hard into the spray by the other ship's forecastle, the immediate spurt of orange tongues as she fired back in earnest.

The *Sparrow*'s foretopgallant mast quivered and then seemed to curtsy downwards into the swirling brown smoke, the furled sail marking its progress as it caught and swung in the criss-cross of rigging before plunging into the sea alongside. Holes appeared in several of her sails, and Bolitho caught his breath as the hammock nettings below the quarterdeck buckled and burst apart from a direct hit.

The enemy was much nearer now, her foretopsail bulging as she stood before the wind, charging down on the sloop which was now less than two cables from her starboard bow.

Tyrrell exclaimed, 'He's done it! Blast th' man, he's going about!'

The *Sparrow* was wearing, her masts swinging upright as she came round violently, the growing light making her sails shine as they flapped and puckered to the strain.

The gunfire had stopped, for with her stern towards the enemy *Sparrow* presented no target at all. Her forecourse was already being unleashed, and as she gathered way through the water Bolitho saw the topmen running out along the yards like black insects until more and still more canvas bellied to the wind. He could see Buckle by the quarterdeck rail, too intent on his work even to watch the labouring Indiaman as she surged past. *Sparrow* was abeam, and then in minutes was well beyond the Indiaman's bows, heading towards the first rays of sunlight from the placid horizon.

Bolitho felt suddenly dry, his limbs very loose, as if belonging to someone else. He watched the *Bonaventure*'s forecourse being brailed up to reveal her great span of poop, the men on her gangways who were waving and gesturing after the retreating sloop. Jeering no doubt. All the madness of intended battle now lost in the confused actions of an unfought victory.

Bolitho walked to the rail and said quietly, 'Remember, Mr Tyrrell, and remember it well. We have to cripple her if we can. Then if a patrolling frigate finds her she can finish what we started.' He gripped his wrist. 'But make sure our people play their parts. If *Bonaventure* hauls off now, she can pound us to pieces without losing a breath!'

The privateer had edged closer, running down towards the quarter so that she would eventually overhaul *Royal Anne* along her larboard side. Her captain was a superb seaman. With all but his topsails clewed up he was handling the heavy vessel with both confidence and skill, and would certainly hold the wind-gage no matter what Bolitho tried to do.

A gun flashed out its long tongue, and Bolitho felt the ball smack into the lower hull, jerking the planks at his feet with savage violence.

He saw bunched figures on the other ship's poop, the wink of sunlight on raised telescopes, and guessed they were examining their victim. It looked much as it had when he had come aboard. Damaged bulwarks and broken rigging. One hatch had been purposefully left open, and several of his men were running about in apparent confusion while Heyward directed their performance from beneath the forecastle.

'Now!'

Bolitho waved his hand, and from the main deck first one then another of the six-pounders hurled its challenge across the narrowing strip of water.

From aft a swivel banged sharply, the canister probably falling harmlessly long before it reached the enemy's side.

The response was immediate. Gun by gun, the *Bonaventure*'s broadside sent ball after ball crashing into the hull. Bolitho was thankful he had sent most of his men below, otherwise they would have been cut down by the fierceness of the onslaught. Timber and planks flew in all directions, and he saw a seaman hurled like a bloody rag to the opposite side his limbs kicking as he died.

Stockdale looked at Bolitho and saw him nod. With a grunt he dashed along the deck waving a cutlass, while Bolitho drew his pistol and yelled after him. When Stockdale ran on towards the halliards he fired, praying that his hand was steady as the shot whined clear above the coxswain's head. Stockdale reached his goal, and with one slash severed the halliards, bringing the big Company flag tumbling down like some bright shroud across the weather rail.

In a lull of noise and gunfire Bolitho heard a voice across the water, magnified and unreal in a speaking trumpet.

159

'Heave to or I'll sink you!'

From forward he heard Heyward urging his men to obey the call, the sudden groan of timber as the ship lurched drunkenly into the wind, her remaining sails flapping and banging in disorder.

Tyrrell said, 'He's going to grapple!'

There were men on the *Bonaventure*'s yards, and as the big hull surged carefully and then more insistently against the side Bolitho saw grapnels flying from a dozen points at once. The men on the yards were busily making fast their lines to *Royal Anne*'s shrouds and spars, so that as both ships lifted and swayed together Bolitho knew the moment to act had arrived.

'Now! Boarders away!'

With a wild chorus of yells the hidden seamen surged up from both hatches and on to the bulwarks, their cutlasses and boarding pikes marking down several enemy hands before they realized what was happening. Moments, seconds earlier, they had seen *Royal Anne* as one more helpless prize, a ship which had struck to them, her flag hacked down by one of her own crew. Then, as if from nowhere, the bulk of Bolitho's seamen came surging up and over the side, their steel bright in the sun, their voices hoarse and wild with the madness of combat.

Bolitho ran to the rail and jerked the lanyard of another swivel, seeing the packed canister scything through a bunch of men on *Bonaventure*'s gangway and blasting them aside in its murderous hail.

Then he was running with the second party and pulling himself on to the shrouds, slashing with his sword at a man's arm on the chains below. Screams and curses, the bang of pistols and rasp of steel, he was dazed by the noise. A man plummeted past him to be held like a tortured animal between the two grinding hulls, his blood running pink in the leaping feathers of foam.

He was on the enemy's deck, his arm jarring as he struck down a man's guard and drove the hilt against his jaw, throwing him back into the struggling figures beyond. Another charged forward with a levelled bayonet, slipped on a smear of blood and took Stockdale's blade across his neck. It sounded like an axe biting into a log.

He yelled wildly, 'Cut the rigging, lads! Cripple the bastard!'

He felt a ball fan hotly past his face, and ducked as another smacked into a seaman's chest right beside him, his cry lost in the other din of battle.

Now he was on a ladder, shoes sliding in blood, his fingers feeling up a rail, conscious of the torn wood where one of the swivels had made its mark. Two officers were parrying aside pikes and swords as they tried to rally their men from the opposite side. Bolitho saw one of them drive his sword into a boatswain's mate, saw the eyes roll with agony as he pitched to the deck below, then he was up and facing the privateer's officer, their swords clashing as they struck and explored their strength and weakness.

'Damn you!' The man ducked and thrust up at Bolitho's throat. 'Strike while you are still alive, you mad bugger!'

Bolitho caught the blade across his basket hilt and levered the man clear, feeling the warmth of his body, the fierceness of his breathing. He yelled back, 'Strike be damned!'

A pistol exploded and the officer dropped his arm, staring blankly at the blood which pumped through his shirt in a bright red stain.

Tyrrell strode past and fired a second pistol into the man's chest. When he turned Bolitho saw that Tyrrell's face was like stone.

He shouted, 'I knew that bastard, Cap'n! A bloody slaver afore th' war!'

Then with a gasp he dropped on one knee, blood running from his thigh. Bolitho dragged him aside, cutting down a screaming seaman and thrusting the blade through his chest in two swift movements.

'*Easy!*'

He stared desperately above the nearest men. Much of the enemy's rigging had been slashed, but the attack had made little impression after all. And his men were falling back around him, the lust to fight and win dwindling to match their numbers.

On every hand, or so it appeared, muskets and pistols were firing down into the retreating English seamen, and he saw Heyward standing astride a wounded man and screaming like a madman as he fought off two attackers at once.

As if from a great distance he saw the American captain watching from his poop, a tall, handsome man who was standing quite motionless, either so confident in his men's efforts or so appalled by his attackers' sacrifice that he was unable to tear his eyes away.

Bolitho hacked a cutlass aside and sobbed aloud as his blade broke within inches of the hilt. He hurled the remains at the man's head and saw him fall kicking, impaled on a pike. In a half daze he recalled the glib trader at English Harbour who had sold him the sword. He would not get his money now, damn his eyes.

To Stockdale he croaked, 'You know what to do!' He had to push him away, and even as he ran from the fighting he was still peering back, his eyes filled with anxiety.

Then there was the distorted voice again, and when he looked up he saw the American captain using his trumpet.

'Strike now! You have done more than enough! Strike or die!'

Bolitho swung round, his heart bursting, his mind sick as he saw a young seaman fall to the deck, his face opened by a cutlass from ear to chin.

Tyrrell was struggling on his injured knee and pointing wildly, 'Look! Stockdale's done it!'

From the main hatch on the Indiaman's deck came a growing plume of dark smoke, spreading and thickening until it seemed to spurt up through the seams like steam under pressure.

Bolitho yelled, 'Fall back, lads! *Back!*'

Then they were limping and staggering across the bulwarks, dragging their wounded, carrying others too crippled to move. There were not many of them, wounded or otherwise.

Bolitho wiped his streaming eyes, hearing Tyrrell gasp with agony as he half carried, half dragged him to the opposite bulwark. Behind him he could hear frenzied shouts, the sudden click of steel as the *Bonaventure*'s men tried to cut away the lashings which they themselves had so skilfully used to hold both ships together. But it was too late. It had been from the instant Stockdale had begun the last and most dangerous act. A short fuse, and then the fire had burst amongst the cargo of rum and the massive barrels of spirits, spreading through the hull at a terrible rate. Flames licked out of open ports and ran along the *Bonaventure*'s tarred rigging like angry tongues, sails vanished into ashes, and then with a bellow one great sheet of flame leapt between the two hulls, joining them finally in a single pyre.

Bolitho peered down at the one remaining boat tethered to the ship's quarter, riding where it had been since taking his orders across to Graves.

'Abandon ship, lads!'

Some clambered down, while others fell headlong, splashing and yelling until they were helped inboard by their companions. Blazing canvas, ashes and gusts of sparks rained across their heads, but as a seaman severed the bow rope and they groped half blinded for the oars Bolitho heard another great explosion, as if from the sea itself.

The Indiaman began to settle down immediately, her masts and spars interlocking with her attacker's to throw flames and sparks hundreds of feet into the air.

He watched his small handful of fit men pulling at the oars, feeling the heat searing his back as he steered the boat away, from the blazing ships. Exploding powder and toppling masts, a ship's hold splitting wide open in an inferno of noise and shooting flames, and later the engulfing sounds of inrushing water. He heard it all, even pictured the general's gold bullion, which someone might discover one day on the sea bottom.

But it was all beyond him now. They had done the impossible. *Miranda* was avenged.

He looked sadly at his men, at their faces which now meant so much to him. At young Heyward, filthy and exhausted, a wounded seaman propped across his lap. Tyrrell, a bloody bandage around his thigh, eyes closed with pain, but holding back his head as if to seek the first yellow bars of warmth from the sun. And Stockdale, who was everywhere. Bandaging and baling, lending weight to an oar, or helping to heave a dead man over the gunwale. He was tireless. Indestructible.

He held out his hand and studied it. It was quite steady, even though every nerve and muscle seemed to be quivering. He glanced at his empty scabbard and gave a rueful smile. No matter. Nothing mattered now.

How long they pulled at the oars, the time it took for the two blazing hulks finally to sink, Bolitho did not remember. The sun beat down on their aching, exhausted limbs, the stroke became slower and more hesitant. Once, when Bolitho peered astern he saw the sea's face covered by a great spread of drifting remains from the ships and the men who had fought across them. But the privateer had managed to launch at least one boat, and before it was blotted out in haze he saw it was crammed with survivors. Perhaps they, too, would know the same despair as *Miranda*'s men.

Then a shadow flitted across his face and he stared round, caught off guard as *Sparrow*'s topsails flashed gaily across the sun's path.

The men in the boat watched silently, unable to speak even to each other. Unable yet to realize they had survived.

Bolitho stood by the tiller, his eyes stinging as he watched her careful approach, the lines of heads along her decks and gangways. She had come for him. Despite the danger, the unlikelihood of his plan succeeding, she had returned to make sure.

Across the water a voice hailed, 'Boat ahoy?'

It sounded like Buckle, anxious maybe to know who had survived.

Stockdale looked at him, his battered face questioning. When Bolitho said nothing he stood up and cupped his big hands.

'*Sparrow!* Stand by for th' captain!'

Bolitho sank down, the last reserve draining from him. He was back.

10. Sea Change

CAPTAIN RICHARD BOLITHO stared at the partly written letter he had been composing to his father, and then with a sigh carried his chair to the opposite end of the table. It was stifling hot, and as the *Sparrow* idled sluggishly on a flat calm she swung her stern very slightly allowing the hard sunlight to reach him and require him to move still further away from the windows.

Becalmed. How used he had grown to this situation. He rubbed his eyes and held his pen above the paper again. It was difficult to know what to write, especially as he never knew when this or any letter might find its way aboard a home-bound vessel. It was harder still to feel involved with that other world in England which he had left in *Trojan* nearly six years back. And yet . . . the pen hovered uncertainly, his own world, so close and so vital in colour and smell in the bright sunlight, and that word *becalmed* would still be too painful, too harsh a reminder for his father of the Navy which he had been forced to leave.

But Bolitho wanted to tell him so desperately, put his thoughts and memories into perspective, to share his own life and thereby fill the one remaining gap in it.

Overhead, blocks clattered and feet thudded on the quarter-deck. Someone laughed, and he heard a faint splash as one of the hands cast a fishing line outboard to try his luck.

His eyes moved from the letter to his open log which lay across the chart nearby. The log had changed as much as himself. Worn around the edges, matured perhaps. He stared at the date on the open page. April 10th, 1781. Three years, almost to the day, since he had first stepped aboard this ship in English Harbour to assume command. Without moving it was possible to glance back through the bulky log book, and even though he did not even touch a page he could recall so many of the things which had happened, faces and events, the demands made upon him and his varying successes in dealing with them.

Often, during moments of quiet in the cabin, he had tried to fathom out some set thread in his life beyond the narrower explanations of luck or circumstance. So far it had defied him. And now as he sat in the familiar cabin where so much had happened he could accept that fate had had much to do with his being here. If, when he had left the *Trojan* he had failed to take a prize *en route* for Antigua, or upon arrival there had been no opportunity for immediate promotion, he might still be a lieutenant in the old ship-of-the-line. And on that very first convoy, if Colquhoun had sent him back to English Harbour instead of going himself, would he have ever succeeded in proving to be more than average in either skill or luck?

Perhaps Colquhoun's fateful decision on that far-off day had been the chance, the offering which had set his feet on the final path.

Bolitho had returned to Antigua not merely as just one more officer rejoining his rightful squadron, but, to his astonishment, as some sort of hero. In his absence the stories of his rescuing the soldiers from Delaware Bay, his running a frigate aground, had been well spread. Then, with the news of *Bonaventure*'s end and his arrival with the rescued passengers, it seemed that every man wanted to see him and shake his hand.

The *Bonaventure* had been even more deadly than Bolitho had realized at the time, and her successes formidable. Her loss to the enemy might mean little, but to the British it was a tremendous lift to their battered pride and morale.

The admiral had received him in Antigua with controlled pleasure, and had made no bones about his hopes for the future. Colquhoun, on the other hand, had been the one man to offer Bolitho neither encouragement nor praise for his achievements in so short a time.

Whenever Bolitho recalled their first meeting, Colquhoun's warnings about the lot of any sea captain, he was reminded of the thinness of margin between fame and oblivion. Had Colquhoun stayed with that first convoy it was unlikely he would have shared *Miranda*'s fate, for he was too shrewd and cautious to take anything for granted. Had he been lucky enough to meet and destroy *Bonaventure* he would have gained the one thing he cared about, just as Commander Maulby had suggested, the unshakeable power of flag rank, or at very least the coveted broad-pendant of commodore. Instead he had stayed where he was, frigate captain, and, with the war changing so rapidly, now likely to lose even his control of the small flotilla. Maulby no longer called him *little admiral*. Today it seemed too cruel, too unjust even for him.

Eight bells chimed out from the forecastle, and without effort he pictured the hands preparing for the midday meal, the welcome ration of rum. Above his head Tyrrell and the master would be taking their noon sights, comparing their findings before bringing them down to the chart.

The year after Bolitho's destruction of the big privateer he had received his next surprise. The admiral had sent for him and had calmly announced that their lordships of Admiralty, like himself, believed in offering *Sparrow*'s commander a chance of exploiting his experience and skill. Promotion to full captain. Even now, after eighteen months of it, he found it hard to accept and believe.

Within the flotilla the unexpected rise up the ladder had caused a great stir. Genuine pleasure from some, open resentment from others. Maulby had taken the news better than Bolitho had dared to hope, for he had come to like the *Fawn*'s laconic commander too much to have their friendship broken. Maulby was senior to him, but had merely remarked, 'I'd like to see the rank go to no other man, so let's drink to it!'

Aboard *Sparrow* the news had had no division at all. They all seemed to share the same pride, the same sense of achievement, which could not have come at a better time for them. For the war had changed greatly even in the past year. No longer was it a matter of patrol or convoy for the army. The great powers had taken their stand, and Spain and Holland had joined France against England in their support of the American Revolution. The French had mustered a well-matched and powerful fleet in the West Indies under the Compte de Grasse, the most effective and talented admiral available. Admiral Rodney commanded the British squadrons, but with the pressures mounting daily he was hard put to spread his resources where they were most needed.

And the Americans were not content to leave affairs to their seasoned allies. They continued to use privateers whenever possible, and a year after *Bonaventure*'s destruction yet another challenger emerged to shake British morale to its foundation. The privateer and ex-slaver Paul Jones, in his *Bonhomme Richard*, defeated the frigate *Seraphis* off the coast of England itself. The fact that the privateer, like the *Seraphis*, was reduced to a battered wreck in the hotly contested battle made no difference. British captains were expected to take on odds and win, and the defeat so close to home did more than many Americans believed possible to take the war and its reasons into English homes as well as their own.

In the West Indies and along the American coast the work of patrolling took on new importance. As Bolitho had always thought, it was far better for the eyes of the fleet to be left unhampered by close authority. True to his word, the admiral had offered him almost total independence, and had given him scope to patrol and seek out the enemy in his own way, provided, of course, his efforts were rewarded with some success.

Bolitho leaned back in his chair and stared at the deckhead. Again the word luck seemed to hover in his mind.

Maulby had scoffed at the explanation. He had once said, 'You are successful because you have trained yourself to think like the enemy! God damn it, Dick, I caught a lugger loaded with contraband which had come from as far south as Trinidad, and even that wretched fellow had heard of you and *Sparrow*!'

It was certainly true about one thing, Bolitho decided, they had been successful. In the past eighteen months alone they had taken twelve prizes and despatched two small privateers with the loss of twenty killed and wounded and very little damage to the ship.

He let his eyes wander round the cabin, less elegantly painted now, even shabby after ceaseless service in all weathers. It was strange to realize that apart from the unexpected promotion, symbolized by the dress coat with white lapels and bright gold facings which swung gently inside the sleeping compartment, there was outwardly little to show for it. And yet he was a rich man, and, for the first time in his life, independent of the home and estate in Falmouth. He smiled ruefully. It seemed almost shameful to become moderately wealthy merely because he was doing the one thing he enjoyed.

He frowned, trying to think of something to purchase if and when they were allowed a stay in port. And they were well overdue for that. Despite her coppered hull, *Sparrow*'s speed had been reduced by a full knot in otherwise perfect sailing conditions by long, clinging weed which defied the copper and their efforts to move it. He would buy some wine perhaps. Good wine, not the bitter-tasting muck which was normally used as the only alternative for foul drinking water. A dozen shirts or more. His mind played with the idea of such luxury. At the present moment he had only two shirts which would bear close inspection.

It might be possible to find a good sword somewhere. Not like the one which had shattered aboard the privateer, nor the curved hanger which he had used since, but something better. Lasting.

He heard footsteps beyond the door and knew it was Tyrrell. He would have known it even if it had been another time, a different watch. For since being wounded Tyrrell had been unable to rid himself of a limp and not a little pain.

The first lieutenant had otherwise not changed very much, he thought. Or maybe the three years had drawn them so close he had not noticed it. Unlike Graves, who seemed to have withdrawn even further and had grown noticeably more nervous after each action or skirmish. Upon his promotion to captain, Bolitho had become entitled to an extra lieutenant, and the appointment fell vacant on the very day the two midshipmen went aboard the flagship to sit for their commissions. Heyward had passed with flying colours, and now, looking back, it was hard to recall him as a midshipman at all. Bethune had unfortunately failed his exams, not once, but three times, and Bolitho repeatedly wondered how best to get rid of him. He had grown very fond of Bethune, but knew that being retained in *Sparrow*'s confined community was only acting against his remaining, if dwindling, chances. His navigation was hopeless, his ability to take charge of the quarterdeck and set the hands to making or shortening sail was dismal to behold. As a marine officer, or even a foot soldier, he would have been adequate. He could obey orders, even if he found them hard to formulate. Under fire he had shown plenty of courage, and a boyish stoicism which was rarely matched even by a seasoned sailor. Now, aged twenty, and with no hope of gaining the commission he so obviously desired, he stood out like a sore thumb. Heyward had tried to help him, more so than Bolitho had imagined he would. But it was no use. The ship's company treated him with cheerful acceptance, as they would a child. His burden had not been eased by the appointment of a new midshipman to take Heyward's place.

Roger Augustus Fowler, sixteen years of age, and with the pouting features of a petulant pig, had soon learned to add to rather than detract from Bethune's misery.

Fowler's arrival had further enlarged the rift between Bolitho and Colquhoun. The boy was the son of the admiral's best friend, and so his appointment to this or any ship was very close to a royal command. The offspring of some influential person could be a great handicap to a young and busy captain, but equally he could open doors otherwise denied by the chain of command. Colquhoun had probably seen the boy's arrival from England as an opportunity in the latter category, and had been outraged when the admiral had chosen *Sparrow* rather than his frigate *Bacchante*.

Fowler had been aboard for eight months and was not popular. It was nothing you could put a name to. Obedient and attentive in the presence of his superiors, he could be equally sharp and sarcastic with seamen old enough to be his father. He had a way of shutting off his expression, using his pale eyes and pouting lips like the extensions of a mask. If he ever reached command rank he would be a tyrant to serve, Bolitho thought.

There was a tap at the door and Bolitho swept his musings into the background.

Tyrrell limped into the cabin and sat down at the table. Against his open shirt his skin was burned almost to mahogany, and his hair had become a shade lighter under forgotten suns. He pushed the calculations across the chart and together they looked at *Sparrow*'s approximate position.

To the south lay the nearest extensions of the Bahama Islands, the countless spans of cays and reefs, treacherous sandbars and islets. Some eighty miles to the west lay the coast of Florida, and to the east the main routes used by ships going to and fro from the Indies and New York. It was a veritable warren of islands and narrow channels, although to the untried eye of a landsman the sea might appear at peace, broken here and there by restful purple humps of land shrouded in low haze. But to the mariner the chart showed much more, and that was less than he required to know the true margin of safety. The occasional dab of white betrayed a reef, the duller patch on the sea's face might represent a cloak of weed across some vast pinnacle lurking beneath the surface, the spines of which could tear the keel from a ship like the string from an orange.

Tyrrell said at length, 'I reckon we've lost th' bugger.'

'Maybe.' Bolitho opened a drawer in the table and took out two long clay pipes. Handing one to Tyrrell he groped for a tobacco bowl and then said, 'Is *Fawn* still in sight?'

Tyrrell grinned. 'Sure enough. 'Bout three miles to th' east'rd.' He tamped down the tobacco in his pipe and added, 'Our masthead lookout thought he saw breakers to th' sou'-west. If so, that would be the Matanilla Shoal, which fixes our calculations, so to speak.'

Bolitho lit his pipe from the hanging smoking-lantern and then walked restlessly to the windows. Once near the sill he felt the slow breeze across his face and chest like air fanned from a blacksmith's forge. When eventually the wind returned to give life to the sails it was to be hoped it came from the south-east as before. It was no time to be driven closer to those deadly shoals. But they had to stay near enough to be able to watch at least three channels while *Fawn* patrolled further to the east. For six weeks, in company with the other sloop, they had been searching for a big blockade runner, a

French *flute* which had been reported out of Martinique and heading north, most likely for the enemy base of naval operations in Newport, Rhode Island. The information from spies, or those merely after recognition or reward, was always open to doubt. But a *flute*, which was a large man-of-war with some of her armament removed to facilitate the fast passage of men or stores, was too important to be ignored.

The flotilla's third sloop, *Heron*, was sweeping somewhere to the south, off the Andros Islands, and Colquhoun's *Bacchante* had, as far as he knew, remained in more open waters to the west, between the Bahamas and the American mainland.

Once away from Colquhoun's supervision, Bolitho had taken the sloops to their present position. On the chart the chance of making contact with a solitary enemy seemed impossible, but he knew by now that if the sea appeared empty, it was in fact divided into channels by sprawling reefs and cays, and was just as much a hazard to enemy as to friend.

'If we take her, it'll be another feather for us.' Tyrrell watched his pipe-smoke drifting through the skylight above him. 'I often wonder if it makes all that difference to th' war.'

'It *all* helps, Jethro.'

Bolitho studied him gravely. How close they had become. Like the use of first names, the ritual pipe-smoking for as long as the tobacco stock lasted, it all seemed to symbolize what the ship had made them.

Time and distance, hours and days spent in every sort of condition, they had all left their mark on *Sparrow*'s company. Even the necessary changes brought about by death and injury, transfer and discharge had seemed unable to break the little ship's hold on their destiny. Over a third of the company were replacements made since he had taken command, and apart from colonists, included a sprinkling of Negroes, some merchant seamen pressed from a home-bound ship, and a solitary Greek who had deserted his own vessel only to be taken aboard a French brig as a captive. The brig, seized as a prize by *Sparrow*, had yielded several new hands, and the Greek had proved to be an excellent assistant cook.

'How long will you give her?'

Bolitho considered the question. 'Another week maybe.

If she doesn't show herself, I think we can assume she's slipped past us, or turned back somewhere. She might have run into one of the patrols further south.'

'Aye.' Tyrrell yawned. 'An' then *we* can get some time in port.'

Feet pounded overhead and they heard Buckle shout, 'Call all hands! Th' wind's a'coming back!'

Then there was a rap on the door and Bethune peered in at them, his round face sweating badly.

'Mr Buckle's respects, sir. The wind is freshening from the sou'-east. *Fawn's* tops'ls are already filling.'

'I'll come up.' Bolitho waited until the midshipman had withdrawn before asking quietly, 'What am I to do about him?'

Tyrrell shrugged. 'He'll not get promoted unless by a miracle. Maybe if we put him in charge of our next prize?' He shook his head before Bolitho could comment. 'Almighty God, the lad'd lose his way *an'* th' prize!'

On deck they found the hands already being mustered while overhead the sails were stirring uneasily, the masthead pendant lifting as the first breeze reached it.

'Man th' braces!' Tyrrell strode to the rail and squinted into the glare. 'It'll be up to us soon, lads.'

Bolitho shaded his eyes to stare at the other sloop as her sails suddenly filled and brought her round in a slow pirouette. Across the sea's glittering face he saw the first ruffle of wind, then felt the sun-dried planking lift under his shoes, the immediate response of blocks and halliards.

The *Sparrow's* decks were like tinder and it made no difference how many times they were doused down. Paintwork was blistered by the heat, and as he turned to watch the busy seamen he realized it was hard to tell the Negroes from his original company.

Lean and sun-dried maybe, he thought, but they looked healthy and bright-eyed, ready for anything.

Tyrrell called, 'Shall I have th' larboard cutter towed astern now, sir?'

Bolitho nodded. Only by towing them alternately could they hope to keep them from drying out and opening their seams. Even half filling them with water on board seemed to have small effect.

'Yes. Tell Mr Tilby to . . .' He checked himself and added, 'Pass the word to the boatswain, if you please.'

After six months, it was still difficult not to speak his name, or expect to see his sweating features peering aft at the quarterdeck.

They had run down a Spanish schooner off the Great Bahama Bank, but had been forced to fire on her when she refused to yield. Then, with grapnels flying like snakes, *Sparrow* had surged alongside in the manner so well practised that it was accepted without comment even by the new men. A few pistol shots, the sight of the half-naked boarders with drawn cutlasses had been enough to quench the Spaniard's resistance and it was all over almost before it had begun. Sometime in the middle of it, while men had dashed to shorten sail and prepare for boarding, as Bolitho had waved his arm to signal the Spanish master to strike and avoid bloodshed, Tilby had died.

Not in the heat and terror of close action or under an enemy broadside, but quietly and without fuss while he stood at the foot of the foremast, his favourite place where he usually kept an eye on the workings of his ship. Dalkeith had examined him and reported that the boatswain's heart had given out, like a clock which had run its course and could take no more.

His death made a deep impression on everyone who had known him. To die in such a way was unthinkable. Tilby, who had survived battles at sea and countless drunken brawls in taverns the world over, had gone without a man seeing his passing.

When Tyrrell had collected his possessions Bolitho had been dismayed to see that there was hardly anything to barter amongst the company and thereby raise money for dependants he might have in England. Two small wood carvings of ships he had once served, and one of them was broken, a collection of foreign coins, and his silver call which had been presented to him by no less a person than Captain Oliver of the *Menelaus* where he had served as a bosun's mate. Poor Tilby, he had not even learned to write his own name, and his language was limited to the profane for much of the time. But he knew ships, and he knew *Sparrow* like his own body.

Harry Glass, the senior boatswain's mate, had been promoted in his place, but like most of the others seemed unable to accept that he was now independent of Tilby's booming voice and ever-vigilant eye.

As he watched the cutter rising from its chocks on the gun deck Bolitho wondered if indeed Tilby had anyone ashore to grieve for him. He touched the sun-heated taffrail and shuddered. He was a captain now, the realization of a dream which had been with him since he could remember. If the war suddenly ended, or other circumstances forced him to leave the Navy, he would drop from his present foothold like a falling stone. Not being confirmed to post-rank, he would end up as a mere lieutenant on half-pay, and all this would just be a mocking memory. But how much worse for those like Tilby. He ran his eyes quickly across the men nearest to him as they worked at the braces to set *Sparrow* before the wind again. They had nothing. A little prize money if they were fortunate, some bounty maybe from a charitable captain, otherwise they would be thrown on the beach less able to face the demands of the outside world than when they had volunteered or been pressed into service. It was unjust. Worse, it was dishonourable to treat men so shabbily, when without their sacrifice and courage their country would have fallen to an enemy years ago.

He began to pace the deck, his chin sunk on his chest. Perhaps one day they could change it. Make the Navy a Service where men from all walks of life would be as glad as he was to serve in reasonable security.

'Deck thar! Breakers on the larboard bow!'

He came out of his thoughts and said, 'Bring her round two points, Mr Buckle. We will give those reefs a wide berth until we are clear.'

'Aye, sir.'

He turned his attention to the other sloop, noting that Maulby had managed to repaint his hull in spite of the heat. *Fawn* was exactly the same colour as *Sparrow*, and to any uncertain eye would appear a twin. It was another part of

Bolitho's hard-won experience. When sailing separately, the fact they looked so similar helped to keep the enemy or his spies guessing. Like the flag locker, which he had stocked with almost every foreign flag in the book. Deception and surprise had been the enemy's game. Bolitho was reaping the benefit of their past success and turning the tables against them.

'West nor'-west, sir! Steady as she goes!'

'Very well.' He glanced at the compass and at the set of the main topsails. 'Not much of a wind, Mr Buckle, but it suffices for the present.'

All afternoon and into early evening the two sloops continued on the same tack, with the wind showing no sign of changing in strength or bearing.

The first dog watch was just drawing to its close and Bolitho was making another attempt to complete his letter when a sail was reported to the south-west. Signalling *Fawn* to remain in company, Bolitho altered course to investigate, but as the newcomer showed no sign of running he guessed it was a friendly ship. The masthead soon confirmed that she was in fact the flotilla's little schooner *Lucifer*, a vessel kept as busy if not busier than any of them, carrying despatches and poking into coves and bays where even sloops found little room to move in safety.

In the dull bronze sunlight she made a pretty sight, with her big fore-and-aft sails spread like wings across her narrow hull as she tacked towards the sloops, her signal flags soaring aloft to break in brightly coloured squares.

Bethune called, '*Have despatches on board*, sir!'

Bolitho looked at Tyrrell. 'Heave to, if you please.' To Bethune he added, 'Make to *Fawn*. *Remain in close company.*' He crossed to the rail as Tyrrell lowered his speaking trumpet. 'You can never be sure. She might have good news for us.'

Tyrrell gripped the rail, grimacing with pain as, with sails slapping fussily, *Sparrow* came up into the wind.

'Damn this leg!' In a calmer tone he said, 'Good or bad, it's grand to see a friend. I was beginning to think we had th' bloody sea to ourselves.'

A jolly-boat was already on its way, and Bolitho saw that

Lieutenant Odell, the schooner's captain, was coming in person, and felt a sudden twinge of hopeful excitement.

Odell clambered up the side and doffed his hat to the quarterdeck. He was a quick, darting young man, and was said to be slightly mad. But he seemed calm enough, and when he reached the cabin handed Bolitho his bulky envelope before saying, 'I have just come from Captain Colquhoun.' He took a glass of wine from Fitch and stared at it. 'He is much excited.'

Bolitho slit open the envelope and ran his eyes quickly over the scrawling hand of Colquhoun's personal clerk.

Tyrrell stood just inside the door, and Bolitho was well aware of Buckle's shadow across the skylight above the table. Not actually eavesdropping, but if he happened to hear anything, well . . .

He looked up and said, 'Captain Colquhoun took a fishing boat and questioned the crew.' He flattened the damp paper on the table. 'That was a week ago.'

Odell held the empty glass in front of him and waited until Fitch had refilled it before saying dryly, 'Actually, *I* caught the boat, sir,' he shrugged disdainfully, 'but the good Captain Colquhoun seemed to take it over, as it were.'

Bolitho eyed him gravely. 'It also states here that the crew provided valuable information about the Frenchman.' He beckoned to Tyrrell and pushed the unfinished letter from his chart. 'The *flute* was sighted here, close inshore,' his finger rested on the western end of Grand Bahama Island, 'right amongst the islets. She was carrying out repairs, according to the fishermen.'

Tyrrell nodded slowly. 'It sounds likely. If th' Frenchman knew a hunt was mounted, he would take th' most hazardous passage amongst th' islands to throw us off. It don't signify he's still there of course.'

Bolitho nodded. 'A week back. Allow another few days before that for the fishing boat to reach the place where *Lucifer* sighted her.' He snatched up his dividers and bent over the chart. 'Thirty leagues from our present position. We could be off the island by noon tomorrow if the wind holds.'

Odell said wearily, 'But I understand that Captain Colquhoun wishes you to flush her out and nothing more, sir?' He smiled. 'Or did I not comprehend the good captain's desires?'

Bolitho sat down and opened the despatches again. '*Bacchante* is to approach by the North West Providence Channel, while we remain to north'rd and harry the Frenchman if he tries to run for it.'

Odell nodded, satisfied. '*Bacchante* can be barely twenty miles from her attacking position by now, sir. I am to find her again and report that I have met you and that you *understand* the instructions.'

Bolitho glanced at him quickly. 'Thank you. I do understand.'

The lieutenant stood up and reached for his hat. 'Then I will return to my ship. I have no wish to be caught in these waters after dark.'

Together they watched the lieutenant being rowed back to his schooner.

Then Tyrrell said heavily, 'Seems clear enough to me. Cap'n Colquhoun is set on taking th' Frog as a prize, all to himself, while we just act as beaters.'

'There is something which bothers me far more.' Bolitho rubbed his chin. 'The fishing boat was a small one, according to the despatches. Too frail to be out in deep water where she might *expect* to find *Bacchante* or some other frigate. It was a mere fluke that she met with *Lucifer*, for as we know, Jethro, schooners in the King's service are rare out here.'

Tyrrell's eyes glistened in the dying sunlight. 'You mean that th' fishermen were looking for *another* ship?'

Bolitho met his gaze. 'Aye.'

'But there's only us an' the *Fawn* between here an' th' inshore squadron, an' their nearest patrol must be four hundred miles away.'

'Exactly.' Bolitho stared astern at the other sloop, her topsails already painted in deepening shadows. 'And who would know that better than some island fisherman, eh?'

Tyrrell breathed out slowly. 'Hell, you're saying *we* was meant to get the information, but once Colquhoun got his hands on 'em they acted for their own safety.'

'I don't know.' Bolitho walked to the nettings and back to the compass, seeing neither. 'But *Fawn*'s captain said something to me a while ago. That our exploits were getting well known, which is another way of saying they have been hurting the enemy.'

Tyrrell nodded. 'A trap. Is it likely?' He waved one hand towards the sea. 'Surely we're not that important!'

'It depends what the enemy intends.'

Bolitho turned away, feeling a chill on his spine. It was a new sensation, uncanny. To think that someone might be discussing him, planning and scheming like runners after a wanted criminal.

But it was certainly how it appeared, how he must anticipate it if he was to prepare himself. Fleets and valuable convoys stayed to the east or west of the Bahama Islands, so it was much more likely the enemy was after one particular prize.

He said, 'We will show a stern lantern for *Fawn*'s benefit tonight. At dawn I will tell Commander Maulby what I think.' He grinned, suddenly amused by his unusual caution. 'Or maybe by that time I will have driven my ghosts away.'

Tyrrell watched him doubtfully. 'To our enemy, th' Frogs in particular, you're like a thorn.' He frowned. 'There's only one way to deal with thorns, you tear 'em out and stamp on 'em!'

Bolitho nodded. 'I agree. We will continue with our new course, but be prepared to treat every event as a trick and a ruse until proved otherwise.'

He looked abeam for the *Lucifer*, but she was little more than a blur in the damp evening haze. He cursed Colquhoun for not supplying more information about the fishing boat, where it came from, or the reliability of its crew. Yet he could almost feel sorry for him. He was obviously beset with anxiety about his own future, and now there was the chance of catching a rich prize, and probably military information as well, he could think of little else.

He went below to his cabin and stared at the chart beneath a gently spiralling lantern. Between his hands the islands, the countless tentacles of reefs and shallows were like the neck of some gigantic bag, around which Colquhoun's flotilla, accidentally or otherwise, were converging to close with the finality of a noose.

Bolitho sighed and turned to lean from one of the windows. In the shaded stern lantern's beam the small frothing wake glowed like blue wool, and beyond it the horizon had faded to mingle with the first pale stars.

Then he touched the scar beneath the lock of hair, noting that it was hurting, throbbing in time with his heart. He knew he was uneasy, more so because he could not find a proper reason for it.

Overhead he heard Graves murmuring as he took over the watch, and Tyrrell's limping step as he walked towards the companion ladder. Normal, regular sounds which usually gave him a sense of pleasure. Now, perhaps because they represented people he had come to know, and not merely extensions of the ship's efficiency, he was suddenly afraid. Not of an enemy or the ever-present shadow of death, but of his responsibility which their trust had given him.

11. Strategy and Spite

BOLITHO was hastily tying his neckcloth when Tyrrell thrust his head through the cabin skylight and called, '*Bacchante*'s just signalled, sir! *Capn's to repair aboard!*'

'I will come up directly.'

He threw on his coat and took a quick glance round the cabin. He did not see Colquhoun very often, but he had learned it best to forget nothing.

On deck he found the gig being swayed over the gangway, and when he glanced abeam he saw *Fawn*'s boat already in the water and Maulby hurrying down into it with his usual agility.

It was early afternoon and the deck burning hot through his shoes. All night, with *Fawn* keeping as close as safety allowed, they had driven south, with the sprawling barrier of sandbars and shallows some ten miles off the larboard beam. But it had taken longer than he had hoped to find Colquhoun's *Bacchante*, and almost as soon as the masthead had sighted her topsails the wind had fallen away to a mere breath, allowing the sun to tighten its grip over them like a furnace.

As he waited for the gig's crew to man their boat he turned to stare across the opposite beam, towards the distorted hump of blue and purple which he knew to be the western tip of Grand Bahama. Colquhoun was taking no chances. He was standing well clear of the land, either to give himself sea-room, or to prevent the enemy from seeing his intentions.

'Ready, sir.'

He ran down to the entry port and said to Tyrrell, 'Keep a sharp lookout for inquisitive craft of any kind. Send a cutter after 'em if they draw near. Don't wait for my orders.'

Then he was in the gig and settling himself on a hot thwart as Stockdale swung the tiller and sent the boat dipping and swaying towards the frigate. *Bacchante* was hove-to, her sails flapping loosely, showing her copper as she rolled unsteadily in the swell. She was a fine ship, he thought. Clean-cut and designed by a craftsman. Thirty-six guns and the ability to live off her own resources for many months, she was, or should be, every young captain's ambition. It did not seem to fit Colquhoun at all.

Stockdale was muttering under his breath, and Bolitho knew he was cursing his opposite number in *Fawn*, who always seemed to manage to get his boat anywhere just that bit faster. The gig turned swiftly, oars backing in close unison, the bowman hooking on to the frigate's main chains as *Bacchante*'s shadow gave them brief respite from the glare.

Bolitho clambered up the side, doffing his hat and regaining his composure while the calls shrilled in salute and a squad of red-coated marines slapped their muskets to the present.

The first lieutenant, a gaunt, harassed-looking man, bobbed his head in welcome.

'The captain is aft, sir. He is preparing his strategy, otherwise . . .'

Maulby stepped from the shade of the gangway and took his arm. '*Otherwise*, my friend, he would have had the good grace to meet us at the entry port, eh?' He laughed at the lieutenant's embarrassment. 'You, sir, deserve rich recognition for your penance aboard this ship.'

Together they strode beneath the poop, automatically ducking their heads despite the ample room above.

A marine stamped his boots together and threw open the cabin door, his eyes never blinking or shifting until both officers had stepped over the coaming.

Colquhoun was standing by the stern windows, studying his watch with obvious impatience.

'So you have arrived, gentlemen.' He sat down at his table. 'Eventually.'

Bolitho relaxed slightly. So it was to be this way.

He replied, 'We had adverse winds overnight, sir.'

Maulby added calmly, 'And I thought you might be closer inshore, sir. We seem to be somewhat, er, out of touch with affairs at present.' He glanced towards his own ship as she rolled uneasily about a cable from *Bacchante*'s quarter. 'But I expect you have a reason for that, sir.'

Colquhoun stared at him fixedly, as if to seek out the truth of his words. Fortunately he seemed quite oblivious to Maulby's sarcasm.

He snapped, 'Look at my chart.' They gathered round and he tapped it with some brass dividers. 'The Frenchman is here. I sent a cutter under sail before dawn to investigate.' He looked up, his eyes triumphant. 'So there's an end to speculation.'

Bolitho leaned closer. What a formidable place. From the western tip of the main island the chain of reefs and bars ran northward for about forty miles to link with the notorious Matanilla Shoal. The latter then turned eastward, enclosing the great span of open water known as the Little Bahama Bank like one monstrous snare. In places the water was only feet deep, and the fathoms were few and far between.

According to Colquhoun's marks on the chart, the French ship had passed through or around one of the cays to rest up on the other side of the island. It was perfect for anyone trying to avoid a skirmish. For on this side and elsewhere in the channel the sea bottom was over two hundred fathoms, and any hope of a close attack was foiled by the steepness of the island's face. Whereas on the other side, within the Little Bahama Bank, the water was very shallow and sandy, ideal for a master who wished to careen his ship and carry out temporary repairs.

'Was your cutter seen, sir?' Maulby did not look up.

'Of course not!' Colquhoun seemed angry even at the simple suggestion. 'My first lieutenant was in charge. He knows what would happen to him if he allowed such carelessness.' He calmed himself with an effort. 'He saw many lights on the water. The cutter pulled through the surf and between two sandbars and watched the enemy at work. She's big, probably a forty-gun frigate with some armament removed. Must have touched bottom and sustained damage sometime after entering the islands.'

Bolitho glanced at his profile. Colquhoun was very excited, there was no doubt about it, despite his efforts to conceal his true emotions. There was a strong smell of brandy, and he guessed he had been celebrating privately the victory already in his pocket.

He asked quietly, 'What do you intend, sir?'

Colquhoun looked at him searchingly. 'I am working on the assumption that the enemy is near finished repairs. Now, he will either continue on passage, or make for Martinique again if he is badly holed and needing greater help. Either way, we must act at once and avoid another chase.'

'I would suggest a boat action, sir. We could cross the bar from two directions and cut her out before they know what is happening. With men and boats from all three ships we can swamp her defences with darkness on our side.'

Colquhoun said mildly, 'With *you* in overall command of the boats, no doubt?'

Bolitho flushed angrily. 'Your frigate is too large by half to be of use in those confined waters, sir! If the Frenchman makes a run for it, or decides to show fight, you will be needed to present your ship to him and without delay.'

'Easy, Bolitho.' Colquhoun was smiling gently. 'You rise quickly to my words. Such haste to speak tends to show guilt more than conviction.'

He turned swiftly before Bolitho could reply. 'You, Maulby, will take *Fawn* across the bar tonight, under sweeps if required, but I want you in position *at dawn tomorrow*.' He leaned over the chart again. 'If the enemy is repaired enough to make sail he will no doubt hope for one of three possible channels. To the north his passage could be adversely affected by wind and tide. South is more likely, in which case *Bacchante* will be well placed to take him as he tacks around the point. But if he is still laid up or careened, you will be able to rake him there and then. He will see no use in firing back at you. Just a few more holes will be sufficient to render him immovable, or long enough for us to present more drastic measures.' He wagged one finger. 'But I know these Frogs. They'll not fight if the odds are so well laid.'

Across his bowed shoulders Maulby looked at Bolitho and shrugged.

Bolitho said nothing, knowing Colquhoun was waiting for

184

him to protest. *Sparrow* was better suited to the task as defined by Colquhoun. Her armament was heavier, and her thirty-two pounders were far more accurate and deadly than *Fawn*'s lesser battery of nine-pounders. He knew that any such suggestion, however, would only bear out Colquhoun's earlier hint that he was greedy for more success and fame, or that he was a better man than Maulby for the mission.

Maulby asked slowly, 'Will you send men overland, sir?'

Colquhoun still did not look at them. 'God in heaven! Where is all this stuff of combat I have been reading in the *Gazette*? I am beginning to wonder at its substance!'

Bolitho said, 'It is a sensible suggestion, sir. I would prefer a boat action by night, but in daylight a force of men, including your marines, would be able to . . .' He got no further.

Colquhoun straightened like a steel spring. 'Enough of this! My plan leaves no room for nervous fumbling about the rocks like a lot of damn lizards! That Frenchman is as good as taken, and I intend to sail her into port intact and with her cargo or whatever ready for closer inspection!'

He walked from the table and stared at a half-filled decanter on his desk. As he reached out for it Bolitho saw his hand was shaking with anger or agitation. His voice was equally unsteady as he continued, 'And *you*, Bolitho, will close from the north. Stay out of sight until the time of attack and then make contact with me for further orders.' His fingers closed around the decanter like claws. 'That is all. My clerk will give you written details of attack as you leave.'

They left the cabin and walked in silence to the quarterdeck.

Maulby spoke first. 'It should be *your* doing, Dick. I agree with you about trying to cut the enemy out, but either way, it is your right to lead if Colquhoun intends to stand offshore.'

Bolitho touched his shoulder. 'I wish you all success, but you know that. You are more than due for promotion, and I hope this will bring it for you.'

Maulby grimaced. 'I'll not deny that I'd relish the chance. But I would wish it done with less bitterness.' He glanced aft. 'That man will be the death of me with his bloody moods.'

Bolitho bit his lip, trying to find the right words.

'Look, John, take good care. I know Colquhoun is desperate

for this victory, but I do not share his scorn for Frenchmen. They fight well, they fight with courage. They are not given to empty gestures, even in the cannon's mouth.'

Maulby nodded, his eyes grave. 'Have no fear. If that Frenchman decides to match gun for gun with me I will haul off and await support.'

Bolitho forced a smile. Maulby was lying to ease his troubled mind. Lying as he would probably do under similar conditions. Before and after a fight at sea there was always room for recriminations and counter-proposals, but once joined in battle there was usually only one thought. To fight, to keep on firing until the enemy broke or the tide turned against you.

'Boats alongside!' The first lieutenant greeted them with a tired smile. 'Is it done, sir?'

Maulby held up his written orders. 'Aye. Done.'

The lieutenant sighed. 'I have made a small sketch which may be of some help for you, sir. The tide-race is bad there, and the surf no better. But if the French could enter, then you should have less hardship.'

The two gigs were hooked on to the chains, and Bolitho said with sudden urgency, 'I will be making sail directly if I am to take station by dawn.' He held out his hand. 'I wish I was coming with you.'

Maulby returned the clasp. 'I, too.' He grinned. 'But at least you will be spared the sight of *Fawn* as she makes Colquhoun both rich and famous in one blow.'

Stockdale stood up in the gig as Bolitho descended the frigate's side, his eyes puzzled.

As the boat shoved off and the oars picked up the stroke, he hissed, 'Then we're not fightin', sir?'

Bolitho sighed. Secret orders, plans of battle, meant nothing to the lower deck. Stockdale had not left the gig, but he and probably every Jack in the flotilla knew what was happening.

'Not this time, Stockdale.'

He had already forgotten Colquhoun's snub, the calculated attempt to drive a rift between him and Maulby. He was thinking of *Fawn*'s task, the chances of success without prolonging the attack so that Colquhoun could blame Maulby for the delay.

'It ain't right, sir.' Stockdale was muttering from the tiller.

Bolitho glared at him. 'Just attend to your work! I have had a bellyful of strategy for one day!'

Stockdale studied the captain's squared shoulders, the way he was gripping his hanger so that the fingers showed white through his tan. *It ain't no use you blowin' off at me, my lad, it still ain't right, an' wot's more, you knows it!*

With his secret rebuff held firmly in his mind Stockdale eased the tiller bar and headed straight for the *Sparrow*.

As the bowman hooked on to the chains Bolitho turned abruptly and said, 'But thank you for your concern.'

Stockdale stood and removed his hat while Bolitho reached for the sloop's side.

He grinned broadly at his back. 'Thankee, sir!'

Tyrrell was no less ready to speak out. 'But that's a strange choice! Commander Maulby's a fine officer, but . . .'

Bolitho swung round. 'Prepare to get the ship under way. Rig the royal yards as soon as we are under command, for I want to make all speed with what wind there is!' He relented again. 'Just do as I *ask*, Mr Tyrrell, and let us have no more of it.'

Buckle ambled across the deck as Bolitho hurried below to rid himself of his heavy dress coat.

'What d'you make of it, Mr Tyrrell?'

Tyrrell frowned. 'That damn Colquhoun! I never took to th' man. Like bloody Ransome, his eyes are slits for the Devil to peer through!'

Buckle shook his head. 'Cap'n's worried, there's no doubt on that.'

'Not for himself.' Tyrrell watched the men hauling at the boat tackles as the gig bobbed above the gangway. 'That is equally certain.'

Bolitho's voice rose sharply through the skylight. 'When you have *finished*, gentlemen, I would be obliged if you would attend to my orders!'

Buckle looked at Tyrrell and grinned sheepishly.

'That's more like it! Our Dick's not the one to brood too long!'

Within the hour *Sparrow* was ghosting slowly to the north-west, her yards alive with canvas, as with all sail set she left her consorts further and still further astern.

The wind rose very slightly, and by the time the first stars appeared above the raked masts they had logged nearly fifty miles. Back along the same course they had used to join Colquhoun with such haste the previous night.

But there was nothing anyone could do about it, and there were some who were inwardly pleased to be spared *Fawn*'s uncomfortable passage through the shoals.

On the quarterdeck Lieutenant Graves leaned against the rail, half watching the loosely flapping sails, partly listening to the creak of the wheel, an occasional voice from his seamen on watch. He was thinking about his home in Chatham and the news he had received in a rare letter from England. His was not a seafaring family, and his father had owned a small but flourishing grocer's shop where Graves and his sister had been born and had grown up together. His mother, a sickly woman, had died a year before *Sparrow* had sailed from the Thames, and in the past years his father had apparently taken to drink. The business had fallen into debt, and his sister, probably out of desperation, had married an impoverished lieutenant in the army garrison.

She had written asking for money, for herself and to try to keep their father from a debtor's prison. Graves had sent all he had, which had been little enough. His share of *Sparrow*'s prize money would help considerably, but until he received more news from home he was unwilling to sign it over when it had been so hard to come by. If only he had been better moulded to dealing with the ways of the Navy. Like the captain, whose seafaring background and famous ancestors put him apart from men like himself. Or even Tyrrell, who seemed indifferent to all authority, although God knew he could ill afford to be so. He remembered exactly when Tyrrell's sister had come aboard. They had been in Kingston, Jamaica, where she had been living with friends, waiting until the *troubles*, as she called them, in America were over. A vivacious, lively girl, with none of Tyrrell's casual attitudes. To Graves she had appeared like some sort of angel, an answer to everything he had ever dreamed. She came from a settled, prosperous family, and as a wife would have given him the chance to better himself, find his rightful place in the world instead of remaining unsure and cautious. Tyrrell had seen his intentions clearly enough, but had neither encouraged nor come out directly against him. Then, the fool had had an argument with Captain Ransome over a man being punished. Graves could no longer remember if the punishment was just or not, nor did he care. All that remained clear was that Ransome had acted swiftly and had used all his charm, which was considerable, and his obvious skill on the girl's defences to break his own chances as well as alienating her brother completely. But Graves still blamed Tyrrell, hated him whenever he thought of her and the way she had looked when Ransome had finally put her ashore in Antigua.

He gripped the rail until the pain steadied him. Where was she now? Someone said she had sailed for America again, others mentioned a passing Indiaman which had gone south to Trinidad. Would she ever think of him? He turned away, angry with himself for daring to hope after so long. Why could he never be confident when it was most needed? Perhaps he had been too long in that damned grocer's shop, hearing his father grovelling to the *quality*, bowing and scraping to customers who ran up bills far greater than his own debts.

The worry about his sister, the uncertainty about himself, had taken their toll in other ways, too. He had sensed it after the fight with the *Bonaventure*, even though he had been aboard *Sparrow* with the rescued passengers. Suppose the captain had failed to grapple her long enough to carry out his wild plan? Would he have had the strength to turn *Sparrow* against orders and attempt to rescue Bolitho and his men? But for Buckle and some of the others he doubted if he would have done so even when both grappled ships had burst into flames. They had witnessed the great pall of smoke from the horizon itself.

And later, when they had closed with the other prizes and had exchanged shots with privateers, he had felt the fear spreading inside him like some loathsome disease. Nobody had noticed. Yet. He shook himself and crossed to the weather side, trying to clear his mind in the cool breeze.

The two midshipmen were standing by the lee nettings, and Bethune said quietly, 'Mr Graves seems worried.'

The new midshipman, Fowler, ignored the comment. 'Now look here.' He had a lisp, which became more evident whenever he was trying to appear innocent before his superiors. Now it was barely noticeable. 'I have to supervise swabbing the cable tier tomorrow.'

Bethune was watching the lieutenant. 'I know. It's your turn.'

Fowler showed his small teeth. 'You do it for me. When we rejoin the fleet I will speak with the admiral.'

Bethune gaped at him. 'For *me*?'

'Perhaps.'

Bethune's gratitude was pathetic. 'Oh, if only . . .' He nodded firmly. 'Yes, I will take charge of the cable party. Anything else I can do . . .'

The youth regarded him coolly. 'I will let you know.'

Throughout the ship the company lived out their hopes and dreams in their own way.

In his tiny cabin Tyrrell was sitting on his sea-chest massaging his wounded thigh, while on the other side of the bulkhead Bolitho finished his letter to his father.

In the dimly lit wardroom Dalkeith was drowsing over a glass of rum, hearing Buckle re-telling a yarn about some woman or other in Bristol, while young Heyward listened to him with his eyes closed.

Right forward above the plunging beakhead, his hair blown by wind and drifting spray, Yule, the gunner, squatted with his back against a stanchion, a bottle between his knees, his blurred mind thinking of Tilby, the good times they had shared together.

Deep in the hold, a lantern above his narrow head, Lock, the purser, inspected a cask of lemons, examining each one like some robber with his booty, while he made notes in a ledger.

And below her pale canvas *Sparrow* held them all. Oblivious to their various troubles and pleasures, indifferent even to the sea. For she needed none of them, and seemed content.

*　　　*　　　*

As soon as Bolitho reached the quarterdeck, he knew the wind was changing against them, and rapidly. He had been in a deep sleep when a master's mate had groped into the cabin to tell him that Lieutenant Heyward was requesting advice.

It was only halfway through the middle watch, and the stars still very bright above the mastheads, but as he hurried across the deck, his bare feet soundless on the damp planking, he heard the topsails shaking violently, the responding chorus from stays and shrouds.

Buckle was beside the wheel, and like himself was wearing only his breeches, evidence, if it was still needed, of Heyward's unwillingness to call for help until it was almost too late.

'Well?' He peered at the slanting compass bowl, seeing the helmsmen's eyes glowing faintly in the binnacle light. 'I'm waiting, Mr Heyward.'

He did not wish to fluster the young lieutenant, and at another time could appreciate his wishing to control his own watch without showing uncertainty. But this was not the time, and in such dangerous waters they would have to act fast.

Heyward explained, 'The wind backed a point or so, and I had my watch trim the yards.' He gestured vaguely above his head. 'But now it has backed at a faster rate, I fear maybe from the north-east.'

Buckle muttered, 'We'll never be able to change tack in time to reach the head o' the shoals, sir.' He glared at the compass. '*Never!*'

Bolitho rubbed his chin, feeling the wind playing across his bare shoulders. Heyward had been foolish to let *Sparrow* have her head like this. Maybe he expected the wind to veer again, as it often did hereabouts, but whatever he thought or hoped, the ship's bow was now pointing almost north-west by north, and she was not holding that course very well either. Every minute was taking them further from the chain of shoals, and it would waste hours of wearing and tacking to fight round again towards their station as Colquhoun had directed.

Heyward said miserably, 'I'm sorry about this, sir. I—I thought I could hold her.'

Bolitho was thinking busily. 'You cannot help the wind. But in future you must learn to call me the moment you are unsure of anything. I'll not think worse of you.' He looked at Buckle. 'What is your opinion? We have four hours before dawn.'

Buckle was adamant. 'Impossible.' He sighed. 'I'm afraid we must remain close-hauled and try to wear ship in perhaps three hours or so.'

Bolitho pictured the chart in his mind, recalling vividly the nearest sandbars, the set of the tide.

'Call all hands, Mr Heyward. We will wear ship directly.'

'But, *sir*!' Buckle sounded anxious. 'We'll never be able to take up our proper course! With the wind staying steady from the nor'-east it's not possible.'

Bolitho heard the shrill of calls below decks, the sudden stampede of feet on gangways and ladders. 'I agree, Mr Buckle.' He paused as Tyrrell came out of the gloom, dragging his leg badly as he tried to buckle his belt. 'I intend to pass *through* the bars.' He looked at Tyrrell. 'If we stay as we are we will be unable to offer assistance if it is needed when daylight comes. Once inside the bank we will at least be able to use the wind if an opportunity presents itself.'

Graves ran to the quarterdeck, his feet very loud above the hushed voices. He had evidently found time to put on his shoes.

Bolitho said, 'Very well. Leadsmen in the chains, and then get the royals and t'gallants off her.' He was speaking fast in time with his thoughts. 'Tell the bosun to unleash the sweeps in case the wind drops altogether.'

Tyrrell nodded. 'Aye, aye, sir. I reckon we stand a fair chance of getting through. Th' set of th' tide is in our favour.' He hesitated. 'When it drops a piece we may find it bothersome.'

Bolitho smiled in spite of his thoughts. 'Well spoken!'

Shouts came along the gun deck where petty officers completed their count of topmen and hands for the braces. So well did most of them know the ship that darkness made little or no difference to them.

Bolitho nodded. 'Shorten sail, Mr Tyrrell.' He lowered his voice. 'Quick as you can.'

Within minutes all canvas had vanished from the upper yards, and with her topsails and courses thrusting noisily to the wind *Sparrow* lifted and staggered in a heavy swell.

Bolitho gripped the weather nettings, watching the thin slivers of spray darting across the gangway, the extreme angle of the yards as with sail and helm Buckle tried to hold her as close to the wind as he dared.

And all the while he was thinking rapidly. Once the ship had gone about the nearest strip of sandbar and shoal would lie some ten miles across the bows. A false estimate of speed and distance, a wrong or careless description on the chart, and he might drive her hard aground. But in his heart he knew the risk was worthwhile. No one could blame him for keeping to his original orders and thereby allow the wind to carry him away from the area. Colquhoun would probably be pleased to have him as far off as possible if only to deny *Sparrow* even the role of spectator for the final act. By ignoring the rigid span of his orders he might lay himself open to reprimand, but with luck he would be better placed to give *Fawn* assistance if the Frenchman decided to fight. With the wind backed to the north-east, Colquhoun would be hard put to remain in his own sector when the time came, and that in itself would offer some excuse for Bolitho's action.

'Ready, sir!'

He tightened his jaw. 'Put the helm down!'

He tensed, feeling the sea dragging against the weeded keel in a strong undertow.

'Helm's a'lee, sir!'

Through the darkness he saw the headsails shaking wildly, heard the tramp of feet as the men hauled steadily at the braces to get the yards round.

'Off tacks and sheets!' Graves's voice was hoarse above the din of canvas and blocks.

'Mainsail haul!'

A man fell in the darkness and a voice yelled harshly to restore calm on the gun deck.

Bolitho gripped the nettings, his body tilting with the hull as *Sparrow* lifted her jib-boom, hesitated and then sliced heavily across the wind.

'Braces there!' Tyrrell was leaning over the rail as if to seek out individual seamen in the gloom. 'Heave, lads! *Harder!*'

Sparrow resisted a while longer, then with sails filling and

193

booming again she heeled over on the opposite tack, the spray
sluicing up over the gangways and drenching the men beneath.

Bolitho had to shout to make himself heard above the noise.
'Close as you can, Mr Buckle!'

'Aye, sir.' He sounded breathless. 'Full an' bye!'

More uncomfortable minutes while men scampered above
and along the gangways. A pull here and belay. Men hauling
busily at halliards, while in the bows the selected hands took
their leads and lines to the forechains in readiness to begin
sounding.

Eventually even Buckle seemed satisfied. 'Sou' by east, sir!'

'Very good.'

Bolitho peered up at the hard-braced yards. Not even a
frigate could sail this close to the wind. Nothing could.

Tyrrell staggered towards him, his shirt plastered to his
body. 'You wanted this, didn't you, sir?' He was shouting,
but his voice was matched by the surge of water alongside.
'You were worried about *Fawn*?' He cursed as his foot slipped
and then clapped his hands to his thigh.

Bolitho supported him and waited for the hull to sway
upright again.

'Easy, Jethro! Is it painful?'

Tyrrell showed his teeth. 'Dalkeith said there might be some
small splinters left in th' bone. Them pistol balls can split open
when they cut into a man.' He stood up gingerly and grimaced.
'Not too bad.'

Bolitho watched the topmen slithering down stays and
shrouds and then said, 'Yes. I suppose I did want it. I cannot
explain my fears.' He shrugged and added, 'So I will not try.'

He pushed his uncertainties away. 'Now, Jethro, I want our
people to have breakfast and a tot of blackstrap. No sense in
waiting for daylight, and I imagine they are too well drenched
to sleep just now.' He ticked off the points on his fingers.
'Then have the fires doused, and muster the hands at quarters.
We will not clear for action, but I intend that every available
man is on deck when we cross the bar.'

Tyrrell was watching him intently. 'What about Heyward?
Are you going to log him?'

Bolitho shook his head. 'He's learned his lesson, so there's no harm done. When I was a junior lieutenant I once fell asleep on watch.' His teeth showed white in the darkness. 'I'm not proud of the fact, but by God I never did it again!'

He moved to the hatch cover and paused. 'I will go below and get into some clothes. It'll never do for our people to see their captain like this in daylight.' He laughed, the sound carrying up to a solitary man working on the main yard. 'I may live like a savage, but I see no cause to look like one!'

Tyrrell turned back to the rail, easing his leg as the pain lanced through it. He had just seen yet another Bolitho. Naked to the waist, his black hair plastered over his forehead, he had looked as young, if not younger than Heyward. In such a moment Tyrrell had been touched by his concern for the hands as he had been impressed by his cheerful recklessness over the approaching sandbars.

Heyward came from the gun deck and waited to resume his duty.

Tyrrell said, 'Dismiss th' watch below. Then have th' petty officers lay aft for instructions.'

Heyward asked glumly, 'Will this go badly for me?'

Tyrrell clapped him on the arm. 'God, boy, *no*!' He laughed at his astonishment. 'You did th' cap'n a favour! If you *had* called him earlier he'd have been forced to change tack. Your *mistake* allowed him to take another course of action.' He strolled away whistling to himself, his bare feet slapping on the spray-drenched planking.

Heyward walked up the tilting deck and joined Buckle by the wheel.

'I don't think I understand.'

Buckle studied him dubiously. 'Well, don't you try, that's my advice.' He shuffled towards the hatch and added, 'An' next time you feels like playing God with my ship, I'd be obliged if you'd pass the word *first*.'

Heyward glanced at the compass and crossed to the weather side. There was more to being lieutenant of the watch than holding a commission, he decided wearily. He looked at the taut mainsail and grimaced. It had been a near thing, and at one time he had felt stricken by the swift change of events, so that he had imagined the ship was running wild, carrying him and all aboard like some uncontrollable juggernaut. Now, in these last moments, he had learned something. If it all happened again he would know what to do. Of that he was quite certain.

Stockdale was waiting in the cabin with Bolitho's shirt, and after handing him a towel asked, 'Did you *really* fall asleep on watch, sir?'

Bolitho rubbed his chest and arms, feeling the salt drying on his lips like another skin.

'Almost.' Was nothing secret from Stockdale? 'But we have to embroider things a little sometimes.'

He stepped out of his sodden breeches and threw them across the cabin. As he continued to towel his naked body he listened to Heyward's measured tread across the deck above.

Then he added quietly, 'I once knew of a lieutenant who beat a man for giving a false report from the masthead. After that the seaman was too frightened to say anything, and when there *was* danger he held his tongue for fear he would get another beating. As a result, the ship was driven ashore and the lieutenant drowned.'

Stockdale watched him warily. 'Serve 'im right.'

Bolitho sighed. Moralizing was wasted on Stockdale.

The big coxswain shook out a clear pair of breeches and handed them across. For another minute or so he did not speak, but his forehead was wrinkled in thought.

Then he asked, 'An wot 'appened to the seaman, sir?'

Bolitho stared at him. 'I am afraid he was flogged for neglect of duty.'

Stockdale's battered face lit up in a broad grin.

'Proves me point then, don't it, sir? There ain't no justice in th' world for any on us!'

Bolitho sat down, one leg still tangled in the breeches. As was often the case, Stockdale had had the last word.

12. A Twist of Fate

LIEUTENANT TYRRELL gripped the quarterdeck rail and peered fixedly along the starboard gangway.

'God damn this mist!' He leaned across the rail, straining his eyes forward in an effort to see beyond the forecastle. 'And God damn our luck!'

Bolitho said nothing but moved to the opposite side of the deck. Since before dawn, when with leads going and every ear and eye pitched to the shouted depths, the sounds of distant surf and the occasional feather of warning spray in the darkness, he had been aware of the thickening sea mist. It was not unusual in these waters at the time of year, but he had expected it to pass quickly, to clear with the first hint of morning sunlight.

Now, as he stared abeam, he knew it was thicker than ever. Moving steadily with the wind, it wreathed between the shrouds and seemed to cling to the rigging like pale weed. Above the topsail yards he could see nothing, and apart from a clear patch of water below the quarterdeck, the sea was equally hidden. Keeping pace with the ship's cautious progress, the mist cut away all impression of movement, so that it felt as if *Sparrow* was suspended in cloud like some phantom vessel.

A voice below the quarterdeck called, 'By th' mark five!'

The seaman's call was hushed as the sounding was passed from mouth to mouth from the leadsmen in the forechains. Once over the bar, Bolitho had ordered the ship to be cleared for action, and with the enfolding mist shutting out both sight and sound, it was necessary to take every precaution.

He glanced at the maintopsail again. It was drawing quite well, taking the sloop steadily across the shallows, the flapping canvas shining with moisture in the grey light to show that somewhere above the mist there was a sun and maybe a sight of land, too.

'Deep four!'

Bolitho walked aft to the wheel where Buckle stood with his men, the mist moving through his splayed legs and making him appear like a spectre.

He stiffened as Bolitho approached and reported, 'She's holding well, sir. Sou' by east as afore.'

From the gun deck came a scrape of wood, and when he turned Bolitho saw one of the long sweeps swaying above the water before coming into line with the rest. He had ordered the sweeps to be run out an hour earlier, for if the wind dropped or they came upon some unexpected shoal, they would be the only means of working clear.

'Deck there!' The masthead's voice seemed to come from the mist itself. 'Ship on th' starboard quarter!'

Bolitho stared upwards, aware for the first time that the mist was tinged yellow like a North Sea fog. Sunlight at last. Far above the deck, isolated by a layer of mist, the lookout had sighted another vessel.

He saw Tyrrell and the others watching him, caught in their various attitudes by the lookout's sharp call.

Bolitho said, 'I shall go aloft, Mr Tyrrell.' He unbuckled his sword and handed it to Stockdale. 'Keep good watch and ensure that the anchor can be dropped instantly if need be.'

He hurried to the gangway, his mind torn between the unexpected sighting of a strange ship and his rising nausea at the prospect of a climb to the lookout.

Then he swung himself out on to the main shrouds and gripped the gently quivering ratlines with as much force as if the ship had been in a full gale. Through the ratlines he saw Graves below on the gun deck, shoulders hunched, his eyes looking neither right nor left.

Bethune was close by him, one hand resting on a twelve-pounder, the other shading his eyes as he peered up at the mist. All along the ship men stood like crude statuary, bare backs shining with moisture which dripped ceaselessly from the sails and rigging, so that they appeared to be sweating, as if they had just been in battle.

Here and there a checked shirt, or the darker blue and white of a gunner's mate, stood out from the rest, as if the artist had found more time to complete their postures before passing on to some other part of the picture.

'By th' mark five.' The chant came aft from the forecastle like a dirge.

In his mind Bolitho pictured the chart. The tide was on the turn now. Soon even the so-called safe channels between the shoals and sandbars would be drawn closer together, like great jaws closing around a capture.

He gritted his teeth and started to climb. When he paused to draw breath the ship had lost her outline in the mist. Only the guns and oblong hatchways stood out with any clarity, and aft by the taffrail Buckle and the others seemed to be cut in halves by the following tendrils of haze.

Up and up. At the maintop he swarmed quickly through the lubber's hole rather than tackle the additional agony of hanging by fingers and toes from the futtock shrouds. A seaman gaped at him as he passed and was still staring as Bolitho increased his rate of climb until he, too, was lost from view.

A few moments later Bolitho stared up at the main topgallant yard with something like awe. For there, above it, clean and empty of cloud, the sky was bright blue, and as he started up the last ratlines he saw the taut stays and shrouds shining like copper in the early sunlight.

The lookout, legs swinging carelessly from the crosstrees, moved over to allow his captain to climb up beside him.

Bolitho gripped a stay with one hand and tried to control his rapid breathing.

'Ah, Taylor, you have a good perch up here.'

The maintopman gave a slow grin. 'Aye, sir.' He had a soft North Country burr, and his homely voice did more than he would have dreamed possible to steady Bolitho's sickness.

He raised a bronzed arm.

'There she be, sir!'

Bolitho twisted round, trying not to look at the vibrating mast as it vanished below into the mist. For a moment longer he could see nothing. Then, as the sluggish wind stirred the mist into movement he saw the raked topmasts and flapping pendant of a frigate some three miles away on the starboard quarter.

He forgot his precarious position, the nausea of the dizzy climb, everything in fact but the other ship.

The lookout said, 'There be breakers yonder, too, sir. I reckon that frigate's on t'other side o' the bar.'

Bolitho looked at him gravely. 'You know her, don't you?'

The man nodded. 'Aye, sir. She's *Bacchante*, Cap'n Colquhoun's command flag is at the fore.' He watched Bolitho's impassive face. 'Anyway, I was in 'er once, two years back.'

Bolitho nodded. He had known it was *Bacchante*, too. Perhaps he had been hoping he was mistaken, that the mist and light were playing tricks.

But there was no doubting Taylor's conviction. It was typical of such seamen as he. Once they had served with or aboard a ship they seemed to know her under any condition. Taylor had only seen the frigate's upper yards, but he had recognized her instantly.

Bolitho touched his arm. 'Keep a good watch on her, Taylor.' He slung his leg over the edge. 'You've done well.'

Then he was climbing and slipping downwards, his mind grappling with this new encounter. Once, when he peered over his shoulder he thought he saw hazed sunlight on the water, further away from the hull. So the mist was thinning after all. But it was too late now, if things went wrong.

Tyrrell was waiting for him by the quarterdeck rail, his eyes anxious as Bolitho jumped down from the shrouds and hurried towards him.

'It's *Bacchante*!'

Bolitho stared past him at the upturned faces on the gun deck, the faint leap of spray as the leadsman made yet another cast.

'Quarter less five!'

He turned to Tyrrell. 'Colquhoun must have stood well clear of land during the night. When the wind backed it caught him out, as it did us. He must have been driven miles along the Channel.' He turned away, his voice suddenly bitter. 'The damn fool should have stayed closer inshore! Now he's useless out there beyond the shoals! It'd take him near half a day to beat back into an attacking position!'

Tyrrell's hand rasped over his chin. 'What'll we do? With

the tide on th' turn we'll have to look sharp if we're to close with th' Frogs.' He glanced at Buckle. 'My guess is we should stand away and try again later.'

Buckle nodded slowly. 'Mine, too. If Cap'n Colquhoun's plan has gone off at half-cock then we can't be expected to do better.'

Bolitho ignored him. 'Pass the word, Mr Tyrrell. Withdraw sweeps and have the guns loaded and run out. Gun by gun, if you please, with as little noise as possible.' He studied Buckle's dubious expression and added quietly, 'I *know* the risk. So brail up the courses and have the bosun prepare a stream anchor in case we have to take the way off her directly.' He thrust his hands behind his back. 'You can think me mad, Mr Buckle.' He heard the sweeps thumping inboard on to their racks and the slow rumble of trucks as the first cannon were hauled towards the open ports. 'And maybe I am. But somewhere out there is a British sloop like ourselves. Thanks to others she is quite alone now, and God knows, if I am *not* mad then *Fawn* is going to need every bit of help she can get!'

The big main course rose billowing and protesting to its yard as men worked busily to bring it under control and lay bare the decks from bow to quarterdeck.

A gunner's mate called huskily, 'Loaded an' run out, sir!'

Tyrrell strode aft, his speaking trumpet jammed beneath his arm.

Bolitho met his gaze and smiled briefly. 'You were faster this time.'

Then together, with their backs to the helmsmen and an apprehensive Buckle, they leaned on the rail and stared directly ahead. The mist was still all around them, but thinner, and as he watched Bolitho knew it was at last outpacing the ship, moving stealthily through the shrouds and away across the lee bow. There was sunlight, too. Not much, but he saw it reflecting faintly from the ship's bell and playing on a black twelve-pounder ball which one gun captain had removed from a shot garland and was changing from hand to hand, testing its perfection or otherwise.

Bolitho asked softly, 'How far now, in your opinion?'

Tyrrell raised his injured leg and winced. 'Th' wind stays

regular from th' nor'-east. Our course is sou' by east.' He was thinking aloud. 'Th' soundings have found no lie in th' chart.' He made up his mind. 'I reckon we're about six mile from th' place where *Fawn* crossed through th' shoals.' He turned and added firmly, 'You'll have to put about soon, sir. You'll be hard aground if you keep on this tack much longer.'

The chant seemed to float aft to mock him. 'By th' mark three!'

Lieutenant Heyward, who was standing very still by the quarterdeck ladder, murmured, 'Holy God!'

Bolitho said, 'If the Frenchman is still there, then there must be ample room for him to work clear.'

Tyrrell eyed him sadly. 'Aye. But by th' time we reach that far we'll be in no position to go about. Th' Frog can thumb his nose at us.'

Bolitho pictured the disembodied masts and yards of Colquhoun's frigate and gripped his hands together to steady his nerves and restrain his rising anger. That fool Colquhoun. So eager to keep the spoils to himself he had failed to anticipate a change of wind. So keen to keep *Sparrow* out of the victory that he had now left the gate open for the enemy to run free if he so desired. *Fawn* could not bring her to battle even if she could catch her.

'An' a quarter less three!'

He grasped the nettings and tried not to imagine the sea's bottom rising slowly and steadily towards the keel.

It was no use. He swung away from the nettings, his sudden movement making Midshipman Fowler start back in alarm. He was risking his ship and the life of everyone aboard. *Fawn* was probably anchored, or had already found the enemy gone. His apprehensions, his personal doubts would cut little cloth with the relatives of those drowned by his risking *Sparrow* for a whim.

He said harshly, 'We will wear ship. I intend to cross the bar and rejoin *Bacchante* as soon as the mist clears.' He saw Buckle nod with relief and Tyrrell watching him with grave understanding. 'Convey my compliments to Mr Graves and have the guns . . .' He swung round as several voices shouted at once.

Tyrrell said tersely, 'Gunfire, by God!'

Bolitho froze, listening intently to the intermitten cracks and the heavier crash of larger weapons.

'Belay that last order, Mr Tyrrell!' He watched as a shaft of sunlight ran down the trunk of the mainmast like molten gold. 'We will not be blind for long!'

More minutes dragged by, with every man aboard listening to the distant gunfire.

Bolitho found that he could see beyond the tapering jib-boom, and when he glanced abeam he saw a writhing necklace of surf to mark the nearest prongs of reef. Perhaps it was the mist, or back echoes from the hidden land, but the gunfire did not sound right. He could pick out the sharper bark of *Fawn*'s nine-pounders from the enemy's heavier artillery, but there were other explosions from varying bearings which seemed totally at odds with the circumstances.

Sunlight swept down across the damp planking and raised more haze from the dripping shrouds and hammock nettings, and then, like some fantastic curtain, the mist was drawn aside, laying bare the drama with each detail sharp in the morning light.

There was the tip of the island, hard blue against an empty sky, and the intermingled patterns of surf and swirling currents to show the nearness of the bar. And dead ahead of *Sparrow*'s slow approach, her hull seemingly pinioned on the jib-boom, was Maulby's *Fawn*.

Further away, with masts and furled sails still shrouded in departing mist, lay the Frenchman, half hidden in shadow, the outline blurred into the landmass beyond. She was firing rapidly, her battery flashing long orange tongues, her flag clearly visible above the gunsmoke.

It was only then Bolitho realized that *Fawn* was still anchored. Sickened, he watched the sharp waterspouts bursting all around her, the occasional fountain of spray as a ball smashed hard alongside.

Buckle called hoarsely, 'He's cut his cable, sir!'

Maulby's men were already running out the long sweeps to try to work clear of the murderous barrage, while their own guns maintained a brisk fire towards the enemy.

Bolitho gripped the rail as *Fawn*'s foretopmast staggered and then reeled down in a great welter of spray and smoke. He heard Tyrrell's voice as if in a dream, saw him pointing wildly, as more flashes sparkled, not from the Frenchman but from the headland and low down as well, probably on some small beach.

What a perfect trap. Maulby must have been caught by the mist, and after making sure the enemy was still apparently moored close inshore, had anchored to await Colquhoun's support. No wonder *Bacchante*'s first lieutenant had reported so much activity. The French captain had taken time to land artillery so that any attacker would be caught in one devastating arc of fire from which there was small chance of escape.

The sweeps were out now, rising and falling like wings, bringing the little sloop round until she was pointing away from the enemy and towards the bar and the open sea.

A chorus of cries and groans came from the gun deck as the larboard bank of sweeps flew in wild confusion, the splintered blades whirling high into the air before splashing around the ship in fragments.

Bolitho raised a telescope and held it trained on *Fawn*'s quarterdeck. He saw running figures, faces magnified in the lens and made more terrible by distance and silence. Open mouths, gesturing arms as men ran to hack away the wreckage and keep at least some of the guns firing. A spar fell across his small encircled world, so that he flinched as if expecting to feel the shock of its impact on the deck. A seaman was running and stumbling along one gangway, his face apparently shot away, his terror agonizing to watch as he fell and was mercifully lost alongside.

Someone had kept his head, and high above the deck Bolitho saw the maintopsail billowing free to the wind, the sudden response beneath *Fawn*'s gilded figurehead as she began to gather way.

He felt Buckle shaking his arm and turned as he shouted desperately, 'We *must* go about, sir!' He pointed frantically towards the glittering water and at a mass of brown weed which glided so close to its surface. 'We'll be ashore this instant!'

Bolitho looked past him. 'Prepare to anchor, Mr Tyrrell!'

He did not recognize his voice. It was like steel against steel. 'Have the cutter swayed out and prepare to lay a kedge anchor directly.' He waited until Tyrrell had run to the rail and the first dazed men had swarmed out along the yards. 'We will remain *here*.'

Moving more slowly, *Sparrow* edged into the shallows, and when she passed above one sandbar it was possible to see her own shadow before the water deepened once more.

Bolitho continued to pass his orders, making each one separate and detached from the next while he forced himself to concentrate, to shut his ears to the gunfire, to shield his eyes from *Fawn*'s slow and methodical destruction.

The cutters were lowered, and as ordered, Glass, the boat-swain, took one of them to lay out a small kedge. With sails brailed up, and loosely anchored from bow and stern, *Sparrow* finally came to rest.

Then and only then did Bolitho raise his glass again and turn it on the *Fawn*. Listing badly, and all but her mizzen shot away, she was still trying to work clear of the bombardment. It was hopeless, for although her rudder seemed intact, and the spanker and crossjack were giving her some sort of steerage way, she was badly hampered by a mass of dragging spars and canvas, and appeared to have few men left who were able to cut it adrift. She was hit again and again, the splintered sections of timber and planking plummeting in the shallows, floating with and astern of her like blood from a wounded beast.

She gave a violent lurch, and as her mizzen came down to join the rest of her spars, Bolitho knew she had driven aground. She was broaching to, her deck tilting towards him as the first savage spines ground into her bilges and keel. It was finished.

He closed the glass and handed it to someone nearby. He saw no individual faces, heard no voices he could recognize. His own was as strange and unnatural as before.

'The Frenchman lies on our larboard bow.' How quiet it was now. The enemy had ceased fire, for as *Fawn* lay gripped on a shoal she was at last out of reach from those guns. Smoke drifted above the headland, and Bolitho pictured the French artillerymen sponging out the muzzles, watching perhaps the unexpected arrival of another sloop. One more victim. 'The range is less than a mile. He is well moored to present a perfect deception.' He knew Tyrrell and the rest were watching him. Transfixed. 'Equally, he cannot hurt us. We on the other hand . . .' He turned despite his guard to see *Fawn*'s beakhead and bowsprit tear away and drop into the swirling current beneath her stem. He continued tonelessly, 'We can hit him, and *hard*!'

Graves was on the ladder, his face pale from shock or at seeing the other ship destroyed so cruelly.

Bolitho looked at him. 'Get the larboard bow-chaser to work. You will open fire when ready. Pass your requirements to the bosun. By using the anchor cables you will be able to traverse at will.' He turned to Tyrrell. 'Have the capstan manned at once.'

Graves was halfway along the deck when Bolitho's voice brought him stockstill in his tracks.

'Fetch Mr Yule! Tell him I want him to build a small furnace where he can heat shot for your gun. Take good care that it is done right and well.' He shifted his eyes to the enemy ship. 'We have time now. Plenty of it.'

Then he walked to the nettings and waited for Tyrrell to come aft again.

Tyrrell said quietly, 'You were right after all, sir. It was *us* they were after. Good God Almighty, it was *us* we just watched being destroyed!'

Bolitho studied him gravely. 'Aye, Jethro.' He recalled with stark clarity Maulby's words to him at their last meeting. Of Colquhoun. *That man will be the death of me. . . .*

He swung round, his voice harsh again. 'What the hell is the delay?'

He was answered by a loud bang from forward, and was in time to see the fall of shot some half cable from the enemy.

An order was passed down the deck and the men at the capstan bars took the strain, tautening the cable very slightly so that *Sparrow*'s bows edged round to give Graves's crew a better traverse.

Bang! The ball shrieked away, this time slapping down in line with the enemy's poop.

Bolitho had to grip his hands to steady himself. The next ball would strike. He knew it would. From then on . . . He beckoned to Stockdale.

'Away gig. Pipe for the second cutter to head for *Fawn*. We may yet pick up some of her people.'

He saw Dalkeith below the ladder, already dressed in his long, stained apron.

Another bang came from the bow-chaser, and he saw the brown smoke billowing through the beakhead, hiding the actual fall of shot. But a voice yelled, 'Got 'er! Fine on th' quarter!'

He said, half to himself, 'Not pop-guns this time, Mr Frenchman! *Not this time!*'

'Gig's ready, sir!' Even Stockdale sounded shocked.

'Take charge until I return, Mr Tyrrell.' He waited for him to drag his leg down to the entry port. 'We will work out of here on the next tide.'

He heard dull hammering as Yule and his mates constructed a crude furnace. It was dangerous, even foolhardy under normal circumstances to consider heating shot aboard ship. A tinder-dry hull, cordage and canvas, tar and gunpowder. But this was not normal. *Sparrow* was anchored in sheltered waters. A floating gun-platform. It was merely a matter of accuracy and patience.

Tyrrell asked awkwardly, 'How long do we keep firing, sir?'

Bolitho swung himself out above the gently slapping cat's-paws and green reflections.

'Until the enemy is destroyed.' He looked away. '*Completely.*'

'Aye, sir.'

Tyrrell watched Bolitho climb into the gig, the quick flurry of oars as Stockdale guided it towards the hulk which had once been *Fawn*.

Then he walked slowly to the quarterdeck rail and shaded his eyes to watch the enemy ship. There was little sign of damage, but the balls were hitting her regularly now. Shortly, the heated shot would be cradled from Yule's furnace, and then . . . he shivered despite the growing sunlight. Like most sailors he feared fire more than anything.

Heyward joined him and asked quietly, 'Did he mean it?'

Tyrrell thought of Bolitho's eyes, the despair and hurt when *Fawn* had been taken by the trap.

'Aye, he did.'

He flinched as a gun fired from the Frenchman's deck, and saw the ball throw up a thin column almost a cable short. Seamen not employed on the capstan or boats were watching from the gangways and shrouds, some even made wagers as to the next shot. As each French ball fell short they cheered or jeered, spectators only, and as yet unaware that but for a twist of fate they and not *Fawn*'s people would have died under those cannon.

Tyrrell continued, 'Colquhoun brought us to this. If our cap'n had been given his rightful position to attack we'd have got clear.' He banged his palms together. 'Arrogant bastard! An' he just sits out there like some sort of god while we finish his mess for him!'

Another bang echoed across the water and he saw a spar fall from the enemy's mainmast. Very slowly, or so it appeared, like a leaf from a tree in autumn.

Midshipman Fowler called, 'Our boats are standing off the wreck, sir!'

He was pale, but as he raised his telescope his hand was as steady as a gun.

Tyrrell looked at him coldly. And there's another one. Like Ransome, like Colquhoun. Without humanity or feelings.

Wreck was how he had described *Fawn*. Yet moments ago she had been a living, vital creature. A way of life for her people and those who would have come after.

Savagely he said, 'Get aloft, Mr Fowler, and take your glass with you! Keep an eye open for *Bacchante* beyond th' reef and watch for her signals.'

If any.

Then as the gun banged out again he made himself walk to the opposite side leaving Heyward to his thoughts.

Bolitho heard the gun's regular bombardment even as the gig hooked on to *Fawn*'s listing side, and with some of his men he climbed aboard.

'The cutter first!' He gestured to Bethune who was staring

at the bloody shambles like a man in a trance. 'Full load, and then the gig.'

Stockdale followed him up the slanting deck, over smashed boats and tangled rigging. Once as they passed a hatchway Bolitho saw a green glow, and when he peered below he saw the sea surging jubilantly through a great gash in the hull, the reflected sunlight playing on two bobbing corpses. Huge patches of blood, upended guns around which the dazed survivors staggered down towards the waiting boats. There seemed very few of them.

Bolitho wiped his face with his shirt-sleeve. *Us*, Tyrrell had said. It was not difficult to understand.

He paused on the quarterdeck ladder and looked down at Maulby. He had been crushed by a fallen spar, his features frozen in the agony of the moment. There was a small smudge of blood on his cheek, and there were flies crawling on his face.

He said hoarsely, 'Take him, Stockdale.'

Stockdale bent down and then muttered, 'Can't be done, sir. 'E's 'eld fast.'

Bolitho knelt over the spar and covered his face with a scrap of canvas. Rest easy, old friend. Stay with your ship. You are in the best of company today.

The deck gave a quick shiver. She was beginning to break up. The sea, the tide and the unlashed guns would soon finish what the enemy had begun.

Bethune's voice came up from alongside where the cutter rose and plunged in a dangerous swell.

'All off, sir!'

'Thank you.'

Bolitho heard the sea crashing through the deck below, swamping the wardroom and on into the stern cabin. One like his own. There was no time to retrieve anything now. He bent down and unclipped Maulby's sword.

He handed it to Stockdale. 'Someone in England might like it.'

He made himself take one long glance around him. Remembering every detail. Holding it.

Then he followed Stockdale into the gig. He did not look back, nor did he hear the sounds of *Fawn*'s final misery. He was thinking of Maulby. His drawling voice. Feeling his last handshake.

Tyrrell met him and then said, 'Mr Yule has th' furnace ready, sir.'

Bolitho looked at him emptily. 'Douse it, if you please.'

'Sir?'

'I'll not burn men for doing their duty. The Frenchman is too badly holed now to get away. We will send a boat across under a flag of truce. I don't think he'll wish to prolong senseless killing.'

Tyrrell breathed out slowly. 'Aye, sir. I'll attend to it.'

When he turned back from passing the order to cease fire he found that Bolitho had left the deck.

He saw Stockdale carrying the sword and wiping it with a scrap of waste, his battered face totally engrossed in the task. He thought of Tilby's two model ships. Like Maulby's sword. Was that all that was left of a man?

He was still pondering about it when *Bacchante*'s topmasts hove in sight and she hoisted her first signal.

It was evening before *Sparrow* was able to close with the frigate. For almost as soon as she had worked clear of the bar the wind veered and gained considerably in strength, so that it was necessary to use every effort to beat clear of those treacherous breakers. In open waters again, with the darkening slab of Grand Bahama some five miles abeam, *Sparrow* reduced sail and hove-to within a cable of Colquhoun's ship.

As he sat in the crazily tossing gig Bolitho watched the frigate and the last signal for him to repair on board being hauled down to the deck. It had been hoisted for some time, but like Colquhoun's previous ones, he had ignored it. Had not even made an acknowledgement.

Spray lanced back from the oars and dashed across his face. It helped to calm him, if only slightly. His sorrow was matched by anger, his self-control by an eagerness to confront Colquhoun.

The gig turned and rose dizzily on a steep swell, the bowman almost pitching overboard as he hooked on to the chains and made fast.

Bolitho clambered up the frigate's tumblehome, for once ignoring the sea which swirled along the hull as if to pluck him away.

Colquhoun was not at the entry port, and the first lieutenant said quickly, 'By God, sir, I am sorry for what happened.'

Bolitho eyed him gravely. 'Thank you. The fault was not of your making.'

Then without another word or a glance at the swaying side party he strode aft to the cabin.

Colquhoun was standing by the windows, as if he had not moved since their last encounter. In the lanterns' yellow glare his face looked stiff and unsmiling, and when he spoke his tone was like that of a much older man.

'It took you long enough! How dare you ignore my signals!'

Bolitho faced him coldly. The anger in Colquhoun's voice was as false as his composure, and he saw one hand twitching badly against his white breeches.

'Your earlier signals were made to *Fawn*, sir.' He saw him start and continued slowly, 'But she was already in pieces and her people mostly killed in battle or drowned when she struck.'

Colquhoun nodded jerkily, his brows tightening as if he was trying to keep a grip on his emotions.

'That is beside the point. You disobeyed my orders. You crossed the bar without permission. You . . .'

Bolitho said, 'I did what I considered to be my duty.' It was no use. He could feel his control slipping away like an icy yard beneath a topman. 'But for your lust after glory we would have taken the Frenchman together, without loss. We had all the advantage, for the enemy knew nothing of your full strength. She was after one prize only. *Sparrow*.' He turned away, trying to hide his grief. 'Because of you, Maulby and his men were killed, his ship lost. Because of your senseless rigidity, your failure to see beyond prize money, you could not help when the time came.' He swung round again, his voice harsh. 'Well, the Frenchman is taken! What d'you want now, a bloody knighthood?'

Surprisingly, Colquhoun's voice was very low, and as he spoke he kept his eyes on some point away from Bolitho.

'I will ignore your outburst.' He paused. 'Ah, I remember

211

now, you have young Fowler aboard. It would have done no good to lose him in battle.' He was speaking more quickly, the disjointed sentences falling from his lips in time with his thoughts. 'The admiral will expect a full report. I shall . . .'

Bolitho watched him, sickened. 'I have the written orders you originally gave me. The ones which were to send me as far from the point of attack as you could invent.' Despite Colquhoun's pathetic explanations and excuses he forced himself to go on. 'If I had obeyed them, or the wind had remained constant, *Fawn* would still have perished. What would you have done then? Sent the little *Lucifer* maybe?'

Colquhoun walked to his desk and pulled a decanter from its rack. Some of the brandy slopped over his hand but he did not seem to notice it.

'I received orders some while back. When we had run the French *flute* to ground, or given up the search, we are ordered to proceed to New York. The flotilla is to be reduced.' He swallowed half a glass of brandy and had to fight to regain his breath. '*Bacchante* will be returned to fleet duties.'

Bolitho stared at him. Any compassion or pity he might have harboured behind his anger was gone with that admission.

In a low tone he asked, 'All this while, and you *knew* we were to go to New York?' He listened to his own voice, wondering how he could sound so calm. 'You thought it was a last chance to prove yourself. A great show of victory, with you entering port, a fine fat prize under your colours! Yet because of your greed you could not see the real danger, and *Fawn* has paid dearly for your ignorance!'

Colquhoun lifted his eyes and watched him desperately.

'In New York things might seem different. Remember, I was the one who helped you . . .' He broke off and swallowed another drink. 'I needed that prize! I've *earned* it!'

Bolitho moved towards the door, keeping his eyes on Colquhoun's quivering shoulders.

He said, 'I sent *Fawn*'s remaining lieutenant to take charge of the *flute*. Surrender was arranged by Lieutenant Heyward.' He made himself keep to the details, if only to stop Colquhoun from pleading. 'The French ship'll not be much use again.

I suggest you send your marines to take charge and await the military, who'll wish to escort the prisoners elsewhere.'

Colquhoun leaned against the stern windows, his voice muffled by the sounds of sea and rudder.

'It will mean a court martial.' His shoulders stiffened. 'You will be ordered to attend.'

Bolitho nodded. 'It would seem so.'

Colquhoun waved one hand towards the cabin without turning.

'All this gone. In just a moment of bad circumstances. Fate.'

'Maulby probably thought that, too.' Bolitho rested his fingers on the door.

Colquhoun pushed himself from the windows and lurched across the cabin.

'So you've won in the end, eh?' His voice cracked. 'You and your bloody *Sparrow!*'

Bolitho saw the man's anguish and answered, 'Three years ago when I was given *Sparrow* I thought command was everything, all a man could desire. Then maybe I would have agreed with your decisions, no matter what they entailed. Now I know better, perhaps after all, thanks to you. Command is one thing. But responsibility, the duty to those who depend on you, is the greater burden. We must share the guilt for Maulby's death.' He saw Colquhoun staring at him incredulously but continued, 'Your folly blinded you to everything but future advancement. My crime was pride. A pride which goaded the enemy into laying a snare for me, and one which cost *Fawn*'s people dearly.' He opened the door. 'I hope I never forget it. Nor you.'

He walked quickly to the quarterdeck and heard the door slam behind him, the slap of a musket as the sentry returned to a more relaxed stance.

By the gangway he found the first lieutenant waiting for him. Across the heaving water, its crests and troughs already painted with shadows, he saw *Sparrow* swaying unsteadily against the first pale stars. A lantern gleamed from her taffrail, and he thought he saw the splash of oars to mark where Stockdale held the gig in readiness. He could have waited in vain. Colquhoun might have made one last gesture by throwing him under arrest for his outburst. That he had not was proof enough of his true guilt. More, that Colquhoun was well aware of what he had done.

He said, 'We are to rejoin the Flag at New York.'

The lieutenant watched the gig bobbing towards the side and replied sadly, 'I'll not be sorry to quit this place.'

Bolitho sighed. 'Aye. A defeat is a bad business. But a victory can often bring the greater pain.'

The lieutenant watched him climb into the gig and pull clear.

So young, yet with so much responsibility. Not for me. Even as the thought crossed his mind he knew it was a lie, and upon looking round the darkening deck he wondered if Colquhoun's error had brought him any nearer to his own promotion.

13. No Better Epitaph

ALMOST IMMEDIATELY after dropping anchor at Sandy Hook, *Sparrow* and her company were thrown into the urgent work of a short but well-deserved overhaul. Under the wintry eye of a senior dockyard officer the ship was careened and the thick growth of weed cut and cleaned from her hull. Bolitho was able to send Lock ashore, and with more careful bribes obtained fresh provisions as well as replacements for some of the fouler casks of beef and pork.

In the midst of all this activity, which continued from dawn to dusk, he was occasionally visited by a scholarly lieutenant of the Commander-in-Chief's staff. He took statements from Bolitho and Tyrrell and compared them with notations in the log at the time of *Fawn*'s destruction, as well as those leading up to the actual attack. Buckle was required to display and explain each section of the charts used, and was instantly reduced to mumbling confusion under the lieutenant's skilful examination. But as one day followed the next, and *Sparrow* regained her original trim appearance, the bitter memories of *Fawn*'s loss, even the display of hot anger in Colquhoun's cabin, became blurred, if not erased from Bolitho's mind.

He had been kept continuously busy with the affairs of his ship, never knowing for sure when his next orders would arrive, and had spent any spare moments studying the wider aspects of the war on land. When the summons to appear at a court martial was delivered to him, it came as something like a shock.

Three weeks had gone by since he had confronted Colquhoun in *Bacchante*'s cabin and almost every day had been occupied with incident and activity.

Only certain details still stood out with stark clarity in his mind. The picture of slaughter and desolation on *Fawn*'s shattered deck. Maulby's face, the flies crawling over his contorted features. Young Heyward's obvious pride at being given

215

the task of receiving the Frenchman's surrender, and the *Fawn*'s one surviving officer who had gone to take charge of the enemy until the marines arrived. Maulby's lieutenant had been like a man coming out of the shadow of death itself. His movements disjointed, his face stricken from the sights and sounds he had endured.

On the morning of the court martial Bolitho stood on *Sparrow*'s quarterdeck with Tyrrell and Buckle, aware of the many watching eyes, of his men, and those on nearby ships at anchor.

Tyrrell shifted his leg and muttered, 'I may be called as witness, but by God I feel like a guilty man!'

Bolitho watched the gig moving towards the entry port, and noticed that Stockdale and the oarsmen were dressed in their best clothes. Conscious, too, of this moment perhaps.

As well they might, he thought grimly. It was Colquhoun's day, but it was not unknown for a drowning man to drag others down with him.

He shifted his gaze to the old seventy-four which lay some three cables distant. The *Parthian*, where he had been given his instructions for rescuing the soldiers and General Blundell's bullion from the Delaware. How long ago it seemed now. An eternity.

The gig made fast and Tyrrell said abruptly, 'That bastard deserves to hang!'

Bolitho followed the others to the entry port, trying once again to find his true feelings. It was difficult to go on hating Colquhoun. His weakness had perhaps been too human, which made it harder to condemn after the first anger had passed.

As eight o'clock came and the bells chimed from each anchored ship-of-war, a solitary gun crashed out from the *Parthian*'s side, and the court martial Jack broke simultaneously from her gaff. It was time.

Graves stood with the rigid side party, his face expressionless as they climbed into the gig. He was not implicated, and Bolitho wondered if he saw his chances of promotion reflected in the court martial flag.

Once through *Parthian*'s gilded entry port and past the marine guard and assembled band, Bolitho felt a rising sense of disgust. The two-decker's quarterdeck was thronged with visitors. Senior officers, some of them military, several prosperous-looking civilians and a solitary artist gave the impression of a carefree outing rather than a trial. The artist, a bearded, intent little man, busied himself from every angle, making quick sketches, dotting in detail of uniform or title, hardly pausing between each capture.

He saw Bolitho and hurried between the chattering throng, his pad already poised in readiness.

'Ah, good sir! Captain Bolitho?' The pencil hovered and then darted down. 'I am so glad to see you at last. I have heard much of your exploits.' He paused and smiled shyly. 'I wish I could have been aboard your ship to take sketches. The people at home need to be told . . .'

Tyrrell murmured, 'For Christ's sake!'

A master-at-arms opened a door and the visitors began to filter aft towards the great cabin. Left isolated and ill at ease in their best uniforms, the witnesses remained on the quarterdeck.

Bolitho said quietly, 'At some other time maybe.'

He turned his head to watch a marine captain with drawn sword marching aft to the cabin. Just the sight of it made him feel sick. The grim array. Like the crowds at Tyburn, or the jeering fools who stood for hours to watch some wretch choking out his life on a village gibbet.

The artist's smile faded. 'I understand. I thought . . .'

Bolitho replied, 'I know what you thought. That I'd be pleased to see a man fall from office!' He did not hide his contempt.

'That, too.' The artist's eyes flickered in the sunlight as he made a quick alteration to his sketch. 'I also imagined you might see your future made stronger by this man's disgrace.' He shrugged as Bolitho turned on him angrily. 'That I am wrong on both counts makes me a fool, and you an even better man than they say you are.'

Bolitho looked at him sadly. 'What *they* say will count for little today.'

A lieutenant called, 'This way, gentlemen.'

They followed him in order of seniority and filed into the ship's wardroom.

The artist passed quickly and vanished towards the great cabin as Tyrrell growled, 'God, what is happening to us? Will they make pictures of th' Day of Judgement, too?'

All morning the wearing business went on. Witnesses were called and evidence mounted. Factual and hearsay, technical or just plain imagination, it seemed to take an eternity to get it down in writing. There were occasional pauses for refreshment and to allow the visitors to stretch their legs on deck.

Throughout the whole morning, Bolitho hardly spoke. Around him, their faces displaying either confidence or uncertainty, the rest of the witnesses waited their turn. Odell off the schooner *Lucifer*, his quick, agitated movements only adding to the tension. *Bacchante*'s first lieutenant and sailing master. *Fawn*'s surviving lieutenant and a blinded seaman who had stood beside Maulby when he had been struck down.

In seniority, or as their value directed, the witnesses dwindled until only Bolitho and Tyrrell remained. Through the open ports Bolitho saw boats plying between the ships and the shore, the haze of smoke from a nearby spit of sand where a man was burning driftwood.

It was stiflingly hot. The first day of May. He pictured what it would be like at home. In Falmouth. Sometimes he thought he would never see it again. Tiny pale dots of sheep on the hills and headland. Noisy cows in the lane below the house, always inquisitive as they passed the gates, as if they had never seen them before. And in the town square, where the coaches loaded up for Plymouth or the horses were changed for another route to the west, there would be plenty of laughter and good cheer. For if the war was a threat, so, too, was winter, and that was well behind them until the next time. Now, the fishermen could put to sea in safety, and the fields and markets would show the evidence of their labours and rewards.

'Mr Tyrrell.' The lieutenant held the door open. 'This way.'

Tyrrell picked up his hat and looked at him. 'Soon now, sir.' Then Bolitho was alone.

It did not take very long. Tyrrell's evidence was purely factual and concerned the times of crossing the bar and commencing the attack. In all events, he was obeying orders. He was safe.

When his call came Bolitho followed the lieutenant into the cabin without remembering hearing his name announced.

It was packed with seated figures, and right aft, behind a table which reached almost from side to side, he saw the officers of the court. In the centre, as President, was Sir Evelyn Christie, flanked by ten captains of varying status and seniority, none of whom was known to Bolitho.

Rear-Admiral Christie eyed him bleakly. 'Your sworn statement has been read and submitted in evidence.'

He sounded clipped and formal, so that Bolitho was suddenly reminded of their last meeting. The difference almost amounted to hostility.

'We have heard of the plan to take the *flute*, of the events leading to her discovery, including evidence given by *Lucifer*'s captain and that of your own officers.' He paused and ruffled through some papers. 'In your statement you said that you had advised your senior officer against a cutting-out expedition of the kind which was eventually employed?'

Bolitho cleared his throat. 'I thought that under the circumstances . . .'

The nearest captain snapped, 'Yes or no!'

'Yes.' Bolitho kept his eyes on the admiral. 'I gave my opinion.'

The admiral leaned back slowly. 'The accused has already stated that is *not* the case. He gave you your orders only after you had insisted that your ship would be better placed to the north of the Bank.'

In the sudden silence Bolitho could feel his heart pounding like a hammer. He wanted to turn his head and look at Colquhoun, but knew that any such attempt would be immediately seen as guilt.

The senior captain at the table said abruptly, 'Were there any witnesses as to what occurred when these decisions were reached?'

Bolitho faced him.

'Only Commander Maulby, sir.'

'I see.'

Bolitho felt the cabin closing in around him, saw the nearest faces watching him like a row of greedy birds.

The admiral sighed. 'I will continue. After leaving the other vessels you proceeded towards your allotted station.'

'Yes, sir.'

The admiral looked up with a jerk. 'Then why did you cross the bar?' He slapped one hand on the papers, bringing a mingled gasp from the spectators. '*Was it guilt?* Did you at last realize that Captain Colquhoun was right and that he needed your support in the south?'

'No, sir.' He could feel his hands shaking, the sweat like ice-rime between his shoulders. 'I have stated my reasons. We lost the wind, I had no option but to tack when I did.' Pictures flashed through his mind like parts of a nightmare. Heyward, ashamed at losing control of the ship. Buckle, doubtful and anxious for her safety as he had told him his intentions. He heard himself add quietly, 'Commander Maulby was my friend.'

The senior member of the court regarded him flatly. 'Really?'

Bolitho turned his head and saw Colquhoun for the first time. He was shocked to see the change in him. He was very pale, and in the reflected light his skin was the texture of wax. He was standing with his arms limp at his sides, his body moving only slightly to the gentle tilt of the deck. But his eyes were the worst part. They were fixed on Bolitho's face, on his mouth when he spoke, and shone with such incredible hatred that Bolitho exclaimed, 'Tell them the truth!'

Colquhoun made as if to step forward, but his escort, the marine captain, touched his arm and he relaxed again.

The admiral snapped, 'That will do, Captain Bolitho! I'll have no exchanges in this court!'

The senior captain coughed discreetly and continued, 'The rest we know. The French deception, and your destruction of their *flute*, all of which is above criticism. Despite obvious dangers you managed to rescue some of *Fawn*'s company, and several of her wounded are now alive and recovering, thanks to your efforts.'

Bolitho watched him emptily. He had done his duty, but the lies already told by Colquhoun about his character, and his statement which only Maulby could confirm, made a mockery of it. He looked down at Colquhoun's sword on the table. His own might lie there soon. He found he cared little about that, but the slur on his name he could not bear.

The admiral looked around the crowded cabin. 'I think we have heard enough before we withdraw, gentlemen?'

Bolitho swayed. A long lunch. More delays. It was torture.

Like most of those present he jerked round as a chair at the rear of the court went over with a loud clatter.

A husky voice shouted, 'No, dammee, I won't keep still! In God's name. I've given me eyes for the King! Ain't I allowed to speak the truth?'

The admiral rasped, 'Keep silent there! Or I will call the officer of the guard!'

But it was no use. Most of the visitors were on their feet, all talking and shouting at once. Bolitho saw that some had even climbed on to their chairs to see what was happening behind them.

The admiral sat speechless, while the rest of the court waited for him to carry out his threat.

The voices died away, and the crowded figures parted to allow the small artist to come aft to the table. He was leading the seaman who had been blinded aboard *Fawn* and who had already stated briefly what he knew of the preparations to cut the cable and escape the French artillery.

Now, in his ragged trousers and borrowed blue coat, with his head tilted as if to sniff out those nearest him, he approached the table.

The admiral said gravely, 'Very well, Richards.' He waited for the people to sit down again. 'What is this you wish to say?'

The seaman reached out and gripped the edge of the table, his bandaged eyes trained above the admiral's head.

'I were *there*, sir. Right there on th' quarterdeck with Cap'n Maulby!'

Nobody moved or spoke except the blind seaman named Richards.

Bolitho watched his hand as it moved vaguely in the air, saw his chest heaving as he relived those last terrible moments.

He said huskily, 'The Frogs had our measure, sir. We was all but dismasted an' with more'n half our brave lads cut down.'

The senior captain made as if to interrupt but the admiral's gold-laced cuff froze him to stillness.

'Th' sweeps was shot away, but all th' time Cap'n Maulby was shoutin' and cussin' in his same old style.' Beneath the stiff bandage the man's mouth twisted in a smile. 'An' he could cuss when given occasion, sir.' The smile faded. 'I were quartermaster an' alone at th' wheel. The master was down an' so was my mate, both killed. The first lieutenant were below havin' his arm off, an' it was then that th' cap'n turns to me an' cries, "*God damn that Colquhoun, Richards! He's done for us this day!*"' His head drooped and his fingers slipped from the table as he repeated brokenly, 'That's what he said. *He's done for us this day.*'

The admiral asked quietly, 'And then what happened?'

Richards waited for a few moments to compose himself. Still nobody moved or even whispered. Beyond the stern windows the wheeling gulls seemed too loud to be real.

Then he said, 'Mr Fox, th' second lieutenant, had just gone forrard, I think to seek some men for th' pumps. Several balls from th' Frog guns ashore came inboard an' killed Mr Midshipman Vasey. He were only fourteen but a good lad when he put his mind to it. When he fell, th' cap'n shouts to me, "*If Richard Bolitho was with us today as he wanted to be, then by God we'd show 'em, artillery or no*"!'

The admiral snapped, 'Are you absolutely certain? He said those very words?'

Richards nodded his head. 'Aye, sir. I'm not likely to forget 'em. For it was then that we was hit again and th' cro'jack yard came down to th' deck. It took Cap'n Maulby with it. He never even cried out.' He nodded again, very slowly. 'He were a good cap'n, even if he did cuss more'n most.'

'I see.' The admiral glanced at his senior captain. Then he asked, 'Do you recall anything more?'

'We struck th' reef, sir. Th' mizzen come down an' a bloody swivel, beggin' your pardon, sir, exploded on th' rail and took away me sight. I don't remember much else till I come-to aboard th' *Sparrow*.'

'Thank you.' The admiral gestured to a marine orderly. 'I will see that you are taken care of.'

Richards groped up to knuckle his forehead and then said, 'Thankee, sir. I hopes you'll forgive me, but I had to speak me piece.'

He was guided between the watching faces, and as the cabin door closed a slow murmur began to grow like combined anger.

The admiral snapped, 'I will not order you to be silent again!'

'Surely you're not going to believe that lying hound?' Colquhoun's voice was shrill. 'That . . . that . . . *half-wit*!'

The marine captain stepped forward to restrain him but faltered as the admiral said calmly, 'Pray continue, Captain Colquhoun.'

'Oh, I knew about Bolitho and Maulby all right! As thick as thieves!' Colquhoun had turned slightly, his arms outstretched as if to embrace the court. 'And I was well aware that Bolitho wanted all the glory for himself. That was why I sent him to the north and gave Maulby the chance to prove himself.' He was speaking very rapidly, and his face was shining with sweat. 'I saw through Bolitho's little game from the start, which was why he tried to condemn me. I knew he wanted to take the Frenchman for himself without giving me time to take up my proper attacking station. An attack overland and with boats indeed!' He stopped, his jaw hanging open with astonishment.

The admiral said coldly, 'So he did *not* agree with your plan of attack, Captain Colquhoun? Your testimony was a lie?'

Colquhoun turned and stared at him, his mouth still open, as if he had just been struck by a pistol ball and was beginning to feel its first searing agony.

'I—I . . .' He reeled away from the table. 'I only wanted . . .' he could not go on.

'March the accused out, Captain Reece!'

Bolitho watched Colquhoun as he lurched past the assembled officers, his gait less steady than the blind seaman's had been. It was incredible. Yet despite what had just happened he could sense neither release nor satisfaction. Shame, pity, he did not know what he really felt.

'You may stand down, Captain Bolitho.' The admiral eyed him calmly. 'It will be placed on record that you and your

223

people acted and behaved in the best traditions of the Service.' He turned to the cabin at large. 'Court will reassemble in two hours. That is all.'

Outside the stuffy cabin it felt like a different world. Faces swam around him, hands gripped him, and many voices called greetings and congratulations.

Tyrrell and Odell, with Buckle bringing up the rear, managed to guide him to a quieter part of the upper deck to await their respective boats. Bolitho saw the small artist and strode across to him.

'Thank you for what you did.' He held out his hand. 'I was hard on you earlier.' He looked round. 'Where is that man Richards? I would like to thank him, too. It took true courage to act as he did.'

'He's already gone across to a transport, Captain. I asked him to wait, but . . .'

He shrugged sadly.

Bolitho nodded. 'I understand. Here we all are, congratulating ourselves, while he has nothing to look forward to and no eyes to see what awaits him either.'

The little man smiled, his gaze on Bolitho's face, as if seeking to discover something.

'My name is Majendie. I would like to speak with you again.'

Bolithᴐ clapped him on the shoulder, forcing a smile.

'Then join me in my ship. If we must wait two hours, then I'd rather do it where I have a sense of freedom.'

The court assembled at the exact moment prescribed, and Bolitho found he was barely able to take his eyes from Colquhoun's sword. It was pointed towards him, the hilt on the opposite side of the table.

The senior captain's voice was lost, too, in his confused thoughts and memories. He heard fragments like 'hazarding the lives of men under your command, the ships used at your direction.' And later: '. . . did lay false evidence to smear the name of a King's officer and thereby bring discredit on this court.' There was a lot more, but Bolitho heard other voices intermingled with the cold summing-up. Maulby, Tyrrell, even Bethune, they were all in it. And above all, the blind

224

seaman, Richards. *He were a good cap'n.* Surely there was no better epitaph for any man?

He jerked from his thoughts as the admiral said, 'The sentence is that you be dismissed your ship and be confined under close arrest until such time you may be transported to England.'

Colquhoun stared at the grave-faced officers and then at his sword.

Dismissed his ship. Bolitho looked away. They should have hanged him. It would have been kinder.

A voice broke the silence, 'Prisoner and escort, quick *march*!'

It was over.

As the orderlies ushered the chattering spectators towards the quarterdeck, Rear-Admiral Christie came round the table and held out his hand.

'Well *done*, Bolitho.' He shook Bolitho's hand warmly. 'I have great hopes for young officers of your cut.' He saw Bolitho's uncertainty and smiled. 'It grieved me to treat you as I did. But I had to have your name cleared of that slur. Right or wrong, it would have marked you for the rest of your service.' He sighed wearily. 'Only Colquhoun could do it, and it took poor Richards to spark the flint.'

'Yes, sir. I see that now.'

The admiral picked up his hat and studied it.

'Come ashore with me tonight. The Governor is holding a reception. A ghastly business, but it does no harm to see 'em enjoying themselves.' He seemed to sense Bolitho's mood. 'Take it as an order!'

'Thank you, Sir Evelyn.'

Bolitho watched him as he walked to his adjoining cabin. An invitation ashore. The admiral could just as easily have sentenced him to ignominy, if fate had not stepped in to aid him.

He let out a long breath. When did you ever cease to learn about such complex matters?

Then he strode out to look for his gig amongst the many boats alongside.

*   *   *

The reception that evening proved to be even more breath-taking and unnerving than Bolitho had imagined it could be. As he handed his hat to a bewigged Negro footman and waited for Rear-Admiral Christie to exchange a few words with another flag officer, he stared up and around the great pillared hall, at the teeming throng of colourful figures who seemed to fill every inch of floor space and a handsome balcony as well. The scarlet coats of the military were very much in the majority, interspersed with velvets and brocades of their ladies, the familiar blue of sea-officers, although Bolitho noted with some alarm that most of the latter appeared to be admirals of one sort or another. Marine officers, too, their white facings and silver buttons distinguishing them from the soldiers, and so many civilians it was a wonder that New York had not come to a standstill. Along one side there were alcoves where Negro footmen and servants were kept busy at long tables, the contents of which were enough to make Bolitho think he was dreaming. The nation was at war, yet those tables were groaning under the weight of food and delicacies of every kind. Meats and huge portions of pie, tempting fruits and a glittering array of silver punch-bowls which were being refilled even as he watched.

Christie rejoined him and murmured, 'Take a good look at 'em, Bolitho. A man needs to know whom he is serving, as well as his cause!'

A footman in green livery met them at the top of the marble stairs, and after a cursory glance addressed the assembled guests in a voice which would have fitted a foretopman in a gale. 'Sir Evelyn Christie, Knight of the Bath, Rear-Admiral of the Red.' He did not bother to announce Bolitho, probably taking him as a mere aide, or some dependent relative.

Not that it mattered. There was no break in the tide of laughter and conversation, and hardly anybody turned to examine the newcomers.

Christie moved nimbly through the fringe of the crowd, nodding to a face here, pausing to pat a sleeve or bow to a lady there. It was hard to see him in his role that morning. President of the court. Answerable to nobody when he passed his sentence.

Bolitho followed the admiral's slight figure until they reached a table at the far end of the hall. Beyond it and the perspiring footmen a doorway opened on to a great lawn, where he could see a fountain shining in the reflected glow of all the lanterns.

'Well?' Christie waited until each had a heavy goblet in his hand. 'What do you make of 'em?'

Bolitho turned to study the press of figures by the alcove, hearing the strings of some invisible orchestra as they joined in a lively quadrille. How anyone could find room to dance he could not imagine.

'It's like a fairyland, sir.'

Christie regarded him with amusement. 'Fools' paradise is a better description!'

Bolitho tasted the wine. Like the goblet, it was perfect. He relaxed slightly. The question had put him on guard, but the admiral's comment had shown that he had no intention of testing him.

Christie added, 'A town under siege, and we must accept that is the true position here, is always unreal. It is crammed with refugees and tricksters, merchants out for quick profit who care little for which side they trade with. And as always in a campaign of any size, there are two armies.'

Bolitho watched him, momentarily forgetting the noise and bustle around him, the despair and anxiety of the morning. As he had believed from the first, Christie's austere appearance hid a rapier-sharp mind. A brain which could sift and examine each challenge and problem, discarding everything that was superfluous.

'*Two* armies, sir?'

The admiral signalled for fresh goblets. 'Drink your fill. You'll not find wine like this elsewhere. Yes, we have the military who daily face the enemy, search out his weakness or try to contain his attacks. Soldiers who live on their feet. Know nothing of clean beds or good food.' He smiled sadly. 'Like those you saved in Delaware Bay. *Real* soldiers.'

'And the others?'

Christie grimaced. 'Behind every great army there is the *organization*.' He gestured towards the crowd. 'The military government, the secretariat, and the traders who live off the fighting like leeches.'

Bolitho eyed the swaying figures outside the alcove with growing uncertainty. He had always mistrusted people of the sort described, but it seemed impossible that it was all so blatant, so dishonest as the admiral had said. And yet . . . he thought of the cheerful, chattering visitors at the court martial. Spectators to a man's disgrace, but seeing it only as something to break the boredom of their own world.

Christie watched him thoughtfully. 'God alone knows how this war will end. We are fighting too many enemies, over too vast a span of the world to hope for some spectacular victory. But you, and those like you, must be warned if we are to have any chance of honour, let alone mastery over our adversaries.'

The wine was very strong, and the heat of the hall helped to break Bolitho's caution.

'But, Sir Evelyn, surely here in New York, after all that has happened since the rebellion, they must be aware of the true facts?'

He shrugged, a weary gesture. 'The general staff is too busy with its own affairs to retain much concern for what is happening here. And the Governor, if we may call him so, spends so much time in chasing giddy young girls and enjoying his mounting riches, that he has no wish to alter matters. He was once an army quartermaster, therefore an accomplished thief, and is ably supported by a Lieutenant Governor who was originally a customs officer in a city which was renowned only for its smuggling!' He chuckled. 'So between them they have tied this place into a bag for their own booty. No merchant or shipmaster can enter or leave without permits, from which our *leaders* reap a rich profit. New York is crammed with refugees, and the Governor decided that city, church and college moneys should be gathered into a fund for their relief.'

Bolitho frowned. 'Surely *that* was in good faith?'

'Maybe. But most if it has been squandered away. Balls and dances, receptions such as this, misses and whores, hangers-on and favourites. It all takes a great deal of money and support.'

'I see.'

In fact he did not. When he thought of his ship, the daily

risk of injury and death with little comfort or relief, the manner in which every fighting man was facing a determined enemy, he was appalled.

Christie said, 'To me duty stands before all else. I would hang anyone who acted otherwise. But these . . .' he did not hide his contempt, 'these maggots deserve no loyalty. If we must fight a war, we should also ensure they have no gain from our sacrifice!'

Then he smiled, the sudden relaxing of the lines around his eyes and mouth altering him yet again.

'There, Bolitho, you have learned the next lesson, eh? First you command respect, then a ship. Next you achieve control of more and larger vessels. That is the way of ambition, without which no officer is worth a wet fuse to me.'

He yawned. 'Now I must be off.' He held up one hand. 'But you remain and continue your education.'

'Will you not stay to meet the Governor, sir?'

Something like panic at the thought of being left abandoned made him show his inner feelings.

Christie smiled cheerfully. 'Nobody will meet him tonight. He merely holds these affairs to pay off old debts and to keep his pot a'boiling.' He beckoned to a footman. 'So enjoy yourself. You have earned it, although I daresay you'd wish rather for London, eh?'

Bolitho grinned. 'Not London, sir.'

'Ah, of course.' The admiral watched the footman approaching with his hat and boatcloak. 'A son of the soil. I forgot.' Then with a nod he moved through the door to merge quickly with the deep shadows on the lawn.

Bolitho found an empty corner at the end of the table, and tried to decide what he should eat. He had to have something, for the wine was doing its work well. He felt unusually light-headed, although he knew that drink was not entirely to blame. By leaving him to fend for himself the admiral had momentarily cut the strings of control. He had given him his head to act and think as he wanted. He could not recall it ever happening like this before.

A thickset post-captain, his face blotchy with heat and good wine, thrust past him and carved a huge piece of pie, adding several other sorts of cold meat to his plate before any footman could assist him. Bolitho thought of Bethune. The plate would have satisfied even his appetite for several days.

The senior captain turned and focused his eyes on him.

'Ah. What ship?'

'*Sparrow*, sir.' Bolitho watched him squinting as if to clear his vision.

'Never heard of her.' He frowned. 'What's yer name, eh?'

'Richard Bolitho, sir.'

The captain shook his head. 'Never heard of *you* either.' He ambled back into the crowd, brushing some of the meat against a pillar without even pausing.

Bolitho smiled. In these surroundings you soon found a proper awareness of your status.

'Why, *Captain*!' The voice made him swing round. 'It is! I just *knew* it was you!'

Bolitho stared at the girl for several seconds without recognition. She was dressed in a beautiful, low-cut gown, the colour of tawny port wine, and her hair, which hung in ringlets across her bare shoulders, shone beneath the chandeliers like silk.

He exclaimed, 'Miss Hardwicke! I did not know you were here, in America.'

He felt as foolish as he sounded, but her sudden appearance had caught him entirely aback. She was lovely, more so than he remembered since that far-off day. When she had defied her uncle, General Blundell, had shouted and kicked as his seamen had carried her bodily from the Indiaman before his fight with the *Bonaventure*.

And yet she was exactly the same. The smile, half amused, partly mocking. The violet eyes which seemed to strip away his defences and leave him like some inarticulate ploughman.

She turned to the tall officer at her side, wearing a frogged jacket of the dragoons, and said, 'He was so young, so *serious*, I think all the ladies on board fell in love with the poor man.'

The dragoon eyed Bolitho coldly. 'I think we must hurry, Susannah. I would wish you to meet the general.'

She reached out and laid a white-gloved hand on Bolitho's sleeve.

'It is good to see you again! I have often thought about

you and your little ship.' Her smile faded and she became suddenly serious. 'You look well, Captain. Very well. A little older perhaps. A little less . . .' the smile crept back again, 'of the boy dressed as a man?'

He flushed, but was conscious of pleasure to match his confusion.

'Well, I suppose . . .'

But she was already turning away as two more escorts pushed from the jostling crowd to join her.

Then she seemed to make up her mind.

'Will you dine with me, Captain?' She studied him thoughtfully. 'I will send a servant with the invitation.'

'Yes.' The words came out in a rush. 'I would like that very much. Thank you.'

She gave a mock curtsy, bringing back the memory of their first meeting like a stab in the heart.

'Then it is settled.'

The crowd eddied and swayed and seemed to swallow her up completely.

Bolitho took another goblet and walked unsteadily towards the lawn. Susannah, the dragoon had called her. It was perfect for her.

He stopped beside the tinkling fountain and stared at it for several minutes. The reception had turned out to be a success after all, and made the morning seem just a blurred memory.

14. Join the Ladies

THREE DAYS after the Governor's reception the *Sparrow* was to all intents ready for sea again. Bolitho had carried out a careful inspection, and under Lock's anxious scrutiny had signed the final manifest for stores and supplies. The last days had been uneventful, almost lazy, and Bolitho found it easier to understand, if not share, New York's apparent lethargy. It was an unreal existence, with the war seen only at the end of a marching column of soldiers, or in some colourful account on the news-sheets.

The flotilla's other surviving sloop, *Heron*, had recently dropped anchor at Sandy Hook, and was now waiting hopefully for a similar overhaul.

On this particular forenoon Bolitho sat in his cabin enjoying a glass of good claret with *Heron*'s commander, Thomas Farr. The latter had been a lieutenant at their last meeting, but Maulby's death had given him a well-deserved promotion. He was elderly for his rank, probably ten years or so older than himself, Bolitho decided. A big, broad-shouldered man, uncouth, and with a ripe turn of phrase which reminded him vaguely of Tilby. He had come to his present appointment by a roundabout route. Sent to sea as a boy of eight years old, he had been in merchant service for most of his life. Coasters and mail-packets, Indiamen and humbler craft, he had eventually risen to command a collier brig out of Cardiff. With England embroiled in war he had offered his services to the Navy and been gratefully accepted. For if his manners and background marked him apart from many of his brother officers, his experience and skill in sail put him well ahead of them. Paradoxically, *Heron* was smaller than *Sparrow*, and like her commander had begun life as a merchantman. Consequently, her armament of fourteen guns was of lesser size. She had already gathered several good prizes, nonetheless.

Farr sprawled untidily on the stern bench and raised his glass to the sunlight.

'Bloody fine stuff! Though give me a tankard of English ale an' you can spit this against a wall!' He laughed and allowed Bolitho to pour another glass.

Bolitho smiled. How things had changed for all of them. Looking back to that moment at Antigua when he had gone to meet Colquhoun it was hard to recall just how the years and weeks had affected them as individuals. Then, as he had looked from Colquhoun's window in the headquarters building, he had seen the flotilla as a whole, had wondered what his new command would be like. So many other doubts and fears had plagued him on that morning.

Now, *Fawn* was gone, and *Bacchante* had sailed only the previous day to rejoin the fleet under Rodney. Her captain had been appointed from the flagship, and Bolitho wondered if Colquhoun had been able to watch her clear the anchorage from wherever he was being held in custody.

Only *Sparrow* and *Heron* remained now. Apart from the little schooner *Lucifer* of course, and she was almost a rule unto herself. She would stay on her stop-and-search patrols of small coasting craft, or continue probing into coves and creeks in search for enemy blockade-runners.

Farr watched him comfortably and remarked, 'Well, you are doing famously, I hear. Reception with the mighty, wine with the admiral! By the living Jesus, there'll be no saying where you'll end up. Probably on some ambassador's staff, with a dozen little girls to dance to your tune, eh?' He laughed loudly.

Bolitho shrugged. 'Not for me, I have seen enough.'

He thought quickly of the girl. She had not written to him. Nor had he seen her, although he had made it his business to pass by way of her residence when he had been ashore on ship's affairs.

It was a fine house, not much smaller than where he had attended the reception. There had been soldiers at the gates, and he guessed that its owner held some sort of government appointment. He had tried to tell himself not to be foolish, so naïve as to expect someone of her background to remember

233

him beyond a momentary meeting. In Falmouth the Bolitho family was much respected, its land and property giving work and substance to many. Bolitho's own recent gains in prize money had made him feel independent for the first time in his life, so that he had lost sight of reality when it came to people like Susannah Hardwicke. Her family probably spent more in a week than he had earned since taking command of *Sparrow*. She was accustomed to travel, even when others were held still by war or lack of means. She would know the best people, and her name would be accepted in any of the great houses from London to Scotland. He sighed. He could not see her as the lady of the house in Falmouth. Entertaining ruddy-faced farmers and their wives, attending local fairs and the rough and tumble of a community which lived so close to nature.

Farr seemed to sense his mood and asked, 'What about the war, Bolitho? Where is it getting us?' He waved his glass. 'Sometimes I get to thinking we will go on patrolling an' running after bloody smugglers till we die of old age.'

Bolitho stood up and moved restlessly to the windows. There was plenty of evidence of power nearby. Ships-of-the-line, frigates and all the rest. And yet they gave an appearance of waiting. But for what?

He said, 'Cornwallis seems intent on retaking Virginia. His soldiers are doing well, I hear.'

'You don't sound too damn confident!'

Bolitho looked at him. 'The army is pinched back to its lines. They can no longer rely on supplies or support by land. Everything must move by sea. It is no way for an army to fight.'

Farr grunted. 'Not our concern. You worry too much. Anyway, I think we should leave 'em all to their own games. We should go home an' smash hell out of the Frogs. The bloody Dons would soon call for peace, an' the Dutch have no liking for their so-called allies anyway. *Then* we can come back to America an' have another go at 'em.'

Bolitho smiled. 'I fear we *would* die of old age if we followed that course.'

He heard a shouted challenge, the scrape of a boat alongside.

He realized that his mind had recorded it, but that he felt at ease, even remote. When he had first come aboard there had been neither sound nor event that had not caught his immediate attention. Perhaps at last he was accepting his true role.

Graves appeared in the cabin door with a familiar sealed envelope.

'Guardboat, sir.' He darted a glance at *Heron*'s commander. 'Sailing orders, I expect.'

Bolitho nodded. 'Carry on, Mr Graves. I will inform you directly.'

The lieutenant hesitated.

'This letter was delivered also, sir.'

It was small, and the handwriting was almost hidden by a seal. *Office of the Military Government.*

As the door closed Farr asked thickly, '*Graves?* No bloody relative of our admiral, I trust!'

Bolitho grinned. With Rodney in the West Indies, and further restricted by bad health, the command of American waters came under the flag of Rear-Admiral Thomas Graves. Lacking the wisdom of Rodney, the hard-won respect of Hood, he was looked upon by most of the fleet's officers as a fair but cautious commander. He believed utterly in the rigid rules of fighting, and had never been known to change one jot of their interpretation. Several senior captains had put down suggestions for improving the system of signalling between ships engaged in close action. Graves had said icily, according to the many stories circulating amongst the fleet, 'My captains know their function. That should be enough for any man.'

Bolitho replied, 'No. Perhaps it would be better if he were. We might know more of what is happening.'

Farr stood up and belched. 'Good wine. Better company. I'll leave you to yer sealed orders. If all the written despatches from all the admirals in the world was laced together we'd have enough to cover the Equator, an' that's a fact! God's teeth, I sometimes think we choke on paper!'

He shambled out of the cabin, refusing Bolitho's offer to see him over the side by saying, 'If I can't manage on me own by now, then it's time I was weighted with a pair of round-shot and dropped overboard!'

235

Bolitho settled down at the table and slit open the canvas envelope, although his eyes rested mainly on the smaller one.

The orders were briefer than usual. Being in all respects ready for sea, His Britannic Majesty's Sloop-of-War *Sparrow* would weigh and proceed at the earliest convenience the following day. She would carry out an independent patrol, eastward to Montauk Point at the top of Long Island and thence via Block Island to the approaches of Newport itself.

He contained his rising excitement with some difficulty and made himself concentrate on the sparse requirements of the patrol. He was not to become involved with enemy forces other than at his own discretion. His eyes rested on the last words. How they reminded him of Colquhoun. So brief, yet concealing the very precariousness of his own position should he act wrongly.

But here at last was something direct to carry out. Not merely harrying blockade-runners or seeking some sly privateer. This was French territory. The fringe of the second greatest sea-power on earth. Beneath the flag captain's scrawling signature he saw that Rear-Admiral Christie had added his own. How typical of the man. A sign of his trust, and the extent of his arm.

He stood up and rapped on the skylight.

'Midshipman of the watch!'

He saw Bethune's face above him and called, 'My compliments to the first lieutenant. I would like to see him at once.' He paused. 'I thought you were on watch earlier?'

Bethune dropped his eyes. 'Aye, sir. That is true. But . . .'

Bolitho said quietly, 'In future you will take your watches as laid down. I suppose Mr Fowler should have been on duty?'

'I promised him, sir.' Bethune looked uneasy. 'I owed him a relief.'

'Very well. But remember my orders. I'll have no *retired* officers in this ship!'

He sat down again. He should have noticed what was happening. Poor Bethune was no match for the Fowlers of this world. He smiled in spite of his concern. He was a fine one to talk.

He slit open the second envelope and came up with a jerk against the table.

My dear Captain. I would be so pleased if you could dine with us this evening. I feel wretched at this inexcusable delay and hope for instant forgiveness. As you read this letter I am watching your ship through my uncle's telescope. So that I shall not be held in suspense, please show yourself.

It was signed, *Susannah Hardwicke.*

Bolitho stood up and winced as his skull collided with a deck beam. Pausing only to lock his orders in the cabin strong-box, he hurried out of the door and up the companion ladder. Her uncle's telescope. So General Blundell was here, too. It would explain the sentries at the gates.

But even this fact did not repress him. He almost collided with Tyrrell as he came limping aft, his arms spattered with grease.

'Sorry I was adrift when you called for me, sir. I was in th' cable tier.'

Bolitho smiled. 'Taking the opportunity of an empty tier to look for rot, eh?'

Tyrrell rubbed his thigh. 'Aye. But she's fine. Sound as a bell.'

Bolitho walked to the nettings and shaded his eyes against the fierce glare. The distant houses were almost lost in haze, their outlines quivering and intermingling as if they were melting in the heat.

Tyrrell watched him questioningly.

'Something wrong, sir?'

Bolitho beckoned to Bethune and took his telescope. It was no better. The one trained upon *Sparrow* was probably a huge affair. Very slowly he raised his arm and waved it from side to side.

Behind him Tyrrell and Bethune stood stockstill, each as puzzled as the other by the captain's strange behaviour.

Bolitho turned and saw Tyrrell's face. 'Er, I was just waving to someone.'

Tyrrell looked past him at the anchored ships and busy harbour craft.

'I see, sir.'

'No you don't, Jethro, but no matter.' He clapped his shoulder. 'Come below and I will tell you what we are about.

237

You will be in charge of the ship this evening, for I am dining ashore.'

A slow grin spread across the lieutenant's face. 'Oh, I *see*, sir!'

They were examining a chart and discussing the sailing orders when they heard Bethune yell, 'Avast there! Stand still, that man!' Then there was a splash and more shouts along the gun deck.

Bolitho and Tyrrell hurried to the quarterdeck again to find Bethune and most of the unemployed hands lining the larboard gangway or clinging to the shrouds.

A man was in the water, arms striking out strongly, his dark hair glossy in the spray and sunlight.

Bethune panted, 'It was Lockhart, sir! He dived overboard before I could stop him!'

Tyrrell murmured, 'A good seaman. Never any trouble. I know him well.'

Bolitho kept his eyes on the swimmer.

'A colonist?'

'Aye. Came from Newhaven some years back. He's done it now, poor devil.' There was no anger in Tyrrell's voice. If anything it was pity.

Bolitho heard the men near him exchanging guesses at the swimmer's success of getting ashore. It was a long way to go.

He had known many deserters during his life at sea. Often he had found room for sympathy, although he had thought their actions to be wrong. Few men would volunteer for the harsh demands of service in a King's ship, especially as nobody ever knew for sure if he would regain his home in safety. Seaports were full of those who had returned. Cripples and men made old before their time in many cases. But as yet, no one had found a better way of crewing the fleet. Once pressed, most men accepted it, could even be relied upon to take others by similar methods. The sailor's old rule, 'If I'm here, why not him?' carried a lot of weight in ships-of-war.

But this was different. The seaman, Lockhart, had seemed nothing out of the ordinary. A good worker and rarely adrift for his watch or station. Yet all the while he must have been brooding over his proper homeland, and the stay in New York had done the rest. Even now, as he thrashed steadily past an anchored two-decker, he was no doubt thinking only of his goal. Some vague mental picture of house and family, or parents who had almost forgotten what he looked like.

A faint crack came from the two-decker's beakhead, and Bolitho saw a red-coated marine already ramming another ball into his musket for a further shot at the lone swimmer.

A growl of anger came from *Sparrow*'s seamen. Whatever they thought of the man's desertion, or of the man himself, had nothing to do with their reaction. He was one of their own, and the marine sentry was momentarily an enemy.

Yule, the gunner, muttered, 'That damn bullock should be shot down hisself, the bloody bastard!'

The marine did not fire again, but sauntered to the end of his little platform to watch the swimmer, like a wildfowler who has given his quarry best for the time being. Or so it appeared. Then as a guardboat swept round the stern of another two-decker, Bolitho knew why he had not bothered to shoot.

The longboat was moving swiftly, the oars sending it through the glittering water like a blue fish. In the sternsheets he saw several marines, a midshipman with a raised telescope trained on the seaman.

Yule observed dourly, "E'll not escape now.'

Tyrrell said, 'It's out of our hands.'

'Aye.'

Bolitho felt suddenly heavy, the pleasure of the letter spoiled by this man's despair. Nobody who had *run* from a King's ship could expect mercy. It was to be hoped he was hanged rather than face the horror of flogging round the fleet. He chilled. If he was to be hanged . . . He stared up at *Sparrow's* mainyard, his eyes desperate. There was no doubt where the execution would be carried out. Even Christie would make sure of that. An example. A warning clear to all aboard and throughout the nearby ships. He tried not to watch the guardboat as it swept down on the tiny, bobbing head.

His own friends, *Sparrow*'s loyal seamen, would be forced to witness the halter being set around his neck before they, and they alone, were ordered to run him up to the yard. After all they had endured together, this sickening act might drive a

239

wedge between officers and men and destroy what they had achieved.

Tyrrell gasped, 'Look, sir!'

Bolitho snatched a glass and trained it beyond the guardboat. He was just in time to see the man, Lockhart, treading water, turning to stare either at the boat or perhaps at *Sparrow* herself. Then, even as the boat's oars backed water and a marine groped over the stemhead for the man's hair, he threw up his hands and disappeared beneath the surface.

Nobody spoke, and Bolitho found himself holding his breath, perhaps like the man who had vanished so suddenly. Sailors were usually poor swimmers. Perhaps he had got cramp. In a moment he would break surface nearby and the guardboat would haul him on board. Seconds, minutes passed, and then at a shouted command the guardboat resumed its leisurely patrol between the anchored ships.

Bolitho said quietly, 'I thank God for that. If he had to suffer, I am glad it was gently done.'

Tyrrell watched him dully. 'That's true.' He turned with sudden anger on the gunner. 'Mr Yule! Clear these idlers off th' gangway or I'll find 'em some harder work for their wits to dwell on!'

He was unusually disturbed, and Bolitho wondered if he was comparing his own fate with that of the drowned seaman.

He said, 'Make an entry in the log, Mr Tyrrell.'

'Sir?' Tyrrell faced him grimly. 'As a deserter?'

Bolitho looked past him at the seamen as they wandered towards the gun deck again.

'We do not *know* for certain he was deserting. Mark him as *Discharged—Dead*.' He walked to the hatch. 'His relatives will have enough to bear without the weight of shame also.'

Tyrrell watched him go, his breathing returning slowly to normal. It would not help Lockhart. He was beyond reach. But Bolitho's order would ensure that his name carried no stigma, and his loss would be recorded with those who had fallen in battle, in fights which he had also suffered without complaint. It was a small distinction. But even so, he knew that only Bolitho would have thought of it.

* * *

240

When Bolitho climbed from his gig he was astonished to find a smartly painted carriage waiting for him on the jetty. A liveried Negro doffed his tricorn hat and beamed hugely.

'Good evenin', Sah.' He opened the carriage door with a flourish while Stockdale and the gig's crew watched in silent admiration.

Bolitho paused. 'Er, do not wait, Stockdale. I will return to the ship in a local boat.'

He was strangely elated, and conscious of watching towns-folk on the road above the jetty, an envious glance from a passing marine major.

Stockdale touched his hat. 'If you says so, sir. I *could* come along with you . . .'

'No. I'll have full need of you tomorrow.' He felt suddenly reckless and pulled a coin from his pocket. 'Here, buy some grog for the gig's crew. But not too much for safety's sake, eh?'

He climbed into the coach and sank back against the blue cushions as with a jerk the horses took the first strain at their harness.

With his hat on his knees he watched the passing houses and people, Stockdale, even the ship, temporarily forgotten. Once, when the coach reined to a halt to allow a heavy wagon to cross ahead of it, he heard a faraway murmur of cannon fire. It was a fine evening, and the steady westerly wind was dry and warm. Sounds carried easily in such conditions. Even so, it was hard to connect the distant gunfire with the brightly lit houses, the occasional snatches of music and song from taverns along the road. Some army battery testing its guns perhaps. But more likely a nervous duel between opposing pickets where the two armies lay in watchful readiness.

It did not take long to reach the house, and as he stepped down from the coach he realized there were other guests arriving, too. Again he called himself a fool for imagining he alone would be entertained this evening.

Servants glided from the shadows, and like magic his hat and boatcloak were spirited away.

A footman opened some doors and announced, 'Captain Richard Bolitho of His Britannic Majesty's Ship *Sparrow*.'

How different from the reception, he thought. As he walked

into a fine, high-ceilinged room he was conscious of comfort and luxury mixed with an air of intimacy which had been lacking before.

At the end of the room General Sir James Blundell watched his approach in silence, and then called gruffly, 'You are an unexpected guest, Bolitho.' His heavy features yielded slightly. 'My niece told me of your arrival.' He thrust out his hand. 'You are welcome here.'

The general had changed very little. Heavier perhaps, but otherwise the same man. In one hand he was holding a brandy glass, and Bolitho was reminded of his stay aboard *Sparrow*, of his obvious contempt for the men who had carried him to safety.

Something of their first meeting must have circulated amongst his friends, for upon Blundell's show of greeting the room came alive again with laughter and noisy conversation. It was as if they had all been waiting to see how Blundell would react. Bolitho's own feelings were of course unimportant. He could always be told to leave.

Bolitho felt the girl's hand on his arm and turned to find her smiling up at him. With a nod to her uncle she steered him towards the other side of the room, the guests moving aside for her as if she were royalty.

She said, 'I saw you today. Thank you for coming.' She patted his cuff. 'I thought you were splendid just now. Uncle can be rather troublesome.'

Bolitho returned her smile. 'I think I can appreciate that. After all, he lost a great deal of bullion because of me.'

She wrinkled her nose. 'I have no doubt he will have recovered it by insurance elsewhere.' She gestured to a servant. 'Some wine before dinner.'

'Thank you.'

He saw several officers, mostly military, watching him intently. Envy, resentment, curiosity, it was all there.

She said, 'Sir James is Adjutant General now. I came out here with him after our return to England.' She watched his face as he sipped the wine. 'I am glad I came. England is full of woe because of the war.'

Bolitho tore his mind from what she had just said of her

uncle. Christie had already spoken scathingly about the Governor and his assistant. With Blundell involved in controlling the city, there seemed little hope of improvement.

As the girl turned to curtsy to a white-haired man and his lady he let his eyes devour her as if seeing her for the last time. The curve of her neck as she bowed to her guests, the way her hair seemed to float across her bared shoulders. It was beautiful hair, Golden brown, like the wing of a young thrush.

He smiled awkwardly as she looked up at him.

'*Really*, Captain! You make a girl feel indecent the way you stare so!' She laughed. 'I suppose you sailors are so long away from civilization you cannot control your ways!' She clutched his arm, her mouth quivering with amusement. 'Do not fret! There is no need to be so serious about it. I really must teach you to accept what is there, to enjoy what is yours by right.'

'I am sorry. You are most likely right about me.' He looked at the marble floor and grinned. 'At sea I can stand upright. Here, I feel as if the deck is moving!'

She stepped back and regarded him searchingly. 'Well, I shall have to see what can be done about that.' She tapped her lips with a slim fan. 'Everyone is talking about you, what you have done, how you faced that awful court martial and made fools of them.'

'It was not exactly like that . . .'

She ignored him. 'Of course *they* will not mention any of this. Some are probably afraid you will turn into a wild, bloodthirsty sea-dog!' She laughed gaily. 'Others see in your success something of their own failure.'

A footman was whispering to the general and she added quickly, 'I will have to leave you to your own devices for dinner. I am hostess tonight.'

He said, 'Oh, I thought . . .' To cover his confusion he asked, 'Is Lady Blundell not here, too?'

'She stays in England. My uncle's habits are those of a soldier. I think she is content to keep them well away from her.' She held his arm again. 'But do not look so sad. I will see you later. We must talk of your future. I know people who can help you. Put you where you deserve, instead of . . .' She did not finish.

A gong boomed and the footman intoned, 'My lords, ladies and gentlemen. Dinner is now served.'

They followed the general and his niece into an even greater room, and Bolitho found himself paired off with a dark-haired little woman who was apparently the wife of a staff officer. He was not present, and with something like gloom Bolitho thought he would be saddled with her for the rest of the evening.

The dinner matched the room. Every course larger, more xtravagantly prepared than the one before. His stomach had ^eong become used to the sparse fare aboard ship and the vary-ling efforts of many sea-cooks. No one else seemed to find difficulty, however, and he could only marvel at the way the plates emptied without any apparent break in conversation.

There were many toasts, with the wines as varied as their reasons for drinking them.

After the loyal toast to King George there were all the usual ones. *Death to the French. Confusion to our enemies. A curse on Washington.* As the wine flowed they became as meaningless as they were incoherent.

The lady at Bolitho's side dropped her fan, but as he bent to collect it she reached below the tablecloth and seized his wrist, holding it against her thigh for several seconds. It seemed like an hour, and he thought every eye at the table must be on him. But she was the only one, and her face was filled with such desire that he could almost feel her control slipping away.

He returned the fan and said, 'Easy, ma'am, there are quite a few courses yet.'

She stared at him, open-mouthed, and then gave a secret smile.

'God what it is to find a real man!'

Bolitho forced himself to take another portion of chicken, if only to regain his wits. He could feel her knee pressing into his leg, and was very aware that whenever she required some-thing from the table she seemed to need it from across his arm. Each time she lingered over the motion, letting her shoulder or breast touch for just a few moments more every time.

He glanced desperately along the table and saw the girl

watching him. It was hard to understand her expression when she was so far away. Part amused, part watchful.

His companion was saying casually, 'My husband is much older than I. He cares more for his damned office than for me.'

She reached for some butter, allowing her breast to touch his sleeve while she kept her eyes on his.

'I expect you have been many places, Captain. How I *wish* I could take a ship somewhere. Away from this place. And *him*.'

At last the meal was over, and with a scraping of chairs the men rose to allow their ladies to withdraw. Even at the last moment Bolitho's companion persisted with her campaign, like a frigate cutting out a ship which was totally outmatched from the start.

She whispered, 'I have a room here. I will send a servant to guide you.'

As she moved from the table he saw her stagger but recover instantly. It would take more than wine to break her, he thought anxiously.

The doors closed again and the men moved their seats closer to the head of the table.

More brandy, and some black cheroots which Blundell said had come from *some damned rascal who tried to avoid his dues.*

'I hear you are now on our local patrols, Bolitho.' Blundell's harsh voice reduced the other guests to attentive silence.

'Yes, Sir James.'

Bolitho eyed him evenly. Blundell was well informed, considering he had only received his orders that forenoon.

'Good. We need a few captains with the will to guard our lifelines, what!' Blundell's features were crimson from the extent of his dinner. 'These damn Yankees have had too much their own way, I say!'

There was a growl of approval, and someone called tipsily, 'Thash th' bloody truth, shir!' He shrank under Blundell's withering gaze.

Bolitho asked quickly, 'Colonel Foley, sir. Is he still in America?'

'He has a battalion under Cornwallis.' Blundell seemed disinterested. 'Best bloody place for him, too.'

Bolitho allowed the conversation to flow around him like a protective cloak. He heard little about the war. Horse breeding, and the cost of keeping house in New York. The affair of some unfortunate artillery captain who had been found in bed with a dragoon's wife. The growing difficulty of obtaining good brandy, even at smuggler's prices.

Bolitho thought of Christie's summing up. *Two armies*, he had said. How true it now seemed. Colonel Foley, whether he was a likeable man or not, was one of those fighting for his country's cause, and his life. Around this table sat a goodly proportion of the other sort. Spoiled, cosseted and completely selfish, he wished he could be rid of them.

Blundell heaved himself upright. 'We will join the ladies, God help us!'

When Bolitho glanced at the ornate French clock he saw it was almost midnight. It seemed incredible that time could pass so swiftly. But despite the hour there was no lessening in the pace. A small string orchestra struck up a lively dance, and laughing noisily the guests pushed and jostled towards the sound of music.

Bolitho walked slowly through the connecting rooms, watching for Susannah Hardwicke and keeping a wary eye open for his earlier companion.

As he passed a book-lined study he saw Blundell speaking with a group of men, most of whom were prosperous-looking civilians. One, very tall and broad-shouldered, stood partly in shadow, but the side of his face which was visible in the candlelight made Bolitho start with shock then pity. It had been scoured away, the skin burned almost to the bone from hairline to chin, so that it had the appearance of some grotesque mask. He seemed to feel Bolitho's eyes on him, and after a quick glance turned his back, hiding himself in shadow.

No wonder he had not joined the others at dinner. It was easy to imagine the agony of that disfigurement, the torment which had left him so scarred.

'Ah, there you are!' She came out of another room and rested her hand on his arm. 'Take me into the garden.'

They walked in silence, and he felt her dress swishing against his legs, the warmth of her body.

'You were absolutely splendid, Captain.' She paused and looked at him, her eyes very bright. 'That poor woman. I thought for an instant you would fall to her.'

'Oh, you saw.' Bolitho felt uneasy. 'She has gone, it seems.'

'Yes.' She led him into the garden. 'I sent her off.' She laughed, the sound carrying through the shrubs like an echo. 'I cannot have her interfering with *my* captain, now can I?'

'I hope you were easy with her?'

'Actually, she burst into tears. It was all rather pathetic.'

She turned inside his arm, her full dress spreading out behind her like pale gold.

'I must leave you now, Captain.'

'But . . . but I thought we were going to talk?'

'Later.' She studied him gravely. 'I have plans for your future, as I told you earlier, did I not?'

'I weigh anchor tomorrow.' He felt wretched. Helpless.

'I *know* that, silly!' She reached up and touched his lips. 'Do not frown. I cannot allow it. When you come back I will introduce you to some friends of mine. You will not regret it.' Her gloved fingers moved gently to his cheek. 'And neither, I trust, shall I.'

A servant appeared through the gloom. 'Carriage ready, Missy.'

She nodded. To Bolitho she said, 'After you have left I will try and clear these dreary people from the house.' She tilted her head and faced him calmly. 'You may kiss my shoulder, if you wish.'

Her skin was surprisingly cool, and as soft as a peach.

She twisted away from him and called, 'Be good, Captain, and take care of yourself. When you return I will be here.' Then she laughed and ran lightly up the terrace into the house.

The coach was waiting for him as he walked dazedly through the shadowed garden and on to the carriageway. His hat and cloak were on the seat, and strapped to the boot was a large wooden box.

The footman's teeth shone in a white crescent. 'Missy Susannah had the kitchen pack some food for you, Sah.' He chuckled. 'Nothin' but the best, she said.'

Bolitho climbed into the coach and sank against the cushions.

He could still feel her skin against his mouth, smell the perfume from her hair. A girl who could drive a man mad, even if he was not halfway there already.

At the end of the jetty he found a waterman nodding over his oars, and had to call several times to attract his attention.

'Wot ship, sir?'

'*Sparrow*.'

Just saying the name helped to steady his racing throughts. Before he stepped down into the dory he turned to look at the coach, but it had already disappeared. Like one more part of the dream.

The waterman was grumbling to himself as he hauled the heavy box down the steps. Not enough to offend a ship's captain, but enough to add slightly to his fare.

Bolitho wrapped his cloak around him and felt the sea-breeze cold against his face. Still westerly. It would be good to get away again. If only to find time to collect himself and examine his hopes for the future.

15. A Good Likeness

THE MISSION to investigate the strength of French shipping at Newport proved to be more difficult for *Sparrow* than Bolitho had expected. The passage from Sandy Hook to the eastern extremes of Long Island showed nothing but promise for a quick completion and an equally swift return. But the weather decided otherwise, and in a savage westerly gale the little sloop was driven and battered continuously, so that Bolitho had to run with it rather than risk damage to spars and canvas.

Even when the wind moderated it took many more days to beat back again, and hardly an hour passed without the need to shorten sail or lay the ship on a tack which would take her away rather than toward her goal.

New York's entertainment seemed a long way behind, and Bolitho found the reality of driving his ship against wind and tide more than enough to occupy his energy. Even so, he found plenty of time to think about Susannah Hardwicke. Pacing the deck, hair whipping in the wind, his shirt often drenched with spray, he remembered their parting, the hint of an embrace which he could recall as clearly as if it had just occurred.

He suspected that his officers knew or guessed what had happened in New York, if only because of their careful silence.

The drudgery of fighting against the wind, the constant demands on every man aboard, were eased in part by the presence of their passenger. Rupert Majendie, true to his word, had arrived within minutes of weighing, complete with sketching and painting materials, and a repertoire of stories which did more than pay for his keep on board. When the sea and wind calmed he would be seen with his pad, sketching seamen at their daily tasks or catching them at their relaxation off watch, dancing or making small models and scrimshaw work. If the weather was less friendly he would disappear below to find fresh scope for his busy hands with only a swinging lantern to guide his pencil or brush. He and Dalkeith had become firm friends, which was hardly surprising. Each came from another sphere of culture and high intellect, with far more to discuss than the average sailor.

At the end of three long weeks, and with each day adding to his frustration, Bolitho decided to wait no more. He called Tyrrell to the cabin and unrolled his chart.

'We will close with the shore at daylight tomorrow, Jethro. The wind is still strong, but I see no other choice.'

Tyrrell let his eyes move across the chart. The approaches to Rhode Island were always a problem with a prevailing westerly wind. To be caught in a full gale might mean being driven eastwards again, and once within the jaws of the mainland and Newport itself there would be little room for manœuvre. Under normal conditions it required patience and understanding. But with the French in control of the area it was something else entirely.

As if reading his thoughts, Bolitho said quietly, 'I'd not wish to be caught on a lee shore. But if we stay out here in open water, we might as well admit failure.'

'Aye.' Tyrrell straightened his back. 'I doubt th' Frogs'll have much in th' way of ships anyway. They depend on their batteries to defend themselves.'

Bolitho smiled, some of the strain slipping from his face. 'Good. Pass the word. I'll want the very best eyes at the mastheads tomorrow.'

But true to Buckle's gloomy prediction, the next morning was something of a disappointment. The sky was clouded over and the wind which made the topsails bluster and crack despite their trim, told there was rain nearby. And yet the air felt sultry and oppressive, affecting the hands as they went to their stations for changing tack. The welcome stay in harbour, followed by the nervous uncertainty of thrashing this way and that at the wind's discretion, had taken their toll. There were plenty of curses and not a few blows from boatswain's mates before *Sparrow* laid herself over on the larboard tack, her plunging beakhead pointing towards the shore once again.

A grey day. Bolitho gripped the weather nettings and

mopped his forehead with his shirt-sleeve. His skin and clothing were wringing wet, as much from sweat as from flying spray.

Only Majendie seemed content to remain on deck willingly, his pencil busy, his thin body and jutting beard dripping with moisture.

'Land ho! Fine on the weather bow!'

Bolitho tried not to show his satisfaction and relief. With the dull visibility and blustery wind you could not be too secure with mere calculations. He looked up at the masthead pendant. The wind had backed slightly. He stared at the pendant until his eyes watered. There was no doubt about it. Good for a steady approach. Not so comforting if they had to turn and run. 'Bring her up a point, Mr Buckle.'

'Aye, aye, sir.'

Buckle dabbed his face with a handkerchief before passing his orders. He would be well aware of the difficulties, Bolitho thought. There was no sanity in worrying him further.

To Majendie he said, 'I hope you are getting it all down. You will make your fortune when you return to England.'

Buckle yelled, 'Nor' nor'-east, sir! Full an' bye!'

'Very good. Hold her so.'

Bolitho walked a couple of paces and thought of the girl in New York. What would she think of him now? Crumpled and soaked to the skin, his shirt more patches than original cloth. He smiled to himself, not seeing Majendie's pencil as it recorded his mood.

Tyrrell limped up the deck and joined him by the nettings.

'I reckon that Newport is 'bout five miles off th' starboard bow, sir.' He looked up with surprise as a shaft of watery sunlight played across the bucking hull like a lantern beam. 'Hell, you can never tell in these waters.'

'Deck thar! Ships at anchor to the nor'-east!'

Tyrrell rubbed his hands. 'Frogs may be assembling a convoy. Our inshore squadron'll catch 'em if we carry th' word fast enough.'

The lookout yelled again. 'Six, no, *eight* sail-o'-the-line, sir!'

Graves staggered from the rail as *Sparrow* lurched sickeningly into a deep trough.

'The man's mad!' He spluttered as spray burst above the

251

nettings and cascaded over him like hail. 'A couple of frigates at most, if you ask me!'

Bolitho tried to ignore the buzz of speculation and doubt around him. De Grasse had a powerful fleet in the West Indies, that was well known. His subordinate, de Barras, who commanded at Newport, had no such strength. His usefulness was placed in frigates and smaller craft and in quick forays against British coastal trade. De Barras had made one attempt to challenge the New York forces off Cape Henry earlier in the year, but the action had been desultory and ineffective. He had retired to his defences and had remained there.

He said, 'Aloft with you, Mr Graves. Tell me what you see.'

Graves hurried to the shrouds muttering, 'That fool. Can't be ships-of-the-line. Can't be.'

Bolitho stared after him. Graves was acting very strangely. It was as if he dreaded what he might discover. Afraid? No. That seemed unlikely. He had been aboard long enough to know the risks and rewards of the game.

'Deck there!' It was another seaman clinging high above the mizzen yard. 'Sail on the larboard quarter!'

'Damn!' Tyrrell snatched a telescope and hurried with it to the taffrail.

Mist and spray, the distance made worse by *Sparrow*'s drunken motion, it took time to find the newcomer.

Tyrrell snapped, 'Frigate. No doubt, sir.'

Bolitho nodded. The other ship was clawing close inshore, coming around the jutting headland with every available sail set to the wind.

Buckle cupped his hands. 'Stand by to come about!'

'*Belay that!*' Bolitho's voice held the master motionless. 'We have got this far. Let us see what there is to see and *then* run.'

Graves came lurching from the gangway, his shirt torn from his rapid descent.

He gasped, 'He was right, sir. Eight of the line. Maybe two frigates, and a whole clutter of supply ships anchored closer in.'

Bolitho thought of his talk with Farr at Sandy Hook, his own reaction at seeing the British two-deckers nearby. Waiting, he had thought, but for what? And were these Frenchmen doing likewise?

Tyrrell said, 'Can't be none of de Grasse's ships, sir. Our patrols, even blind ones, would've seen 'em!'

Bolitho met his stare. 'I agree. It's a gathering for something. We must inform the admiral directly.'

Buckle shouted, 'Frigate closing fast, sir. Less than three miles, by my reckoning.'

Bolitho nodded. 'Very well, run up French colours, and prepare to come about.'

The flag rose swiftly to the gaff, to be greeted by an immediate blast of cannon from the frigate's forecastle.

Bolitho smiled grimly. 'He is not deceived. So hoist our own, if you please.'

Buckle crossed to Bolitho's side, his features screwed tight with worry.

'I think maybe we should wear ship, sir. That Frenchman'll be up to us afore we knows it otherwise.'

Bolitho shook his head. 'We would lose too much time. The frigate might chase us all the way to Nantucket or run us aground.' He swung on Graves. 'Clear away the bow-chasers. Load but do not run out.' He clapped him on the forearm, seeing him start with alarm. 'Lively, man! Or Mr Frenchman'll be aboard for grog!'

Men scampered wildly to their stations, some pausing only to peer over the hammock nettings at the other ship which was driving purposefully towards the larboard quarter. She was much nearer, but in the bursting spray her hull was almost lost to view. Only her bulging courses and topsails displayed her captain's eagerness to do battle.

'Ready about!' Bolitho had his hands on his hips as he peered aloft at the slashing pendant. 'Stand by on the quarter-deck!'

'Put the helm down!' He felt the deck stagger, and wondered how *Sparrow* would appear to the enemy. Running? Preparing to fight?

He almost fell as the ship heeled and tilted still further to the thrust of sail and rudder.

'Helm a'lee, sir!' Buckle added his own weight to the wheel.

Headsails flailing about like mad things, yards bending to the contest between braces and booming canvas, it was a

253

picture of confusion as *Sparrow* heeled sickeningly round into the wind. The sea surged up and over the beakhead, and men fell cursing and sprawling, some being washed into the gun deck scuppers like corpses.

Majendie clung to the nettings, his pad already sodden with spray as he stared transfixed at the sloop's wild turn across the wind.

Tyrrell's voice rose above the pandemonium like a trumpet. 'Braces there! Heave, my lads! Bosun, drive 'em hard today!'

Bolitho tried not to watch his ship's torment, but concentrated instead on the frigate. As *Sparrow* swung and plunged round on to her new tack, the wet sails thrusting her over until the lee gangway was awash, he saw the enemy's topmasts appear suddenly above the starboard bow. Barely a mile between them, but the violent turn had had the desired effect. Instead of closing comfortably on *Sparrow*'s larboard quarter, she now lay across the opposite bow and on a dangerously converging tack.

'Starboard chaser!' Bolitho had to repeat the order before young Fowler heard him and scurried forward to find Graves.

He yelled at Tyrrell, 'He must be made to think we are going to fight!'

Faintly from forward he heard the squeal of chocks as the gun crew hauled the thirty-two pounder to its port. It would not be easy for them. With the ship lying hard over it would be like dragging it uphill.

'*Fire!*'

The smoke whipped inboard above the forecastle as the bow-chaser roared its challenge at the enemy.

Nobody reported a fall of shot, and at such at angle it was likely the ball had passed clean above the other ship.

Bolitho felt his jaw tighten into a grin. The enemy's forecourse was being brailed up, her topgallants disappearing as if by remote hand as they shortened sail to fight the impudent *Sparrow*.

'Fire!'

Again the gun hurled its heavy ball into the murky confusion of sea and drifting spume.

Bolitho looked at Buckle. 'Stand by!' He strode to the rail

and touched Tyrrell's arm. 'Get the forecourse on her! Hands aloft and loose t'gallants! 'Tis time for a little prudence!'

As the great foresail billowed and then hardened to the wind Bolitho felt the hull steady and hold firm to its thrust. Right above the deck the topmen were busy releasing the topgallant sails, so that as he peered aloft the mainmast seemed to be bending forward like a tree in a storm.

When he turned towards the French frigate again he saw that his plan had worked well. She was trying to reset her foresail, but the momentary pause to present her broadside had cost her dearly. She was plunging past the *Sparrow*'s quarter a full three cables clear.

By the time she had regained her control of wind and tack she would be well astern. Also, *Sparrow*'s sudden manœuvre had now given her the wind-gage.

A ripple of flashes spouted from the frigate's side. Balls plunged into the sea nearby, although with so many white-horses on each beam it was hard to tell shot from spray.

Overhead a ball whined between the masts, and a seaman fell from the mainyard, hitting the sea alongside without surfacing until he was far astern.

Majendie said hoarsely, 'The poor fellow! God rest his soul!'

Bolitho nodded. 'Aye. That was bad luck.'

He stared along the gun deck where his men worked like demons to retrim the yards and secure halliards which were swollen with damp. Hardly one of them had looked up as the man had fallen. Later perhaps they would mourn. But maybe, like himself, they were thanking God that *Sparrow* had answered their call, had not scorned their efforts to drag her into the wind and risk demasting or crippling her to lie an easy prize under the enemy's guns.

'Steer due south, Mr Buckle. We will gain some room before we attempt to wear.'

Buckle gazed astern. The frigate was going about, the heart gone from her original challenge.

'There he goes, God rot him!' Buckle grinned at his helmsmen. 'Thought we were going to surrender without a fight, did he?'

Majendie watched Bolitho's strained face. 'Many would

have done, Captain. Even I, a landsman, know you were badly matched.'

Bolitho forced a smile. 'But we did *not* fight, my friend.' He glanced briefly astern. 'Not *this* time.'

He shut the picture of the falling topman from his mind. It was to be hoped he died instantly. To see his ship sailing on without him would make his last moments on earth worse than death itself.

'Now, fetch Mr Graves and the lookouts. We will put all our information together.' He caught Majendie's arm as a deep plunge all but threw him down the quarterdeck ladder. 'Steady there! I may want you to make some sketches for the admiral. It seems the fashionable thing to do these days.'

When at last he was satisfied with *Sparrow*'s course and trim he walked aft and looked for the land. But it was lost from view, and he guessed that rain covered the headland and the frigate which had so nearly caught them in a trap.

He stripped off his shirt and mopped his neck and chest with it. Majendie watched him and then peered glumly at his sodden pad. That, he decided would have been the best sketch of all.

Bolitho read carefully through his prepared report and then thrust it into an envelope. Stockdale stood beside the table, a candle and wax ready to seal it, now that it seemed there was nothing more to add.

Bolitho leaned back and stretched his arms. For two whole days they had fought their way south-west, losing sight of land and intent only on gaining advantage over the wind. Tacking back and forth for hours at a time to record but a few miles in actual progress. It had been hard work for everyone, but now that the wind had decided to back still further *Sparrow* had at last been able to turn towards the mainland. With luck they would anchor at Sandy Hook tomorrow. He glanced at the open log book and smiled. It was sobering to realize that in the time it had taken to reach Newport, fight the adverse weather and return to Sandy Hook by this frustrating and delaying method, he could have sailed his ship clear across the Atlantic to Falmouth with days to spare.

'Will I seal it now, sir?' Stockdale watched him patiently.

'I think so.'

He closed his eyes, memorizing the statements he had obtained from Graves and the lookouts. They differed in small details, but one thing was clear. It seemed more than likely to expect a combined Franco/American attack on New York, and soon. He found some satisfaction in the fact that if the weather had delayed his swift return, then it would equally hamper the enemy.

'Deck there! Sail on th' weather bow!'

Bolitho pushed Stockdale's candle aside. 'Later.' Then he hurried from the cabin.

Because of the *Sparrow*'s need to gain advantage from the wind they had driven far to the south-west. Now, having at last found the wind's favour, the compass pointed north-west by north, with Sandy Hook some ninety miles ahead. The afternoon was hot but clear, and even from the deck it was possible to see the small pyramid of canvas to show that the other vessel was standing on a converging tack.

'Bring her up a point. Steer nor'-west.'

He took a glass from Bethune and steadied it above the nettings.

The masthead called, 'Brigantine, sir!'

He looked at Tyrrell. 'Ours probably.'

It was the only sail they had sighted since narrowly avoiding action with the French frigate. It was always good to meet a friendly ship, and he would pass some of his news across to her, in case she was making for the north and might pass too close to the enemy's squadron at Newport.

With the wind blowing keenly it did not take long for both ships to draw near one another.

'He intends to pass to lee'rd.' Bolitho raised the glass again.

Brigantines were untidy looking ships. Square-rigged on the foremast, and with a schooner's fore-and-aft sail on the main, they appeared ill-designed, but were known capable of outdistancing even a frigate under good conditions.

Bolitho said, 'Signal her to heave to. I will speak with her master.'

Tyrrell said, 'Anyway, she's English. No doubt about that.'

Flags soared up the newcomer's yards and broke to the wind.

Bethune shouted, 'She's the *Five Sisters*, sir!' He fumbled with his book while Fowler stood a little apart, his mouth set in an expression of disdain. 'Shown here as under warrant to the Governor at New York.'

'Thought as much.' Tyrrell frowned. 'Law unto themselves, and crewed by some real rascals, I can tell you.' He sighed. 'Still, a warrant keeps 'em safe from th' press and risking their precious necks.'

The brigantine had crossed *Sparrow*'s bows and was moving steadily on the starboard tack. Bolitho could see the red and gold flag at her fore, the trim semblance of order usually found in a government sponsored vessel. She was drawing closer, and would eventually pass less than half a cable clear.

Bolitho saw Majendie and Dalkeith by the nettings. The former scribbling frantically, the surgeon peering over his shoulder with obvious interest.

'She's heaving to, sir.'

The brigantine was coming up into the wind, her canvas aback and the big mainsail diminishing steadily as the seamen took charge of it.

Bolitho nodded approvingly. It had been well executed.

'Luff, Mr Tyrrell. I will hail her while she rides under our lee.'

The crash and boom of flapping canvas made any sort of conversation difficult, for as *Sparrow* turned closer into the wind and her way was reduced to a crawl, every sail and shroud seemed intent on drowning Bolitho's voice.

He held the speaking trumpet in both hands and shouted, '*Where are you bound?*'

Across the short wave-crests he heard the reply.

'Montego Bay! Jamaica!'

Tyrrell remarked, 'Bit off course, I'd say.'

The voice came again. 'We were chased by a Spanish frigate yesterday. Gave him the slip during the night, but you might report him for me.'

The brigantine was falling downwind, her yards moving restlessly to show her master was eager to be on his way.

Bolitho lowered the trumpet. There was no point in detaining her longer. And he would get precious little thanks for so doing by the New York authorities. It was odd to realize that she probably came under the control of men like Blundell, who knew nothing and cared less for the sea.

He heard Dalkeith murmur, 'By God, that captain's face! I've never seen such cruel burns and know a man to live!'

Bolitho snapped, 'Give me that glass!' He snatched it from the astonished surgeon and levelled it on the other ship's poop.

Through the black rigging and loosely flapping sails he saw him. His coat collar was turned up to his ears despite the heat, and his hat was drawn firmly almost to eye-level. Bolitho realized that the brigantine's captain had not only lost half his face, but an eye as well, and he was holding his head at a stiff, unnatural angle as he trained the remaining one on the sloop.

So the brigantine had something to do with Blundell. He could picture them murmuring together in the study, the scarred face half hidden in shadow.

Buckle called worriedly, 'Permission to get the ship under way, sir? We're riding a bit close.'

'Very well.'

Bolitho waved to the men on the brigantine's deck and turned to watch Majendie again. He was hanging on the nettings, scribbling and shading, smoothing out and adding detail even as the *Five Sisters* reset her foresail and began to gather way downwind.

Dalkeith grinned. 'Not bad, Rupert! I daresay some of our naval companions will assist you with detail of rigging, eh?'

Tyrrell limped over to him and peered across his narrow shoulder. He seized the pad and exclaimed, 'Holy God! If I didn't know for sure . . .'

Bolitho strode to his side. The picture was of the brigantine's poop, with officers and seamen caught in realistic attitudes, even if, as Dalkeith had hinted, the details of rigging were imperfect.

He felt himself go cold as he saw Majendie's drawing of the ship's captain. Distance and scale had wiped away the terrible scars, so that he stood out like a figure from the past. He looked at Tyrrell, who was still watching his face.

259

Tyrrell said quietly, 'You remember, sir? You were too busy fighting and guarding me from attack.' He turned to stare at the other ship. 'But after I took that ball in my thigh I had plenty of time to watch *that* bugger.'

Bolitho tried to clear the dryness from his throat. With stark clarity he saw the fury and hatred of battle as if it had been yesterday. The *Sparrow*'s seamen being cut down and driven from *Bonaventure*'s decks. And the privateer's captain, standing like some detached onlooker, calling on him to strike and surrender

He snapped, 'Put the ship about! Hands aloft and set t'gallants!'

To Majendie he added softly, 'Thanks to you, I think we may solve a mystery today.'

The instant *Sparrow* showed her intentions, and even as the fore topgallant sail bellied from its yard, the brigantine also increased her canvas and headed away.

'Clear for action, sir?'

'No.'

He watched the jib-boom edging round until it fastened on the brigantine's starboard quarter like a bridge. In fact she was two cables clear and showed no sign of losing her lead.

'It must be quickly done. We will go alongside and grapple. Tell Mr Graves to loose off a ball from the larboard bow-chaser, Lively now!'

Buckle said grimly, 'We're overhauling him, sir.'

Bolitho nodded. Tyrrell understood what was happening, but so far nobody else had even hinted surprise at his actions. To all intents he was chasing a government vessel with which, minutes earlier, he had been exchanging pleasantries.

Bang. The bow-chaser's black muzzle lurched inboard on its tackles, and Bolitho saw the waterspout shoot upwards within a boat's length of the brigantine's side.

'She's shortening sail now!' Buckle sounded satisfied.

'Pass the word for Mr Graves to muster a boarding party!' Bolitho watched narrowly as the other ship began to yaw heavily in a procession of troughs. 'Mr Heyward, take charge of the gun deck! Mr Bethune, accompany the second lieutenant!'

Men scampered to the larboard gangway, cutlasses bared, and some carrying muskets above their heads to avoid misfiring into their companions.

'Steady, Mr Buckle!' Bolitho held out his hand and looked up at the yards. Sails were vanishing briskly, and as the fore-course rose booming and writhing to its yard he saw the brigantine slipping under the larboard bow, as if both ships were being drawn together by hawsers. '*Steady!*'

Along the gangway picked seamen swung their grapnels, while others scurried forward to fend off the first contact.

Across the shortening range Bolitho heard, 'Stand away there! I command you to keep clear! I will have the law on your head!'

Bolitho felt his tension easing. If he had harboured doubts they were gone now. There was no mistaking that voice. Too many of *Sparrow*'s seamen had died that day aboard *Bonaventure* for him ever to forget. He raised the trumpet. 'Take in your sails and bring to *instantly*!'

He heard the grumble of chocks and guessed the brigan-tine's crew were well able to see the big thirty-two-pounder as it was run out again.

Warily, and with great skill, both vessels slowly edged round, their progress through the choppy water falling almost to nothing, their seamen taking in canvas and trimming yards in harmony with the change of rudder. It was perfectly done, and with little more than a shudder *Sparrow* nudged against the brigantine's hull and ground forward before coming to rest with her bowsprit level with the other's foremast. Grapnels flew from the gangway, and Bolitho saw Graves waving his men forward, and Bethune swinging out on the fore shrouds, his dirk seeming too small for so heavy a midshipman.

Tyrrell rested his hands on the rail and said, 'She carries a deck cargo as well.' He pointed to a large canvas hump below the forecastle. 'Booty for th' master, no doubt!'

Even as he finished speaking, and as the first seaman jumped out and down on to the brigantine's bulwark, the deck cargo revealed itself. Hands tore the canvas away to uncover a sturdy twelve-pounder which was rigged in the centre of the deck, its bulk controlled by tackles and ring-bolts.

The crash of its explosion was matched only by the shriek of grape-shot as it burst with terrifying impact along *Sparrow*'s gangway. Men and pieces of flesh flew in bloody profusion, and through the rolling bank of brown smoke Bolitho saw some of them smashed to the opposite side of the deck.

Then came the shouting, and from the brigantine's poop and main hatch he saw some fifty men charging to the attack.

He groped for his hanger, but realized he had forgotten to bring it from the cabin. Everywhere men were shouting and screaming and above it all came an increasing rasp of steel, the bang and whine of musket fire.

A seaman fell bodily from the nettings and knocked Tyrrell against the rail. His leg doubled under him and his face contorted with pain.

Bolitho yelled, 'Take charge, Mr Buckle!'

He snatched a cutlass from the dead seaman's belt and ran to the gangway. His eyes smarted in smoke, and he felt several balls fan past him, one severing a netting like an invisible knife.

The brigantine stood no chance against *Sparrow*'s cannon. But, grappled together like this, the fight could easily turn against them. He had done this very thing himself and knew the odds.

He vaulted wildly on to the main shrouds and then saw with astonishment that Graves was still below him on the gun deck. He was yelling at his men, but seemed unable to follow them. Of Bethune there was no sign, and he realized that Heyward had gone forward to meet a rush of boarders who were trying to climb across the beakhead.

He slipped and almost dropped between the hulls, and then with a gasp he was on the brigantine's deck. A pistol exploded beside his face, nearly blinding him, but he slashed out with the heavy cutlass, felt a brief impact and heard someone scream.

'The poop!' He thrust his way between some of his men and saw Bethune using a musket like a club, his hair blowing wildly as he tried to rally what remained of his boarding party. 'Take the poop, lads!'

Somebody raised a cracked cheer, and with fresh heart the seamen lunged aft. Feet and legs kicked and swayed above groaning wounded and corpses alike. There was no time to reload muskets, and it was blade to blade at close quarters.

Through the struggling, interlocked figures Bolitho saw the ship's wheel, a master's mate standing alone beside it, while others lay in various attitudes of death around him to show that aboard *Sparrow* someone had mustered a few sharp-shooters in the maintop.

Then, all at once, they were face to face. Bolitho, with his shirt torn almost to his waist, his hair plastered across his fore-head and the cutlass outstretched towards his enemy.

The other captain stood quite motionless, his sword held easily and angled across his front. Close to, his face was even more terrible, but there was no doubting his agility as he suddenly darted forward.

The blades came together with a sharp clang. Sparks flew as they ground inwards until both hilts locked and each man tested the weight of his adversary's arm.

Bolitho looked into the unwinking eye, felt the heat of his breath, the quivering tension in his shoulder as with a curse he thrust Bolitho back against the wheel, withdrawing his sword and striking forward in two swift movements. Again and again, strike, parry, guard. The cutlass felt like a lead weight, and each movement became an agony. Bolitho saw the other man's mouth set in a grim smile. He knew he was winning.

Beyond the rail the fighting continued as before, but above it he heard Tyrrell yell from the quarterdeck, 'Help th' cap'n! For Christ's sake, *help him*!'

As they circled each other like jungle cats, Bolitho saw Stockdale slashing and hacking to try to reach him. But he was fighting at least three men, and his bellows were those of an anguished bull.

Bolitho lifted his cutlass and levelled it at the other man's waist. He could raise it no further. His muscles seemed to be cracking. If only he could change hands. But he would die if he attempted it.

The sword flicked out, its point cutting through his sleeve and touching his skin like a white-hot iron. He could feel blood running down his arm, saw the man's single eye gleam-ing through a mist of pain like some glowing stone.

The brigantine's captain shouted, 'Now, Cap'n! This is the moment! For *you*!'

He moved so quickly that Bolitho hardly saw the blade coming. It caught the cutlass within inches of the hilt, turned it from his fingers like something plucked from a child, and sent it flying over the rail.

There was a loud crack, and Bolitho felt the ball pass his shoulder, the heat so fierce it must have missed him by an inch. It struck the other man in the throat, hurling him aside even as the sword made its final lunge. For a moment longer he kicked and convulsed in his blood and then lay still.

Bolitho saw Dalkeith throw one leg over the bulwark and climb up beside him, a pistol smoking in his hand.

Throughout the two ships there was stricken silence, and the brigantine's crew stood or lay to await quarter from their attackers. Bolitho said, 'Thank you. That was close.'

Dalkeith did not seem to hear him. He said brokenly, 'They killed Majendie. Shot him down like a dog as he tried to save a wounded man.'

Bolitho felt the surgeon's fingers on his arm as he ripped his shirt into a deft bandage.

Majendie gone, and so many others, too. He looked down at the dead man by the bulwark. If he had kept his head he might have got away with the deception. But for Majendie he certainly would have done. Perhaps, like himself, he had never forgotten that day aboard the privateer, and once more fate had decided to end the memory in its own way.

He turned to survey the two vessels. There was much to be done, a lot to be discovered before they reached Sandy Hook.

Some of his men gave a hoarse cheer as he walked to the bulwark, but most were too spent even to move.

Anger, disgust, as well as a sense of loss, flooded through him as he walked amongst his gasping seamen. To think men had died because of treachery and to gain riches for others who remained aloof from blame.

'But not *this* time!' He spoke aloud without realizing it. 'Somebody will pay dearly for today's grief!'

Then he thought of the girl in New York and wondered how he could protect her when the truth became known.

264

16. One Man's Loss . . .

REAR-ADMIRAL SIR EVELYN CHRISTIE rose from behind
a table crammed with documents and leaned forward to offer
his hand.

'Welcome.' He gestured to a chair. 'Good to meet you
again.'

Bolitho sat down and watched the admiral as he moved
towards the stern gallery. It was stiflingly hot, and even though
there was a regular breeze across Sandy Hook, the air in the
flagship's great cabin was lifeless.

Christie added abruptly, 'I am sorry to have kept you so
long. But the politics of high command are no area for a
young captain.' He smiled. 'Your courage is beyond doubt,
but here in New York they would eat you alive.'

Bolitho tried to relax. For three days after dropping anchor
he had been to all intents confined to his ship. Once his report
had been spirited to the flagship and his wounded landed for
care ashore, he had been left in little doubt as to his own
position. No actual command had been issued, but the
Officer-of-the-Guard had told him that his presence aboard
would be in everyone's best interests until word from the
admiral.

He began, 'If I have done wrong, sir, then . . .'

Christie looked at him sternly. '*Wrong?* Quite the reverse.
But you have certainly set a fox amongst the geese this time.'
He shrugged. 'But you did not come aboard to hear what you
already know. Your action in capturing the brigantine *Five
Sisters*, the seizure of certain documents before her master
could dispose of them, far outweigh individual discomfort
elsewhere.'

'Thank you, sir.' He was still uncertain where Christie's
comments were leading.

'It now seems evident that the brigantine's master, one

Matthew Crozier, intended to pass information either to an enemy vessel or to some spy along the coast. That would explain his being so far off course, his excuse of avoiding a Spanish frigate. But there can be no doubt as to his main mission. Whilst on passage for Jamaica he was to deliver a message for the Compte de Grasse at Martinique. My people have examined the despatch most thoroughly.' He eyed Bolitho steadily. 'In it they found full details of our defences and all available ships-of-war. Deployments, both sea and military, even to the extent of our strength under Cornwallis.' He picked up a document and studied it for several seconds. 'One way or t'other, this will be a year to remember.'

Bolitho shifted in his chair. 'How could a privateersman like Crozier obtain a warrant to work for the British?'

Christie smiled wryly. 'He owned the brigantine. It was no doubt purchased by his own side. The crew were hand-picked. The sweepings of a dozen ports and almost as many countries. With small vessels in such demand his deception was not so very difficult. Even on his official voyages he was apparently smuggling.' He turned away, his shoulders suddenly rigid. 'Mostly for those in power in New York!'

'May I ask if they are to be punished?'

Christie turned and shrugged. 'If you mean General Blundell, then you may be assured he will be leaving America very soon. After that I am equally certain he will be saved by influence and powerful friends at home. Distance and time are great healers where the guilty are concerned. But others will certainly go to the wall, and I have been told that the Military Command intends to use your discovery to rid itself, in part at least, of the parasites who have lived too long off its back.'

He smiled at Bolitho's grave features. 'Pour some madeira. It will do us both good.' He continued in the same unruffled tone, 'Admiral Graves is well pleased with you. He has sent the schooner *Lucifer* to Antigua to inform Admiral Rodney of the situation here. Patrols have been ordered to Newport to watch de Barras's squadron, although, as you well know, it is hard to see what is happening there. In fact, everything is being done with the forces available to watch over local waters to see which way the tiger will pounce.'

He took a glass from Bolitho's hand and asked, '*Sparrow*, is she in good repair?'

Bolitho nodded. It was still difficult to keep pace with the small admiral. 'My carpenter has almost completed repairs to the gangway and . . .'

Christie nodded briskly. 'In any case, *that* can be finished at sea. I want you to take on full supplies, for three months at least. My flag captain has it in hand. He might even find you some seamen to replace those lost in battle. I have sent *Heron* to the south'rd again, but my other inshore patrols are too well spread for comfort. I need every available ship, especially yours.' He smiled. 'And you.'

'Thank you, sir.' He put down the glass. 'Newport again?'

The admiral shook his head. 'You will join Farr and his *Heron*.'

Bolitho stared at him. 'But, sir, I thought you needed ships to watch de Barras?'

Christie picked up the decanter and examined it thoughtfully. 'I may do so later. But for the present I want you out of Sandy Hook. Away from those who will try to bring you down. You have made enemies by your actions. As I said just now, you are no match for the devious ways of politics.'

'I am prepared to take that risk, sir.'

'*I am not!*' Christie's voice was hard. Like it had been at the court martial in this very cabin. 'To you, your ship and her affairs are paramount. But I must think on a wider scope, and my superiors wider still. If it is thought best for you to lead my whole squadron against de Barras, then that is how it will be. And if your ship must be sacrificed like a tethered animal in a snare, then that, too, will be ordered!' He relented. 'Forgive me. That was unpardonable.' He waved one hand above his charts. 'The enemy is powerful, but not so that he can attack everywhere at once. He can strike against New York, for deprived of it we have no pretence at government in America. Or he can turn his iron on General Cornwallis's army in the field, for without that we are just as pointless. Either way there will be a battle, and I believe that a sea fight will decide our course and that of history for years to come.'

Feet pounded overhead and Bolitho heard the bark of

commands, the scrape of tackles and blocks. Even the old *Parthian* was preparing to sail, to show her readiness for whatever the enemy intended.

Bolitho stood up.

'When can I expect my orders, sir?'

'Before sunset. I would advise you to contain your, er, other interests, until some later date.' He proffered his hand. 'The heart is a fine thing, but I would prefer you to rest your judgements on the brain.'

Bolitho walked out to the sunlight, his mind buzzing with all Christie had said and the greater part which he had left unspoken. It was all so unfair. A sailor stood to his gun in battle until told otherwise. Or he struggled aloft in a shrieking gale, frozen with icy spray, and scared half to death. But he obeyed. It was the way of things, or had been in Bolitho's experience. Until now.

Yet Blundell's kind ignored such distinctions, could and did use their personal authority for gain, even when the country was fighting for its life. No wonder those like Crozier could prosper and achieve more results than an army of paid spies. Crozier had been doing his duty in the only way he knew. By ignoring the dangers, Blundell had committed little better than treason.

He stopped by the entry port and stared at the waiting gig with sudden anxiety. So why had he not told Christie of Crozier's presence in Blundell's house? There would have been no hiding from conspiracy had that piece of news been released. He swore under his breath and signalled to Stockdale.

Fool, fool! Perhaps he should have told her first. To allow her time to disassociate herself from her uncle's affairs.

The flag captain joined him by the port. 'I have had the water hoys sent over to *Sparrow*. Another lighter will be alongside within the hour. If your people turn to with a will, you should have all the stores aboard before dusk.'

Bolitho eyed him curiously. Such calm assurance, yet this captain had not only his own ship and the whims of an admiral to consider, he must concern himself with the needs of every officer and man in the squadron. He was jolted by his discovery. It was like seeing Christie's charts on the cabin table.

To all but himself, *Sparrow* and her company were just a tiny part of the whole.

He doffed his hat to the shrill calls and shining bayonets and clambered down to the gig. He said nothing as the boat pulled lustily across the anchorage, and Stockdale for once seemed content to leave him in peace.

He was in his cabin with Lock studying the latest return of ship's stores when Graves entered to announce the arrival of another hoy carrying fresh water.

As the purser scuttled away to watch over the casks before they were lowered into the hold, Bolitho said, 'I was meaning to have a word with you, Mr Graves.' He saw the lieutenant stiffen, the way his fingers locked into his coat. Poor Graves. He looked like an old man, and even his tan could not hide the shadows under his eyes, the pinched lines at each side of his mouth. How did you begin to ask an officer if he was a coward? He added, 'Are you troubled about something?'

Graves swallowed hard. 'My father is dead, sir. Some weeks back. I just received a letter.'

'I am sorry to hear that, Mr Graves.' Bolitho watched his face with sudden compassion. 'It is harder to bear when you are out of reach, as we are.'

'Yes.' Graves did not even blink. 'He had been, er, ill for some while.'

The door swung open and Tyrrell limped noisily into the cabin. He did not appear to see Graves as he exclaimed, 'By God, Cap'n! I've had news!' He leaned on the table, all his excitement and pleasure welling out of him in an uncontrollable flood. 'My sister. She's safe an' well! I met a man who was a trapper in th' county. He said she's living with our uncle. That's about twenty mile to th' north of our old farmstead.' He grinned widely. 'Safe! I still can't believe I'm awake.' He turned and saw Graves for the first time. 'Oh hell! I'm sorry. I forgot myself with th' fair excitement of it all.'

Graves was staring at him glassily, and his fingers had screwed his coat into two tight balls.

Tyrrell asked, 'What's wrong? You sick or something?'

Graves muttered, 'I must go. If you'll excuse me, sir.' He almost ran from the cabin.

269

Bolitho stood up. 'It *was* good news, Jethro.' He looked at the open door. 'I am afraid Graves just brought some of a sadder note. His father.'

Tyrrell sighed. 'I'm sorry. I thought maybe it was something I said. . . .'

'In what way?'

Tyrrell shrugged. 'No matter. He was once in hopes of courting my sister.' He smiled at some secret memory. 'It all seems a long way back now.'

Bolitho tried not to think about Graves's stunned expression.

'One day you'll be able to join your sister again. I am very glad for you.'

Tyrrell nodded, his eyes dreamy. 'Aye. One day.' He nodded more firmly. 'I don't feel quite so lost any more.'

Midshipman Fowler stepped neatly over the coaming and removed his hat. 'The lighterman brought you a letter, sir.' His lisp was very pronounced. 'He insisted I give it to you myself.'

'Thank you.'

Bolitho held it in his fingers. Like the other one which he had locked in his strong-box. Her own hand.

He opened it quickly and then said, 'I'll be ashore for an hour. Maybe longer. Call away my gig.'

Fowler ran from the cabin, his sharp voice calling for the boat's crew.

Tyrrell asked quietly, 'Is it wise, sir?'

'What the hell do you mean by that?' Bolitho swung towards him, caught off guard by his question.

Tyrrell frowned. 'I met several people when I was ordering some new cordage, sir. It's well known all over New York what you've done. Most are laughing fit to burst that your action has unmasked these bloody scabs and traitors. But some think you'll be in real danger while you're here. There'll be plenty more quaking in their beds. Wondering what you discovered, an' when th' soldiers are going to bang on *their* door.'

Bolitho dropped his eyes. 'I'm sorry about my anger. But have no fear. I've no intention of parading my back for the benefit of that sort.'

270

Tyrrell watched him as he snatched up his hat and fretted impatiently for Fitch to adjust his swordbelt.

Then he said, 'I'll rest easier when we're at sea again.'

Bolitho hurried past him. 'And that will be tonight, my cautious friend. So stir yourself and watch over the provisions!' He smiled at Tyrrell's concern. 'But beware. There may be an assassin hiding in the salt beef!'

Tyrrell saw him over the side but remained by the rail for a long while, despite the sun and the pain in his thigh.

There was a small carriage waiting for Bolitho at the end of the jetty. It was a shabby affair and not in the least like the one which had carried him to the general's residence. But the driver was the same Negro, and as soon as Bolitho was inside he cracked his whip and urged the horses into a brisk trot.

They rattled through several narrow streets and then out into a quiet road which was lined by sturdy houses, most of which seemed to be occupied by some of the city's refugees. The buildings had lost their façade of well-being, and where there had been gardens there were piles of discarded boxes and sorry-looking vehicles. At many of the windows he saw women and children staring out at the road below. They had the lost look of uprooted people with little to do but wait and hope.

The coach wheeled through a pair of sagging gates and towards another such house. Except that this one was empty, its windows bare in the sunlight like blind eyes.

For an instant he recalled Tyrrell's warning, but as the coach slid to a halt he saw the girl beside the house, her gown reflected in a partly overgrown pond.

He hurried towards her, his heart pounding in time with his shoes.

'I came as fast as I could!' He took her hands in his and studied her warmly. 'But why must we meet here?'

She tossed her head, throwing the hair from her shoulder in the way he had remembered in the weeks he had been away.

'It is better so. I cannot bear the watching eyes. The sneers behind my back.' There was little emotion in her voice. 'But we will go inside now. I must speak with you.'

Their shoes rang hollowly on the bare boards. It had been a fine house, but now the plaster was flaking and the walls were heavy with cobwebs.

She walked to a window and said, 'My uncle is in serious trouble, but I expect you know. He was perhaps foolish, but no more than many here.'

Bolitho slipped his hand beneath her arm. 'I do not want you to be involved, Susannah.'

His insistence, or the use of her name, made her turn and face him.

'But I *am* involved, as you put it.'

'No. The smuggling and other offences could have had nothing to do with you. Nobody would ever believe it.'

She stared at him calmly. 'Nor does it matter. But one hint of treason would ruin my uncle and all connected with him.' She gripped his arm. 'That man, Crozier, have you spoken of his presence at our house? Please, I must know. For if you remair silent, all may yet be well.'

Bolitho turned away. 'Believe me. I can save you from that. Your uncle will be sent to England. There is no reason why you cannot remain here.'

'*Here?*' She stood back from him. 'What use is that?'

'I—I thought, given time you might see your way to becoming my wife.' In the empty room his words seemed to come back to mock him.

'Marry you?' She brushed her hair from her forehead. 'Is that what you thought?'

'Yes. I had cause to hope.' He watched her despairingly. 'You hinted that . . .'

She replied sharply, 'I hinted no such proposal, Captain! If things had gone as I had planned, well then maybe . . .'

He tried again.

'But nothing *need* change for us.'

She continued as if he had not spoken. 'I did think that with some help from my friends you might one day amount to something. A position in London, perhaps even a seat in Parliament. All is possible if the will is there.' She lifted her eyes to his face again. 'Did you really expect me to marry a sea-officer? Live from day to day waiting for one ship after

272

the other to drop anchor? There are other lives beyond your miserable Service, *Captain!*'

'It is my life.' He felt the walls closing in on him. The air forced from his lungs as if he was drowning.

'The path of duty.' She walked to the window and looked down at the carriage. 'You were a fool to think of my sharing such an existence. An even bigger one if you continue to do so!' She turned easily, her eyes flashing. 'There's more to living than catching some poor smuggler in the King's name!'

Bolitho said, 'I did not tell of Crozier being with your uncle. But it is certain to come out when the authorities have finished their inquiries.' He added bitterly, 'Rats always turn on one another when the pickings are few.'

She breathed out slowly, one hand resting lightly below her heart. 'Stay a few minutes while I go to my carriage. I have no wish to be seen here.'

Bolitho reached out his arms and then let them drop to his sides. He was defeated. Had been so for longer than he had understood.

Yet in the dusty sunlight, as she stood watching him, her violet eyes holding him at a distance, he knew that if there was anything he could do or say to keep her he would use it.

She moved to the door. 'You are a strange man. But I can see no future for you.' Then she was gone, her shoes fading on the staircase until he was quite alone.

He did not remember how long he stood in that empty room. Minutes? An hour? When at last he walked down the stairs and into the overgrown garden he realized that even the shabby carriage had gone. He crossed to the pond and stared at his own reflection.

If she had been angry, or frightened, anything he could have recognized, he might still have known what to do. There had not even been contempt. She had dismissed him with no more thought than if she had been rejecting a useless servant.

A foot scraped on stone and he swung round, seeing in those seconds four dark figures lined against the ragged bushes.

'*Easy*, Cap'n!' One of them had a drawn sword, and he saw the others were also well armed. 'There's no sense in strugglin'!'

Bolitho backed up to the pond, his fingers on his hanger.

Another of the men chuckled. 'Aye, that's right, Cap'n. Somewhere for us'n to hide yer corpse when we've done with you. Most considerate, eh, lads?'

Bolitho remained quite still. He knew it was useless to bargain with any of them. They had the looks of professional criminals, men who worked for a fee, no matter what the final cost might be to them.

He was suddenly very calm, as if their arrival had driven away his other despair like a cold wind.

'Then I'll take a couple with me!'

He snatched out his hanger and waited for them to attack. Two carried pistols, but there were probably military patrols nearby and a shot might bring them running.

Steel clashed with steel, and he saw the leader's grin fade to an intent frown as they locked blades together. He ducked as one man struck at his neck, twisted his hanger and slashed him across the face, hearing him scream as he tumbled back into the bushes.

'Damn you, you bloody bastard!' Another dived forward, his sword sweeping under Bolitho's guard. But it glanced from his belt buckle and he was able to thrust him aside with the hilt, catching him on the jaw with such force it almost tore the hanger from his grip.

The garden swam in a mist of pain as something struck him savagely on the forehead, and he realized that one of them had hurled a stone. He hit out with the hanger but felt it pass through air. Someone laughed, and another called hoarsely, '*Now*, 'Arry! In the guts!'

Feet pounded through the shrubs, and Bolitho was pushed aside by someone in a blue coat who shouted, 'At 'em, lads! Cut 'em down!'

Swords grated and sparked, and a body rolled thrashing into the pond, the blood staining the surface like red weed.

Bolitho lurched to his feet, realizing that Heyward and Tyrrell were driving the two attackers against the house, while Dalkeith stood watchfully nearby, his beautiful pistols shining in the sunlight.

Heyward brought his man to his knees and jumped back to let him roll silently on to his face and stay there.

The sole survivor threw down his heavy sword and yelled, 'Quarter! Quarter!'

Tyrrell swayed awkwardly on his crippled leg and said harshly, 'Quarter be damned!'

The sword took him in the chest, holding him to the wall for an endless moment before allowing him to slide beside his companion.

Tyrrell sheathed his blade and limped to Bolitho's side.

'All well, Cap'n?' He reached out to steady him. 'Just in time, it seems.'

Heyward stepped over one of the corpses. 'Someone wanted you dead, sir.'

Bolitho looked from one to the next, the emotion rising to mingle with his understanding.

Tyrrell grinned. 'You see, I was right.'

Bolitho nodded heavily. *Someone wanted you dead.* But the worst part was knowing that she had realized his peril, and had done nothing. He glanced at the corpse sprawled in the pond.

'What can I say? How can I find words?'

Dalkeith murmured, 'Let's say it was for Rupert Majendie, too.'

Tyrrell slipped his arm over Heyward's slim shoulder for support.

'Aye, that'll do.' He glanced at Bolitho and held his gaze. 'You've done plenty for us. An' in *Sparrow* we look after our own!'

Then together they walked out to the road and towards the sea.

17. Mistaken Identity

BOLITHO leaned back in his chair and stared wearily at the open log. He was stripped to the waist, but could feel no benefit in the overheated cabin. He touched his mouth with the pen, wondering what he should write, when there was nothing to report. Around and above him the ship swayed and dipped in a gentle south-easterly breeze, and he pitied the watch on deck, sweating out another day of relentless glare and fierce sunlight. Even the *Sparrow* seemed to be voicing her protest. The timbers groaned and trembled to the motion, dried out by salt and heat, and through the open windows he saw the carved scrollwork by the sill splitting open, the paint flaking away to reveal bare wood.

Once on station north of the Little Bahama Bank he had anticipated being recalled to more active duty within a matter of weeks. But like most of his men, he had long since given up hope. Week followed week, with *Sparrow* and her attendant sloop, *Heron*, dragging their wearying patrol through July, each dawn bringing an empty horizon, and every hour tightening its grip on their small, isolated existence.

And now it was August. Perhaps Christie had insisted on three months' supplies because he had had no intention of recalling *Sparrow* until the end of that time. Maybe they had all been forgotten, or the war was over. It was as if the whole patrol area had been drained of movement. Unlike their last visit to the Bahama Banks, when they had taken prizes or had gossiped with lawful merchantmen, they had seen nothing. Their routine varied little, Usually they kept *Heron's* topsails just within sight below the horizon, and on a parallel tack swept back and forth well clear of reefs and shoals. With the masthead lookouts of both sloops able to see one another, it was possible to sweep an area some sixty miles wide, unless the weather changed against them. Even a real storm would

276

be welcome. But the agonizing discomfort was getting everyone down, not least himself.

There was a tap at the door and Dalkeith entered, his round face shining with sweat. The forenoon watch had half run its course, and Bolitho had found it necessary to meet the surgeon at this time every day when he had completed his inspection of the sick.

He gestured to a chair. 'Well?'

Dalkeith groaned and shifted his bulk carefully to avoid the glare from the open skylight.

'Two more down today, sir. I've got them below. A few days' rest might revive 'em for a while.'

Bolitho nodded. It was getting serious. Too much heat and not enough fresh food or fruit. Lock had already opened the last barrel of lemons. After that . . .

Dalkeith had been carrying a glass of water which he now stood on the table. It was the colour of tobacco juice. Without comment he took a flat bottle from his pocket and looked at Bolitho for permission to pour himself a stiff glass of rum.

Again, it was one of their little routines. Although how the plump surgeon could stomach rum in this heat was beyond Bolitho.

Dalkeith smacked his lips. 'Better'n this water.' He frowned. 'If we can't get a fresh supply of drinking water I'll not answer for the consequences, sir.'

'I'll do what I can. Maybe we can close with some small island and find a stream. But I am not too hopeful hereabouts. Was that all?'

Dalkeith hesitated. 'I'm supposed to hold my peace, but friendship and duty rarely go hand in hand. It's the first lieutenant.'

'Mr Tyrrell?' Bolitho tensed. 'What about him?'

'His leg. He tries to pretend it's all right, but I'm not happy about it.' He dropped his eyes. 'Worse, I'm getting anxious.'

'I see.' He had noticed Tyrrell's limp getting more pronounced, but whenever he had mentioned it he had replied, 'It'll pass. Nothin' to bite on!'

'What d'you advise?'

Dalkeith sighed. 'I can probe for more splinters. But if that

277

fails . . .' He took another swallow of neat rum. 'I might have to cut it off.'

'Oh God.'

Bolitho walked to the windows and leaned out over the transom. Below, the sea looked very clear, and he could see small darting fish in the rudder's frothing wake.

Behind him he heard Dalkeith add firmly, 'I could do it, of course. But it would have to be while he is still strong. Before the pain and this damn heat gets him down like some of the others.'

Bolitho turned, feeling the sun across his bared back.

'I was not doubting your ability. You've proved that more than enough.'

Dalkeith said grimly, 'I was at a fine hospital in London before I left England.' He grimaced. 'We practised on the poor and worked for the wealthy. It was a hard training ground, but very useful.'

'Will you return when the war is over?' He tried not to think of Tyrrell being held on a table, the saw poised above his leg.

Dalkeith shook his head. 'No. I'll settle out here somewhere. Maybe in America, who can tell?' He gave a wry smile. 'I am afraid that I had to leave England in somewhat of a hurry. A matter of honour over a lady.'

'I have wondered these three years where you found your skill with pistols.'

Dalkeith nodded. 'Unfortunately, I shot the wrong man. His death was considered a greater loss than mine, so I caught the packet from Dover, and eventually, two years later, I arrived in the Indies.'

'Thank you for telling me.' Bolitho massaged his stomach with the palm of one hand. 'I will see what I can do to obtain a berth in another ship, if and when we are ordered home.'

The surgeon lurched to his feet. 'I would appreciate that.' He watched Bolitho doubtfully. 'And Tyrrell?'

'I'll speak with him.' He turned away. 'In God's name, what do I say? How would I feel if it were me?'

Dalkeith rested his hand on the bulkhead until *Sparrow* had completed a slow uproll.

'I can't answer. I'm just a surgeon.'

'Aye.' Bolitho looked at him gravely. 'And I'm just a captain.'

Midshipman Bethune clattered through the wardroom and paused outside the cabin.

'Mr Graves's respects, sir. *Heron* has signalled she has sighted an unknown sail to the east'rd.'

'Very well. I'll come up.'

Dalkeith waited for Bethune to go. 'Recall to New York, sir? If so, I could take Tyrrell to a hospital. They have facilities, proper care.'

Bolitho shook his head. 'I fear not. That sail will be from the south'rd to be on such a bearing. Friend or foe, we have yet to see.'

He heard Dalkeith sigh as he left him and hurried up the ladder to the quarterdeck.

He glanced quickly at the helmsman who called hoarsely, 'Nor' nor'-west, sir!' His lips were cracked in the heat.

Graves reported, 'Our masthead has not sighted her yet, sir.' His mouth jerked at one corner and he added quickly, 'Could be anything.'

It was an empty comment, but Bolitho knew it was merely to cover his embarrassment. He had seen the growing strain on Graves perhaps worst of all. Now the twitch in his jaw laid bare his inner torment like the mark of some disease.

'Very well. Call the hands and prepare to run down on *Heron*. Get the t'gallants on her and lay her on the starboard tack.' He saw Buckle climbing wearily through the hatchway and called, 'A sail, Mr Buckle! Maybe it'll bring us luck today!'

The master pouted. ' 'Bout time, sir.'

Bolitho heard the familiar limping step and turned to see Tyrrell walking from the larboard gangway.

Tyrrell grinned. 'A sail, did I hear, sir?' He shaded his eyes as he watched the men mustering at their stations. 'Now there's a thing indeed!'

Bolitho bit his lip. It made it more painful to see Tyrrell's new contentment. To know what must be done. That was if Dalkeith knew his trade. And he did.

On the horizon he could see *Heron*'s sails glinting brightly, and knew Farr would wait for him to join him. To break the monotony if nothing else.

Within the hour the stranger had identified herself. It was the *Lucifer*, her great schooner sails spread like wings as she ran before the wind, the spray bursting above her jib-boom in a lively silver pattern.

Fowler was in the lee shrouds with a telescope, his small, piggy face glowing with heat.

'From *Lucifer*. *Have despatches on board*.' He looked down at the quarterdeck as if proud of his revelation.

'Heave to, Mr Tyrrell.'

Bolitho watched the mad dash aboard *Lucifer* to shorten sail and put her about before running down beneath *Sparrow*'s lee. A fine little vessel. Had she been his instead of *Sparrow*, he wondered if his life would have been changed to the same extent.

He saw the haste with which the schooner's boat was being hoisted out above the water. Something acted like a small warning in his mind, and he said, 'Signal *Heron*. Captain repair on board.'

'Aye, aye, sir!' Fowler snapped his fingers and continued to do so until the flags had broken from *Sparrow*'s yard.

Farr's gig hooked on the chains within minutes of *Lucifer*'s jolly-boat.

Odell had come aboard in person, and as he removed his hat to the quarterdeck and darted a sharp glance at Bolitho's bare torso, Farr climbed up beside him and said cheerfully, 'By God, what brings you here, man? Were you pining for us in Antigua?'

Odell walked a few paces clear and then faced them.

'The French are out, sir.'

For a moment nobody spoke. Bolitho held the words in his mind, yet was also aware of those about him. Stockdale by the hatchway, slightly stooped as if to hear better. Buckle and Tyrrell, their faces showing astonishment and more. Relief perhaps that the guessing was over.

'Come below.'

Bolitho led them to his cabin, the heat and the drudgery of patrol forgotten.

Odell sat on the edge of a chair, his features giving little hint of strain at driving his command all those miles from Antigua.

Bolitho said quietly, 'Now tell us.'

'I carried the despatches to the fleet as ordered.'

Odell had a quick, erratic manner of speaking, nodding his head in time with his words. It was not hard to see how he got his reputation for being slightly mad. A man on a knife-edge, Bolitho suspected. But there was no doubting the accuracy of his report.

'Admiral Rodney despatched a fleet of fourteen ships-of-the-line to assist our forces at New York.'

Farr muttered, 'By God, that's more like it. I've no stomach for our Admiral Graves.'

Odell's eyes flashed dangerously at the interruption.

He snapped, 'Rodney has sailed for England. He is a sick man. Hood commands the reinforcements.'

Farr was unabashed. 'Ah well, even better, I've served Admiral Hood and respect him.'

Bolitho said, 'Let us hear all of it. I suspect there is more.'

Odell nodded. 'The Compte de Grasse set sail with some twenty sail-of-the-line. The patrols reported that he was escorting the season's convoy clear of the islands.'

Bolitho said, 'That is quite usual, I believe.'

'Yes. But de Grasse has not been seen since.' The words fell into the cabin like round-shot.

Farr exclaimed, 'A whole fleet! Disappeared? It's bloody impossible!'

'But fact.' Odell glared at him. 'Admiral Hood's ships must have passed this area well to the east'rd. And there are several frigates searching elsewhere.' He spread his hands. 'But of de Grasse there is no sign.'

'God!' Farr looked at Bolitho. 'What d'you make of that?'

Odell said testily, 'I could relish a glass, sir. I am as dry as a pauper's loaf.'

Bolitho opened his cupboard and handed him a decanter.

He said, 'Hood will join with Graves at Sandy Hook. They will still be outnumbered, but can give good account if de Grasse chooses to head their way.'

Farr said less firmly, 'And Hood will show the damn Frogs, eh?'

Bolitho replied, 'His fleet is larger than Admiral Graves's. But Graves is senior now that Rodney has gone home.' He looked at Farr's anxious face. 'I am afraid Graves will lead our forces if and when the time comes.'

He turned to Odell, who was drinking his second glass of wine.

'Do you know anything else?'

He shrugged. 'I understood that Admiral Hood will examine Chesapeake Bay while on passage to New York. Some believe the French may strike at Cornwallis's army from the sea. If not, then New York is to be the melting pot.'

Bolitho made himself sit down. It was strange to be so moved by Odell's information. For months, even years, they had expected some great confrontation at sea. There had been skirmishes and bitter ship-to-ship actions in plenty. But this was what they had all known would happen sooner or later. Who commanded the waters around America controlled the destiny of those who fought within its boundaries.

He said, 'One thing is certain, we are doing no good here.'

Farr asked, 'Are you saying *we* should join the fleet?'

'Something like that.'

He tried to clear his mind, put Odell's brief facts into perspective. De Grasse could be anywhere, but it was ridiculous to imagine he had sailed back to France, his mission left incomplete. Without his presence in the Indies, the British would be able to throw every ship and man into the fight for America, and de Grasse was astute enough to know his own value.

He moved to the table and pulled a chart from its rack. It was close on seven hundred miles to Cape Henry at the mouth of Chesapeake Bay. With the wind remaining friendly they could make landfall in five days. If Admiral Hood's ships were lying there he could request further orders. Sloops would be more than useful for searching close inshore or relaying signals in a fleet action.

Bolitho said slowly, 'I intend to head north. To the Chesapeake.'

Farr stood up and exclaimed, 'Good! I'm with you.'

Odell asked, 'Are you taking full responsibility, sir?' His eyes were opaque.

'Yes. I would wish you to remain here in case any ships come this way. If they do, you can come after us with all haste.'

'Very well, sir.' Odell added calmly, 'I would like it in writing.'

'Damn your eyes, you impudent puppy!' Farr thumped the table with his fist. 'Where's your bloody trust?'

Odell shrugged. 'I trust Captain Bolitho, have no doubts, sir.' He gave a quick smile. 'But if he and you are both killed, who is to say I only obeyed orders?'

Bolitho nodded. 'That is fair. I will do it directly.' He saw the two men watching each other with open hostility. 'Easy now. Right or wrong, it will be good to move again. So let's not start with disharmony, eh?'

Odell showed his teeth. 'I meant no offence, sir.'

Farr swallowed hard. 'In that case, I suppose . . .' He grinned broadly. 'But by God, Odell, you push me to the limit!'

'A glass together.'

Bolitho wanted to go on deck, to share his news with Tyrrell and the others. But he knew this moment was equally vital. Just a few seconds, which each would remember when the other ships were mere silhouettes.

He raised his glass. 'What shall it be, my friends?'

Farr met his eye and smiled. He at least understood, 'To us, Dick. That will do fine for me.'

Bolitho placed his empty glass on the table. A simple toast. But, King, Cause, even Country were too remote, the future too uncertain. They had only each other and their three little ships to sustain them.

With legs braced against *Sparrow*'s uncomfortable, corkscrewing motion, Bolitho levelled a telescope across the nettings and waited for the shoreline to settle in the lens. It was close on sunset, and as the dull orange glow withdrew beyond the nearest shoulder of land he forced himself to concentrate on what he saw, rather than what he had anticipated from his charts. Around him other glasses were also trained, and he heard Tyrrell's heavy breathing at his side, the squeak of a pencil on Buckle's slate by the wheel.

Within a few miles of Cape Henry, the southernmost cape at the entrance of Chesapeake Bay, the wind had backed sharply, and backed again. A full day had been added to their previously fast passage, and as they had clawed desperately from a lee shore, had fought to obtain sea room, Bolitho had watched the bay fading across the quarter with something like anger.

And now, after their long beat back towards the entrance, he was faced by a new decision. To lie offshore until dawn, or take his chance and thrust between Cape Henry and the northern headland in what would certainly be total darkness.

Tyrrell lowered his glass. 'I know this entrance well. There's a great middle-ground which reaches into th' bay. With care you can pass either side, but with th' wind under our coat-tails I'd suggest trying th' southern channel. If you stay to lee'rd of th' middle ground you can hold mebbe three miles clear of Cape Henry.' He rubbed his chin. 'If you misjudge and tack too far to south'rd, you'll have to move lively. There are shoals off th' cape, an' bad ones at that.'

Bolitho shifted the telescope to watch some dancing red flashes far inland.

Tyrrell remarked, 'Cannon. Good way off.'

Bolitho nodded. If Tyrrell was feeling the strain of drawing so near to his home territory he did not show it.

Tyrrell continued, 'Up beyond York River, I reckon. Heavy artillery, by th' looks of it.'

Heyward, who was standing nearby, said, 'No sign of any ships, sir.'

'There wouldn't be.' Tyrrell was watching Bolitho. 'Just around Cape Henry lies Lynnhaven Bay. Good shelter where big ships anchor sometimes when there's foul weather around. No, you'd not even see a fleet from out here.' He paused. 'You'd have to go inside th' old Chesapeake.'

Bolitho handed the glass to Fowler. 'I agree. If we wait longer the wind might veer. We'd be on a lee shore again and lose more time fighting clear from it.'

He turned to look for *Heron*. Her reefed topsails were still

284

holding the fast fading sunlight, but beyond her the sea was in deep shadow.

'Show the signal lantern to *Heron*. Captain Farr knows what to do.'

He turned to Tyrell.

'The place is badly charted.'

Tyrrell grinned, his eyes glowing in the dull light. 'Unless things have changed, I reckon I can take us through.'

Fowler called, 'Signal passed, sir!'

Bolitho made up his mind. 'Alter course two points to starboard.' To Tyrrell he added slowly, 'I hate entering any bay like this one. I feel more secure in open sea.'

The lieutenant sighed. 'Aye. Th' Chesapeake is a brute in many ways. North to south it measures close on a hundred an' forty miles. You can sail a fair-sized craft right up to Baltimore without too much hardship. But it measures less'n thirty across, an' that's only where the Patowmack flows into it.'

Buckle called, 'Course sou'-west, sir.'

'Very well.'

Bolitho watched the nearest headland of Cape Charles losing its bronze crest as the sun finally dipped behind a line of hills.

'You may clear for action, Mr Tyrrell. Better safe than sorry.'

He wondered briefly what Farr was thinking as he tacked to follow *Sparrow*'s shadow towards the dark mass of land. Doubt, regret, even mistrust. You could hardly blame him. It was like groping for coal in a shuttered cellar.

Under his shoes he felt the planks quiver to the hurrying seamen, the thud of screens being torn down and mess tables dragged clear of tackles and guns. There was another difference he had found in *Sparrow*. Even clearing for action had a sort of intimacy which was lacking in a ship-of-the-line. In *Trojan* the hands had scurried to quarters, urged on by the drums' staccato beat and the blare of a marine's bugle. Sometimes you never knew men who did not serve in your own watch or division. But here it was entirely different. Men nodded to each other as they dashed to their stations, a grin here, a brief touch of hands there. In many ways it made death harder to accept, a man's cries too personal to ignore.

'Cleared for action, sir.'

'Good.' Bolitho gripped the nettings and watched the tiny feathers of surf far abeam. 'Alter course another point.'

'Aye, sir.' Buckle was muttering to his helmsmen. Then, 'Sou'-west by south, sir.'

'Hold her steady.'

He moved restlessly below the great spanker, seeing a faint glow on the boom from the compass bowl.

There were already plenty of stars in the velvet sky, and there would be a moon on the water in a few hours. But by then he must be inside the bay.

Tyrrell joined him by the wheel. 'It's a strange feeling. My sister'll be no more than fifty miles from where I'm standing. I can still remember it clearly. Th' York River, th' place in th' woods where we used to get together as kids. . . .' He turned and said sharply, 'Let her fall off a point, Mr Buckle! Mr Bethune, take some men forrard and trim the foreyard again!' He waited until he was satisfied with the ship's head and the bearing of the nearest cape and continued, 'It's a funny business all round.'

Bolitho agreed. After the first few weeks he had not thought much about Susannah Hardwicke. Now, as he pictured an unknown girl out there in the darkness beyond the occasional flash of gunfire, he realized how their lives had become merged. Tyrrell's sister, and Graves's secret longings for her. Dalkeith's affair of honour which had cost him his career and almost his life. And himself? He was surprised he could still not examine her memory without regret and a sense of loss.

When he looked again he realized that Cape Charles had merged with the shadows. A quick glance at Tyrrell reassured him. He seemed relaxed, even cheerful, as he stood where he could watch the compass and the set of the spanker overhead. But for the treacherous span of middle-ground, they could have sailed boldly between the capes with a comfortable four miles or more on either beam.

Tyrrell said, 'We will alter course again, with your permission, sir.'

'She's in your hands.'

Tyrrell grinned. 'Aye, aye, sir.' To Buckle he called, 'Steer west by north, full an' bye!'

Then he cupped his hands and yelled, 'Pipe th' hands to th' braces!'

With the helm down and the seamen hauling at the braces, *Sparrow* turned her bows towards the land. Voices called in the gloom, and above the decks the paler shapes of arms and legs moved busily about the yards.

'West by north, sir!' Buckle peered at the flapping sails as the ship heeled still further, close-hauled on the starboard tack.

Tyrrell limped from side to side, his arm darting out to catch a man's attention, or his voice sending another to pass his orders right forward where Graves was equally busy.

'Right, lads! Belay there!' He cocked his head as if to listen to the chorus of shrouds and vibrating halliards. 'She's loving it!'

Bolitho walked up to the weather side and felt the cold spray across his face. Tyrrell had come and gone through these capes many times in his father's schooner. Perhaps that memory, and the realization that his sister was now safe and close at hand, made him forget the purpose of their mission, the chance of danger with each passing minute.

'Breakers on the weather bow!' The lookout sounded nervous.

But Tyrrell called, 'Breakers be damned! That'll be th' middle-ground.' His teeth gleamed in the darkness. 'True as a bloody arrow, if I do say so myself!'

Bolitho smiled at his excitement. *Breakers be damned!* He had used much the same phrase and tone when he had driven his sword through the man who had almost killed him beside the pond.

The massive, looming shoulder of Cape Henry hardened from the darkness on the larboard beam, and for a brief instant Bolitho imagined they were too close, that the wind had thrust them further downwind than Tyrrell had allowed.

He dragged his eyes to the opposite side, and through the spray and across the deep inshore swell he saw a revolving patch of white. The middle-ground was clearly marked by the swirl of broken water, but if Tyrrell had misjudged his approach it would have been too late to avoid it.

Tyrrell shouted, 'Once saw a damn fine Dutchman aground there! She broke her back!'

Buckle muttered, 'That's bloody encouraging!'

Bolitho peered astern. 'I hope *Heron*'s seen our entrance.'

'She'll be fine.' Tyrrell hurried to the side and studied the darker wedge of land. 'She draws less and is better to handle close-hauled.' He patted the rail. 'But *Sparrow*'ll do for me!'

'Take in the forecourse, if you please.' Bolitho pitched his ear to the sea's changing sounds. The hollow boom of surf against rocks, the deeper note of water exploring a cave or some narrow gully below the headland. 'Then the spanker.'

Under topsails and jib *Sparrow* crept deeper into the bay, her stem rising and plunging across tiderace and swell alike, her helmsmen tensed at the wheel, fingers sensing her will almost as soon as she did.

Minutes dragged by, then an half-hour. With eyes straining into the darkness, and other men poised at gun-port tackles and braces, the sloop tacked delicately below the cape.

Then Tyrrell said, 'No ships here, sir. Lynnhaven lies abeam now. Any squadron at anchor, ours or th' Frogs, would be showing some sort of light. To deter an enemy, if for no other reason.'

'That makes good sense.'

Bolitho walked away to hide his disappointment. Odell had been right to ask for written orders, for if Bolitho had misjudged Hood's whereabouts this badly he could be equally at fault for quitting his proper station in the south.

A series of dull explosions echoed across the water, and one bright stab of flame, as if some powder had been accidentally fired.

He ran his fingers through his hair, wondering what he should do next. Sail on for New York? It seemed the only solution.

Tyrrell said quietly, 'If we are to beat clear of th' cape, then I suggest we wear ship now.' He paused. 'Or anchor.'

Bolitho joined him by the compass. 'Then we anchor. We must make contact with the army. They at least should know what is happening.'

Tyrrell sighed. 'It's hard to think that there's a damn great

288

army out there across our bows. Poor bastards. If they are in Yorktown as Odell was led to believe, then they are well placed. But it'll be no comfort if they come under siege.'

'Let's waste no more time.' Bolitho beckoned to Fowler. 'Show the lantern again. Captain Farr will anchor when he sees the signal.'

The topsails stirred noisily as *Sparrow* turned obediently into the wind, her anchor throwing up a sheet of spray like some disturbed water-spirit.

Buckle called, 'Easy with that light, Mr Fowler! Enough is enough!'

Tyrrell dropped his voice. 'No matter. We'll have been sighted from th' moment we weathered th' cape.'

Bolitho looked at him. It was not difficult to picture some scurrying messenger or a mounted man riding through the darkness to warn of their arrival. He felt much as he had done in Delaware Bay. Cut off and restricted, with only the vaguest idea of what was happening.

Tyrrell said, 'I can take a boat, sir. If th' army is encamped in th' town, then they'll be well shielded around th' next spit of land along York River.' He sounded suddenly on edge. 'God, this quiet disturbs me more'n gunfire! My grandfather was a soldier. Used to make my flesh creep with his yarns of night fighting.'

Bolitho watched the topmen sliding down to the deck, seemingly indifferent to the closeness of land or a possible enemy.

'Rig boarding nets and have half the twelve-pounders loaded with grape.'

Tyrrell nodded. 'Aye. An' I'll put some good hands on th' swivels, too. No sense in being rushed by some crazy boat attack.'

He waited and then asked, 'Shall I go?'

'Very well. Take both cutters. Mr Graves can command the second one. Mr Fowler will go with you in case we need any signals made.'

A voice called, '*Heron*'s anchored, sir!'

But when Bolitho looked across the nettings he could see nothing. The lookout must have caught a brief glimpse of her reefed topsails as she edged around the cape, or the splash of her anchor when she let go.

Tackles creaked and jerked as both cutters were swayed over the gangways before the decks were sealed off in a web of nets. That could be left safely to the boatswain. Not too taut to afford a grip to some daring boarder, just slack enough to confuse him, to allow a pike or bayonet to catch him before he could slip free.

Men shuffled across the deck, and he heard an occasional clink of steel, the thud of oars being released from their lashings.

Graves came aft, his breeches white in the darkness.

'You know what to do?' Bolitho looked at each in turn. 'Mr Tyrrell will lead. Muffle your oars, and watch out for enemy pickets.'

Graves sounded breathless. 'How will we recognize our own soldiers?'

Bolitho could imagine his mouth jerking uncontrollably and was tempted to keep him on board. But Tyrrell was all important. He knew the lay of the land like his own cabin. It needed an experienced officer to back him if things went wrong.

He heard Tyrrell reply calmly, 'Easy. Th' Frogs speak French!'

Graves swung round and then controlled himself with an effort.

'I—I didn't ask for your sarcasm! It's all right for you. This is your country.'

'That will do!' Bolitho stepped closer. 'Remember, our people are depending on you. So let's have none of this bickering.'

Tyrrell eased his sword in its sheath. 'I'm sorry, sir. It was my fault.' He rested his hand on Graves's shoulder. 'Forget I spoke, eh?'

Fowler's voice came up from the boats. 'All ready, sir!'

Bolitho walked to the gangway. 'Be back by dawn.' He touched Tyrrell's arm. 'How is the pain now?'

'Hardly feel a thing, sir.' Tyrrell stood back to allow his men to clamber into the cutters. 'A bit of exercise will do me good.'

The boats shoved off and pulled steadily into the darkness. Within minutes they had vanished, and a watchful silence settled over those who stood at the loaded guns on either beam.

Bolitho sought out Stockdale and said, 'Have the gig lowered. I may want word carried to *Heron*.' He saw Bethune's plump outline by the rail and added, 'You take the gig and pull round the ship. I will signal if I need a message passed.'

Bethune hesitated. 'I would have willingly gone with the first lieutenant, sir.'

'I know that.' It was hard to believe that in the midst of all this confusion Bethune had managed to see his choice of Fowler as a personal slur. 'He is very young. I need all the *men* I can get to manage the ship.' It was a lame explanation, but it seemed to suffice.

It was cool under the stars, and after the heat of the day, a gentle relief. Bolitho kept the seamen in short watches, so that those not on lookout or standing at the guns might snatch a few moment's rest.

Likewise, the officers stood watch and watch, and when he was relieved by Heyward, Bolitho squatted against the mainmast trunk and rested his head in his hands.

He felt someone gripping his wrist and knew he must have fallen asleep.

Heyward was crouching beside him, his voice a fierce whisper. 'Boat approaching, sir, maybe two.'

Bolitho scrambled to his feet, his mind grappling with Heyward's words. Surely they were not returning already. They could not even have reached the first part of their destination.

Heyward said, 'It's not the gig. She's away on the starboard quarter.'

Bolitho cupped his hands round his ears. Above the slap of water alongside he heard oars and the squeak of a tiller.

A boatswain's mate asked, 'Shall I call a challenge, sir?'

'No.' Why had he said that? 'Not yet.'

He strained his eyes and tried to pick out the splash of oars amidst the lapping cat's-paws of the bay. It had to be Tyrrell returning for he was coming straight for the ship without caution or hesitation.

A thin shaft of moonlight had made a small rippling pattern across the water, and as he watched a longboat glided into it, the oars moving unhurriedly.

Before it slid once more into shadows Bolitho saw the gleam of crossbelts, some soldiers wearing shakos crowded in the sternsheets.

Heyward gasped hoarsely, 'Holy God, they're French!'

The boatswain's mate whispered, 'There's another one astern of 'er!'

Thoughts and wild ideas flooded through Bolitho's mind as he watched the boats' slow approach. Tyrrell and his men captured and being returned for parley. The French coming to announce that Yorktown was theirs and to demand *Sparrow*'s surrender.

He moved quickly to the gangway and cupped his hands. '*Ohe! du canot! Qui va la?*'

There was a babble of voices from the boat and he heard someone laughing.

To Heyward he snapped, 'Quick, recall the gig! We'll catch these beauties with any luck!'

The first boat was already grinding alongside, and Bolitho held his breath, half expecting one of his own men to fire.

From a corner of his eye he saw a cream of spray, and thanked God that the gig's crew had kept their wits. It was sweeping around the stern, and he could imagine Stockdale willing his men to pull with all their strength.

Heyward came back, the signal lantern still in his hand.

Bolitho shouted, '*Now!*'

Even as the first men appeared on the chains and clung uncertainly to the nets, a line of armed seamen leapt on to the gangway with levelled muskets, while Glass, the boatswain, swung a swivel gun and trained it threateningly.

There was a chorus of shouts and a musket stabbed fire through the night. The ball slammed into the rail and brought a savage fusillade of shots from Heyward's marksmen.

Glass depressed the swivel and jerked the lanyard, changing the crowded boat into a screaming, bloody shambles.

It was more than enough for the second boat. The crash of musket fire, the devastating hail of canister from Glass's swivel were sufficient to render the oars motionless. Hardly a man moved as the gig tore alongside and made fast, and across the choppy water Stockdale bawled, 'Got 'er, sir!' A pause and he called again, 'There's a dozen English prisoners in this 'un!'

Bolitho turned away, feeling sick. He saw Dalkeith and his mates climbing down to the boat alongside and pictured the whimpering carnage he would find there. It could just as easily have been the second boat, and the canister would have carved its bloody path amongst their own people.

He said harshly, 'Get those men aboard, Mr Heyward. Then send the gig to *Heron*. Farr will be wondering what the hell we are about.'

He waited beside the entry port, as with boarding nets lifted the first dazed men were pushed or hauled aboard. The second boatload, French and English alike, came with obvious relief. The French glad to have been spared their companions' slaughter. The English redcoats had different reasons, but their stunned disbelief was pitiful to watch.

Bedraggled and filthy, they were more like scarecrows than trained soldiers.

Bolitho said, 'Take the prisoners below, Mr Glass.' To the redcoats he added, 'Have no fear. This is a King's ship.'

One, a young ensign, stepped forward and exclaimed, 'I thank you, Captain. We all do.'

Bolitho gripped his hand. 'You will get all the rest and help I can offer. But first I must know what is happening here.'

The officer rubbed his eyes with his knuckles. 'We were taken several days back. It was a skirmish with one of their patrols. Most of my men were killed.' He rocked on his feet. 'I still cannot believe we are saved. . . .'

Bolitho persisted, 'Is General Cornwallis holding Yorktown?'

'Yes. But as I expect you know, sir, Washington and the French general, Rochambeau, crossed the Hudson some weeks back to the head of Chesapeake Bay. They have a great army massed around Yorktown. A musket behind every tree. But when we heard that an English squadron had looked into the bay we thought we were relieved. I understand a little French and heard the guards speaking of their arrival.'

Heyward said, 'Hood's ships.'

Bolitho nodded. 'When was this?'

The ensign shrugged. 'Three days back. I have lost count of time.'

Bolitho tried to shut out the pitiful cries alongside. He knew little French. Little more than he had used to deceive the boat, but sufficient to recognize pleading. A man being held while Dalkeith got busy with his knife.

Three days back. That fitted what Odell had reported. Hood must have taken a quick look into the bay, and finding no sign of de Grasse had pushed on for New York.

The ensign added weakly, 'The French are expecting their own fleet. That was why, when someone hailed them in their own language, they . . .'

'*What?*' Bolitho seized his arm, his voice harsh despite the man's condition. 'Expecting their own fleet?'

The ensign stared at him. 'But I thought . . . I imagined our ships had gone to fight them off, sir!'

'No.' He released his arm. 'I fear that when they reach New York and discover their mistake it will be too late.'

'Then the army is done for, sir.' The ensign walked unsteadily to the rail. 'All this.' He shouted across the dark water. 'All for *bloody nothing*!'

Dalkeith appeared on deck and with a brief nod took the officer's arm.

Bolitho said, 'Take care of them for me.'

He turned away. They would be prisoners again very soon unless he could decide what to do.

Buckle was watching him anxiously. 'What about Mr Tyrrell, sir?'

'D'you imagine I've not thought about him?' He saw Buckle recoil. 'We will pass the word to *Heron* immediately. If she can work clear tonight Farr must carry the news to Admiral Graves. There might still be time.' He saw the purser hovering by the hatch. 'Fetch some paper and I will write a note for Farr.'

To Buckle he added, 'I'm sorry I abused you. It was a fair question.'

He looked towards the land. 'We will weigh at first light

294

and move closer inshore. Have the sweeps ready in case the wind loses us. I'll not throw Tyrrell and his men away without a fight.' He remembered the lieutenant's words in that far off garden. *In* Sparrow *we look after our own.* He added quietly, 'We've all come too far together for that.'

Dalkeith crossed the deck as Bolitho walked to the taffrail. To Buckle he whispered, 'What's the captain going to do?'

Buckle shrugged. 'Something crazy, I expect.'

The surgeon wiped his hands on a piece of waste. 'But you approve, nonetheless?'

Buckle grinned. 'Don't make much difference what I think, does it? But I s'pect he'll think of something.' He added vehemently, 'I bloody well hope so, for all our sakes!'

18. Only the Brave

STOCKDALE padded across the quarterdeck and held out a pewter mug.

"'Ere, sir, Some coffee.'

Bolitho took it and held it to his lips. It was barely hot, but cleared the dryness from his throat.

Stockdale added thickly, 'The galley fire was doused, so I 'ad to warm it on a lantern in the shot locker.'

Bolitho looked at him. Was it imagination, or were Stockdale's features growing more distinct in the gloom? He shivered. More likely he had been too long on deck, waiting and wondering. Yet he could do no good by pacing the deck and going over his ideas again and again.

'It was a kind thought.' He handed him the mug. 'I feel awake now.'

He peered up at the rigging and furled sails. The stars were still there, but paler. That was no illusion.

'Where is the wind?'

Stockdale considered the question. 'As afore, sir. Nor' nor'-east, if I'm not mistook.'

Bolitho bit his lip. He had already decided it was so. Stockdale was usually right, but his confirmation did little to help.

He said, 'Rouse the master. He is by the hatchway.'

Buckle sprang to his feet, wide awake at Stockdale's first touch.

'What is it? An attack?'

'Easy, Mr Buckle.' Bolitho beckoned him to the rail. 'The wind has dropped, but still too far north'rd to help us.'

The master said nothing and waited to see what the captain had in mind.

'If we are to be of any use, we must drive higher into the bay. It would take hours of tacking back and forth, with little to show for our pains. But if we stay here at anchor we can help neither the first lieutenant nor ourselves if an enemy arrives.'

Buckle yawned.

'That's true enough.'

'So call all hands and run out the sweeps. We will get under way and not wait for the dawn.'

Buckle pulled out his watch and held it against the compass light.

'Hmm. It'll be a hard pull, sir. But the current will not be too much against us.'

He walked to the nettings and kicked a shadowy figure who was sleeping soundly on the bare planks.

'Up, boy! Tell Mr Glass to call the hands. Jump to it!'

Bolitho went quickly to his cabin and concentrated for several minutes on his chart. Recalling what Tyrrell had told him, and adding the information to what he knew already, he settled on his plan of action. Beyond the cabin he could hear the tramp of feet at the capstan, the regular clink of a pawl as the cable came inboard.

He put on his coat and adjusted his swordbelt. How strange the cabin looked in the solitary lantern's light. Cleared for action like the rest of his ship, the guns creaking gently behind their sealed ports, powder and shot, rammers and sponges, all within easy reach. But no one stood near them, for like the remainder of the gun deck, every hand would be needed to raise anchor and man the long sweeps. The latter had got them out of trouble before. This time they might do the same for Tyrrell and his men.

He left the cabin and ran swiftly up the ladder.

It was lighter. There could be no doubt about it. A sort of greyness above Cape Henry, and he could see the swirl of currents well clear of the hull.

He saw the long sweeps swaying above the water on either beam, the men hunched around them, chattering quietly while they awaited an order from aft.

Heyward touched his hat. 'Anchor's hove short, sir.' He sounded tense and very alert.

Bolitho strode from side to side, watching the ship's swing towards the shore, the ripple of water below the gangways.

'How does it feel? From midshipman to first lieutenant with barely a pause?'

He did not hear Heyward's reply, and knew he had only asked the question to cover his own anxiety. If the men lost control of the sweeps he would have to anchor immediately. Even then he might be driven too close inshore for comfort.

From forward he heard Bethune's cry, 'Anchor's aweigh, sir!' The patter of feet as men ran from the capstan bars to add their weight on the sweeps.

Then Glass's voice, 'Steady! *Stand by!*'

Bolitho gripped his hands together until the fingers almost cracked. Why the hell was he leaving it so late? In a moment the ship would be aground.

'Give way all!'

The sweeps swayed forward, dipped and then came steadily aft.

Behind him Bolitho heard the wheel easing gently, and Buckle's quiet cursing as he endured the tension in his own style. He tried to relax his muscles. Glass had been right to make sure of that first stroke. But it was one thing to know it, another to remain aloof in the face of danger to his ship.

Up and down, forward to aft, the sweeps creaked busily but without undue haste, until Buckle called, 'Steerage way, sir!'

'Good. Hold her due north, if you please.'

Heyward removed his coat. 'I'll go and lend a hand, sir.'

'Yes. Make sure we have every available man working. Those redcoats as well, if they have the strength.' He checked him as he ran for the ladder. 'There is no need to tell the soldiers we are heading *towards* the enemy, Mr Heyward!' He saw him grin. 'They'll find out soon enough.'

Buckle and a solitary seaman stood at the wheel, and Bolitho walked right aft to the taffrail without speaking. He saw the nearest cape more clearly now, the pattern of white-caps at its base to mark some small cove. An empty place. When daylight came, and *Heron* was seen to be gone, his men might question his action, and rightly. But if their presence was to be of any use to the admiral, then they must learn everything possible. The released soldiers had told them much. But a lot could have changed since they had been taken. He smiled grimly. He was deluding himself. But for Tyrrell and the others, would he really have remained here in the bay?

He heard shouts on deck and someone speaking in French. Heyward was more than a good companion, he was proving to be an excellent officer. Without further consultation, and at the risk of his captain's displeasure, he had released the French prisoners and put them to work. All strong, beefy soldiers who had led a fairly comfortable life guarding prisoners, they would make a small but significant difference to the heavy sweeps.

Some gulls rose screaming angrily from the water where they had been sleeping as the *Sparrow* moved amongst them at a slow but steady crawl. Time dragged by, and Bolitho saw that the soldiers' coats were red again instead of black as they had appeared in the darkness. Faces regained personality, and he was able to see those who were standing the strain and others who were being relieved at more frequent intervals to regain their breath.

A blacker shadow loomed and held firm across the starboard bow. That must be the inner side of Cape Charles, he decided, with Tyrrell's middle-ground some distance below it.

'Bring her up a point, Mr Buckle.' He heard the helm squeak. 'We must pass the cape with the mainland to larboard. There'll not be too much water in the channel, so hold her steady.'

'Aye, sir. Nor' by east it is!'

The ship was heading almost directly into the wind, and he could feel it on his face, smell the land and its freshness in the dawn air. But it was more sheltered, and he was relieved to see the sweeps were still moving in unison, although the actual progress was probably less than a knot.

He sought out the young ensign and called him aft. He arrived panting on the quarterdeck, and Bolitho said, 'Look abeam. How near are your outposts?'

The soldier peered across the larboard nettings and raised one arm.

'That bit of land, sir. That'll be the turning point. A lot of sand there. We lost some barges a few weeks back when they ran ashore. A mile or so further and you'll be able to see the mouth of York River just beyond a pair of small islands.'

Bolitho smiled. 'I expect you're surprised we're heading this way.'

The ensign shrugged. 'I am past surprise, sir.' He stiffened. 'I heard a bugle. That'll be our lads.' He tapped the rail with his fingers, his face engrossed. Then there was a long-drawn-out trumpet call, which sent a cloud of gulls flapping and squeaking from the land. He said, 'The Frogs. Always a minute behind our reveille.'

Bolitho tried to break him from his mood. 'What of the Americans?'

The ensign sighed. 'They have artillery over the river. They'll start firing at first light. More effective than any damn bugle!'

Bolitho turned towards Buckle. 'We will keep on this course as long as our people have strength for it. The wind will favour us when we finally go about, but I want to get as far above York River as I can.'

He looked aloft and saw the masthead pendant for the first time.

It was flapping gently astern, but showed no warning of a strengthening wind. If it got up now, his men would be unable to hold the stroke. Even with Tyrrell's boat crews it would have been hard. Without them, impossible.

When he glanced abeam he saw the overhanging spur of Cape Charles, and far beyond it, like a thin gold thread, the horizon. Showing its face to the sun which was easing into view, parting sea from sky, night from day.

There was a muffled bang, and seconds later he saw the tell-tale white fin of spray to mark where a ball had ploughed into the bay.

The ensign remarked indifferently, 'They'll never reach you at this range. You've a good half mile to play with.'

'Where is the battery?'

The soldier studied him curiously. 'Everywhere, sir. There are guns right round this sector. Yorktown and its approaches are hemmed in a ring of iron. Our army has the sea at its back.' He suddenly looked very young and vulnerable. 'Only the fleet can bring relief.'

Bolitho pictured Farr's *Heron* making all haste towards New

York. Even there he might find Hood gone, perhaps further still to Newport to contain de Barras.

He thought, too, of Odell's solitary vigil in his *Lucifer*. If the French did come by way of the little used Bahama Channel, he would need no encouragement to make sail and run.

He blinked as a shaft of sunlight played across the distant cape and coloured the yards and stays like honey. He pulled out his watch. Tyrrell should have made his contact with Cornwallis's pickets and be on his way back to Lynnhaven by now. By weighing and putting the men to the sweeps, their meeting should have been brought forward by an hour at least.

Glass ran up the ladder, his chest heaving from exertion.

'Can't hold 'em much longer, sir!' He peered down at the sweeps, at their sluggish rise and fall. 'Shall I put the rope's end to 'em, sir?'

'You will not.' Bolitho looked away. There was no malice in Glass, nor was he prone to unnecessary force. It was just that he did not know what else to do. 'Tell them. Another half hour. Then we make sail, or anchor.'

Glass shifted awkwardly. 'It'd be better from you, sir.'

Bolitho walked to the rail and called, 'One more turn of the glass, lads!' He heard groans, the mingled curses and gasps from those still hidden in shadow. 'It's that or leave our people out there to fend for themselves! Remember, it might have been you!'

He turned away, not knowing if his words had achieved anything but resentment.

Glass watched critically and then spat on his hands. 'That done it, sir! Better already!'

Bolitho sighed. The stroke looked as weary as before, but if the boatswain was satisfied, then . . .

He swung round as a voice called, 'Boat, sir! Fine on the larboard bow!'

Bolitho gripped the rail. 'Just the one?'

'Aye, sir.'

'Bring her round two points to larboard.'

Bolitho tried not to think about the missing boat. He felt the hull yaw, the stroke failing as the helm went over.

The soldier said quietly, 'No closer, I pray you. You'll be in cannon-shot before long.'

Bolitho ignored him. '*Pull*, lads! Come on, do your damn-dest!'

One man fell exhausted from a loom and was dragged away by Dalkeith.

The lookout yelled. 'It's the second cutter, sir! Mr Graves!'

Dalkeith heaved himself up the ladder and stood at the rail. 'I *know* what you're thinking, sir.' He did not flinch under Bolitho's cold stare. 'He'd not leave you. Not for anything.'

Bolitho looked past his shoulder at a patch of land. In the strengthening light he saw tall trees and a round hill beyond. They were motionless. The sweeps were only keeping *Sparrow* steady against wind and current. In a minute she would start to pay-off and drift inshore. They had done their best. It was not enough.

He snapped, 'Damn your eyes, Mr Dalkeith! I'll not be lectured by you!'

He leaned over the rail. 'Mr Heyward! Stand by to let go the anchor!'

Bolitho waited while men ran to the call and Glass sent others to bear down on the flagging sweeps where exhausted sailors had fallen to the deck. He heard a bang and saw a ball ricochet across the water to throw up a plume of spray very close to the approaching cutter. The boat was moving rapidly towards him, and he could see Graves by the tiller, his hat awry as he beat out the time to his oarsmen.

'Ready, sir!'

He chopped with his arm. 'Let go!'

Even as the anchor took grip and the hull swung carelessly to the cable, he yelled, 'Withdraw sweeps! Mr Glass, *get those men on their feet!*'

Dalkeith stood his ground. 'You can't blame yourself, sir.'

He met Bolitho's gaze stubbornly. 'Curse me if you will, but I'll not stand by and see you torment yourself.'

The cutter was hooking on to the main chains, and he heard Graves shouting at the men on deck to make fast his lines.

He said quietly, 'Thank you for your concern. But there is no one else *to* blame.'

He made himself wait by the rail until Graves had scrabbled aboard, and then called sharply, 'Lay aft, if you please! The boatswain can deal with the cutter.'

Graves hurried towards him, his face twitching violently.

Bolitho asked, 'Where are the others?' He kept his voice very calm, but was conscious of his whole being screaming at Graves's stricken face.

'We grounded in some shallows, sir. Both boats separated. It was the first lieutenant's idea. A patrol of soldiers had signalled where we should secure the boats, but there was some shooting. Enemy marksmen, I believe.'

'And then?' He could feel others standing nearby, see Heyward's frozen expression as he listened to Graves's quick, erratic account.

'In the darkness we were all trying to take cover. I lost a man, and Tyrrell sent word for us to stay hidden in a creek.' He shook his head vaguely. 'The balls were flying everywhere. Tyrrell was going to meet one of the officers. They knew we were coming, apparently. Their scouts had seen us.' His mouth jerked uncontrollably. 'We stayed there waiting, and then there was more firing, and I heard men charging through the brush, there must have been a platoon or more!'

'Did you not think of going to assist Mr Tyrrell!?'

Graves stared at him, his eyes blank. 'We were in mortal danger! I sent Fowler to find the others, but . . .'

'You did *what*?' Bolitho reached out and gripped his coat. 'You sent that boy on his own?'

'He—he volunteered, sir.' Graves looked down at Bolitho's hand on his coat. 'When he failed to return I decided to'—he raised his eyes, suddenly composed—'to obey your orders and withdraw to the ship.'

Bolitho released his hold and turned away. He felt sick and appalled with what Graves had done. The lieutenant's pathetic defiance made it worse, if that were possible. He had obeyed orders. So his crime was acceptable.

A puff of smoke rose above the nearest spit of land, and he saw the ball drop within half a cable of the ship. Even now, some officer might be ordering up a heavier gun. One which would make short work of so promising a target.

He heard himself say, 'Tell Mr Yule to run out the larboard bow-chaser and lay it on that gunsmoke. He will fire with grape until I order otherwise. It might cool their eagerness.'

He walked past Graves without a glance.

'Have the cutter manned at once.' He looked down at the silent seamen on the gun deck. 'I want volunteers for . . .' He swallowed as the assembled men moved towards the side as if drawn by wires. 'Thank you. But just a boat's crew. Mr Glass, see to it at once!'

To Heyward he added, 'You will remain here.' He did not look at Graves. 'If I fall, *you* will assist the master in getting the ship under way, understood?'

Heyward nodded, his eyes filling his face.

Dalkeith touched his arm. '*Look*, sir!'

It was the other cutter, or what was left of it. Even in the poor light it was possible to see the splintered gunwale, the few remaining oars which moved it so very slowly on the uneasy water.

There was a bang and another waterspout shot skyward just beyond it. The hidden gun had shifted to a smaller but closer target.

Bolitho flinched as Yule's crew fired their first shot from forward, saw the trees quiver as if in a freak gust as the packed grape scythed towards the drifting smoke.

'A glass!'

He hardly dared to raise it to his eye. Then he saw the cutter, the scars in its side left by musket balls, the lolling corpses still propped between the remaining oarsmen. Then he saw Tyrrell. He was sitting on the gunwhale right aft, someone draped across his knees as he steered the boat past the white patch left by the enemy's ball.

He said quietly, 'Thank God.'

The bow-chaser hurled itself inboard again, dragging him from his thoughts, his overwhelming relief.

He shouted, 'Mr Bethune, take the cutter and assist Mr Tyrrell!' He looked for Buckle. 'Get the hands aloft and prepare to loose tops'ls!'

All exhaustion and dread at Graves's report seemed to be fading as men tore to their stations. The cutter was pulling from the side, Bethune standing upright as he urged his crew to greater efforts.

Dalkeith said, 'Well, sir . . .' He got no further.

One of the topmen who had reached the uppermost yard before his companions yelled, 'Deck there! Sail comin' around th' 'eadland!'

Bolitho snatched a glass and trained it above the nettings. She was standing well out from the bay, but was already tacking frantically towards Cape Henry. It was the *Lucifer*.

Odell would be shocked to find no fleet, nor even *Heron* at anchor. He tensed. There was damage to the schooner's mizzen, and she was handling sluggishly as she tried to beat closer to the entrance. She must have been caught unprepared by another ship, perhaps under cover of darkness. There was no mistaking the flapping rents in her great foresail, the uneven spread of rigging.

He saw flags breaking to the wind, and held the glass motionless while his lips spelled out the brief signal.

He turned to Buckle. '*Enemy in sight.*'

'God A'mighty.'

'Mr Heyward!' He saw him swing round from the capstan.

'Stand by to cut the cable! We will not recover the boats, but make sail as soon as our people are aboard!'

He heard a chorus of shouts, and when he turned aft he saw *Lucifer* folding her great sails like the wings of a dying bird. She must have risked everything to reach him with her news, even to make that one vital signal. She had driven too close and had struck the shoals which Tyrrell had described so vividly.

He made himself walk to the rail and look for the boats. Tyrrell's cutter was almost awash, but Bethune was there, and he saw the wounded being hauled across, a patch of scarlet to mark at least one soldier in the party.

Several more guns were firing now, and balls threw up tall splashes in pale sunlight like a line of leaping dolphins.

Some of the topmen gave a ragged cheer as Bethune cast the waterlogged cutter adrift and headed back towards *Sparrow*.

Bolitho turned towards Graves who was standing much as before. 'Take charge of your guns.' He kept his voice formal without understanding why or how. He could picture *Lucifer's* frail hull breaking up on the rocks and Tyrrell's shattered boat trying to reach *Sparrow*. He could even see young Fowler, a mere child, running through some unknown woods while shots shrieked all about him. 'Do your duty. That is all I ask of you.' He looked away. 'All I will ever ask of you again.'

He heard the boat grind alongside and saw Tyrrell and the others being dragged through the entry port, being clapped on the shoulders and bombarded with questions and cheers.

Bolitho strode towards him and saw with sudden despair that Tyrrell was carrying Midshipman Fowler. It must have been his body across his legs in the boat.

Tyrrell looked at him steadily and gave a tired grin. 'He's all right, sir. He was crying fit to break his heart, an' then fell asleep in th' boat.' He handed the midshipman to some seamen. 'Worn out, poor little bugger.' He saw Graves and added flatly, 'But he's got guts. Plenty of 'em.' Then he strode forward and gripped Bolitho's hands. 'He's not th' only one, it seems.'

A new voice drawled, ''Pon my *word*, I knew we'd meet again!'

It was Colonel Foley. A bandage round his throat, his uniform in tatters, but somehow remaining as impeccable as Bolitho remembered him.

Bolitho said, 'I, too.' He looked at Tyrrell. 'We are in for some warm work today, I fear. *Lucifer's* done for, and we must leave quickly if we are to avoid her fate.'

'Aye.' Tyrrell limped towards the wheel. 'I'd guessed as much.'

A cry from aloft brought every eye towards the headland. Very slowly, their yards braced round in the sunlight, a frigate and a deep-hulled transport were passing level with the wrecked schooner.

Bolitho said simply, 'Sooner than I thought.' He looked at Heyward. 'We will cut the cable.' To Tyrrell he added, 'Then you may pass the word to load and run out.'

The cutter and its dead oarsmen drifted away from the side, a discarded reminder of their sacrifice.

Bethune hurried aft, his face glowing with excitement.

Bolitho said, 'Well done. I'll see you a lieutenant yet, despite what *you* do to the contrary.'

He felt suddenly composed, even relaxed. 'Run up the colours! We'll show the army we're not leaving them to no purpose!'

The cable cut, and with her topsails bellying to the wind, *Sparrow* tilted round in a tight arc, the thunder of her canvas drowning the gunfire from the trees, her seamen too busy even to think beyond their work and the need to reach the open sea.

By the time *Sparrow* had gone about and settled on her course towards the capes, there could be no doubt in anyone's mind as to the enemy's intentions. Even as Tyrrell reported all guns loaded and run out, Bolitho raised his glass to examine yet another ship as she rounded the southern headland. One more heavy transport, and beyond her he could see the billowing topsails of a protective frigate.

Tyrrell said, 'God's teeth, a fleet and nothing less!'

Buckle called, 'Steady as she goes, sir! Sou' by west!'

The first transport had already dropped anchor, and through his glass Bolitho saw her boats being lowered with swift precision, the glint of sunlight on weapons and uniforms as soldiers clambered down ladders and nets in a manner which spoke of much practice. He shifted his glass to the second large vessel. She, too, was crammed with soldiers, and there were limbers on her upper deck, and her yards were festooned with heavy tackles, the kind used for lowering horses into boats or lighters.

Colonel Foley drawled, 'We heard Rochambeau was expecting reinforcements. It would appear they have arrived.'

Bolitho glanced at him. 'What is your mission now?'

'If you can get me to New York I have despatches for General Clinton. They may not help Cornwallis, but he will be glad to know what is happening here.' He gave a brief smile. 'I heard that you dealt severely with our old friend Blundell? Not before time.' He raised one eyebrow. 'You met his niece again, I understand?'

Bolitho watched the jib-boom swing very slightly and settle on the out-thrust wedge of headland. How could they speak so calmly and detachedly when death lay so close at hand?

He replied, 'Yes. She will be in England now.'

Foley gave a sigh. 'I am relieved. I recognize all the signs, Captain. She wanted you to quit the Service and join her train of admirers, eh?' He held up one hand. 'Do not bother to reply! It is plain on your face, as it must have been on mine.'

Bolitho smiled gravely. 'Something of the sort.'

'When she tired of me I was sent to serve under Cornwallis. A favour as it turned out. And you?'

Tyrrell stepped back from the rail. 'She almost had him killed!'

Foley shook his head. 'A formidable woman indeed.'

'Deck there! Ship-o'-the-line roundin' the cape!'

Bolitho felt a chill on his spine as he thought of Odell's dash from the south. Day by day and at each dawn he would look astern at the pursuing ships. It must have been a nightmare for every man aboard.

The boats from the two transports were pulling towards the land now, and he could see the hulls deep in the water as testimony of the numbers they carried.

'Set the t'gallants, Mr Tyrrell. We will need all our wind today.'

Foley drew his sabre and turned it over in his hands. 'You are not merely running away, I take it?'

Bolitho shook his head. 'Those two frigates are shortening sail, Colonel. They intend to rake us when we attempt to clear the middle-ground.' He pointed towards the anchored transports. 'There is our course. Close inshore, where we'll be least expected.'

Foley grimaced. 'Or welcome, I suspect.'

Bolitho looked at Buckle. 'When we go about you must lay her as close as you can to Cape Henry.'

'Aye, sir.' Buckle was peering through shrouds and stays, his eyes fixed on the ships.

Bolitho raised his glass again. The two frigates were under minimum canvas standing before the wind with some difficulty as they waited for the small sloop to dash past them. Less than a mile now. He watched them narrowly, noting their drift, the sun gleaming on their broadsides and on the raised telescopes of their officers.

He snapped, 'How many boats in the water?'

Bethune called, 'At least thirty!'

'Good.'

Bolitho imagined the packed soldiers who would be watching *Sparrow*'s apparent dash for safety. A spectacle to drive away their own doubts and fears of what lay ahead on the American mainland.

Bolitho drew his hanger and held it above his head. Along the gun deck he saw the crews crouching at the tackles, each captain peering aft, a slow-match held ready. In the maintop two swivels were training this way and that, a seaman squatting on the barricade with fresh canister cradled to his chest. Curiously, as he ran his eyes quickly over his command, he was reminded of Colquhoun's words so long ago. *When all others are looking aft at you.*

He heard a sharp bang, and seconds later the high-pitched whine of a ball whipping overhead. One of the frigates had fired a ranging shot. But he kept his eyes on the nearest transport as she swung to her cable, her high poop towards the beach. Aboard the frigates the gun crews would be betting with each other. How many balls would they get off before the *Sparrow* was overwhelmed by their cross-fire or she struck her colours?

He brought down his hanger with a flourish.

'*Now!*'

The wheel creaked noisily, and as men hauled at the braces to retrim the yards, *Sparrow*'s stem began to turn. Bolitho held his breath, watching the frigates slipping further and further down the larboard bow, while the nearest transport and then the great spread of oared boats swam across the jib-boom, and beyond them the land opened up as if to receive their onrushing charge.

'Hold her!'

Bolitho ran to the nettings, his mind hanging on to Tyrrell's words of Lynnhaven Bay, the depths and currents, the dangers and margin of survival.

Buckle's helmsmen cursed and spun the wheel against the opposite thrust of wind and sea, and as spray leapt above the beakhead Bolitho saw the nearest boats careering off course, the realization and horror of his intentions at last only too clear.

Gunfire thudded across the bay, and balls whimpered and splashed very near to the hull. But the two frigates had been taken by surprise, and as *Sparrow* lunged towards the shore, Bolitho knew that within minutes she would be screened from their fire by the first transport.

He could feel the madness surging through him like fever, and as he yelled down at the gun deck he knew it was infectious, saw the men poised at their open ports like half-naked demons.

'*Stand by!*' The hanger was above his head again. 'Full depression!'

He saw the nearest muzzles dipping towards the creaming water, the gun captains dancing from side to side while their men stood ready with charges and fresh shot for the next barrage, and the one after that.

'As you bear!' The hanger hovered, holding the fresh sunlight like gold. '*Fire!*'

The air was blasted apart by the ragged broadsides from either beam. As the dense smoke swirled inboard, and the gun crews yelled and cheered above the squeak of trucks, the clatter of handspikes and rammers, Bolitho saw the next spitting tongues from forward, the double shotted charges smashing into boats and soldiers, the whirl of splinters and spray. Above the decks the braced topsails quivered to each explosion, the smoke fanning out on either side in a choking fog while the guns roared out again and again.

Sharper cracks from muskets, the metallic bangs of swivels, made words impossible. It was a nightmare, a world in torment. Boats lurched into the hull and Bolitho felt the deck shake as *Sparrow*'s stem smashed into a launch, breaking it in two and spilling out the overloaded soldiers in a kicking, screaming profusion.

A transport was firing now, her upper tier cutting over the scattered boats and slapping through *Sparrow*'s canvas like great fists.

A ball burst through the nettings, and Bolitho heard shrill screams as two seamen were pulped against the opposite side. He saw Fowler walking dazedly past the dismembered corpses, his face set as if in deep thought. He noticed that he was snapping his fingers.

The hull gave another great lurch, and below his feet he felt the enemy's iron smashing through the gun deck, the attendant rumble of a twelve-pounder being overturned.

Another longboat lurched down the starboard side, some men firing with their muskets, others scrambling over the frantic sailors at the oars. Balls thudded into the rail and bulwark, and a seaman fell choking on blood as one took him in the throat.

Bolitho ran to the side and wiped his streaming eyes to peer astern. The surface was littered with smashed boats and drifting woodwork. Men, too, some swimming, others fading beneath the water under their weight of weapons and equipment.

Foley was reloading a musket and shouting, 'A few less for our boys to fight!' He leaned over the nettings and shot down a soldier even as he stood to fire at the sloop.

Bolitho strained his eyes towards the shore. It was near enough. Almost too close.

'Bring her about!' He had to repeat the order before Buckle understood.

With blocks screaming and her yards braced round once more, *Sparrow* heeled dangerously on the larboard tack, her bows seemingly pointed straight at the land.

And there was the second transport, swinging drunkenly across the bow, her gun-ports already flashing and tearing the air apart with shot.

A ball ripped through the quarterdeck rail, splitting it apart like matchwood, and cutting down a master's mate who was yelling to the hands at the mizzen braces. Blood splashed across Bolitho's breeches, and he saw other men falling on the gun deck, the protective nets above it jerking with fallen cordage and torn canvas.

A quick glance aloft told him the masthead pendant was streaming almost abeam. They were as close to the wind as they could be. Enough or too little made no difference now. There was no room to go about, nor time to change tack.

Tyrrell yelled, 'Rake that bastard's poop!' He gestured to the nearest gun captains. 'Grape! Bring them down!'

He stared at Bolitho, his eyes glazed with fatigue, the fury of battle.

'She's coming round!' He caught a seaman as he dropped from the nettings, his face a mask of blood. 'Another for th' surgeon!' He turned to Bolitho again and then gave a short cry, his hands to his thigh as he fell.

Bolitho knelt beside him, holding his shoulders as more balls blasted splinters from the deck. Tyrrell stared up at him, his eyes dark with pain.

''S'all right.' He gritted his teeth. 'It's th' same bloody leg!'

Bolitho saw Dalkeith stooping and running across the deck, some of his men at his back.

Tyrrell added weakly, 'I knew it had to come off. Now there's no excuse, eh?' Then he fainted.

From the littered gun deck Graves watched him fall, although his mind was cringing to the noise and the stench of death.

He screamed, 'Run out!' He thrust at a wild-eyed seaman. 'Point! *Ready!*' He stared fixedly at the towering sails of the transport as it rose ponderously abeam. '*Fire!*'

The deck lurched beneath his feet, and he saw two men blasted into crimson fragments, their screams cut short before they reached the stained planking. But somewhere in his reeling mind he was thinking of Tyrrell. He must be dead, *God rot him.* His sister would be all alone now. One day, maybe sooner than the others realized, he would find her. *Take her for himself.*

A gunner's mate gaped up at him, his mouth like a black hole as he bellowed, 'Look out, sir! For Christ's sake . . .' His words were lost in the grating crash of timber as the main topgallant yard plunged through the nets like a great tree. It gouged into the planking and further still to the deck below. As its trailing rigging and severed halliards thundered between the blazing guns Graves died, his body impaled under the broken spar.

At the quarterdeck rail Bolitho saw him die, and knew that the months of patrol duty, the storms and the fights, had at last broken the yard which they had once fished so carefully after another battle, a thousand years ago.

But Heyward was there, his voice rallying the gun crews as

the anchored transport faded into the smoke, her hull pitted with holes from the bow-chaser's merciless bombardment.

The wind fanned the smoke aside, and with something like disbelief he saw the sheer of Cape Henry pulling back like a huge door, the horizon glittering beyond it in welcome.

Fowler slipped and fell on some blood and sobbed, 'It's no use! I can't . . .'

Bethune strode towards him. 'You can and you damn well will!'

The young midshipman turned and blinked at him.

'*What?*'

Bethune grinned, his face black with powder smoke. 'You heard me! So jump to it, *boy!*'

'Mr Buckle!' Bolitho winced as some stray shots shrieked through the shrouds and brought down more lengths of cordage. 'I want you to . . .'

But the master took no notice. He was sitting with his back to the hatchway, hands to his chest as if in prayer. His eyes were open, but the spreading pattern of blood around him told its own story.

Glass and a solitary seaman stood at the unprotected wheel, their eyes wild, their legs straddled amidst dead and dying.

Bolitho snapped, 'As close as you can. *Lucifer*'s remains will guide you clear of the shoal.'

As sunlight enveloped the sloop from stem to stern, and her yards swung yet again to take her out of the bay, Bolitho saw the great array of ships coming down from the southern horizon and filling the sea. It was a fantastic spectacle. Squadron by squadron, the ships-of-the-line appearing to overlap as they headed purposefully towards the Chesapeake.

Foley murmured, 'De Grasse. I have never seen such a fleet.'

Bolitho tore his eyes away and hurried to the taffrail. There was no sign of pursuit from the bay, nor had he expected one. The two frigates would be guarding their new anchorage and trying to rescue some of the soldiers who had escaped *Sparrow*'s fury. He turned towards the wheel where Heyward and Bethune stood watching him.

'We will wear ship directly.' He saw Dalkeith and called. 'Tell me!'

Dalkeith eyed him sadly. 'It's done. He's sleeping now. But I am confident.'

Bolitho wiped his face and felt Stockdale steady his arm as the ship pitched heavily to the freshening wind.

So much still to do. Repairs to be carried out even as they avoided the oncoming might of France. To find Admiral Graves and tell him of the enemy's arrival. To bury their dead. His mind felt numb.

Yule, the gunner, clattered up a sagging ladder and barked, 'Any spare hands, sir? I need 'em for the pumps!'

Bolitho faced him. 'Get them elsewhere.'

He looked around at the sprawled bodies caught in their various attitudes of death.

'Only the brave lie here.'

He looked up, startled, as from high above the deck he heard someone singing. Beyond the pitted canvas and dangling rigging, to where the topgallant yard had splintered apart before falling to kill Graves, he saw a solitary seaman working in the sunlight, his marlin-spike glinting as he spliced a broken stay. The sounds of sea and booming sails were too loud for him to hear the words, but the tune seemed familiar and strangely sad.

Foley joined him and said quietly, 'If they can sing like that, after what they've done.' He turned away, unable to watch Bolitho's face. 'Then, by God, I *envy* you!'

314

Epilogue

TWO DAYS after fighting out of the bay, *Sparrow*'s lookouts sighted the van of Admiral Graves's fleet bearing down the coast of Maryland. The occasion was both exciting and bitter, for with many of her company wounded or killed it was hard not to feel emotion. Well ahead of the fleet, her signal flags rippling in the sunlight. *Heron* stood before the wind, a small symbol of what they had endured and achieved together.

Bolitho could remember the moment exactly, as with his men he had waited on the splintered quarterdeck while his signals were passed to *Heron* and repeated to the flagship.

When the reply had been received, Bethune had turned, his face suddenly matured.

'*Flag* to *Sparrow*, sir. *You will lead. Yours is the honour.*'

For an admiral who disliked superfluous signalling, Admiral Graves had done them proudly.

Once again, *Sparrow* had gone about, her torn sails and battered hull acting like a pointer to the great ships-of-the-line which followed obediently in her wake.

Once in sight of the bay, and with the knowledge that the French were still there, *Sparrow*'s role had become that of a mere spectator to a battle which was to leave its mark on all who took part. A warning to young officers like Bolitho, a grim lesson to the hidebound who had for so long fought by the book, a book which had become outdated by hard experience.

Perhaps Admiral Graves had expected, even hoped, up to the last moment that the French had quit the Chesapeake or at worst de Barras's smaller squadron would be there, having slipped past his patrols and escaped from Newport some days earlier. *Sparrow*'s signal had put paid to any such belief, and the sight of such a grand array must have filled him with misgivings. But if his fleet was inferior to de Grasse's in both ships and guns, he had much in his favour. The wind gave him the advantage, and as Tyrrell had so often predicted, the treacherous middle-ground between the Chesapeake's capes was soon to show its impartiality to those who braved it.

With the British bearing down on the bay, and de Barras's reinforcements not yet in close company, de Grasse decided to weigh and meet them in open water. An adverse wind and tide, the dangerous spit of middle-ground, soon told him he was unable to leave his protective anchorage as a complete fleet. Squadron by squadron, his ships fought their way around Cape Henry, with *Lucifer*'s skeleton close by as a warning to the foolhardy or the careless.

This should have been Graves's great opportunity. To signal *General Chase* and allow his captains to fall on the enemy before he could reassemble and proclaim his superiority. Had there been a Hawke or a Keppel in command there was little doubt in anyone's mind that the effect would have been devastating.

But once again Graves faltered, his mind grasping the written word of the 'Fighting Instructions' and seeing no other alternative.

His flagship hoisted the rigid signal to form line of battle, and it remained flying throughout the action. The delay allowed de Grasse to assemble his fleet and when the two adversaries finally drove together it was impossible for the rearmost British ships even to engage. By evening, failing light forced the fleets to disengage, and driven by a strong northeasterly both soon lost contact.

When at last Graves was able to re-form his squadrons, the French had beaten back into the Chesapeake. They did not leave it again, and after further hesitation Graves ordered his frustrated captains to sail for New York.

Helpless and beyond reach of the action itself, Bolitho had watched much of the tactics and guessed far more of what was happening. He left the deck at regular intervals to speak with Tyrrell in the sickbay, holding his hand as he tried to describe the sequence of events.

He could recall each visit exactly. Tyrrell's face very pale in the lanternlight, his mouth clenched against the agony. And around him, groaning or sobbing quietly, the others who had suffered, and some who were beyond pain.

Tyrrell had said hoarsely, 'That's th' army finished.' He had gripped Bolitho's hand with some of his old vigour. 'But *we* did what we could!'

Later at Sandy Hook, as *Sparrow* had carried out repairs and Bolitho had received orders to sail for England with the admiral's despatches and news of the battle, the blow had fallen.

Cut off from the sea, his ammunition and supplies exhausted, Cornwallis and his whole army had capitulated.

True to his reputation, General Washington had allowed the British to surrender with both honour and dignity, but it was a crushing defeat, nevertheless.

Couriers who had brought the news of the surrender told of the British military band which led their soldiers into Washington's camp. They had been playing 'The World Turned Upside Down,' which gave some hint of what they thought about their situation if nothing else.

Under low cloud and a steady drizzle *Sparrow* weighed and turned her stern to Sandy Hook for the last time. Her company reacted to their sailing orders with mixed feelings. Some mourned old friends whom they had buried at sea or left crippled to await more comfortable transport. Others were almost afraid of what they might find in England after so long. And there were plenty who turned their backs on America and dreamed only of that moment when they would step ashore in their own country, thankful at being spared the pain and despair, grateful even to see the leaden sky above the mastheads.

When not required on deck Bolitho spent much of the voyage alone in his cabin. It made contact less painful, the losses of familiar faces easier to bear.

He could remember his last handshake with Tyrrell as he had said his farewells at a New York hospital. Dalkeith had been there, too, and it had been a sad parting. It was still hard to think of Tyrrell with one leg, nor did he want to. One thing seemed certain, Tyrrell was without despair.

'After this, I'm going home.' He had said it several times. 'I don't know how or when, but by th' Lord I'll get there!'

Dalkeith had been appointed to an accommodation ship off

Sandy Hook, and had added quietly, 'Reckon they'll need a good doctor, too, eh, Jethro?' He had given his deep chuckle. 'So here's me hand on it!'

Bolitho shivered and pulled his coat more closely across his body. It was cold and very damp, and the bulkhead was dripping with condensation. He glanced at the open log book. It was the first day of January 1782, another year for all of them. He stood up and walked slowly from the cabin, his legs taking the pitch and plunge without conscious thought or effort. Over three and a half years since he had stepped into this ship which had become so much a part of him.

He climbed the ladder and saw Heyward at the weather nettings. It would be worse for him. He had been aboard since she had commissioned five years back. He walked across to him, seeing the grey mist swirling through the dripping shrouds, the spray bursting high above the gangway.

'Well, Mr Heyward, the English Channel. Yonder, with any sort of luck, lies the Isle of Wight. We will anchor at Spithead before dark.'

Heyward looked at him steadily. 'It's a strange feeling, sir.' He shrugged. 'I'm not sure if I want to leave the ship now.'

Bolitho nodded. 'It is often the case. *Sparrow* is no different from the rest of us. She needs a proper overhaul in the yard, and she is to be fitted with these new carronades we keep hearing about. She'll not be the same after this.' He saw Bethune climbing from the gun deck, his jaw working on a stale biscuit. 'I doubt if any of us will.'

'Land ho! Fine on th' starboard bow!'

Bolitho took a glass. 'Wight. You'd better let her fall off a point.' He watched Heyward hurry to the rail with his speaking trumpet. It could have been Tyrrell.

Then he looked around the rain-soaked deck at the seamen by the mizzen braces, their faces and arms even darker in the hostile grey light.

A tan-sailed yawl bobbed past, a bearded man waving from the tiller. On the other beam he saw a smudge of land through the drizzle and mist. England. He gripped the rail hard. After so long and so much.

'Steady as she goes, sir!' Heyward joined him again.

Bethune stood on his opposite side and murmured, 'I feel as if I've grown up in *Sparrow*.'

Bolitho thrust his arms around their shoulders.

'We *all* did.'

Then he turned away and said formally, 'Muster your anchor party and tell the gunner to prepare a salute.'

He began to pace slowly up and down the weather side, seeing the busy seamen around him, and many more. Buckle and Tilby, Graves and the artist Majendie.

He paused and touched the rail, the scars where balls had cut down so many of his men.

A frigate loomed through the mist on an opposite tack, her flags very bright against the murky backcloth.

Fowler called, '*What ship?*, sir.'

Bolitho nodded. 'Hoist our number.'

Sparrow, sloop-of-war, had come home.

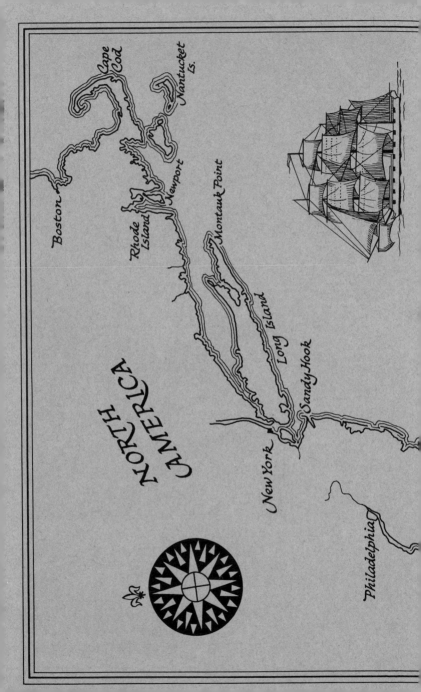